CHILDREN OF EDEN

CHILDREN OF EDEN

Michael Beeney

The Book Guild Ltd
Sussex, England

Any perceived similarity between characters created in this novel and in real life is purely coincidental and supports the contention that reality can be stranger than fiction.

The Book Guild Ltd
25 High Street,
Lewes, Sussex

First published 1999
© Michael Beeney, 1999
Set in Baskerville
Typesetting by Keyboard Services, Luton, Beds

Printed in Great Britain by
Bookcraft (Bath) Ltd, Avon.

A catalogue record for this book is
available from the British Library

ISBN 1 85776 430 7

He beamed in from Vulcania,
She, from a spot between Mars and Venus,
Two wandering spirits on an astral plane,
Looking for a place to land.

She claimed previous lives,
Was it Egyptian, Roman – or both?
He had no recollection to offer,
But would have guessed Neanderthal man.

It happened on planet Earth,
This interstellar rendevous,
Mind and body locked in sweet resonance,
In the perfect equation – balanced with love.

Will it last forever, this magical union?
How long is forever – in this world or the next?
Only fleeting milliseconds in the grand design,
As transient spirits blown on a celestial wind.

But they will leave their mark,
Before passing on to other dimensions,
And the products of their union, fledgling spirits,
Will travel the infinity of space and time forever.

Michael Beeney

CONTENTS

1	Receptacles	1
2	*Empress of the Seas*	39
3	The Table	65
4	Gene Machine	85
5	Delivery	109
6	Confession	133
7	Vapour Trails	147
8	Ship's Nurse	199
9	Breaking the Rule	221
10	True Love	271
11	Revelations	287
12	Blood Test	309
13	Harley Street Revisited	321
14	New Love	359
15	Forbidden Love	379
16	The Wedding	407

PREFACE

When the woman saw that the fruit of the tree was good for food and pleasing to the eye and also desirable for gaining wisdom, she took some and ate it. She also gave some to her husband, who was with her, and he ate it. Then the eyes of both of them were opened, and they realised that they were naked; so they sewed fig leaves together and made coverings for themselves.

Then the Lord God said to the woman, 'What is this you have done?' The woman said, 'The serpent deceived me and I ate.' So the Lord said to the woman, 'I will greatly increase your pains in childbearing; with pain you will give birth to children. Your desire will be for your husband, and he will rule over you.'

To Adam he said, 'Because you listened to your wife and ate from the tree about which I commanded you, "you must not eat of it":

Cursed is the ground because of you;
through painful toil you will eat of it
all the days of your life.
It will produce thorns and thistles for you,
And you will eat the plants of the fields.
By the sweat of your brow you will eat
your food until you return to the ground,
since from it you were taken,
from dust you are
and to dust you will return.'

Genesis 2 and 3

CHAPTER 1

RECEPTACLES

And the Lord God said, 'The man has now become like one of us, knowing good and evil. He must not be allowed to reach out his hand and take also from the tree of life and eat, and live for ever.' So the Lord God banished him from the garden of Eden to work the ground from which he had been taken.

Genesis 3: 22

Sex is the purest form of human felicity, the cordial drop in the otherwise vapid cup of life.

Erasmus Darwin (1731–1802)

The male of the species will copulate with a single female for prolonged periods attaining many ejaculations. With time (the actual time depending on the species) the rate of copulation decreases and actually ceases. If at the time, a new female is presented to the male, he may start copulating with this new female to a significantly greater extent than would have occurred had the original female been removed and re-introduced. Thus, the novelty of a new partner triggers further and greater sexual activity, overcoming any sexual fatigue or satiation that occurred with the original female. This is the 'Coolidge effect' – one day, President and Mrs Coolidge visited a government farm. Soon after arrival they were taken on separate tours. When passing chicken pens she asked if the rooster copulated more than once each day. 'Dozens of

1

times' was the reply. 'Please tell that to the President' she requested. When the President was told about the rooster he asked, 'Same hen every time?' 'Oh no Mr President, a different one each time.' The President nodded slowly, 'Tell that to Mrs Coolidge.'

Journal of Sexual Medicine, 1988

*Life can little else supply
But a few good fucks and then we die*

John Wilkes (1727–1797)

The term 'priaprism' derives from the greek god Priapus and refers to a prolonged painful erection of the penis.

'In Englishe' it is named as an involuntary standing of a man's yerde. To cure, first annoynte the yerde and coddes with the oil of Iuniper and agnus castum, brayed and made into a playster and laid upon the stones. If be the erection of the yerde to synne thence must leap into a great vessel of cold water and place nettles in the codpiece about the yerde and stones. If this doth fail thence must apply leaches to the yerde.

Dr Andrew Boorde
Brevery of Health, 1490

In Manila's Mabini Street the bar girls are masterful in their erotic display of posturing provocation. Enticing glossy pictures offering scantily clad 'hostesses', respectably disguised in description but nonetheless unequivocal sexual merchandise, gaudily decorate every bar entrance. There is one where a rapidly flashing neon red proclaims: 'VERY EXCLUSIVE ALL WELCOME'. Inside, celluloid becomes flesh. Nymphets cavort, gyrate and provoke in the murky smoke-filled gloom, struggling to keep time with the incessant throb of ear-splitting disco music. They shamelessly display their pudenda, barely covered by skin-tight bikini pants illuminated surreally by the prismatic change of strobe lights. Each Venus bulge invites the glassy-eyed punters to sample what is on offer. They sit motionless on stools bolted to the floor, encircling the stage like a pack of hyenas savouring an imminent kill. They soak up the crude eroticism cascading over them greedily and with no hint of self-consciousness. To prevent a customer's attention straying even for a moment, perhaps to take in the continuous video nasty flickering on monitors strategically placed in every corner, the girls frequently improvise even more daring and erotic gestures which assume no imagination and dispel any lingering doubt as to the services on offer. Most are barely 16, slim, supple and hot. They don't speak. Their language is plain enough: 'Kiss my kiki and me eat your titi' – 'Lick my pussy and me suck your cock'. Their semaphore is perfect: 'Strictly business. You want, you can have.' There is a price, of course (which is more than reasonable and less than a tank of gasoline). 'Orgasm guaranteed'. Even if a man is sucked into this vortex of impending carnality against his will and with no desire, he is unlikely to leave alone. The 'instant' eroticism is as intoxicating as the San Miguel beer – and that's dynamite guaranteed to blow anyone's head off...

This man is in good condition, broadshouldered and slim, with hardly an ounce of fat, but his grey sideburns, receding hairline and crow's-foot wrinkles around the eyes put him well into middle age. Worn, craggy features display clearly a face of experience and the restrained smile reveals a veritable man of the world perfectly adjusted to such seedy surroundings. Every movement, each little gesture reinforces his natural rapport with this exotic watering hole as if he himself is an integral part of the show, a natural extension of the stage and an indispensable player in the very unsubtle sexual display just a few feet in front of him.

But his passive demeanour, sitting quietly on a stool, belies the subdued posture of the predator – taking his time, waiting patiently to make his move – as soon as he feels the whims of his circulating hormones reach a critical level. If this is a game, then he is the player, coach and referee all rolled into one, as are the rest of the hungry carnivores. Like them, he definitely calls the shots.

Occasionally his smile breaks into a full grin, generous lips framing a good set of natural white teeth that have resisted the ageing process. But it is a choreographed smile showing his emotions are firmly under control. A slow deliberate raising of the eyebrows with an exaggerated quizzical look and a slight tilting of the head to one side communicates fluently with the girls the common language of impending contract, a contract which is clearly sexual and infinitely more eloquent than the articulated world.

Sharply angled and proud cheekbones are widely separated by a prominent nose, scarred and flattened from a youth of body contact sports and balanced by a square uncompromising jaw. There is no excess flesh. It is a trim if not gaunt look and a testament to the frequent gym workouts and determination

to defeat the aforementioned ageing process. .. he stood
upright at the bar he would be around six feet tall. ..... broad
shoulders taper to a narrow waist and flat midriff and almost
boyish hips. Such physical features contrast markedly with the
majority of the surrounding males. Their grossly protuberant
bellies, fat arses and flabby crimson faces advertise without
shame the ravages of years of uncompromisingly degenerate
excesses in dives like the Blue Hawaii. They positively bulge
from their sweaty T-shirts and ridiculously ill-fitting tight jeans
either convinced of their rugged manly attraction or contemptuously complacent with the confidence that the girls
were economic captives regardless.

But this male, as intent as any other on the parade of
tantalising nymphettes, has managed to minimise the degenera-
tive process. Apart from his well-trimmed grey side burns, the
main head of hair is a natural dark brown and still generously
abundant. It is cut neatly but maintained long enough on the
top to sweep back with a suggestion of a parting on the left
and finish as a flourish of small curls at the back of the neck.
It is kempt, but with a hint of raffishness that even at his
age could still arouse the interest of the opposite sex, no
matter how respectable they themselves might think they
are . . .

Once in a while more as an acknowledgement to the girls up
front, his piercing grey-blue eyes flash, twinkle and sparkle
which together with the controlled smile sends a clear message
to the sexual fodder impatient to do business.

But at odd moments, and one has to be quick to detect it in
the murky, smoke filled atmosphere, there is a paradox. It is
revealed as a fleeting expression more natural than contrived,
which conveys a mixture of emotions, the overall message of
which is one of distaste if not moral indignation. One might
also detect a sense of guilt and contrition and a clear recognition of the reality behind the grim gaiety of the forsaken
humanity parading before him. It is a profound expression
and most certainly rarely witnessed in this sort of location. The
clamouring carnivores would regard it as a wholly inappropriate consideration, an entirely misplaced sympathy for

5

the sexual supplicants displaying their all before them. That is, if they cared to deflect their attention even for a second. They wouldn't be interested in any social analysis of the wretched reality behind the glittering display, a wretchedness imposed by a desperately impoverished existence which forces these young girls barely out of puberty to sell themselves in such a degrading fashion.

But such sensitivities in the man are fleeting and swiftly suppressed. Such considerations are counterproductive to the agenda tonight. Strike such negative thoughts from the consciousness. Who needs guilt? Merely a figment of religious propaganda – that's all it is. These lithesome beauties will benefit handsomely from his generosity anyway, so what the heck. And the real bonus for them is that he most certainly isn't a fat, sweaty, smelly, totally inebriated repulsive creature like so many of the other punters who trawled the sexual watering holes. At least he is clean and fresh and still reasonably firm and supple. And furthermore, despite the onesidedness of the sexual transaction will endeavour to generate some sexual satisfaction for the sex slave object of his desire.

He is dressed in a casual and ageless fashion – purely functional to suit such a hot and humid location. Pristine white, loosely fitting T-shirt with well-tailored equally loose fitting pale blue cotton beach trousers and a pair of spotless yellow espadrilles on his sockless suntanned feet. His only symbol of affluence or hint that he has immeasurably more funds than the average Filipino, or more to the point, Filipina, is the Rolex watch on his right wrist.

Understatement is the overall message. Enough understatement so as not to attract the wrong sort of interest (muggers in the dark streets), but not so much as to suggest he might be limited in the thickness of his wallet or the alacrity he is sure to display when he is being encouraged to part with his dollars.

He sits captivated, simply ogling, his eyes feasting greedily on the exquisite dishes parading before him. He is taking his time. There is no need to rush with such an abundant and varied choice. He is perched on one of the stools with his chin cupped in his hands and propped up by elbows positioned on the edge of the shiny yellow metallic bar. There is a mug of cold beer in front of him. His eyes move between two of the dancers in the line-up, one on the extreme left and the other just right of centre. He cannot make up his mind which one to take. But then, in the final analysis, it doesn't matter! He has more than enough money for Third World prices – he'll take both to his hotel and enjoy double the pleasure!

Oh, such uninhibited carnality! The mere thought is enough to initiate a sensation of firmness in his crotch. In this sexually anarchic environment of the Third World no natural instincts suffered from the conditioned repression one might associate with the established order of the First World. It was simply a matter of pure unrestrained sexual indulgence and guaranteed carnal activity with the subject (or perhaps 'object' might be a more appropriate term) of one's whim. The money was insignificant. The sheer numbers of 'objects' competing desperately to earn a few dollars kept the price down and ensured their enthusiastic cooperation to please the customer.

He is savouring every juicy second. The blast of the disco saturates his auditory senses. It conveniently serves to block out any chance of conversation with those of similar intent who sit alongside. He didn't come to talk – certainly not with men. But then, their purpose is identical and they likewise do not wish to make anything more than a passing polite acknowledgment for fear of missing the action up front.

The action up front is beginning to sizzle as the girls, in particular the two who are being closely observed by the man, vie desperately for his undivided attention and the opportunity of being selected. He knows the drill all too well. When his desire is sufficiently fired up by their display, then he will get them off of the catwalk with the mere wink of an eye and purposeful nod of the head – and along to the bar to start the serious business of making dollars. Alternatively, an imperious beckon with the hand is all that is needed to stop them in mid-bend or lateral twist and cause them to scamper off the stage and around to the front of the house to make personal contact with their would-be benefactor.

He definitely decides to have both. At an appropriate

moment he will signal such an intention, but in the meantime he is content to savour the anticipated pleasure and squeeze every last drop of contrived sensuality from the two competitors.

Images from past encounters are recalled, and one particular memory brings a wry smile to his face. His suppressed laugh and prolonged grin signal an affirmation to both girls that it could be their lucky night. They respond with unbridled enthusiasm; the one on the left protrudes her tongue, and the one on the right massages her breast as a promise of things to come. They are happy at the prospect. After the bar owner has taken his cut, they can pay their rent and buy a few groceries and maybe still have a few dollars left to send back to parents and younger brothers and sisters who eke out a wretched existence in the Northern Province.

He recalls the first time. It was a stopover in Manila on his way to Australia, which not only made a break in the never-ending journey but also gave an opportunity to investigate first-hand some of the wild tales he'd heard of the sexual delights to be found in the Philippines. But when he had arrived that first time, tired and jet-lagged after a seemingly endless flight, Manila airport had hardly promised such pleasures. The intense heat and humidity, not to mention the heaving masses of people in the arrival area, cast doubt on the wisdom of his decision to stop over. Tired, irritable, hot and sweaty, with increasing paranoia and hostility to the threatening throng, he'd begun to wish he'd simply stayed on the plane and flown on to Sydney.

And he'd not even booked a hotel! If it hadn't been for the tranquilliser he'd taken on the flight, which had compounded his fatigue but at least dulled his senses, he would have been desperately anxious. After an endless crawl through immigration it had been such a relief to retrieve his one bulging valise from the creaking carousel and head towards the exit. One final check by a disinterested customs man in a scruffy, ill-fitting uniform, who cursorily waved him through, and he had emerged into the mayhem of the outside arrival hall.

If it had been organised chaos on the customs side, that had been nothing short of riotous assembly. He'd stood motionless in a daze for a moment, completely overwhelmed by the throng. But any doubts about finding a hotel had been rapidly dispelled. Within seconds he had been encircled by dozens of placards animated aggressively by highly vocal touts offering the very best and the cheapest hotel in Manila. He had been totally bewildered, and although the tranquilliser still exerted its calming effect, his confusion and uncertainty as he recoiled defensively had only served to reinforce the gesticulations of those vying for his attention.

He had tried to scan what was on offer. But there were just too many, and he didn't really care which hotel, as long as it provided a clean safe haven for the night. One placard waver had a sort of restrained dignity and stood out from the rest.

'"Silahis International"?' he'd said to the man behind the board.

'Yes sir – the finest of hotels – guaranteed international standard, double room with kingsized bed, fridge and mini bar, three restaurants, twenty-four hour coffee shop, fitness centre, exclusive massage parlour ... and just for you sir, a fifty per cent discount...'

'OK, OK,' he'd answered quickly, not bothering to speak to the others who were still jostling around him, 'which way?'

'I'll take your bag, sir. Please follow to the courtesy car.'

On reflection, he wasn't sure if it had been the man's more dignified approach, the offer of a 50 per cent discount or the mention of an exclusive massage parlour which had clinched the deal, but when he'd flopped into the back of the air-conditioned Toyota sedan he'd felt relieved and pleased that it had seemed so easy.

On the ride to town it was dark and there had been a distinct lack of street lighting, so he hadn't been able to see much of the surroundings as the 'luxury sedan', seemingly devoid of suspension, rattled down the road. He remembers clearly hoping that the hotel's air-conditioning would be more sophisticated than the open windows of the Toyota, through which gusts of hot, stale and at frequent intervals, frankly faeculent air assaulted his nostrils.

The Silahis had not disappointed him. It appeared as a huge concrete monolith brightly lit and beckoning as the car pulled off Roxas Boulevard and onto the narrow slip road to the entrance. He had climbed wearily out of the back seat and onto the steps, thinking only of crisp sheets and sleep. After tipping the driver he'd turned to his bag, only to see it being fought over by two gaily clad bellboys smiling ear to ear. One conceded when he'd grimaced, and saving face, led him and his rival into the lobby.

Check-in had been straightforward, although the 50 per cent reduction he'd been offered at the airport was offset by sales tax, government tax and one or two other hidden tariffs which brought the final charge up to the original figure. But it hadn't mattered. He'd arrived.

The elevator had seemed to stop at every floor on its way to the tenth, and he'd had time to read the glossy notice highlighting the facilities available in the hotel: shops first floor, corporate dining room second, pool and fitness centre third, Jacuzzi steambath and oriental massage (including VIP option) fifth, business centre seventh, nightclub and disco eighteenth.

He remembers the twinge of expectation he'd felt for the first time as the elevator door opened on the tenth floor, and although sleep had been the priority, he knew it wouldn't be too long before he was investigating the services available on the fifth floor.

He'd stripped in seconds, leaving his clothes on the floor, and crawled into bed. Sleep had been almost instantaneous. It had been deep-dream sleep punctuated by startling erotic images, tantalising as reality, and he had eventually awoken with an astonishingly hard, aching erection.

He had felt ravenously hungry. He would fill his belly first and then investigate the services on the fifth floor. The coffee shop on the ground floor served hot meals around the clock, and he'd had a huge cheese and onion omelette with a stack of french fries and freshly squeezed orange juice, wolfed down in a matter of minutes.

When he'd got into the lift and pressed the button to the fifth floor he'd felt a surge of butterflies. He'd not been quite sure what to expect. He'd never experienced a massage parlour before, and so when he'd walked through the door on which 'Health Spa' was stencilled in thick black lettering, an acute sensation of vulnerability and uncertainty had threatened to overwhelm him.

He'd entered directly into a reception area. Behind a chest-high solid-looking counter stood two women. One was grey-haired, old and wrinkled, but the younger one was very pretty. Sensing his awkwardness, they'd both smiled warmly and asked which particular service he desired.

Feeling momentarily tongue-tied, he'd simply blurted out, 'A massage, please.'

'Of course, sir. We have the very best, and so many beautiful girls who can please you I am sure . . .'

'Uuuh – yes, of course, uum, I really don't . . .'

'Sir can pick a number, any one of these.'

The old woman had pointed to a wooden board hanging on the wall behind the desk on which hung dozens of numbered keys. It had seemed so matter-of-fact and unerotic, his eyes scanning along the numbers as if they represented a lucky dip at a funfair sideshow. He'd stared silently at the board for a long time, which had brought a prompt from the old lady.

'Number 89 is very good, sir, will make you very happy.'

'Well – uuh, maybe. Maybe, I really don't know, I . . . maybe 101 . . . I'm not sure . . .'

'Sir is very wise. He has made very good choice. Marilyn very beautiful **and** very experienced.'

'Well, perhaps . . . I'm not sure. Maybe if I come back . . .' He was getting cold feet; his nerve was going and it didn't seem quite the right thing to be doing. He wished he'd flown directly onto Sydney.

'She will do **ALL** for you . . .'

'OK, OK. Marilyn – please.'

'This way, sir.'

He had followed the old lady rather meekly through a thin semi-lucent curtain and along a dimly lit passage with cubicles on either side, which had reminded him of the municipal swimming baths in his childhood. There had been a slight

11

feeling of trepidation, marginally exceeded by a guarded expectation of impending pleasure of a sexual nature. At the end of the passage she'd pulled back another curtain to reveal a small cubicle, bare except for a simple wooden bench which took up most of the space. A single orange lightbulb on one wall threw a dull amber glow across the bench, which was barely covered by a thin white sheet with a solid-looking pillow placed at one end. In one corner there was a small locker with a key inserted in the open door. Inside was a tiny tablet of white soap and a neatly folded towel.

'Thank you sir. Marilyn will be along soon. If you would like to get undressed ... you can have a shower next door.' There had been a moment's hesitation before she turned.

'Oh yes – uuh, thank you, thank you.'

Uncertain of tipping levels in such circumstances, he'd given her a 20-peso note which, from her effusive thanks as she'd disappeared through the curtain, made him realise later was more than expected.

He'd leaned against the bench feeling vulnerable and slightly nervous, and had to remind himself that it was sure to be safe in a first-class hotel. Even so, he had waited a few minutes, uncomfortable in the solitude, before starting to slowly remove his clothes. He'd placed them in the open locker and then wrapped the minuscule and virtually transparent worn towel around his midriff. It was so small it had hardly extended around his waist, smaller as it was in those days, and had barely covered his genitals. He'd waited in an anticipatory posture, half-sitting on the edge of the bench, feeling anything but sexually aroused.

The silence had been punctuated by a variety of sounds from adjacent cubicles, mainly guttural utterances, which strongly suggested more activity than simple massage was taking place.

And then he'd been aware of a not unpleasant odour of sweet perfume momentarily overcoming the musty warm body smell which had hit his nostrils when he'd entered the cubicle area. He'd sensed it was a forewarning of a female presence nearby, if not the impending arrival of the aforementioned Marilyn. It had made his pulse quicken in nervous expectation.

There had been a sudden swish of the curtain and Marilyn, number 101, had appeared. He remembers clearly how he'd jerked his head up suddenly, not unlike a startled beast under imminent threat. It had made his pulse race even more, alerting him fully from the still semi-somnolent daze of his deep sleep and enabling him in an instant to absorb the persona standing in the doorway. Her aura was friendly yet slightly intimidating. In the dim semi-darkness she'd hesitated for a moment, leaning with one hand above her head against the door frame before entering. The other hand and its long spindly fingers flashing bright red, perfectly manicured nails was pressed firmly into her hip in a subdued pose of theatrical titillation and perhaps a promise of things to come.

She was short, around five feet one, not fat, not thin, but more what he would describe as 'compact', displaying the generous figure, accentuated by the tight-fitting white tunic, of a woman in her mid-thirties. The tiny white plimsolls and well-fitted white trousers demonstrated undoubtedly the garb of a technician – and with the posture, clearly a technician with a wealth of experience.

In the gloom of the cubicle her mere presence had automatically raised tenfold the level of his expectation. Her shiny red fingernails flashed again as she'd moved her hand from her hip to slowly stroke her chin, with her head tilted sideways, barely suppressing a tight smile in a contrived inquisitive posture as if to survey the task facing her and her intended *modus operandi*.

Her rather plain face was compensated for by her cheek-bones, prominent and gracious, and dark, heavily mascared eyes – the softer, smouldering eyes of the South-east-Asian female, warmer and more sexually inviting than the sharp uncompromising eyes of the Chinese. Her lips were full and carefully rouged with glossy vermilion, and in the instant he took all this in at the first glance they had parted in a slow and deliberate manner, breaking into a restrained smile as if to say: 'Not all at once – we will take our time.'

After this brief pose at the doorway she set to work, greeting him with a cheerful 'Hi!' and at the same time propelling herself towards the bench to adjust the pillow in an automatic

13

fashion, as if that was the first move in a well-rehearsed sequence. Very demonstrably and unquestionably, she was going to be in charge.

She'd spoken good English in a relaxed and unhurried manner, initiating the conversation with a brief question-answer interlude which he was later to learn was the standard patter of all sex workers. It determined the intended length of stay, the name of a client's hotel and the country of origin – information which had important financial implications when it came to remuneration.

And then, quite matter-of-factly, she had instructed him to lie on his front. Did he want the 'hard' massage or the 'routine'? He'd asked what the hard entailed, and when she'd said it included walking on his back he'd swiftly opted for the routine. 'Oil or powder?' With hardly a moment's hesitation, he'd whispered 'Oil'. Slithery lubrication seemed potentially more natural, and therefore potentially more erotic, than powder.

She'd started on his back, high up over his shoulders and around the neck. He'd felt nothing in particular at first as she'd smoothed effortlessly over his shoulder blades, pressing her oily palms firmly down on his spine. Her hands moved in a slow deliberate circular motion, applying pressure at certain points and pushing his chest quite forcibly into the couch. It had in fact made him wince once or twice and could hardly have been described as sexually arousing.

He'd begun to wonder if the 'special VIP service' was nothing more than a marketing ploy, a tempting lure designed simply to extract more money from an unsuspecting client. But then, quite without warning, her soft warm hands had moved downwards to the small of his back, and then slithered outwards around his loins. It invoked a tingling sensation all the way down his spine, accompanied by a gentle surge of penile tumescence. Sensing his arousal, slight as it may have been, she'd smoothed her hands back to the centre and massaged his spine for a few moments. But then slowly her fingers came down the lumbar curve a second time, sliding effortlessly on a film of oil as far as the rise of his buttocks.

14

That had set of a furious bombardment of sensory impulses to the pleasure centre in his brain and almost instantaneously transformed his semi-turgid organ into a curved rod as hard as rock. He'd automatically shifted his pelvic posture to accommodate the stiffened member – a subtle but positive signal to the effectiveness of her technique which she must have recognised a thousand times before.

With a deft flourish, she'd swept a hand under the top of one thigh, barely stroking the contents of his crotch with her fingertips. It had been such a fleeting and gentle contact he'd thought it might have been that she'd touched those parts merely by accident. This uncertainty of her intent had added a certain piquancy to the sensation, as if it could have been unintended or even illicit. Her hands had then moved swiftly over the back of his thighs and with increasing pressure, down as far as his knees – away from the erogenous zone signalling that indeed, the brush with his genitals had been nothing more than an accident. But she was the consummate professional. His disappointment had been shortlived. With an abrupt reversal of direction and passing upwards along the outside of his thighs, her slippery spindly fingers probed underneath, if only for a second. This time, they unambiguously caressed the organ and scrotum before passing on to his lower back.

'Turn over please,' she'd said quietly and confidently, well aware of his intense arousal. Her feigned start at the sight of his erection had been as predictably on cue as it must have been for the countless clients who had been through 'her hands'. And the expected silent penitent apology with his eyes had naturally drawn her question as if from a well-worn script, superfluous as it was in the circumstances.

'Sir would like "special sensation"?' she'd said, as might a waitress offering to sprinkle ground pepper on his salad. Simultaneously, she'd nodded her head towards his groin with a suppressed smirk and a more than devilish twinkle in her eyes.

An unintelligible sound, half-sigh half-grunt, accompanied by a restrained nod of his head, had been the affirmative response to make her reach for the lubricant. With several

15

squirts from the plastic container, which would have been more at home in an automobile repair shop, she'd anointed his jacked-up phallus as if lubricating a rusty piston rod. Grasping it wholly and firmly in her fist, she began masturbating him slowly and methodically. Her strokes hadn't even reached double figures before he had ejaculated copiously, spurting jets of watery grey seminal fluid in the air. She'd misjudged the exact moment and direction, and the first spurt had spattered on her snow-white tunic just below one breast. Her instant withdrawal and the hard-to-conceal look of disgust on her face defined the reality of the charade as she'd hastily disappeared through the curtain.

He'd then passed into the twilight consciousness of post-ejaculatory fulfilment, only vaguely aware that she had left the cubicle. She'd returned a few minutes later, having regained her composure.

'Coffee sir?' she'd said with a smile. It wouldn't have done to upset the customer when a hefty tip was in the offing.

That had been the first time. It had etched an indelible trace on his memory when the recall of so many other subsequent encounters had long faded. It had convinced him that sexual pleasure could be purchased in an impersonal, unemotional and purely technical fashion which did not necessarily exploit or harm anyone. There would be sexual relief for the client and suitable financial remuneration for the technician. It was strictly a business transaction, plain and simple.

The images of that first night in Manila now flood back. He remembers giving Marilyn a more than substantial tip (judging by her gleeful reaction) and then getting into the lift and going down to the lobby, feeling lightheaded and incredibly relaxed. He'd simply wanted to walk, and he'd left the hotel waving aside the offer of a taxi and headed off into the night.

The sensation of euphoria had been exquisite and all-consuming. Robot-like, as if in a semi-trance, he'd not been conscious of heading in any particular direction. But he can recall passing through an intertwining muddle of streets, drawn imperceptibly it would seem, towards a bright glow in the night sky. His instincts were guiding him. The intense light above the dark night told him there was something there to which he must yield – a primeval force older than mankind itself which had to be obeyed. A force that reigned supreme over all other forces. So powerful a force it could drive men and women to total distraction.

Even after all these years and his trance-like state at the time, he can still recall vividly how his scrambled thoughts had attempted to analyse, to rationalise, to dissect piecemeal the mystery of this force, to define its awesome power, to challenge its contemptuous arrogance and bring it under the control of the thinking processes and the free will – to relegate it to the mere subservient animal force that it was. Could it not indeed be brought to heel and made subservient to the free will? Had not the human species become unique in its evolution of the brain? Had it not developed an intellectual power far and above that of animals? Did this not represent the ultimate power – the ultimate control?

No. NO. NEVER. The power of the sexual force, so dominant in the behaviour of animals, had not diminished. It would never yield. It had scant regard for its intellectual opponent. With utter contempt for mankind's cerebral development it imposed its own will and agenda for behaviour in a time-honoured fashion, unchanged since the first asexual organisms had crawled out of the swamp and started looking for a mate.

The force was at work that first night in Manila. He remembers clearly the girls looming spectre-like from the shadows in the semi-glow, their painted faces and lingering coquettish smiles flashing signals that were plain and unequivocal in their message. And eyes that had searched for a hint of a biological contract, a quick deal to be struck in seconds – an offer awaiting an immediate response. There had been so many. Almost a continuous stream, offering, it would seem, unlimited sexual services judging from some of the accompanying gestures. Anything you like. Where you like. With as many as you like. **Immediate – now**.

Were not these shadows in the night the perfect means of

assuaging this, the most powerful of man's instincts? Minimal social preliminaries. No involvement of the higher centres of the human brain. A simple uncomplicated physical act contracted and paid for on the spot. No possible regard for the consequences. Total submission to the force. Acquiescence to an animal lust which at a whim, cast aside the intellectual sensitivities as if they counted for nothing.

Were not these creatures simply convenient mechanical devices, no more than suitably animated vaginal orifices – mere receptacles in which to insert his aroused organ – available (at a modest price) for instant sexual gratification? Enthusiastic. Uninhibited. Anonymous. And above all, disposable – disappearing into the shadows of the night after the act.

Ahead on his left he had been able to make out the large bright yellow letters surrounded by flashing orange lights of the 'Blue Hawaii', and as he got nearer, the smaller letters, '*Taste our exotic paradise, sample our beautiful girls*'. His pace had accelerated with his pulse as the other establishments had come into view – on the opposite corner, a little further along the street, the bright red neon sign of the 'Firehouse', claiming to be the 'hottest spot in town', next door, a flashing beacon highlighting the 'Pitstop', 'Asia's legendary nightclub', then the 'Aussie Bar', the 'Hollywood Agogo', the 'International Club', 'first for young beautiful girls' … the carnal watering holes came thick and fast.

He'd hesitated momentarily as he passed the entrance to the 'Blue Hawaii'. Three scantily-clad pubescents, miniskirts to just below the crotch, were standing motionless outside. His attention, fleeting as it was, had activated their animation automatically and they had started to pull open the huge black door. In a chorus, they'd beckoned in shrill, child-like voices: 'You like plenty plenty girls, plenty plenty jig-a-jig. You look, you see!'

He'd irresistibly peeked in. Writhing torsos of near-naked girls had focused his attention in an instant. The multi-coloured flashing lights and heavy megawatts of deafening disco sound had mesmerised him for a moment. It had been

18

enough to consolidate the capture and the trio of giggling pubescents had confidently ushered, if not pushed, him through the door. Once inside, he'd not been allowed to ponder his decision to enter. A pretty waitress had plucked him from the arms of the pubescents and guided him to a velvet-cushioned recess before he could change his mind.

'Drink, sir?'

'Beer, please.'

Hardly had she turned away than another female had appeared. She hadn't been particularly attractive, but her firm young body and the skimpy bikini pants which delineated her vulval anatomy to maximum effect had been enough for him to acknowledge her arrival.

'Where you from? Where you stay? How long you stay?'

He recalls answering politely but uninterestingly. If she had been the only female around then she would have been more than welcome. But it was like being a fox in a henhouse. The choice of pretty, libidinous females had appeared to be unlimited, positively overwhelming. In the few seconds it had taken for his visual awareness to adjust to the changed light, his eyes had fixed on a lithesome apparition whirling in a near frenzy at the far side of the bar on an elevated section which served as a stage. What a figure! It stood out even amongst the mass of near-perfect anatomies which filled the place. Absolute perfection! Dark. Petite. Ultra-slim but delicately muscular. Extremely pretty – and a wild look in her flashing eyes. Untamed. **Animal**. The perfect animated vagina. Cavorting, provoking, tempting – **inviting**.

The girl now looping her skinny brown arms around his neck had recognised the glint in his eyes, and had resigned herself to the rejection that was about to follow. Trying to salvage what might be supposed a long-extinguished self-esteem, she'd cheerfully volunteered that everybody said Sharon had the best arse in the 'Blue Hawaii'.

'**That** she has,' he'd nodded in glazed agreement, more to himself, confirming to the girl that she had been rejected before even she'd been given the chance to sell herself.

'I fetch her for you,' she'd said forlornly.

She'd threaded her way through the mass of inebriated males in a matter of seconds to reach the stage. Sharon had leapt down immediately as if prescient of an impending contract. After a brief exchange Sharon had looked over in his direction and smiled diffidently. And then his messenger had slipped away, disappearing into the heavy throng. For a brief moment he'd experienced a small tinge of sympathy, if not a slight pang of guilt for her apparent selfless gesture. But then he'd assumed it was an expected duty mutually agreed by all the girls – a sort of house rule reinforced by an *esprit de corps* which brought business to the bar and therefore benefitted everyone.

Such negative thoughts had been rapidly dispelled as Sharon had glided eagerly towards him. As she got nearer, the diffident self-conscious smile suggested a demureness which made her even more alluring.

'Hello. Where you from? Where your hotel? How long you stay?'

It was becoming quite clear that the response to the standard three questions served not only as a convenient opener of social intercourse (which would lead to a more intimate kind of intercourse, they hoped) but also gave a clear indication of the financial potential of any impending sexual contract. He was later to learn that the girls preferred Americans, who were the most generous, but were wary of Europeans, especially Germans, and Australians, who had a reputation for being tight-fisted. Japanese were probably the highest payers of all, but there could be language problems if they didn't speak any English. Five-star hotels naturally raised the tariff. A prolonged stay could lead to what might be described as a 'steady relationship' – an extended contract with bonus.

'I'm from England, on my way to Australia, staying at the Silahis – five days, maybe more ... not sure yet ... it depends ... sit down.' He was learning fast.

The shyness, contrived or otherwise, hadn't stopped her sidling up so close that her bare thigh pressed firmly into his – or grasping his hand uncompromisingly and placing it in her lap. Despite the recent 'relief' from the massage at the hotel,

20

his penis had stirred immediately. Conversation, after that first brief exchange where the important information had been gleaned, more or less ceased, especially as it had been almost impossible to speak above the deafening disco noise. Besides, further conversation was irrelevant. It was hardly the occasion to explore aspects of her personality or intellect. His objective had been quite clear – he'd simply wanted to play with her like a new toy, explore uninhibitedly her body and then fuck her wilfully, with scant regard for her feelings or identity as a human being. If ever a woman could be described as nothing more than a mere sex object then Sharon, the shy nymphette in the 'Blue Hawaii' represented just that.

With his hand firmly settled in her groin he'd planted a full open-mouthed kiss on her lips. God, how he remembers so vividly that sensuous kiss, as if it were only yesterday – and a tongue which had probed so far down his throat he'd almost swallowed it.

'I fetch Mamasan,' she'd said confidently, pulling away abruptly, knowing he was well and truly hooked. It was time for business.

The floor manager had materialised in an instant.

'Bar fine 250 pesos. Drinks 350 pesos, please sir.'

'Fine – OK. Keep the change.'

'Thank you, sir. You are very generous, sir.'

The three pubescents had giggled as they'd ushered them both through the heavy black door and into the street. They'd then set off in silence and she'd placed one tiny hand in his quite naturally, as if they'd been familiar lovers. At the time, he hadn't known the street names, but now he remembers it was Del Pilar that they had strolled down, away from the flashing neon signs and girlie bars, aiming approximately in the direction which he hoped would take him back to the hotel.

At the first intersection they'd turned right and gone down a dimly lit street which had made him feel a little nervous. But she had seemed relaxed enough, and he'd assumed must have gone down that street many times before. Within minutes they'd reached Roxas Boulevard, the busy highway skirting the bay, along which most of the large hotels were situated. He'd recognised the Silahis just a couple of blocks down and had automatically quickened his pace, anxious to get back to the secure surroundings of the luxury hotel. By the time they'd reached the slip road which led up to the main entrance he was hot and his shirt was soaked through with sweat.

It had been such a relief to sink into the soft chair and enjoy the coolness of his air-conditioned room.

'Help yourself to a drink,' he'd said after she'd already opened the fridge door. It was clearly a familiar routine.

'I like Silahis,' she'd confessed with childlike candour, sensing his bemusement.

He hadn't wasted much time. Preliminaries and foreplay he knew he could contemptuously toss aside. 'Come here,' he'd instructed, as a Lord and Master might his sex slave.

She'd sat on his lap dutifully, and he had thrust his hand immediately and without ceremony beneath her short skirt. His fingers delved and probed roughly between her legs, not expecting any resistance. There had in fact been a slight momentary resistance which, in the circumstances, had surprised him. But then perhaps, he had been just too arrogant and too mechanical in his approach with scant regard for her feelings or participation in the procedure. She'd actually fidgeted and pulled his hand away with a facile comment to pre-empt his expected annoyance.

'No. I shy.'

His initial irritation had quickly turned to mild amusement at what he'd interpreted as a half-hearted attempt to tease. It wouldn't have been financially expedient to engender annoyance in a client at such an early stage, especially one with the potential of the Silahis.

Token resistance over, when his hand had gone up the second time (as a conciliatory gesture, slower and perhaps with more grace) she'd parted her legs dutifully by the time his probing fingers had reached her mons pubis. As if her routine was about to begin in earnest, she'd placed one hand matter-of-factly on his crotch and commenced a firm massaging motion.

'You very handsome,' she'd said cheerfully, as if it had been the next line in the script.

He remembers a cynical smile and muttering more to himself he bet she said that to all her 'boyfriends'. He'd then stood up and in the process, scooped her into his arms and carried her over to the huge double bed. He'd then simply let go of her. She'd dropped unceremoniously, bouncing on the bed in a giggling fit as her legs splayed open to expose a tiny pair of pale lemon panties, which were so thin and transparent that he could plainly discern the midline cleft bisecting her smooth-shaved pubic mound.

The first copulation had been almost as fast as the pigeons on the tarmac roof.

In his early years at medical school he'd had a perfectly discreet view from his tiny attic room out onto the rooftops. When he was fed up trying to memorise the function of this muscle or that, or wrestle with the complexities of yet another biochemical cycle, he'd gaze out of the window at the intersecting rooftops and let his mind wander. Being a medical student hadn't been fun all the time, and the reality of trying to pass the too frequent exams had been a strenuous grind. The pigeons had no such preoccupations to distract them from their purpose in life. Even if they had been aware of his attention, it hadn't affected the courtship sequence he'd witnessed that day so many years ago.

He'd observed incredulously the lightning speed with which the male had leapt onto the female's back, with a minimum of flutter you might say, stay quietly positioned for about five seconds and then abruptly fly off. It had made him question why they had bothered at all. He remembers philosophising at the time – if that fleeting and mechanical act represented the culmination of their whole *raison d'etre* (assuming transferring the genes was their main task in life), then it hardly seemed worth taking part in the unending rigours of survival ... but then, there he had been, in a dimly lit, musty-smelling hotel room in an exotic Asian city, acting out exactly the same ritual. It had been no different.

He'd ripped his clothes off in a matter of seconds and stood over her almost threateningly with an erection which had demanded instant satiation. Without warning he'd lunged at

23

her as she lay back passively, seizing her legs around the knees and roughly parting them to reveal that area of the anatomy in which he was most interested. He'd simply aimed in the approximate direction of where he thought her opening should be, probing the flimsy edge of her undergarment with his eager phallus until it found its target. Maybe a chronic pelvic infection had left her permanently moist – his abrupt action had hardly represented significant foreplay – as his organ had slotted into her orifice with little if any resistance, accompanied by a not-so-convincing gasp simulating sexual excitement.

He had always been proud of his 'self-control' and ability to delay ejaculation to accommodate a woman's rising passion. Perhaps the combination of his fever-pitch unbridled lust and the business nature of the transaction had released him from any such consideration, and he'd yielded totally to the all-consuming reflexes to pump semen into her without restraint. The few seconds to completion had been equalled by the few pelvic thrusts necessary. It had been pure animal indulgence unrestrained by the complexities of human social evolution.

She hadn't minded his speedy climax. In fact, premature ejaculators were to be positively encouraged. Like most purveyors of business sex, she would have certainly held the view, the quicker, the better.

He smiles again as the time-softened memory of that first night in Manila fills his thoughts. He looks up at the two girls on the stage, reminding them briefly with his eyes that they will definitely be earning money tonight, so as not to fret or get impatient with his tardiness. They acknowledge and respond enthusiastically, licking their heavily rouged lips and making lurid pelvic movements which clearly promise the full sexual service.

Sharon and that first night dominate his thoughts again. His smile broadens as the reminiscence becomes clearer. Any relief she might have experienced from such a brief coital act and the thought that her work was over for the night had been obliterated over the next four to five hours. He'd certainly been horny in those days, with a physical condition more than able to match that horniness. His penis had resumed full functional tumescence within ten minutes and he had been raring to go again. After she had returned from the fridge with another beer he'd jumped on her from behind, whipping away the towel as she was about to settle down, comfortably reclining against a bank of pillows to watch some ghastly Philippine soap opera on the in-house TV channel.

This time, she had been genuinely resistant and not a little irritated, as if she had completed her work for the night and was entitled to 'switch off' the service. It had only been his forcefulness which had reminded her of the financial realities of the situation. It brought her to her senses and made her curl up in a ball to allow the insertion of his rigid organ from the rear position. His pelvic thrusts had started slowly in a controlled fashion and continued in a steady rhythm unabated for at least five minutes before he'd felt the pleasure of approaching climax. When he had eventually come with a stupendous shudder and a loud uncontrolled cry, he'd almost shot her off the edge of the bed, to where she'd progressively shifted with his forceful thrusting.

She'd quickly rolled over onto her front and jumped up to scuttle to the shower for the customary post-coital douche – obviously not sharing the post-climactic fulfilment which had made him fall back in a semi-exhausted daze. She'd returned after a few minutes, and without speaking resumed her previous reclining position to pick up the threads of the TV drama, as he'd lain motionless on his back concentrating his abundant physical reserve for another attack.

The third assault, after a respectable 30-minute armistice, had been met with unequivocal overtly hostile resistance.

'You too horny,' she'd said, 'too much sex – you hurt me,' and more as an afterthought, 'you pay plenty.'

She'd hoped to dampen his energy and resolve with her hostility and threat of raising the tariff, but he'd quickly convinced her that she was to be well rewarded over and above what she might expect from the average punter.

The next few hours had been pure mechanical sex with nothing more than an animated vagina, a well-lubricated receptacle into which he could bury his solid organ. Any pretence at mutual pleasure, any spark of enthusiasm on her part had been extinguished by the fourth (or was it fifth?) copulatory act. He'd gone through all the positions as if wading his way through a sex manual, and by five a.m., when he'd fallen back exhausted and she'd returned from the bathroom for the umpteenth time, he was ready for sleep.

He'd remembered to leave the card outside his room ordering breakfast, and a gentle knock on the door had awoken him. How good that fresh coffee had tasted – and the strawberries! As he'd looked out over Manila Bay at the distant haze of what he now knew to be the island of Corregidor, he'd felt so perfectly at peace with the world. He'd been able to satisfy pure untainted physical lust with a suitably erotic receptacle, a barely humanised mechanical device with which he was able conveniently to dissipate his pent-up sexual energy.

He'd given not a moment's thought to the fact that there might be another human being involved. He'd simply given free rein to the primal forces he knew existed in everyone – without constraint, uncomplicated by any aesthetic or 'spiritual' consideration – if ever there was such an element which separated man from the beast. In that hotel on that hot humid night, he had been nothing more than pure untainted beast.

When he'd lifted his valise onto his lap to get the money, she'd seen the 'DR' title boldly displayed on the side. It had generated an immediate torrent of words. Despite her limited vocabulary, in the space of a couple of minutes she'd described in detail a physical profile which included a slightly smaller left breast with an intermittently inverting nipple (which he'd been surprised not to have noticed) and the fact that she had a partial urethro-vaginal prolapse.

She hadn't been able to say 'urethro-vaginal prolapse', but with a combination of hand movements and rather lurid posturing he'd been able to deduce that is what she'd probably had. She'd been extraordinarily wet at one stage, which in his drunken haze he'd assumed was sexual arousal, but on cold, sober reflection was probably urinary incontinence which would have been consistent with a prolapse.

Her physical profile thus confessed, and the strawberries polished off, he'd had to decide whether to see her again or dispense with her as one might with a used condom. The decision hadn't been difficult. It was quite clear that there was an unlimited supply of sexual fodder within a short walk of the hotel, and he could send her on her way confident there would be as many beautiful replacements as he cared to chose.

Money. She sensed there was to be no 'long-term' relationship and smiled cynically as he'd handed her 500 pesos.

'You butterfly,' she'd said in a softly contemptuous manner, referring to the punter who sampled the field, flitting from one whore to the next.

'When you come back to the Philippines?' she'd asked, swiftly pocketing the cash. He'd said maybe next year, like General MacArthur, 'I shall return.'

'I will look for you,' she'd replied with a conviction that had been almost touching.

He'd escorted her to the lift still swathed in the towel. The normally servile bellboy had frowned. She'd waved as the door had closed. Five days and countless penile receptacles later he'd caught a plane to Sydney, feeling so sexually replete he'd felt confident he'd never be distracted by women again.

The girls up front get more lewd and daring as they sense he is well and truly hooked. It is essential they hang on to their catch lest another more attractive and provocative creature makes an eleventh-hour steal.

He throws a patronising smile at the two girls on the stage to keep the pot boiling and continues with the indulgence of reminiscence.

His world travels as a ship's doctor over the next five years had simply reinforced his philosophy that most men, when stripped of the civilised veneer and the complex repressions of modern society, will yield quite simply and naturally to the powerful instinctive forces which induce the male of the species to copulate with females. The reward, instant sexual gratification, could be obtained using a convenient disposable animated sex machine, a simple penile receptacle in which to deposit their ejaculate without further consideration – as many

27

and as often as possible, if given free rein to do so. He was confident that, given the same opportunity he had discovered for himself, most men would behave in the same way.

His peripatetic behaviour had simply reinforced this philosophy and taken him to every known sexual paradise in the Far East, not once but dozens of times to indulge his sexual whims. Though he certainly had his critics, those observers who were quick to take the high moral ground and dismiss his lifestyle as base and degenerate and most certainly not consistent with civilised man.

Well, they could damn well think what they like! He had 'rationalised' his 'base' behaviour a long time ago, and it was water off a duck's back. He had seen no reason to change it in the past and, indeed, had no intention of changing it one iota in the future. His presence in the sleazy 'Blue Hawaii', an environment in which he felt naturally at home, transfixed on a stool gawping at a row of disposable sex machines, bore eloquent testimony to the fact that he was addicted to a life of sexual abandon.

His job with the shipping line had given him ample scope to indulge in such carnal watering holes where, when and with whom he liked. Had it been a cop-out? Sure. He could have completed his specialist postgraduate training and settled down to a life of conventional medical practice in a conventional English town, leading a perfectly conventional lifestyle as expected of a doctor in a 'respectable', *conventional* community.

For what purpose? So he could play the eternal game of genetic roulette and throw his tuppence-worth into the biological wheel of fortune on the promise of immortality?

But what a filthy trickster nature was! Using the lure of sex, it had evolved a genetic programme designed to seek out a partner with whom to splice the genes, but alas, the programme did not end there – oh no! It included a permanent social commitment, an eternal provider function for the offspring which drained the very life blood. It was a part of the process of degeneration and regeneration – the 'natural' wearing out and replacement by fresh growth – the death of old wood to make way for the eager young saplings. The selfish gene had evolved and perfected this scheme for immortality a long time ago, with scant regard for individuals.

He was not going to be a part of that game – or at least, he would only play the game up to a certain point; experience the natural pleasures that enticed humanity in the same way as animals, but avoid the traps – the burdens of parenthood or fixed social ties to one ageing female partner. Perfect!

Sure – he was paying lip service to the primal instincts which compelled men to pursue women in order to copulate with them and so deposit their seed in their wombs. But he was having the last laugh over nature. He'd scattered his seed far and wide, with a nonchalant contempt for the process of reproduction which never needed to concern itself with the consequences. Carefree orgasms! That had been his motto. As many and as often as he liked – and with the most beautiful women the world could offer. He had triumphed over nature. He had exposed it as the trickster that it was. Never could it lure him into its carefully laid trap. Never would he succumb to its subtle enticements or yield wholly to its unwritten command.

A peanut strikes him on the forehead. It brings him back to the moment. He looks up at the stage. The girls are getting impatient. His facial signals have indicated a contract, but he is taking too long to initiate the ritual negotiations. The peanut, momentarily annoying, brings a wry smile to his face. How apt! How perfectly symbolic! They were only monkeys anyway. Mere animals. Fuck machines. Repositories for his ejaculate – yes, simple penile receptacles – suitably animated. He had vanquished nature and would take all the pleasure and none of the pain.

The nod. Two nods. The girls scamper down the wooden steps faster than a man can blink. He's never seen such eagerness. It could only serve to increase the pleasure.

Distraction. Commotion. Intrusion through the deep red velvet curtain veiling the entrance. He looks up. It couldn't be a brawl. That was almost unheard of on the strip where men came to get women and could never be disappointed.

Ah ha! Police raid. He recognises the characteristic gesticulations and threatening posturing of the vice squad, frequent visitors to each and every bar on the strip. Although plain-clothed and casually dressed like ordinary punters, their intimidating aura and the defensive posture of the management is unmistakeable.

The heated exchange of the confrontation ceases as abruptly as it had begun. Smiles all round. Effusive good humour. An invitation to sit. Brisk gestures to waiters to bring drinks – most certainly not Coca-Cola, but the best brandy in the house.

They had been quick tonight in agreeing the tariff, despite the brief argument at the entrance. Perhaps fees had been unilaterally raised and the management had initially objected. Now it is all smiles and handshakes as the four plainclothes policemen are ushered to a dark recess on the other side of the bar with a good view of the stage. Waiters scurry. Four lithesome females appear from nowhere. They are eagerly welcomed as they slot into place, one beside each man.

He chuckles cynically to himself. Social policing. Community harmony. Perfect empathy with the guardians of the law, that's what it was – get to know your local policeman, the man on the beat. What better way than to wine and dine him and let him fuck your staff? It was a gilt-edged insurance policy, the best protection money could buy.

The girls arrive.

'What your name?' says one.

'Harry – what's yours?'

'Me Dolores. She Isabella.'

'Where you from?'

'England.'

'Where you stay?'

'The Intercontinental in Makati.'

'How long you stay?'

'Three or four days – maybe more.'

'What you do?'

'In business.'

He knows that anyone who gives that reply to an enquiry,

30

polite or otherwise, means 'mind-your-own-fucking-business'. But then Dolores and Isabella are not to know that. He had stopped admitting he was a doctor a long time ago, after one of his visits to Thailand. It had made him feel uncomfortable with the thought that such a responsible, upstanding pillar of society, whose true vocation was to give succour to those in need, should be seen taking advantage of the wretched plight of the Third World poor, whose desperation drove them to sell sex in order to simply survive.

Apart from the vaguely moral sensitivity, on a more pragmatic level, he'd found it often modified the attitude and enthusiasm of the response from the object of desire – as if an invisible barrier had been erected which had the same effect as the small grille between the priest and the sinner in the confessional box. But in place of a list of sins confessed, he'd get a barrage of complaints, imaginary or otherwise, which tended to block or at least dampen the sheer visceral indulgence of the proceedings.

'What kind business?'

'Import–Export. Antiques. Historical artefacts – you know the sort of thing.'

That silences them. Their vocabulary and conceptual expression of the English language is virtually exhausted after the usual question-answer routine that determines punter potential.

He tires of the preliminaries, brief and mindless as they are, and is keen to get moving.

'How much bar fine?'

'250 pesos ... each.'

'Go fetch Mamasan.'

Isabella shoots off at breakneck speed, leaving Dolores to move closer in appreciation of his sweeping offer to take both and his seeming lack of concern to fork out 500 pesos for their release from the bar. Such business potential has to be carefully cultivated and protected, although he hasn't yet verbalised his intention of taking them both back to his hotel. She places one hand on his waist and states rather than asks, in a cheerfully expectant manner:

'I come too?'

'Of course, my dear.'

The ageing Mamasan, probably an ex-bargirl, approaches with her notepad primed.

'You take Isabella AND Dolores?'

He nods sanguinely, reaches for his wallet and hands her five crisp 100-peso bills and settles the 350 peso drinks' bill with a handful of grubby 20-peso notes which includes a generous tip.

The contract confirmed, the girls disappear behind another velvet curtain on the other side of the bar and within minutes reappear ready to go. The similarity to a 'fast food' take-out service is compelling.

They emerge into the street. It is two a.m. and still bustling: beggars everywhere; cripples hideously deformed; groping hands; desperate clawing hands; grubby wretched children in filthy ragged vests selling chewing gum and one cigarette at a time – such hopelessness. Security guards cradle their pump-action shotguns slouched under the awnings of the currency exchange offices. These are especially numerous in the red light area – instant sex means instant cash requirement, and the girls would never take travellers' cheques.

It is steamy. The temperature is still in the eighties. The odour of open sewers hangs heavy in the air. They walk slowly along Mabini Street and take a left turn at the first intersection opposite the Las Palmas hotel. His steps are carefully measured to be sure of where his feet will land. The pavement is uneven and there are gaping holes.

And the bodies. Wrinkly old men and wrinkly old women clinging to a life that has rejected them cruelly, praying that the end will be swift and painless. There are young women too, with tiny, fragile-looking babies, who have set up home on the sidewalk. Their bedroom is a carefully positioned cardboard box, their possessions no more than a filthy threadbare blanket and a pile of crinkled newspapers.

He feels a little drunk and dissociated from the squalor and wretchedness literally at his feet. It is as if it is completely natural in this exotic location to see beggars and homeless souls living on filthy pavements next to an open-sewer drain.

'You take taxi?'

'I want walk while – get fresh air – you understand?'

The two girls can barely disguise their disapproval, silent as it is, but are careful not to antagonise.

'OK. OK. We walk.'

'Not far to Midtown hotel. Then we take taxi – Intercontinental.'

He talks their pidgin. It comes out naturally and seems more appropriate.

The connecting side street to the Midtown hotel is much less illuminated. There are no bars, only shops and offices shuttered and impregnable with padlocks and chains. It is deserted and quiet. The limited lighting makes walking on the pavements that much more hazardous. There seemed to be no shortage of manholes in Manila but a serious shortage of manhole covers. The scrap value gave them a short half-life for their intended purpose, and their swift disappearance caused great danger for the unsuspecting pedestrian – perhaps more danger even than the muggers who could slip out of the shadows wielding knives or machetes if they spied a vulnerable prey.

Oblivious of the perils the dark night might thrust upon them, they cross the road arm in arm at the next intersection as the brightly lit front entrance of the Midtown hotel comes into view.

The outline of a lone figure, vaguely European in the dim light, crosses the road towards them. He is tall, with broad shoulders, and his straight-backed jaunty stride causes the three of them to simultaneously look up as if he radiated some invisible signal to his presence. As he draws alongside, the girls, seeing that he is definitely European – and young and handsome cannot resist offering demure smiles. And then, to reassure their new-found patron of their unwavering loyalty they increase the vice-like grip on each arm and cry out, as if in rehearsed unison: 'He very handsome ... just like you, Harry!'

For a moment, his eyes meet those of the young man, who looks no older than 18. In that split-second, there is invoked in him a strange sensation. It is odd – entirely unexpected and

33

quite inappropriate in the circumstances. It continues to dominate his consciousness even after they have passed each other without so much as a cursory acknowledgement. He cannot relate the feeling to previous experience, but perhaps it is the San Miguel beer.

The figure was a total stranger, a fleeting apparition in the half-light of a Manila backstreet who would hardly warrant a first glance, let alone a second. And yet, as they'd passed and briefly eyeballed each other, he'd definitely felt something he simply could not explain. It was as if a sensor, some long-forgotten memory deep within his subconscious, had been momentarily activated. It was eerie – non-threatening, but still faintly alarming. He is unable to categorise the feeling as fear, anger, pleasure, love, hate, or indeed any emotion that might be familiar from past experience.

The two girls, despite their contrived frivolity and total preoccupation with keeping him amused and in good humour, sense the strange effect exerted by the young man. They launch into a giggling dialogue implying that their presumed sponsor might have a sexual profile broader or more deviant than initially apparent. He notices their reaction and his mind is jolted back to the reality of the moment. He laughs loudly.

'No, no – NO! I promise. Me not like that ... me ALL man,' he says imploringly in the feeble parody of their pidgin which is far from convincing.

They do not understand. But then they do not care. He is still firmly sandwiched between them, the butter on their bread and hopefully the provider of enough cash to pay the bills for the next month.

'How very odd ... very odd indeed,' he mutters more to himself as they reach the grand front entrance to the Midtown hotel. A bellboy pulls at the huge glass door and ushers them in with a flourish.

'It's OK – we only want taxi!'

'Thank you, sir.'

He blows a whistle and waves to the first cab in a line of black Toyota Corollas snaking around into the slip road.

'Black taxi, sir – very good.'

'Yes, I know – meter that works, very good.'

He hands him a 5-peso note.

'Thank you, sir.'

He blows the whistle again, only more vigorously. Harry stands silently and allows himself a faint smile. Visitors to Manila soon learn to avoid the yellow cabs. They are self-employed and invariably forget to switch on the meter, if indeed there is one. To avoid the wrangling which inevitably follows at the destination, most passengers pay the arbitrarily inflated fare. Black taxis are strictly controlled with all the journeys metered correctly. Harry had learnt that lesson a long time ago.

'Let's go. Intercontinental please,' he says, motioning to the girls.

Dolores climbs in first as Isabella holds back to enable their benefactor to sit between them. He ducks down and slides in easily on the plastic seat. Isabella completes the sandwich, pushing him with her backside in a show of flirtation.

He acknowledges it with an automatic grin and then leans forward to stretch over the driver's shoulder. He sees his identity disc prominently displayed on the dashboard: 'Alfredo Romero 626120'.

'Alfredo – can you take a right at the first intersection and go down...'

'Sorry. Slowly ... speak little English.'

'Don't worry – just cross over here and take the next turning towards Del Pilar ... and not the left to Makati ... that's it ... down there...'

He thrusts his hand over the driver's shoulder to make sure he is understood. The girls look puzzled. He is aware of their mild concern, but cannot explain something he does not understand himself. He presses the driver.

'As quick as you can please, Alfredo.'

He flops back in the seat, looking first at one and then the other.

'I'm sorry ladies ... I don't know what it is but I must find out ... I must ask ... I simply must...'

They look at him in silence and then each other. They force

35

a plastic smile and then shrug their shoulders in a gesture of faintly alarmed curiosity. His expression is a mixture of perplexity and mild agitation. He takes on a distant preoccupied stare for a moment, oblivious and unresponsive to the two lithesome creatures who start to entwine their limbs and bodies around him in a fashion more workmanlike than passionate.

The cab slows at the Del Pilar intersection.

'There! There! Stop! STOP!' he shouts.

He fumbles clumsily through the thick wad in his wallet and thrusts a crumpled 20-peso note into the hand of the driver.

'Keep the change.'

He jumps out, turning to his two companions and calling loudly and earnestly:

'Come on girls – out. OUT.'

Dolores, looking even more puzzled, does as she is bid although tardily, with a look of bemusement and guarded resignation. Isabella, equally bemused but not able to conceal a faint alarm, follows on the other side.

The taxi drives away, leaving all three standing motionless on the corner as if the next move is uncertain. His attention is drawn to the food vendor's stall just a few yards along the pavement, where, under clouds of steam and acrid smoke, hunks of chicken quarters and other less identifiable pieces of meat sizzle and spit. The aroma of onions and exotic spices saturates the warm humid air. At the distant end of the stall stands a man with his back to them in animated conversation with three girls.

'That's him. That's definitely him.'

He hesitates, doubting for a moment his certainty, but then takes a couple of bold steps towards the man and gently taps him on the shoulder.

'Excuse me . . .'

The man spins round with lightning speed. There is a more than tangible aura of irritation and imminent hostility. He is clearly not pleased that the intense intercourse with the intended object or objects of his desire has been so rudely and unexpectedly interrupted. Besides, such uninvited taps on the

36

back are likely to be dangerous. He assumes a defensive posture which transforms into one of aggression immediately he realises no impending assault.

'Yeah?'

He is plainly an American. Probably a GI from Clark Airbase or maybe a sailor from the naval base at Subic Bay.

'Oooh-oh, I-I-I'm awfully sorry ... I really thought you ... uuuh, were an old friend of mine ... sorry...'

The man remains still, cocked ready for action, but then shrugs as if to say he is doing a favour but beware.

'OK pal ... forget it.'

He turns back slowly to resume his conversation with the ladies of the night.

'We go now, Harry?' begs Dolores with the controlled impatience of a professional who simply wants to get on with the job in hand.

He is still confused and doesn't respond immediately. Isabella reinforces the exhortation of her partner.

'Harry – we go?'

'What d'ya say? Oh-oh ... sorry ladies...' he says with a puzzled look on his face, 'yes, yes ... of course ... c'mon, what are we waiting for – let's go.'

CHAPTER 2

EMPRESS OF THE SEAS

No man will be a sailor who has contrivance enough to get himself into a jail, for being in a ship is being in a jail, with the chance of being drowned ... a man in jail has more room, better food, and commonly better company.

Samuel Johnson (1709–1784)

What men call gallantry and gods adultery
Is much more common when the climate's sultry

Don Juan, Lord Byron (1788–1824)

The first requisite of a gentleman is to be a perfect animal.

Friedrich Nietzche (1844–1900)

'Hello Barry – good to see you!'

'Lovely to see you back, Doctor – welcome aboard.'

It is always the same feeling when he returns and boards the ship. From the moment he steps gingerly onto the frail and rickety aluminium gangway and ducks his head into the shell door opening, just above the water line, it is as if he is entering the very innards of a huge, black-hulled steel beast and experiencing invariably a perception that he is returning to a vast metal womb, which like its natural counterpart, protects and provides for all within. It is a totally self-sufficient organism. It might just as well be another planet. As he steps inside the shell door the world outside evaporates in an instant.

'I'll use the elevator, I think, Barry.'

'Right you are, sir. Let me take your bag.'

The Master-at-Arms grabs the handle of the battered leather valise and turns towards the elevator. Despite his advancing years, he is an agile, tall and straight backed man, with an unmistakable military bearing, a conspicuous testimony to 30 years in the Royal Navy. A thick, luxuriant grey-black beard and an exuberant handlebar moustache curled ostentatiously at each extremity give him a grandeur which is well-suited to a Master-at-Arms on a luxury cruise liner. It is one of the many nautical images which passengers are conditioned to expect, and his authoritative presence on the gangway never fails to impress.

'A good leave, I trust, Doctor?'

'Very enjoyable. Very enjoyable indeed, Master-at-Arms!'

Images of Manila, still fresh in his mind, are invoked and bring a smile to the doctor's face. He winks at the distinguished-looking security officer, who returns a wink of acknowledgment.

They wait a few moments, and then the elevator door opens.

'Michelle!'

'Harry!'

Eyes are riveted to the curvaceous outline of a striking brunette in her mid-twenties leaning against one side of the elevator. As one of the ship's photographers, Michelle is one of the most popular crew members. Bubbly and gregarious, she is easy-come-easy-go with her favours, especially sexual favours, which probably accounts for the fact that she is decidedly more popular with the men on the ship than the women.

'Thanks, Barry. See you later.'

'You're welcome, Doctor. Take care now.'

The elevator doors close.

'Harry, it's great to see you – I really missed you...'

'Yes, I missed you too. How on earth did you manage to survive so long without...?'

'Well, it wasn't easy, but – you know...'

The elevator starts to move upwards and they embrace passionately. He stands back and shamelessly fondles her breasts as if assessing the ripeness of watermelons.

'Michelle, you know you've got the best tits on board,' he pronounces solemnly as if he is an unchallenged authority on such matters.

'So you keep telling me, Doctor.'

He continues to fondle them with almost clinical detachment. Michelle does not object. Michelle never objects. She is perfectly attuned to her sexuality and the potent effect she exerts on men. She uses such natural talents plainly and simply, unaffected by pretension or the complexity of behavioural self-analysis, simply for the physical pleasure that can be harvested.

The elevator door opens. A man and woman, a couple of

aged passengers well into their late seventies, appear startled as the groping hands are quickly retracted.

'Good morning. Excuse me, sir, madame – see you later, Michelle.'

He throws the valise over one shoulder and makes his way along the narrow alleyway on the upper deck towards the aft end and the officers' quarters. Beads of perspiration run down his neck. Sydney is hot in January and the air-conditioning of the 20-year-old ship is not so effective in port, when the great mass of steel lies motionless at the mercy of a baking sun.

He always finds it a struggle rejoining the ship and carrying his case from the quayside down on six deck to the officers' accommodation high up on the quarter deck at the stern. It is the only time he uses the elevator. When the ship is at sea it is invariably monopolised by passengers or stewards and cleaners. Then, it is much quicker to run up the stairs and benefit from the gratuitous exercise at the same time.

Slightly breathless and feeling the strain in his legs despite using the elevator, he eventually reaches the cool comfort of his quarters. He sinks into the low soft armchair with a sigh of relief. An image of Michelle, or more precisely, an image of Michelle's massive breasts, is still fresh in his mind. Maybe tonight. He'll call her later.

Feeling tired and content to sit and daydream, his thoughts drift as the distant hum of generators induces a feeling of somnolence. Somnolence soon turns to rumination and the continually recurring thoughts about his life, his very existence and what it all means. There are always the same questions, but there are never any satisfactory answers.

What was the purpose? Maybe there was none, but if there was, how could one discover and fulfil such a purpose? And if there wasn't, then what justification could there be for anything?

To start with, what the hell was he doing here? Stuck in a small metal box staring out of a plate-sized porthole at a featureless sky, surrounded by scores of other similar small boxes. Was this the freedom he had yearned for when cooped up in classes or half-asleep on a tedious ward round at medical school? A freedom that might reveal the reason for it all?

The seeds of doubt had been sown in those early days when he had begun to question everything. Towards the end of his initial student training and shortly before qualifying as a doctor, he had started to feel uneasy about conventional patterns of life and the predictable mould into which, like everyone else, he was becoming inexorably shaped. Could it have been simply that he had been unable to cope with the pressure, the stresses and strains of a particularly demanding occupation?

No. Most certainly not. He'd always had confidence in his mental and physical resilience and had never shirked adversity or avoided a challenge. Purpose. That was the fundamental question which formed the basis for his doubts. The reason for it all. The ultimate aim. What the hell was it? He had asked himself time and time again, but the immediate preoccupations of the moment, the never-ending distractions of daily activity, had prevented him from delving too deeply into areas of thought and philosophy which most of his friends and classmates dismissed as negative and cynical, if not downright barmy.

Despite these ideas, he had launched himself vigorously and enthusiastically into the rigours of post-graduate training, determined that he would follow his chosen career right through to the bitter end. One eminent professor at the medical school had been unequivocal in his advice to young supplicants to the profession. 'ACE' was what he had called it – Ambition with a capital 'A', Commitment with a capital 'C' and Enthusiasm with a capital 'E' was the key to success. These were the qualities considered admirable and unquestionably appropriate to the fresh new emerging generation of doctors. It promised to be a hard slog, but well worth while. The seniors thought so and felt it their duty to pass on the same spirit to the juniors.

For a while it had looked as though tradition would triumph. The smouldering feelings of disenchantment with a system so clearly defined and laid down by others, were buried beneath a

44

pile of commitment that demanded all-consuming instant attention. But the seeds of doubt had already been firmly implanted, and although for a while dormant, given time and the right moment would undoubtedly germinate, burst forth and release him from the shackles of conventional existence. He would evolve a new being, develop a fresh consciousness and establish a revitalised soul in resonance with nature.

He would perceive his existence in a different light, recognise and develop a new set of values, fresh values, absolute values of existence based on the natural senses, and not on the accepted ideologies handed down from one generation to the next without question.

As he began to lock in to the perpetual grind of conventional life, the hub of which was work, work and more work, the seeds of doubt began to shoot. At first it was slow, but they soon gathered momentum and finally were able to burst through and shatter the tough outer shell of conformity and state their case boldly. They demanded answers.

Work. What did it mean? Every second, every minute, every hour of the day had to be filled with some meaningful activity. 'Meaningful' as judged by the accepted norms – getting up at the prescribed hour and rushing out to join the commuter stampede, to get stuck in a traffic jam or squashed into a sardine-packed train and arriving at the workplace with stress levels already approaching maximum.

Stress, stress and more stress. Did humans really need it to survive, or was it detrimental to health? Granted, there was a minimum of stress to be experienced in order to prime the organism into optimal function, to boot the computer into function mode. Maybe if stress was removed completely, the result would be total inertia of the animal and perception of the environment zero. But too much stress? The never-ending stress of the rat race. Was that not damaging to the organism, compounding damage that would eventually destroy? How on earth could there be any meaning to that?

But it was the pathway that the vast majority of people took from the first breath. Once they had embarked on the treadmill of life, they were at the mercy of forces which would ultimately destroy them. It was a one-way ticket to the same destination – death and oblivion for all as if they had never existed. Such futility!

He remembers telling patients how 'stress' kills and to try to rule it out of their lives. But how on earth could ordinary people be expected to resist the mighty forces of convention?

There were a few who had begun to challenge the work ethic of the industrialised societies, but the simultaneous evolution of the consumer ethic ensured that the work ethic would still reign supreme.

Civilised man had lost it. He could only see as far as the walls of the box he had built around himself. He could not see outside the box, into the far distance, the outside world, the very nature of things.

Alas, once in place, securely contained within the box, it was exceedingly difficult to escape. Yet he, Harry Lester, with his oft cynical cry that life became repetitive after the first breath, had made the fateful decision to attempt such a thing. With supreme effort, overcoming all the forces ranged against him, he had made his move.

His chosen escape route had been the sea. He'd turned his back on his career and on the set of values he had been expected to blindly follow. The adventure, glamour and larger-than-life images that centuries of tradition had nurtured about the seafaring world had been, it seemed to him at the time, the perfect escape. In one fell swoop he would smash the mould of convention into which he had almost firmly, inextricably been set, liberate his mind and set off down a path of spiritual enlightenment. He would distance himself as far away as possible from the routine, the repetitive and the unending tedium of conventional lifestyles.

Giving notice to quit his hospital job had caused a minor reverberation, and when colleagues totally enmeshed in the career struggle learnt he had found a job with a shipping company as a doctor on a passenger liner they assumed he had completely flipped. He'd cocked a snook to all and sundry, and not a tear was shed when he finally left.

In the beginning it had been like he had imagined. But as he was later to realise, it was simply because it was different. After a short while, his vision had cleared and the true nature of a life at sea became evident. It became apparent that one set of constraints had been replaced by another – less obvious, less conventional, but still constraints. The ship was a parody of life ashore, a well-defined microcosm of the society he'd striven to escape from. It was a replica of social organisation on land, except it was limited physically by the dimensions of the hull and the surrounding expanse of ocean.

Ships, especially modern cruise ships, bore little resemblance to the rotting hulks of the 18th century with their pressganged crews, but the notion was essentially correct. Prison. There may have been the luxury and freedom of movement on board, but the box of social convention he had deserted ashore had been replaced by another space of not exactly the same dimensions, but a box nevertheless.

But at least the opportunities for researching the sensual path of enlightenment had been more readily available. First there was alcohol – consumed when he liked, as much as he liked. And then there was sex – as freely available as the alcohol – with an almost infinite range of partners around the world.

And so, despite the realisation that there were still some rules and restrictions which curtailed his total freedom of choice, he had been willing to accept the constraints, especially in view of the generous leaves he could take away from the ship at frequent intervals.

His life became a compromise. Two or three months on the ship followed by one or two months ashore on leave, completely free to do as he wished. In any one year, the total leave amounted to five months, which had to be better than any sort of working life ashore.

And how the time flew! It hadn't taken long to settle into a new pattern of life. One, two, three – the years rolled by in an almost timeless fashion until here he was, ten years on, alone with his thoughts, still indulging in a lifestyle which he admitted, by most conventional criteria was considered decadent and unwholesome and totally aimless. But what did he care?

The clanking of a gigantic crane with a container swaying perilously beneath it jolts him from his ruminations. He stares out of the porthole and then looks at his watch. Christ! Ten minutes to five. In port, he was supposed to attend an evening clinic at five o'clock. And it was his first day back. There was just time for a quick shower and to change into his uniform. He'd switch his mind into gear on the way to the ship's hospital below on six deck. The nursing sister would be expecting him.

'Evening, Suzanne.'
  'Harry! You're back!'
  'And delighted, of course.'
  'Well, it's good to see you.'
Suzanne Richards is the senior nurse on board the *Empress of the Seas*. There are three nurses in all, a pharmacy dispenser and two general assistants, not to mention Dr Harry Lester, to provide the medical care for a crew of over 1000 and a passenger complement of nearly 2000.

The nurses invariably come from London teaching hospitals. Most are in their late twenties or early thirties and have done a wide range of jobs before. The shipping line considers it expedient to employ those with a broad experience and of a more mature age, to cope with the peculiar, if not unique, environment of cruise ships. Only very occasionally will they take on a girl relatively fresh from her training and still in her early twenties. When that happens it is usually because of an unforeseen crisis in staff numbers and a ship needs a nurse urgently.

Miss Richards is 29 and has certainly been around. She's worked in locations all over the world, from the cold forbidding expanse of Northern Canada inside the Arctic Circle to the dusty fierce heat of the Simpson Desert in Southern Australia, with Eskimos in the former and Aboriginal tribes in the latter. She'd qualified at the Charing Cross hospital in London but had spent most of her life in jobs abroad. Taking a job on a ship had seemed about the only thing she hadn't done, and a luxury cruise liner had to be the most comfortable way to continue her itinerant lifestyle.

Her professional competence is not in doubt, and she has the demeanour of efficiency combined with a tireless good-natured humour that seems to be the traditional expectation of those in the nursing profession.

If there is one big attraction for girls who are not married and are still considered footloose and fancy-free, it is that the vast majority of the ship's company is made up of men. Suzanne has many admirers – understandably. She is very tall and has long blond hair which she ties up in the day at work but is only too happy to let down on her nights off. She has a large face with prominent cheekbones, an aquiline nose and sensuous lips that threaten to devour. With her statuesque five feet eleven inches, well-filled out top and bottom, she exudes a powerful sexual force which few men can resist.

Harry has not tried. He would admit he has been tempted on occasion, but he has always managed to obey the golden rule – never to tamper with other staff on a casual basis, especially in a department as small as the medical. The potential disruptions and disharmony it might cause were just not worth the trouble. They both acknowledge this rule without ever having to speak it. The rule didn't preclude a serious, more permanent affair, where a well-understood commitment existed – but dabbling was definitely out. He gets on well with all three nurses but feels no compulsion to deepen the relationships, and so he adheres strictly to the golden rule.

'Well, my dear Suzanne, I didn't expect to see any patients down here tonight – what with the attractions of a night on the town in Sydney. What have we got?'

'Three passengers, four crew members – and there should be a couple of more passengers who said they will come down later.'

'What do the crew want? They know it's only genuine emergencies in port.'

'I think Brian can answer that question better than I...'

'Oh, I see – must be the first casualties of Tahiti – yes, it's about five days now since we left that exotic paradise – where all the girls are gorgeous and have all got the clap...'

'Precisely, Harry.'

49

'Well, let's make a start. I'll see the passengers first and then the crew.'

A head with short-cropped grey hair appears around the door. It is Brian Kilroy, the amiable dispenser-cum-technician. The crew members with a venereal complaint usually see him first, and if they have a penile discharge he takes the necessary swab and produces a stained slide to see whether they have gonorrhoea or not. They are then told to report to the doctor.

Venereal diseases are a frequent problem on board, particularly during cruises around the Far Eastern ports where sexual services are on offer openly and abundantly to anyone who stepped ashore. Despite the regular medical propaganda that emanated from the medical department about the risks of sexually transmitted diseases in exotic locations, few crew members could resist the temptations in the girlie bars of Thailand or the Philippines.

Dr Harry Lester is an expert in treating VD. God knows, he's had it enough times himself. At medical school, despite the free and easy sex (at any one time there were over 800 young nurses at the teaching hospital) VD hadn't seemed to be much of a problem. It wasn't until the mid-seventies just after he'd qualified, that he got his first dose from a Gulf Air flight attendant in a casual and shortlived affair. It hadn't concerned him too much and was easily treated. However, it had raised his threshold of awareness to the risks of sexually transmitted diseases. From that time, he'd effectively prevented the almost certain infections associated with a promiscuous, peripatetic lifestyle by taking handfuls of antibiotics *before* intended exposure. With all the casual sexual activity he desired around the world he'd become indifferent, if not smug, even when cruising the heavily contaminated sleazy carnal watering holes of South East Asia.

But now, in the eighties there were disturbing stories emerging. It had been reported there was a new kid on the block – a deadly infection with no known cure – a virus which attacked the body's immune system mercilessly until eventual death. It all sounded a bit dramatic and fanciful, a spectre of demonic

50

doom promoted gleefully by the moral brigade, that element of the establishment which deprecated sexual freedom and viewed sexually diseases transmitted as the wages of sin if not divine retribution. Perhaps this new virus would become the very nemesis of all sexual warriors. Only time would tell.

At the moment it seemed pretty specific and limited, the only reports describing its emergence in the homosexual communities on the West Coast of California, centred around Los Angeles and to a lesser extent similar East Coast communities in New York. There were also cases reported in intravenous drug abusers. Thus far, it appeared it was simply a disease of these lifestyles and should not raise any alarm in heterosexuals. Straightforward, old fashioned heterosexual activity, no matter how rampant, is safe.

Although he is faintly uneasy, he is determined not to allow it to cramp his style or curtail his sexual forays when and where he likes. Still, it did no harm to increase the doses of his preventative antibiotics against the conventional infections on the scientific basis that a healthy, well-protected and minimally exposed immune system will be more than capable of dealing with a pathetic little virus which can only attack those of an alternative sexual persuasion or who stick dirty needles into themselves.

'Can I show you a positive slide, Doctor?' says Brian.

They walk to the far side of the clinic where there is a small room which serves as a laboratory.

'It's already under the microscope, Doctor, if you'd care to look.'

The doctor leans over and peers down the eyepiece of the microscope.

'Very nice too, Brian – beautifully stained intra-cellular diplococci – a classic case of gonorrhoea. How bad was the discharge – as it's now nearly a week since we left Tahiti?'

'Very heavy and thick, Doctor – I cannot recall seeing such a bad infection.'

'What does he do on board?'

'Would you believe he's a chef in the Columbia grill?'

'What?'

51

'I've warned him that you'd be rather annoyed, Doctor...'

'Put the bastard off work – I'll bollock him when he comes in to see me. Suzanne says there are three others to see – anything interesting?'

'A mechanic who is an alcoholic and is going to request you grant him compassionate leave because he claims his wife is carrying on with another man...'

'We'll see about that.'

'A stewardess with a sprained ankle – and, ahum – Geoffrey Smallpiece – you know – the old queer steward from the penthouse suites. Says he's got a personal problem he'd rather discuss with you in private.'

'Let's get started, then.'

The first passenger is called and the grind of consultations begins.

'Good evening, Mr Brenner, what can I do for you...?'

After the grateful steward has shuffled out, nodding his head in appreciation, Suzanne appears.

Harry speaks: 'That's more than enough for the first day back. I'm getting out of here. Listen Suzanne, I'll be downstairs in the gym if you need me for anything. I've got an hour session before the cocktail party tonight, which should take care of the calories, know what I mean?'

Harry makes a supreme effort to keep in shape, if only to balance the social excesses. The unending round of cocktail parties and the glut of sumptuous food on offer inevitably piles on the calories, and keeping a normal weight and shape isn't easy. Harry's genetic advantage of being on the slim side makes his task that much easier.

At six-thirty in the evening the gym is usually deserted except for one or two regular enthusiasts. It is better if there are only men. Not that he likes to watch men exercise, but the presence of lithe, supple female forms bending, twisting, grunting and exposing themselves in tightly fitting leotard costumes invariably distracts him from his purpose. But then, he would have to admit, his self-disciplined approach to such exercise is primarily for the purpose of maintaining his youthful body image so that he can continue to attract and success-fully proposition such females, despite being well into his fifth decade.

Tonight, the gym is empty. He can set about his usual routine undistracted. First a warm-up ten minutes before working his way round the full circuit of exercise machines and finishing with 20 minutes of hard pedalling on the bike.

Vest soaked through and rivulets of sweat pouring down his forehead, he is nearly finished pedalling when she comes through the glass-door entrance. Harry glances sideways at the mirror and wipes the sweat from his face.

Slim. Very slim. As he likes them. Nicely shaped legs. A narrow waist and a small, inconsequential bust, but that doesn't matter. Overall, a conscientiously preserved body on the down-ward side of 40. In fact, on second glance, as she comes closer, her facial lines put her closer to 50. A plain but not unattractive face, with prominent cheekbones and sensual lips.

He looks up absentmindedly with perfect timing, as if it is mere chance that he has noticed her entrance. He smiles an unaffected smile.

'Hi there!'

'Hello.'

The black leotard fits neatly and highlights her slender curves. The wrinkles on her neck, not visible at the door, confirm her age is nearer the 50 mark. His exercise routine has all but finished, so he feels no conflict in seizing the oppor-tunity. She hasn't started yet, so it shouldn't be considered impertinent.

'Just joined the ship, have you?' he asks blandly.

'Yes. Had an awful flight from LA. Can you believe it took nearly twenty hours through Honolulu and Fiji?'

She speaks in a relaxed and natural fashion with a familiarity which one might expect to see in old acquaintances, not total strangers meeting for the first time on a cruise ship in the Pacific.

'You must be exhausted.'

'I always find I get over the jet-lag much quicker with a session in the gym.'

53

'How long will you be staying on board?'

'A couple of weeks – until Hawaii. I really need the break – the pressure at work has just been too much this year, and if I hadn't grabbed this opportunity then I think I'd have gone nuts.'

'Doesn't your husband need to work off his jet-lag too?'

'I'm travelling alone.'

'Really?'

The surprised intonation of his one-word response and the questioning look invites her to elaborate her answer. Harry is confident that she will, with little restraint. It never ceases to amaze him how quickly a total stranger could be encouraged to launch into an intimate personal conversation revealing details of their lives which they mightn't even reveal to close family or friends.

It was the isolation factor of cruising. It was as if the ship was a remote island, or even another planet far away from their own earthly world, encapsulated in a time warp of absolute discretion, where it was confidently assumed that all secrets would remain safe and all fantasies could be realised without fear of discovery. It was probably one of the most important attractions of cruising. It provided an escape, if only a temporary one, into a different world where the normal social constraints, habits, conventions, rules and moral values could be temporarily ignored. Then, and only then, when all the inhibiting factors had been discarded, like a chrysalis shedding its cocoon, could full rein be given to the basic animal instincts. As far as Harry was concerned, these instincts were lurking in everyone regardless of their demeanour, and if the circumstances were right, could be suitably activated. The cruise ship served as the perfect catalyst for such a transformation.

'I divorced five years ago. I have a grown-up family – two sons and a daughter who lead their own independent lives now. I am a senior fashion editor and my work schedule is pretty demanding. So, getting away on a cruise ship is a heavenly break for me. Away from the office, all the pressure and all the people I know, lovely as they are, I can get lost.

Become completely anonymous. Out of the spotlight. It's very relaxing, you know.'

'Um – I understand.'

Harry raises his eyebrows in acknowledgment and moves his head in measured agreement. And then there is a subtle twinkle in his eye and a broad smile appears. He has seen it all before. Observed the signs and symptoms. Recognised the syndrome and accurately diagnosed the condition. It was going to be easy, so easy from here on in.

He senses a firm enough foundation has been laid for future activity and he need prolong the conversation no further.

'Well – uuh, I mustn't stop you exercising. Maybe we can meet later – for a drink or something?'

She hesitates for a second, perhaps not quite having yet totally shed her chrysalis coat. Harry decides to play his trump card to perform the *coup de grâce* before her residual jet-lag compounds any trace of uncertainty. Before she can answer, he speaks:

'Anyway, please excuse me, I'll have to run now – check by the hospital . . .'

'Are you feeling alright?'

'Fit as a fiddle – oh I'm sorry, I'm the ship's doctor.'

It rarely fails, although he feels a twinge of guilt in using such a ploy, as if it is cheating. Her eyes light up. Ship's doctor, indeed! Decades of Hollywood role models had conditioned a Pavlovian response to that piece of innocent information. Ship's doctor! Degenerate. Hard-drinking. Wild. Exuberant. And above all, a womaniser. The charm of the devil himself. Her face gives an immediate affirmative answer, but before she can speak, Harry continues, to make it even easier for her:

'It's the Captain's cocktail party for passengers joining in Sydney. Starts around seven forty-five. See you there?'

'I will most certainly look forward to that, Doctor.'

'The name's Harry – please call me Harry.'

'And I'm Janine. Janine McAllister. So pleased to meet you – Harry.'

* * *

He slips through the service door, discreetly situated behind a curtain to the left of the stage. It is 8.30 and the Captain's cocktail party in the Grand Lounge is in full swing. In fact, the huge room which is used for the variety shows on board is literally heaving. There must have been a lot of fresh embarks in Sydney. It is a sea of glittering sequins and shiny black tuxedos. A cacophony of human sounds mixed with the chinking of glasses and the steady background throb of the orchestra. To his right, Harry sees the long line of passengers waiting patiently to have their individual picture taken with the Captain. It is a slow and laborious process, and most of the hour-long cocktail party will be spent waiting patiently in line. But the picture is important. It will be used as the centrepiece for the album back home. After all, this was an expensive trip on an illustrious cruise liner, the flagship of the fleet nonetheless, and meeting the Captain (with photographic evidence) puts a seal on the impression of their importance, status and privilege as cruise people.

The officers are dressed in traditional mess kit, black trousers, patent leather shoes and a white cotton bumfreezer jacket, not unlike the waiters, but carrying prominently the officers' gold bars of rank to ensure there is no misunderstanding as to their exalted position on board the *Empress*. The Doctor has the three gold bars of senior rank, with red in between to signify 'medical'. It is always an easy conversation opener for passengers who might feel ill at ease with so many distinguished looking characters on show.

'Hello, and may I ask what you do on board?'

'I'm the Doctor,' invariably eases tension and opens up a conversation, as if the medical man is a trusted old confidant with whom they can discuss their most intimate personal details. Unfortunately, the response more often than not gets out of hand, and he is arraigned with a list of symptoms or medical problems on which he is expected to pass an expert opinion. It is usually at that point that he exercises his host prerogative to excuse himself with a 'Must mingle, circulate, promised to see somebody – lovely to meet you – we'll have a drink sometime...'

Reality merges with fantasy. Myth and legend of the seafarers' world generates the appropriate questions and answers. The cocktail parties on board, and especially the Captain's, are an essential part of the elaborate charade where passengers and ship's crew play their respective parts. They act out their roles, subconsciously adhering to an age-old script that even first-time cruisers seem to know.

Tonight is no exception.

'Good evening.'

'Nice to meet you. Have you just joined?'

'Yes – uuh, will the weather be fine when we sail?'

'Of course! I think there's only a force two or three forecast – bit of a stiff breeze – you won't even feel the ship move.'

'More champagne, madame?'

'Excuse me – must mingle.'

He is not too concerned with rooting out the young blood tonight, for he has the lady in the leotard in mind. Although she is not exactly youthful, she is well-preserved and the opportunity has presented itself. Even if something better materialises she will be worth the experience, at least for one night. By now she must be getting disappointed. The cocktail party is nearly over, and the guests will soon be leaving for dinner. The anticipation of meeting the doctor has faded with his non-appearance. Perhaps he was simply being polite in the gym, and his remark about seeing her at the party had been casual and unintended.

He spies her. She is alone, looking over heads and appearing a little forlorn. He will put an end to her agony and gain her undying gratitude.

'Hello!'

'Well, hiya!'

'Have a good workout – Janine, isn't it?'

'I think I overdid it on the treadmill or I'm still suffering from jet-lag.'

'It was a pretty long flight you had. It'll take you a few days to recover.'

'Well, I guess I'll get an early night after dinner.'

Is that the cue to fix up the rendezvous before retiring for the night? Maybe, maybe not. There's no rush. It's a dead cert.

'Harry – it is Harry, isn't it?'

'Yeah.'

'You know something, I've been on lots of cruises and – well, I've often wondered, I mean I've always wanted to ask someone like yourself, you know a mature professional, a doctor – I mean, don't you ever get fed up with this life, the continual travelling, the transient lifestyle, never staying in one place long enough to get to know people – to form relationships? I hope that's not too personal a question, but do you know what I mean?'

'I know exactly what you mean. It is, I must admit, a rather odd, almost antisocial occupation in a way. I suppose it might even be considered a trifle decadent or maybe wholly degenerate to some. Trouble is, I've gotten used to it. Been at sea for far too long. Well and truly hooked. They say when you first go to sea, if you stay for longer than two years, it's too late – your heart is captured for ever. Well, I don't think I could ever be that romantic about it, but I have to confess, after a while, the lifestyle assumes a sort of seductive quality, and before you know where you are you've been at sea for years – a veritable old sea dog.'

'Tell me about working on a cruise ship. So much socialising, being nice to passengers all the time, always in the public eye – you must get fed up with it, surely?'

'Yes, I do. Of course. Especially cocktail parties! "Never was so much said, by so many, for so long, about so little" – that's my definition, with apologies to Winston Churchill. But you tell me, Janine, why do you come on a cruise ship – what's the appeal?'

'Aaah, that would be telling. I suppose I know it will be guaranteed escapism from my normal world. A chance to wind down and take stock of my life. Without all the distractions, a real opportunity to think about so many things – you know, contemplate a little, if that doesn't sound too corny.'

'No. Not at all. I know exactly what you mean. And it's true.

But I think you have to admit though, that life on board cruise liners panders primarily to the – shall we say "non-spiritual" side of man – and woman, of course.'

'Do you really think so?'

'Quite honestly, the whole operation on these floating palaces of pleasure is geared to furthering hedonistic pursuits – or put more crudely, satisfying the animal instincts. Sun, booze and sex, if you will. Not necessarily in that order, of course, but you know what I mean.'

'You may be right, Harry, but you make it sound so, well – so basic, so animal. We are human beings, after all...'

'Veneer, my dear. Simply the veneer of recent civilisation barely camouflaging our animal heritage.'

'But surely, a man of your education and intellect must have some, shall we say, spiritual leanings. You're not all animal – are you?'

'Of course not. Of course not! But there is a little animal in all of us – maybe more in some than others. In my mind, for the vast majority of mankind, life is a constant duel between two opposing forces – the mind and the flesh, emotion and logic, the reflex response or the cold analytical appraisal, abstract values versus the material ethic – I suppose ultimately, it is the spiritual nature of man versus the animal component he finds difficult to control. These are the two protagonists of human existence which dictate our conscious and subconscious experience.

'Animal is destructive, dissipative. Spiritual is creative and yearns for immortality. Man's conflict in life is to arrive at a balance of these two forces, establish a truce and some sort of viable stability...'

'That sounds like a lecture in philosophy or ethics.'

'Ha ha, Janine, I'm sorry if it sounded a bit pompous and expert, but in this job you get plenty of time to meditate on such things.'

'I'm sure you do, I'm sure you do.'

'But as I said before, working on a cruise ship does tend to pander to that part of the spectrum of human behaviour which is pleasure-seeking – more animal than human, I'm afraid. And

I do confess, there are times when I feel frustrated and unworthy, as if I am unchallenged and unfulfilled and there is an imbalance between the two forces...'

Janine purses her lips, pondering a measured response. Harry has little more to say. As far as he is concerned the quarry is well and truly ensnared, and it is now just a matter of the logistics of the final assault. As if in cahoots, and with perfect timing, the orchestra stops playing and the cruise director takes the microphone just as she is about to speak.

'Ladies and gentlemen, could I have your attention please...'

It is the final stage of the cocktail party, when the senior officers and the Captain are introduced. Each will come forward to the platform when their name is announced, and they will form a line in front of the babbling assembled throng. There they will stand, hands clasped behind their backs, pristine in their starched white mess jackets and gold bars, smiling selfconsciously at a roomful of adulating passengers, and blinking at the continuous barrage of flash bulbs. The Captain will be naturally last and will make his customary speech of welcome.

Each character gets a brief, one-liner introduction. It is showbiz.

'And the man who operates the rubber bands, ladies and gentlemen, the chief engineer, Mr Steve Hart.'

Applause.

'The gentlemen who makes sure all your creature comforts are attended to, the hotel manager, Mr John McDuff.'

Applause. One or two wolf whistles.

'And here is the guilty man who guarantees to send you home at least six pounds heavier, the food manager, Gordon Philpott...'

Thunderous applause. Whistles and bravos.

Food is a major preoccupation on cruise ships. Most passengers consume everything put before them voraciously. There is ample choice and some take two of the main courses. Three main meals a day, not to mention the sumptuous midnight buffet, greedily consumed by some passengers only a couple of hours after dinner, provide Harry with more than enough patients with every sort of digestive upset imaginable. After a few days of serious eating they will come to the clinic in their droves, with heartburn, flatulence and constipation at the top of the list of complaints. Some simply block up completely. They shove food in at one end faster than it can be eliminated at the other. By about the fifth or sixth day they appear in the clinic, feeling rather sorry for themselves and not a little embarrassed, exhorting the doctor to rid them of their excessive load and deflate their abdomens. Harry always shows the sympathy and compassion expected of a healer, although his management of such problems can hardly be described as gentle. He attacks from both ends, pouring a combination of fierce laxatives down their gullet whilst firing a variety of blockbuster suppositories into the outlet. The results are usually dramatic and swift.

Perhaps the cruise director recognises the subliminal logic in his line-up order, for Harry is next to be announced.

'And now, ladies and gentlemen, someone I hope you will not have to meet professionally although he is always happy to meet you socially, our ship's doctor...'

'Excuse me, Janine, I'll be back.'

Conventional medical education had not prepared Harry for this sort of charade. It was pure entertainment, a part of the flamboyant myth and romance of the sea. Although there are times he gets fed up with the spectacle and cringes, visibly self-conscious as he joins the line, he has to remind himself that it is a timely piece of gratuitous exposure in the most glamorous and prestigious of circumstances, and is therefore a golden opportunity to attract approaches from female passengers who might wish to take advantage of his nautical charms in more intimate surroundings at a later stage in the cruise.

'And finally, ladies and gentlemen, the master of the *Empress of the Seas*, and Senior Captain of the fleet, Captain Alan Bennett.'

He gets the biggest reception, for he represents the very pinnacle of all that is connected with the magic and fantasy of the sea. The aroma, the flavour, the taste, the ephemeral spirit, the very ethos, the ultimate romantic image of the seafarer.

He gives his brief speech, which is word-perfect and always the same, except for the inevitable comment on the weather which even he is unable to programme into the cruise itinerary.

And then it is over. When the Captain leaves the stage the party dies rapidly. With scant regard for order or grace, the shiny sequins and funereal tuxedos surge to the exits, barely able to conceal their urgency to get to the dining tables.

Harry looks from his elevated position on the platform and sees Janine waiting expectantly for him to return. He catches her eye and motions that he is on his way. It only remains to formulate the final strategic details before going to the restaurant to join his table for dinner. She greets him.

'What happens now?'

'The party's over, and it's feeding time.'

'Uuuh – I don't feel like eating much now. It's always the same after a work-out.'

'I'm afraid I don't have a lot of choice, Janine – my public await me at the table.'

'Tell me, Harry, a serious question, I hope you don't mind me asking – but are you married?'

'Good heavens, no!'

'Why do you say it like that?'

'It's going out of fashion, isn't it?'

'I guess you might be right. I divorced my second husband five years ago, and would never do it again. Although I don't regret it, as I do have two beautiful children from my first husband. Have you ever been married?'

'No.'

'I must confess, I always wanted to spend my life in one happy marriage. But in both cases it didn't work. In my first marriage I felt stifled. He was one of those old-fashioned types, you know – wanted me to stay at home and mind house. I had been a successful interior designer, and although I'd looked forward to having children and a certain amount of domestic bliss, I still wanted to keep my career. He didn't see it that way.'

'And the second one?'

'It was sort of rebound. He was very dashing and handsome

and kind of swept me of my feet. It was all a bit of a whirlwind romance, I guess. But he hadn't told me about his alcohol problem or the violent tantrums. I'd always said I would never let a man beat me, and the one black eye was enough for me to leave him. So, there you have it. I threw myself back into my career, and now I feel as fulfilled as I guess I'll ever be.'

'And you're on a cruise ship, on vacation, having successfully escaped from the strait-jacket of convention and boring reality for a brief excursion into the realm of illusion and fantasy.'

'Harry, that sounds almost like a well-worn script – I'm sure you've said it before to scores of women.'

'One or two maybe, but not as many as you might think.'

'It must be a regular routine – different woman every voyage, a girl in every port, isn't that what they say?'

'Clichés, my dear, mere clichés. Not true at all.' The twinkle in his eye clearly belies the validity of his denial.

'In all honesty, I lead a pretty boring life these days. Maybe I'm maturing, or shall we just say getting older. I'm still at sea because it's my living now. I try to avoid all the razzmatazz of cruise life now – just do my job, visit the gym three times a week and go to bed early, invariably alone – truly.'

If she believed that, she would believe anything. But then it suits her to believe. Maybe he is different. He's OK. He's safe and not a philanderer like so many of them … on the other hand, he does have a twinkle in his eye, a devilish gleam…

She takes the lead.

'I'm going to the show tonight, Harry. Will you be busy?'

In this strange, unreal environment it seems natural for her to make the play. After all she is the passenger, and is merely availing herself of the ship's amenities. She also knows that time is limited. The conventional social moves in the courtship ritual must be conveniently manipulated or even totally dispensed with to accommodate the brevity of a cruise. It is as if they are suspended in a time capsule where normal time is compressed and all life events within are magically speeded up.

'Well, I've nothing planned. I feel pretty tired now after the work-out. It's been a long day and I've still got to spend a while entertaining my dinner guests ... quite honestly, I was thinking of going straight to bed after dinner – but maybe we could meet for a goodnight drink in the Midships' Bar?'

'Oh, I'd love that.'

It's in the bag. All he will have to do after dinner is have one drink in the Midships' bar and then whisk her down to his lair for the final act. He looks at his watch.

'Gosh. It's time to go, Janine – my table awaits. Look forward to seeing you after dinner.'

'Yes, I must get to the Princess grill before it's too late – I guess I could eat a little something. Bye Harry, see you later.'

CHAPTER 3

THE TABLE

And when Rachel saw that she bare Jacob no children, Rachel envied her sister; and said unto Jacob, give me children, or else I die.

Genesis 30: 1

And Judah took a wife for Er his first born, whose name was Tamar. And Er, Judah's first born was wicked in the sight of the Lord; and the Lord slew him. And Judah said unto Onan, go into thy brother's wife, and marry her, and raise up thy seed to thy brother. And Onan knew that the seed should not be his; and it came to pass when he went in unto his brother's wife, that he spilled it on the ground, lest that he should give seed to his brother. And the thing that he did displeased the Lord: wherefore he slew him also.

Genesis 38: 6–11

'Good evening, Dottore, and welcome. Your table awaits.'

'Good evening, Romero.'

The Assistant Maitre d', smooth and unctuous as olive oil, greets Harry at the entrance to the Columbia dining room.

'How many tonight, Romero?'

'Eight, sir. Your regular guests and three new embarks – and umm, a transfer from the Princess Grill.'

'Anyone interesting?'

'They all seem very nice, sir.'

'You know what I mean, Romero – anything young and tasty, and female of course?'

'Haaah, Dottore, I am truly sorry, no ... but they are all very charming.'

'I'm sure they are. Now, who's the transfer from the Grill?'

'Ah yes, sir. That is Miss Edwards. I think you know her already?'

Romero casts Harry a fleeting glance with a barely discernible shrug of the shoulders that says he is sorry but it is not his fault.

'I will lead the way, Dottore.'

Romero, immaculate in his black tails and white bow tie, threads his way skilfully between the tables. Harry follows two steps behind, looking right and left and nodding in a detached manner as heads swivel to track his course.

They reach the table. Romero stands aside and ushers Harry to his seat in front of the pillar with mirrors. As he sits, he inclines his head to the circle of expectant faces.

'Good evening everybody. I'm Dr Harry Lester, the ship's medical officer. Please call me Harry.'

When he is settled in his seat, Romero springs forward and with a flourish, spreads the napkin onto his lap.

'Thank you, Romero.'

'*Bon appetit*, ladies and gentlemen,' chirps the suave Italian as he backs away, inclining his head deferentially before making a sharply executed about-turn.

All eyes now fix on Harry. Hushed for a moment, they wait for his lead as an orchestra awaits the baton of the Maestro. His eyes sweep swiftly round the table. Tap! Tap! He can begin.

'I trust everyone had a good day in Sydney?'

His mundane enquiry, designed as a tension-diffuser, is an anticlimax, but serves the purpose. Before anyone can respond, he continues. There are some new faces and he wants to make them feel he runs a relaxed and informal table.

'I know some of you have joined today, so you must be feeling pretty worn out. Well, I already know Edith, Hal, Benjamin and Sophie – and Lulu! I must say, it is a pleasant surprise to see you Lulu. I thought you were in the Princess Grill – anyway, I'm sure you've already introduced yourselves and told our new guests that you're doing the full sentence without remission...'

The first laugh – exaggerated in its nervous intensity, perhaps – it wasn't that funny.

'Now may I say hello to our new guests?'

Harry leans across to his immediate left. The smoke swirls in front of his eyes and causes his nose to twitch involuntarily. He can barely disguise his natural repugnance with a look of instant disapproval.

'It's Louise. Louise Laycock. Pleased to meet you.'

She quickly inserts the extra-long filter tip into her mouth and draws in deeply, unable to disguise her nervousness. Harry's eyes continue to send the signal. He moves his head to her left.

'Melville Laycock. Happy to meet you, Doctor – Harry.'

He can see Harry's discomfort and fidgets in his chair.

'Where are you from, Melville?'

'Dayton – Ohio, in case you didn't know.'

'Oh I know Dayton, Melville, although I must say I've never been there. Haven't you got snow at the moment?'

'Sure thing. Guess that's why we're here – on this beautiful ship of yours.'

'Nice to meet you both.'

Harry's transparent smile scrambles the otherwise clear message that he would probably stand idly by if Louise self-immolated from her cigarette.

'And how is Edith this evening?'

'Not at all at my best I'm afraid, Doctor – Harry...'

She is self-conscious and slightly uncomfortable with the public intimacy of 'Harry'. Edith Baxter is a widow in her late fifties and displays all the stigmata of a sheltered middle-class upbringing. Convent school and ladies' finishing college and all the conditioning that they imply, have imposed on her a rigid and stifling ideology which has left little room for social adaptation and tolerance.

'...it was far too hot in Sydney and the tour bus broke down. The food laid on at the hotel was ghastly and quite frankly the cabaret absolutely third-rate. If only...'

'Never mind, Edith. A few nice relaxing days at sea before Singapore.'

'I'll need to come and see you, Harry,' she says almost threateningly with an intense seriousness. 'When are you free?'

'For you, any time.' He knows that will make her blush and quickly adds, 'Any time after nine in the morning. There is no need to make an appointment. You won't have to wait long, I promise.'

A new face. Harry tilts his head sideways, inviting a self-introduction.

'Desmond Simpson.'

'Nice to meet you, Desmond – where are you from?'

'Connecticut. Harvard, to be exact.'

'You're probably too old to be a student, with all due respect, so therefore you must be a teacher – am I right?'

69

'Spot-on. Professor of Ancient and Medieval History.'

The clipped tones, very slightly effeminate, and the vaguely coquettish smile are enough for Harry to diagnose that the professor's sexual orientation is probably at variance with the rest of the table. Harry smiles and turns to the painfully thin figure sitting next to the portly academic.

'Aaah – Mrs Edwards – Lulu, it really is nice to have you join us!'

Harry knows, and she knows he knows, that she's been relegated from the exclusive Princess Grill, the domain of the wealthiest passengers, to the relatively humble first-class restaurant. No doubt she's got drunk to the point of incontinence just once too often for the other passengers. It is a regular arrangement, and when her behaviour reverts to a more predictable pattern she will be returned to the grill. His tone and facial expression carries with it all the necessary nuances to make it clear to Lulu that her secret is safe with him, providing she behaves herself.

'Harry darling, I couldn't stay away from you a moment longer.'

That's the spirit my dear, he thinks. Play the part and there'll be no ugly scenes.

The heiress to the Reynolds tobacco company, wealthy beyond belief since her first wet nappy, she had led a charmed and privileged existence but one which had failed to give her happiness or fulfillment. Four childless marriages and four charlatan husbands who'd tried to drain her wealth, but each of whom had eventually been sent packing, had left her a pitiful, lonely alcoholic without family or heirs, forever sentenced to cruising around the world on luxury liners, searching in vain for a companion who might fit the bill. It could never be. She is destined to drown in her own alcoholic solace. She would be tragically pathetic if not for her wealth. Without her vast fortune she might be a bag lady in a New York slum.

'And how are the Rosenthals this evening?'

'Fine thanks, Harry. Had a good day shopping. Spent far too much though – at least Sophie did.'

70

'Benjamin, honey – we only live once. And we've got to buy presents for the grandchildren.'

'Yes, but my dear, we've already...'

They bicker incessantly. Edith Baxter hates them. They willingly reciprocate her feelings, an eye for an eye...

He is a retired urological surgeon who once had a plush office on Fifth Avenue and was attending specialist at Mount Sinai hospital. She is matriarchal and dominating, and a little witchlike with old age. At times, they show a native New York earthiness, which is considered coarse by Edith's rigid code, and over a period of weeks has fuelled her initial disapproval and distaste to quite overt hatred. They rarely address each other across the table, but prefer to denigrate with loud criticisms and insults conveniently aimed at Harry, who sits as unofficial mediator in the middle. He has long passed the embarrassing stage and simply ignores their continued animosity as if it didn't exist. Edith's dogged vitriol suggests an element of anti-Semitism, but is carefully disguised. It would need to be on a ship carrying so many wealthy Jewish passengers.

'And how's Hal this evening? Did you have a good day?'

'No. I can't say I like these wealthy ports. No bargains. Nobody to haggle with – know what I mean, Harry?'

'That's a pity – I'm sorry.'

'I can't wait for Thailand. You can make some great deals there. Couple of years back I bought a beautiful hand carved golden eagle in teak wood – it must o' stood at least four feet tall – for just thirty dollars. I beat him down from three hundred. I guess he was good at carving but no damn good at the business of making a profit.'

'Sure, Hal. But maybe that eagle took a long time to carve, maybe weeks or months, and there was a large family to feed and you had more than enough money to give him the modest price he was asking...'

'Harry, you've got no business sense at all. Besides, it's a principle with me – I won't be cheated.'

'No, I'm sure you won't.'

Hal Van Dicky is borderline eccentric, but at times he

71

displays a mean, if not vicious, streak which is not normally associated with eccentrics. He never ceases boasting about his financial expertise or gains on the stock market, his numerous retirement pensions and insurance deals which net him huge lump sums and hefty regular annuities. At frequent intervals he volunteers his monthly net income as something around 10,000 dollars, but still has the gall and insensitivity to boast about cheating a poor indigenous trader out of maybe ten dollars. Harry consoles himself that if there is divine retribution then Hal should hit the jackpot when he finally shuffles off his mortal coil.

Harry has gone round the table. He leans back and smiles.

'So welcome, everybody – old and new, so to speak. I trust you all have a pleasant and relaxing cruise from Sydney to Singapore.'

He looks over his shoulder. It is the signal for the waiter to take the orders. Sean, a young Irishman in his early twenties with piercing blue eyes, heavily streaked blond hair and a discreet gold earring, flounces from behind the dumb waiter.

'Good evening, ladies and gentlemen,' he says in a soft, delicate Irish accent, 'you can choose from the menu, but I'd recommend our two specials tonight. The Lobster Thermidor or the Beef Wellington.'

Louise Laycock is undecided. The choice is difficult. The Lobster would be nice and more calorie-conscious, but the Beef Wellington and its sumptuous pastry is a temptation hard to resist. She is going to have caviare as an *hors d'oeuvre*, so maybe another fish course would be too much. Sensing her dilemma, and the anxiety of the waiter to take the orders, Harry prompts, 'The Beef Wellington is usually very good. A few extra calories won't do you any harm.'

'I'll go with anything the doctor recommends,' she says, relieved that the agonising choice has been made for her.

She stubs out her cigarette screwing the butt firmly into the glass ashtray, which generates a final plume of acrid smoke. The glossy packet of Lights and gold cigarette lighter are prominently displayed just to the left of her wine glass and indicate that it will not be her last.

72

Although he hasn't said anything against her smoking, Harry's aversion is plain to see. But she is probably hardened to the acrimony of anti-smokers and takes a mischievous pleasure in the opportunity to antagonise. He will make his point soon enough.

Sean reappears with a large tray carrying the *hors d'oeuvres*. Everyone seems relaxed now and can commence the serious business of eating. But first Harry must go through the ritual of answering the standard questions that most new passengers feel compelled to ask. As if on cue, when Louise leans forward to scoop up her first mouthful of caviare she turns to Harry.

'How long have you been at sea, Doctor – I mean Harry?'

'About ten years.'

'What did you do before that?'

'Worked ashore in a hospital.'

Melville chips in.

'Do you like being at sea, Harry?'

'Not particularly...'

Puzzled faces.

'Have you ever taken an appendix out on board?' enquires the Professor of Ancient and Medieval history.

'Yes. It doesn't happen too often, but twice in the last year.'

'How many people die on board?'

'One a month on average.'

'Have you ever delivered a baby on board?' asks Louise.

'Yes – once.'

'Have you ever...'

Those who have been on board for a few weeks are able to recognise the pattern of interrogation, and smile with smug amusement as the fresh new embarks put the doctor through the same ritual. They are gloating sadistically, not interrupting, to allow the entertainment to continue so that they can compare Harry's performance with the last.

Sometimes, if he is in an affable mood, Harry will expand his answer and feed the assembled throng with an anecdote or two, but this evening he is not so inclined.

There is a pause in the barrage. Louise rests her fork on the plate and stretches to the glossy packet. Her nicotine level needs a top-up. Harry senses the time is right to make a stand. She plays into his hand.

'You don't mind if I smoke, do you Doctor?' she says with gentle sarcasm.

'Well, yes. Actually I do, very much so.'

Gulp. Her hand rests on the cigarette lighter.

Harry intends to register his distaste and disapproval unequivocally.

'Louise, with all due respect, smoking is a filthy habit which is socially and physically very offensive. Tobacco is a dangerous drug, and certainly in the Western world, by far the most preventable cause of premature death known, and in the Third World only exceeded by war and famine. Passive inhalation of someone else's unfiltered smoke is even worse – and you ask me if I mind! What do you expect me to say?'

'You know, Harry is right, Louise,' says the Professor softly but authoritatively.

Everyone looks up, and there is even a momentary pause in the Rosenthals' mechanical eating action.

'Smoking has got to be one of the more bizarre habits practised by mankind. I think most would agree, if the weed was discovered in modern times it would not be legalised at all. As the learned doctor said, it kills a lot of people – in fact, I read somewhere it has far more victims than all the so-called dangerous drugs put together. Quite honestly, it seems pretty inconsistent of society to persecute drug dealers as heinous criminals and social pariahs when the presidents of the giant tobacco companies are exempted from moral criticism or legal redress.'

Louise stares blankly at Desmond. She is not really in the same league to win an argument against such a learned and well-practised foe. But she has conviction on her side and the unalterable perception that there is nothing morally reprehensible with smoking. She is also prepared to hit below the belt.

'We all have our own particular vices, I guess,' she says

74

pulling a face of mock resignation and looking Desmond straight in the eye. Like Harry, she has presumed Desmond's sexual orientation and is making it more than clear in her subtle innuendo that she hasn't adopted the increasingly permissive philosophy towards homosexuality of modern times.

There is a stony silence.

Benjamin Rosenthal is sufficiently distracted from his plate.

'But c'mon, Professor, you know as well as I do that the so-called recreational drugs are responsible for a great deal of human misery.'

'Sure, but don't forget, nobody forces these poor junkies to take these drugs. God knows, there is so much adverse publicity against such harmful substances that it's a wonder anyone in their right mind would ever consider such a thing.'

'Yes, I agree. But the drug dealers get a lot of their customers at a young and impressionable age.'

'And the manufacturers of cigarettes are not guilty of the same strategy?' Harry interjects, in clear support of Desmond.

'C'mon, Harry – you know it's not quite the same ball game ... to start with, the sort of drugs we're talking about can alter the normal behaviour to such a degree that these people become unable to cope with life ...'

'Sounds a bit like alcohol, Benjamin.'

'No. It's not the same.'

'It is an irony that every law-abiding respectable citizen, like yourself for instance, almost as a conditioned response, vehemently condemns the world of so-called drug abuse, conveniently ignoring the fact that they are probably smoking or drinking themselves to an early grave.'

'It's a matter of free choice, Harry.'

'Well, the same could be said for recreational drugs.'

'You mean allow all those evil criminals to destroy our young folk?'

'No, Louise, I wouldn't do that. But then why should the producers and purveyors of tobacco and alcohol be allowed to profit enormously from their trade whilst drug peddlers are hounded as criminals of the worst kind? It's just inconsistent and plainly illogical.'

75

'I'm sorry, Doctor, I cannot agree with such a thing. Surely you are not saying legalise drugs?'

'Well, it's an option worth considering.'

'Banning an activity which is seen to give pleasure, at least in the first instance, only makes people crave more and resort to devious means to experience it. And be sure not to forget the dangers of legalised substances. The wretched creature lying in the gutter that you might associate with the drug scene of inner cities could just as well be the town drunk of respectable suburban America.'

'But surely it's not on the same scale?'

'Oh I think it is, Louise,' chips in Desmond, 'alcohol abuse is more widespread, affecting all age groups and all levels of society in a more pervasive way than other drugs. Quite frankly, the manufacturers and distributors of cigarettes and alcohol should be indicted for mass murder. The tobacco companies, which might be losing the battle in our society where the health lobby seems to be outmanoeuvring their own powerful lobby, are now aiming their marketing efforts and sales campaigns in the direction of vulnerable, ill-informed and backward Third World populations. In those countries there are no prohibitive laws on advertising or ethical standards of marketing. It really is a death sentence for thousands.'

'That's a wicked thing to say, mister. Absolute hogwash!'

Lulu, the Camel heiress and living embodiment of all that is destructive in alcohol and nicotine, rocks forward unsteadily, momentarily awakened from her semi-stuporose state to vigorously defend the hand that has fed her since the cradle. The learned Professor has not been on the ship long enough to know of her silver-spooned background courtesy of one of the giant tobacco families, and is taken by surprise with her aggressive defence of the family business. Harry quickly recognises the innocent *faux pas* and rescues the situation before Desmond is able to retaliate.

'Lulu's family were in tobacco, Desmond, and I think she is a little hurt by what you are saying.'

'Well, I apologise, Miss Lulu, if I have offended you but, well … you see the point I am trying to make. Our values

76

and perceptions of human behaviour are not entirely consistent...'

Lulu falls back in her chair. It really is too much effort to engage in such a serious conversation. All she wants to do is eat and get back to the exclusive Princess Grill bar, where she can sink a few more gin and tonics before bedtime. Hal Van Dicky, who has been sitting silently, decides to take up the cudgel on Lulu's behalf.

'So, Doctor, I think you were about to say that we should be selling heroin in every corner shop to anyone who wants it.'

'Yes, Hal. I guess that is exactly what I mean.'

'Well you're plumb crazy, mister.'

'But with such legalisation of drugs it would be very necessary for there to be at the same time an intensive never-ending campaign by the government, using the media and all those forces which can influence social behaviour, to explain and warn and make crystal clear the foolhardiness and self-destructiveness of the drug habit. That might sound difficult to achieve, but I believe it is more than feasible once the criminal element has been effectively removed.'

'I agree with Hal, Doctor. With all due respect, I think yours is a dangerous idea,' says Melville.

'I think you both underestimate the deterrent effect of not just self-destruction but more importantly social isolation from the rest of the tribe.'

'"Tribe"? What do you mean?' queries Melville.

'Go ahead, buy your fix of heroin or take your dose of crack for one dollar, but don't forget, you'll loose your self-respect, your education, job, friends, family, health. You'll slide down a slippery slope of abject misery which will end ultimately in death. In short, the whole drug scene has got to be completely deglamorized, debunked as something stupid, but if you really want to prove you've got no brains then go ahead, by all means ... it's your choice.'

'Harry, we print warnings on cigarette packets and people still die from cancer and heart disease.'

'Those habits should be deglamorized too. It's the wickedness of marketing, the selling of a product for immense profit

77

and hang the consequences to society. I'm talking about a media-orchestrated campaign without the glamorization of the "illegal factor" to be overcome, of such intense indoctrination against drugs, that it would influence and, I believe, convince the vast majority of ordinary people. There will always be a small minority of individuals who will abuse drugs whatever social rules are in place, but at least it would be easier to contain their behaviour if drugs were legalised.'

For a moment it is silent and nobody minds the silence. They are content to take mouthfuls of their starters, which have been neglected during the animated exchange. Harry can see how the camps divide. The Professor's pragmatic liberalism is strenuously opposed by the staunch conservatism of Hal, supported less vigorously by the Laycocks, Melville and Louise, whose code of ethics are well-defined, inviolable and not subject to re-evaluation or change. Now that everyone is suitably charged, he cannot resist the opportunity to challenge Hal's perceptions on the world. He gulps a mouthful of Piesporter and gets set to speak.

'Drug dealers are one thing you know, Hal, but there is another group of people in this world who really are wicked beyond belief.'

Hal juts out his chin towards Harry, suspicious that he is going to say something provocative.

'And who may they be?'

'Surely a man of your wisdom can guess.'

''Fraid you've got me, Doc, I've no idea – give me a clue.'

'A man with your military background – you did some time in the Marines didn't you, Hal?'

'I served my country in Korea – certainly. But I still don't know what you're getting at.'

'Arms dealers. The wickedest, most evil humans on this planet. Now they really do make fortunes out of human misery and do literally get away with murder – mass murder at that.'

'You really are crazy tonight, Doc.'

'No, it's quite true. It's a question of one's perception of reality.'

'What do you mean?'

'Well, those entrepreneurs who make their living from trading in arms exploit the natural tendency of all human beings to argue. Face it, there is in human nature a vicious element, which is manifest in aggression, violence or war against one's neighbour, and when certain conditions prevail this natural tendency is encouraged to flourish by the interference of arms merchants. Put simply, if I argue with my neighbour there is always a danger of escalation before resolution of the argument...'

'Doc, I really think you're making this far too complicated...'

'Let me finish, Hal. I know it's a bit long-winded, but I'm trying to pin down how, or just why we allow these purveyors of death free licence to carry on their evil trade. In some inexplicable way they seem to be able to carry on their filthy, despicable, murderous dealings in instruments of mass destruction, seemingly immune to the moral precepts that condemn individuals involved in the drug business. Why should they be able to make enormous profits from peddling commodities which kill and maim far more people, innocents young and old alike, than any amount of illicit drugs can do? They are faceless creatures rarely in the spotlight. They carry on their anti-human activity without fear of prosecution, supported by government institutions and the personal vested interests of easily bought politicians. This business...'

'Hang on a minute, Doc – I think you're way out of line...'

'Let me finish, Hal, then you can say your piece. As I was saying, this business, entirely legal remember, enables tin pot dictators with serious psychopathic personality problems, ruthless oppressors of human rights, to impose their destructive will on so many defenceless unfortunates. The bitter irony is that the those who make the huge profits from such evil business attain the highest social order and respect. Their wealth and extravagance give them the power and social muscle to guarantee they become pillars of the establishment and members of the ruling class.'

Harry is undoubtedly on form. It is a good performance which everybody, with the exception of Hal – and Lulu, who has gone to sleep – has appreciated.

79

'That sounds very neat, but with all due respect it's a load of garbage...'

'Ha ha, Hal, I've got you riled now.'

'Look. It's simple – you're forgetting we need arms manufacturers AND dealers to protect us from aggressors. If we had no arms industry we would be hopelessly vulnerable as free nations of the world.'

'I'm talking about the uncontrolled arms trade to any tyrant who puts up enough money or borrows it from the so-called civilised financial institutions, without any regard to the consequences or the human abuse he is going to carry out.'

'Well, I admit that's difficult to control in any free trade system – but people have got to be allowed to do business...'

'But, I'm saying the arms dealers are worse than the drug dealers. How simple it is to divert attention away from this exclusive brotherhood of purveyors of death by vilifying the activities of drug merchants, the net results of which pale into insignificance. At least with drugs, the individual has the choice, well-informed, one hopes – but with hostile bullets, there is no choice.'

Hal is silent. This discussion has gone on too long.

Harry speaks: 'Well, folks, these are far too serious matters to be talking about on a luxury cruise liner sailing through the South Seas...'

Harry is about to make a whimsical comment on the rare, almost raw rack of lamb when Louise beats him by a whisker as his lips begin to move.

'Doctor...'

'Do call me Harry, Louise.'

'Harry, are your wife and children in England?'

That's perfect, he thinks.

'No. Actually, I'm not married.'

'Really? I can't believe that – how old are you, if you don't mind me asking?'

'Let's say forty-ish.'

'Well, you certainly look younger than that Harry.'

'But how come you are not yet married – you're good-looking and eligible – it seems such a waste if you don't mind me saying...'

'Thank you, but I really am too young to settle down.'

Harry diverts his eyes for a moment from Louise and catches a discernible glint in Desmond's eye, a flicker of hope that perhaps the doctor's sexual orientation might accommodate his own gender preference. Harry senses this and quashes such a fancy instantly with a tit-for-tat glint.

'I'm not a homosexual, either,' he says with an impish grin.

It invokes a genuine belly laugh from around the table, including Desmond. Everyone seems aware that on cruise ships homosexuality, if not exactly appropriate, seems some how more acceptable, even normal within such an environ- ment as if it is to be expected from seafarers. Even in less permissive times, when it was illegal and considered shockingly deviant and socially repugnant, the practice was tolerated at sea as if the strict moral constraints didn't apply in the nautical world.

The tone of Harry's denial is not derogatory. It is neutral and inoffensive. He can see that Desmond is aware of the nuance and is appreciative. Louise continues.

'So you've no children, Harry? No heirs. No one to carry on your line. That's a shame. Really Harry, I think the purpose of life is to – to, procreate. Don't you ever want to get married and have children?'

'I'm not sure – I'm still thinking about it.' He senses Louise wants a fuller answer.

'The whole ritual of the mating game is nothing more than a clever ploy by nature, or to be more specific, the chromosomes and genes – the very substance of life – to replicate and thereby perpetuate themselves for their own selfish reasons. That replication process, immortalisation if you like, seems to be greatly enhanced if the said genes are spliced with a completely different set. You know, the improvements of mixed breeding bringing out the best qualities and deleting the worst by the ruthless machinations of natural selection...'

Louise fall back in her chair with a look of bemusement and disbelief at his cold, rational scientific assessment. But Harry continues with his thesis.

'...and so these amorphous, characterless-looking genes set up an enormously complex system, which at one end of the scale is seen as simple asexual differentiation of very primitive life forms – you know, slime in the swamp – and at the other end develops into the complex elaborate social manipulations and well-engrained ritual behaviour patterns of advanced life forms, as observed in human coupling. Furthermore, social evolution, that is, development of group behaviour in the human animal, has resulted in the marriage concept as an important, nay vital part of our social structure...'

'God – that's way over my head and it sounds so cold – and, and – unromantic. How can you be so...'

'Louise, the whole scheme from beginning to end is a lure, a confidence trick by these "simple genes" of ours so that they can compete effectively with all the other life forms in existence on this planet for the limited resources available.'

Harry leans forward, eyeball to eyeball with Louise.

'Well, I can tell you, I've seen through their game. They're not going to use me. No siree!'

'I'm a little lost, Harry, but you mean you're still not going to have anyone to carry on your...'

'If I need immortality, then I'm confident that in the near future it may be possible to clone, you know, self-replicate, without the need for the social complexities of splicing or sharing one's genes. Sure, my genes are not perfect, but that's their problem. It's not my fault. I suppose there is definite room for improvement, but it certainly won't benefit me. And what a stressful haphazard business it is, in selecting the "right" partner. Who needs it? For what? The genes might get their immortality and maybe improved quality, but all I get is an earlier death.'

'I'm sorry, Harry, but I really am confused. You make it sound so cold and calculating. It isn't like that at all. You really are very cynical – or you're just making fun of me. After all, I only asked if you wanted to get married and have children!'

'I'm sorry, Louise. I did get a little carried away.'

Louise is shaking her head in amazement but, like a bulldog, she refuses to let go her tight grip.

'So Harry, you have no offspring. No heirs. You'll die on this earth, and there will be no one to carry on your line. Doesn't that make you feel kind of sad? Doesn't it make life seem so, so – well, futile?'

Harry pauses and tries to assume a dramatic posture by taking a deep breath and puffing out his chest. He stares at his napkin, then looks up slowly towards Louise like a thespian about to deliver the punchline.

'Who said I said I had no offspring anyway? I didn't.'

'Oh Doctor, you've a secret – you – you rascal! You've been hiding something all the time. Leading me on. That's not fair. You've been playing with us. C'mon, confess.'

'If you insist.'

Harry rubs the bristles on his chin with the tips of his fingers and tries to suppress a smile.

'I have to go back a long way...'

'Good evening, Doctor, ladies and gentlemen. I am sorry to interrupt, but the executive chef, Monsieur Dubisson, would like to honour your table tonight with Banana Flambé Surprise.'

The Assistant Maitre d' distracts everybody from the dramatic confession Harry is about to make.

'It is sizzled in a particularly delicious liqueur sauce which I am sure will not disappoint you.'

All heads turn dramatically toward Romero, standing immaculately like a cardboard cut-out behind the portable stove. He produces a lighter and ignites the gas. Blue flames immediately envelop the solid copper pan. He carefully adds more oil and the pan begins to sizzle and spit as it rapidly gets hotter. Then he adds the bananas, each peeled with a flourish and sliced expertly down the middle, almost in one continuous movement. He pours some liqueur directly into the pan, and then with absolute confidence flicks on the lighter. There is an immediate whoosh and a spectacular flame, which threatens to incinerate the entire table. But he has done this so many times before without any risk, and there is a spontaneous cheer from everyone as they realise it is a slick show.

Louise licks her lips in anticipation as Melville cranes his head forward to see the flaming bananas.

The Rosenthals stare with concentrated purpose, almost Pavlovian in their response as the blue flames settle and the bananas turn a light brown. Eating has become a serious business in their lives. In fact, now well into their retirement, it is probably the most important aspect of their whole existence.

Hal Van Dicky shows a restrained enthusiasm for the performance and even Lulu moves her head slightly, more though in reflex as Romero drains the last contents from the bottle into the pan.

God, how they are all so easily distracted, thinks Harry. He has seen it countless times before and shows only a polite acknowledgment to the Assistant Maitre d'. A mechanical smile appears on his face. It is a mask which belies the agility of his thought. His mind dwells on Louise's probing question, naïve as it may seem to her – no offspring, no heirs, no one to carry on the line? His memory straddles the years effortlessly. It must be 15, no 20, at least 20 years now – but oh, how he remembers it so clearly – as if it were only yesterday...

84

CHAPTER 4

GENE MACHINE

Man's evolutionary purpose is to deposit as many spermatozoa into as many wombs of as many women as possible.

Mantissa, John Fowles

Why, why, why had he drunk so much? His head is about to explode and he feels sick. He has puked three times already. The soft warm mass next to him snores loudly, signalling the inevitable. He just had to get up and perform. Impossible! Why the hell had he allowed her to come back to college hall? He knew damn well that he was on the bank in the morning. Alcohol again. Fuels the passion, obliterates the control. And worse! He was double-booked. Christ! It only happened once in a blue moon, and it had to be on a day like today.

The bed creaks as he swings his legs awkwardly from under the sheet and on to the cold lino floor. The mass stirs reflexly, subconsciously, arms reach out blindly, hips and pelvis slide forwards, offering, submitting.

'You can't have anymore, for Christ's sake! You've just about drained the whole bloody tank – damn it!'

He speaks more to himself rather than the amorphous form buried beneath the blanket. She is still submerged in the twilight sleep of early morning and can only be vaguely aware of his anguished utterances.

He sits forward on the edge of the bed, stifling a groan as his head falls forwards into his cupped hands. Oh God! Why had he succumbed to those bastards in the bar? Never again. Never. Absolutely never. Alcohol. Damn poison! A dangerous drug. A very dangerous drug indeed! What time is it?

He gropes for his watch in the semi-darkness – seven-thirty. He'll be late. Bloody hell. He must be early for Aubrey-Taylor's ward round at nine o'clock. He's got to see Trudi, the ward clerk, to allocate the new patients. Shit. He'll never make it.

He tries to stand, easing himself slowly into the upright position. A lazy semi-erection offers a glimmer of hope. But he feels dizzy and flops back onto the edge of the bed, letting his head fall into his hands again. Semi-erection? He could build on that, he is sure. He must. He gently strokes his aching scrotum and loosely grasps the penile shaft. Ouch! It is sore. But what else could he expect? Not once – but three bloody times he'd copulated with Debbie. He'd quite literally expunged his last drop of semen into her reproductive tract.

He tries getting up again. Successful this time, he staggers blindly to the toilet. He stands over the pan with a great urge to urinate, but with the semi-erection only a trickle comes out. His bladder feels full. It should be. He'd drunk enough the night before. He pushes his buttocks backwards and the trickle becomes a moderate stream. Aaaah! Such relief. By the time the stream finishes in a dribble, the erection is all but gone. The urge to vomit persists and his head continues to pound unmercifully. Oh shit, he'll need that erection, or half-erection in a minute. He fondles the lifeless organ with increasing pessimism.

The magazines. Don't forget the dirty mags. His only chance. Under the bed. Christ! She's got to go. NOW.

'Debbie. DEBBIE. You've got to get up. C'mon. Wakey wakey.'

'Uuuhh?'

He shakes her roughly by the shoulders.

'For Christ's sake, girl, get up. I've got to perform and get down to Harley Street in half an hour. Please. PLEASE, Debbie!'

'Uuuhh.'

Arms outstretch.

'Come back to bed, darling. Just one more time.'

'For fuck's sake. You know I've got to take whatever pathetic specimen I can salvage to the Wank Bank – and pretty soon.'

'Come here, Harry. I'll do it for you. It'll be alright. Come here, darling.'

'You know that doesn't work. It ends up on the floor. This is serious business.'

He has his own special technique which doesn't waste a drop of the precious commodity.

'Debbie, you know I have my own special way to maximise...'

'Oooh, do tell me, Harry darling, it'll make me feel more horny...'

'For Christ's sake, Debbie, please. It's going to be difficult enough as it is. Now look, you must go – NOW.'

He yanks at one arm and pulls her to a sitting position.

'Don't be too rough, Harry, it only makes me more horny,' she says provocatively.

'Look here, this is no joke, Debbie. I've double-booked as well. I've got Crowther and Shirley Mason. Whatever I can produce – and it's not going to be very much, I'm sure – I've got to split in half. It will be like feeding the five thousand without even any breadcrumbs. I need more than a bloody miracle.'

'Ha ha – what you need is an automatic sperm dispenser – ha ha ha!'

'Very funny, I'm sure – now get out of my bed and bugger off, will you? – Or I'm likely to get violent.'

'Promises, promises.'

'Please, Debbie. Be reasonable. How do you think I can afford all that booze that WE drank if I don't produce the goods?'

'OK. Point taken. I'm going. I'm going. Where are my jeans?'

'On the floor where you crawled out of them last night.'

'And my panties?'

'Look in the bed. Please, Debbie. I've got about five minutes, that's all.'

'Aaah. One pair of panties – under the pillow.'

He takes a grey-looking towel, damp and grubby from the back of the chair and wraps it around his waist. Debbie pulls on her panties unceremoniously, trying not to fall in the effort. With some difficulty she wriggles into the tight jeans as he holds the T-shirt open, ready for her to place her head through.

'There! That didn't take long, did it?'

'Thank God for that. Right, I'll see you later on the ward. Go.'

He kisses her on the forehead and with a sweep of one arm ushers her briskly out of the door of room 502, Student's Hall of Residence, Barts Hospital Medical College, London.

As the door closes his mind immediately concentrates on the job in hand. The porn. Where's the porn? He bends down slowly and thrusts a hand under the bed pulling out a handful of glossy magazines.

The glossy mags, thank God for the glossy mags! Just look at this stuff! Page after shiny page of much more than any textbook of gynaecology could offer. These specimens were unlikely to suffer from any women's diseases, except perhaps the odd infection. They are young, beautiful, and perfectly formed. Their anatomical specifications are the absolute best on offer. Designed by nature with man in mind. Crafted by eons of evolution to lure the male into parting with his seed.

The quality of the pictures is excellent. The colours lurid and the focus on intimate anatomical detail ultra-sharp and uncompromising. But they are only images – two-dimensional representations of the real thing. And animation they have not. It is for the imagination to breathe life into them, the fantasy of the voyeur, to set them in motion – enough motion and eroticism to give him a lasting erection and a productive ejaculation. But it won't be easy. Apart from the dreadful hangover, this voyeur feels completely drained. Totally non-sexual. Far too much alcohol, very little sleep and excessive fornication with the three-dimensional, spontaneously animated real article. He stares forlornly at the gorgeous pin-ups. Nothing, but nothing, can raise his sexual interest this morning.

The specimen pots. Don't forget the specimen pots! He pulls open the bottom right hand draw of the desk and takes out a dark brown perspex container which fits neatly into one fist. Two! He needs two!

Oh please, please soft little organ, just hard enough to

squeeze out the last few drops, that's all. There has got to be a little left in the sperm factory.

The infertility clinics insisted that donors abstained from sexual activity for at least three days before producing a specimen to ensure a good quality sample, both in sperm count and volume. In practice, a 24-hour period seemed to be adequate, at least for the super-studs who masturbated each and every day (at least once) and fornicated in between without any quality-control complaints from the clinics. Their testes were conditioned to work overtime, generating billions of sperms and copious volumes of semen every week as good as any factory production line. The regular donors had to be young and healthy, otherwise they would not have lasted long.

These clinics had only become established and begin to mushroom in the mid-sixties as Artificial Insemination by Donor was becoming more accepted as a preferred alternative to adoption by childless couples. To be more precise, the infertility had to be limited to the male, who usually had a very low sperm count or none at all. There were rare cases when the sperm count was enough but the woman still failed to conceive. In those cases it was assumed there was some sort of incompatibility factor present, either sperm antibodies or a hostile mucous substance at work to prevent fertilisation. It was a sad state of affairs for couples who had usually been trying for a pregnancy a considerable time prior to referral to the specialist clinic.

Altruistic motives he had none. Before getting on 'the bank' he had struggled on a meagre grant. His parents had been poor and he had been lucky enough to gain a place at one of the country's most prestigious medical schools on the wave of educational opportunity that had swept through the post-war period of the Fifties and Sixties. This trend had intensified to a peak by the mid-Sixties, when the universities were being filled with talent from what was considered by those of a previously privileged minority as the 'lower classes'. His school credits had certainly been a good enough standard to gain a place on merit and qualify for a government grant. The only problem was that the student grant, which was means-tested on parental income, was barely enough to live on, even though he received the maximum because of his father's low weekly wage.

Most of it was swallowed up in his board and lodging. There was hardly enough left to buy the expensive medical books he needed. As for cash to spend on leisure, that was out of the question. The 'wank bank', as it became affectionately and gratefully known to those who signed up, proved to be a decisive factor in his successful passage through medical school.

Out of hundreds of male students at Barts only a handful sold their semen. Coming from more substantial backgrounds, most didn't need the extra income, or maybe they were just too damn lazy to get up before lectures to produce a sample which had to be taken by hand to the clinic in Harley Street. There were a few who rejected the idea as morally suspect, but were probably too self-conscious to be seen to indulge in such a practice openly.

He had been elated when he'd passed the screening – the blood tests and genetic evaluation. The technicalities of the procedure hadn't quite reached the sophistication of racehorse breeding – there was certainly no stud register – but the clinics, albeit in a more casual fashion, did attempt to match the donor with the potential parents. The idea of using medical students, apart from being a conveniently attainable source, assumed that they had a more than adequate intelligence quotient, good health and physique, unquestionable social responsibility and therefore, good quality genes. Eye and hair colour might be matched with the husband, but this was no more than a superficial gesture which often went astray, with cock-ups in the donor appointment schedule. Often it was necessary to bring in a last-minute emergency donor, and such attempts at physical matching were invalidated. The only essential need for matching was race. There were stories of medical students playing tricks by substituting semen from African students, but he had never seen such a thing.

All these considerations, or indeed any thought about the unique nature of the service he was providing, were forgotten

92

once he had enrolled. All he cared about was the £3 'a shot' he received. It made a considerable difference to his income and standard of living, and that was all that mattered.

After signing on at one clinic he'd soon learnt from the small band of donors of two other clinics, and had soon signed up with both. The money doubled, trebled and occasionally quad-rupled in a good week. But it had been then that the problems had started. Double bookings and even occasionally triple on the same day, could follow unplanned nights out with girl-friends, too much alcohol and the inevitable squandering of his precious natural resources. It came as no surprise to eventually get complaints from the clinics about the quality of samples.

It was then he'd begun to discipline his social life to suit the priorities of the clinics. He would always make sure of produc-ing a good sample for a firm booking and try to limit his social excursions to the weekends, to accommodate unforeseen appointments.

He had not planned to see Debbie. But now that he had momentarily lapsed in his social discipline, there was absolutely no way he could cancel at this late stage or 'sub-contract' out to a last-minute substitute. In fairness to himself, he had deliberately avoided seeing her for two days. His scrotum had swelled and the sperm factory had been fit to burst. He'd had more than enough to provide for a double booking and not get any complaints on the quality. Damn Debbie! Why had she rung him to say she had to see him about 'something'? She knew full well that he couldn't keep his hands off her whenever they met, especially after a few drinks. This had to be the last time he got into such a dreadful situation.

He looks down at the limp appendage – sore and devoid of any sexual feeling. His head still throbs and the nausea comes in waves. He flops into the threadbare armchair and leans over slowly to pick up a glossy magazine from the pile he'd scattered on the table.

The pictures, the poses, the prominent pudenda, the tits, the buttocks all served one purpose and one purpose only for the customers who purchased such magazines. It was quite simply

93

designer masturbatory material. He had often wondered just how many variations the producers of this erotica could possibly introduce week after week in order to maintain a profitable circulation. Big tits, a gaping vagina, a forest of pubic hair, a never-ending parade of pulchritudinous wenches – after a while they all looked the same and the stimulatory effect subsided considerably, especially as he was wanking so often and to order that there was precious little desire left to arouse.

From his physiology classes he had learnt that persistence of a stimulus which generated an electrical impulse down a sensory nerve fibre, if continued at the same intensity for long enough, ceased to have the same effect as the initial stimulus. There existed a state of so-called 'tolerance' of the stimulus. The sensor mechanism in the stimulated organ had simply got used to the unabating stimulus and ceased to be excited. He remembered at the time applying this same strictly physiological concept to every phenomenon, including human relationships. He'd deduced that the same tolerance effect occurred with girlfriends, and he'd got it firmly implanted in to his head that to stay with one stable partner for too long would be very likely to induce the same numbing effect as the tolerance phenomenon of the nerve impulse. It certainly appeared to be the case with the glossy lovelies splayed out before him, but then the dimensions of these relationships were limited to the thickness of one page.

And he shouldn't forget the refractory period, another phenomenon of physiology which so often thwarted his sexual stamina. If he was praying for the tolerance effect to reverse, if only for a moment, then there was still the refractory period to contend with. This was the immediate period after an electrical impulse had passed down a nerve fibre when that nerve could not possibly be made to transmit another impulse, no matter how strong the stimulus. It existed for a defined period of time and represented the 'recovery' phase of the nerve when the chemical conditions necessary to transmit the impulse had to recharge. Well, it was the same with sex, he'd thought. The post-ejaculatory period was certainly a refractory phase. It was that awful empty feeling that men seemed to experience more than women just after orgasm, when nothing, but nothing, could possibly excite them – or make the nerves to their genital apparatus work, although he had observed that the length of his own post-ejaculatory refractory period varied considerably, depending on the 'sexual attraction quotient' of the particular partner at the time.

It seems now, as he sits back in the armchair trying to induce a feeling of sexual arousal, that he is suffering a double dose of tolerance and refractory period. It is hopeless. The magazines strewn before him cease to offer anything but a tiny glimmer of hope for sexual stimulation. He flicks backwards, forwards randomly, desperate for the slightest genital tingle. Nothing. Curses to Debbie!

He drops a magazine, his organ totally flaccid, and lurches sideways towards the bedside cabinet and opens the top drawer. If only he had taken two tablets before going to sleep, he wouldn't have had such a hangover. Sleep? Rutting with Debbie half the night had precluded such a luxury!

He opens the pill pot and takes out two large pink tablets which he places on his tongue. Water. Water. God! He's thirsty. Where's the cordial? Aaaah. There, on the cabinet, Robinson's Lemon Barley, just what he needs. He stands up wobbles and teeters towards the sink, pours an inch of pale lemon cordial into a tall glass and then fills it half-full with tap water.

Oooohhh! Delicious! The two tablets are swilled down in an instant. The psychological effect is immediate – certainly before any pharmacological effect is possible. The headache evaporates as if by magic and with it the intense nausea.

He suddenly becomes more optimistic and hopeful that he will be able to perform the necessary mechanics. It is a self-fulfilling enthusiasm and initiates the pudendal arterial surge and the eagerly awaited tumescence of his organ.

His right hand rushes to assist. Slowly. Start slowly. Not too hard. Judicious massage, backward, forward, pulling the prepuce and shaft skin gently over the coronal edge and the glans. (His anatomy classes are redefining the nature of his body and swelling his vocabulary rapidly, so that by the time he graduates it will be doubled).

God, how desensitised it feels. But he is confident in his virility and continues patiently until the sensation of impending climax approaches.

His penis throbs and an uncontrollable shudder passes through his whole body as the orgasmic sensation reaches the pleasure centre in his brain. Then the pain. Super-sensitivity. Ouch! Ouch! Poor little shrinking penis. Used and abused so much. He looks down hopefully. Oh no, that just won't do. It is not nearly enough for one acceptable specimen, let alone two! And it almost certainly contains only one or two pathetic little sperms, swimming around valiantly but knowing they face a hopeless task.

He knows that the volume of semen in one ejaculate depended largely on the prostate and seminal vesical glands deep inside the perineum, and not the number of individual sperms that came along the vas deferens duct from the testes. These two glands added important nutrients, fructose, minerals and the like, as well as giving substance to the ejaculate, acting as a slimy protective vehicle to transport and keep alive the sperms on their long perilous journey. Ejaculating emptied the petty cash box, which had to wait for replenishment from the main store. The rate of replenishment increased with a greater frequency of ejaculations in an effort for the production line to cope with the extra demand, but there was a limit. A fourth ejaculation within the space of six hours couldn't possibly be expected to yield very much.

Carefully he reaches for the pot, and with the sharp plastic rim scoops up the two opalescent drops from just below his umbilicus. They are so inconsequential they don't even run down the inside of the pot. He knows that the clinics will analyse a sample under the microscope if the volume is well below par, especially from one of their proven donors, as it implies recent sexual activity instead of the required period of abstinence. Looking down the microscope, they would see a pathetically inadequate sperm count. But conversely, if the volume looked adequate they would assume that the three-day 'no sex' rule had been conscientiously observed and so they would not bother to check the sperm count.

Volume. Volume. That's what he desperately needs. His head is clearing. The Brufen tablets are working well. His mind is working. A brainwave! An absolute brainwave! What happened to a good volume specimen of semen after it had been left standing for half an hour? It liquefied. The viscous, grey-yellow-white effluent 'melted' and homogenised into a light grey, opalescent liquid. And that was how the clinics received it about an hour after production. Their judgment on the quality of the sample from a proven donor was based simply on the observable volume in the plastic pot. If it looked over 5 ml they didn't need to go through the trouble of checking a sample from a plainly cooperative donor.

A light grey, opalescent liquid. Of course! Why the hell hadn't he thought of it before? Robinson's Lemon Barley! Perfect. It looked exactly the same as the liquefied semen – even more so in a brown tinted semi-lucent plastic pot. Salvation. God bless Wimbledon and all those years of Robinson's exposure at the Centre Court.

Careful. Not too much. He mustn't overdo it or they'll expect it every time. He carefully decants about 10 ml into the metal top of the bottle and then transfers about half directly into each plastic pot. Wow! It looks perfect. Absolutely the genuine article! He feels relieved and pleased, not so much because it will get him off of the hook, but because it is such a brainwave. He must keep it a secret from the others.

As he presses the white lid of one pot firmly in place he cannot suppress an uninvited thought. Conscience. He experiences a definite sensation of guilt. The woman. The recipient. The anonymous, faceless and eternally grateful innocent victim of this fraudulent sample. She will have undoubtedly already gone through enormously stressful trials, traumas, heartaches and disappointments to end up in a Harley Street clinic. There, she will submit to the final indignity of having a plastic syringe thrust into her vagina and some total stranger's semen squirted into her posterior fornix. It is not exactly the usual romance and passion associated with making babies. But it is desperation. And today, a very special, supremely important day for her, when she hopes her prayer for new life will be answered with the joy of pregnancy, the miracle of birth and parenthood, there is, unknown to her, the cruel irony of a specially selected specimen, 'guaranteed' fertile, which is in fact 99 per cent lemon cordial. How cruel and merciless life can be!

But as quickly as this distasteful negative thought skims across his mind, he dismisses it. Pragmatism. That was the rule he was learning each and every day in medical school. There was little room for sentiment. That was a luxury few could afford.

The second pot. Snap on the lid tight. There. Must keep these precious little samples safe and warm until delivery. He looks at his watch. Christ! 7.45. He'd better get a move on.

Safely on the elevator going up to Oxford Circus tube station, he is able to relax a moment and ponder his brilliant idea. Two pots intact, warm and snug! He is pleased. The clinics were hardly likely to complain about these samples. Not that volume! They won't even bother to check the sperm count or sperm motility – the volume speaks for the quality from a proven donor who has dutifully obeyed the rules of sexual abstinence. Just as well. He is on his final warning from Dr Bodkins at 52 Harley Street. There had been too many duff samples in the last few months. They'll be pleased with this one, he is sure! It will be assumed if the woman doesn't fall pregnant after this offering from one of their best donors, then it is her fault. Never mind. You can try again next month, dear!

Dr Crowther at 17 Harley Street was more lenient with his donors, aware of some of the logistical problems encountered in producing samples, especially at short notice. But even he had given Harry a gentle warning to ensure he followed the strict rules of abstinence. Fortunately, his pretty dark-haired nurse, Liz had a soft spot for him and had been able to get him off the hook when he turned in bad samples. He had toyed with the idea of asking her out, but the risk of mixing business with pleasure had held him back. If they fell out, then it would be the end of that clinic and the regular weekly income it yielded.

The consequences of his activity and the end results of his 'donations' to the clinics were never considered. But for once, as he crosses the square and turns into the southern end of Harley Street, he indulges the fantasy of the possible end product of his mission (although today there was hardly likely to be an end product with samples of almost 100 per cent Lemon Barley). When he's grown up, what would such an individual say to an inquiry about his origins?

'Oh yes – I began, or at least half of me began in a brown perspex pot, carried in a warm coat pocket travelling on a short journey along the underground, and then into a plastic syringe and squirted up into the posterior fornix of my mother's vagina, carried forth on a wave of Robinson's Lemon Barley!'

God forbid! Poor bastard! Some ignominious start to life.

52 Harley Street. Dr Reginald Bodkins. He rings the bell. Miss Rhodes, the prim middle-aged secretary, opens the door. Besides a snooty affectation, she cannot disguise a thinly veiled contempt, if not disgust, for the purveyors of semen.

'Can you wait a minute please, Mr Lester?'

'Sure.'

He knows she is taking the sample to Dr Bodkins, who will look at the volume and decide whether to pay him, give him a final, final warning or strike him off the books once and for all.

Within half a minute she returns, looking a little flushed.

'Yes, Mr Lester, that's fine. I'll give you your three pounds now.'

'And my next appointment?'

'I suggest you phone later today or tomorrow.'

'Thanks. Bye.'

Phew! Off the hook. God bless you, Robinson's Lemon Barley.

On to number 17. It will be no problem now.

Liz opens the door.

'Hi, Liz! Your friendly milkman calling with an extra pint of full cream.'

'Come in,' she says with a wry smile.

He knows she cannot share with her the full irony of his cheerful greeting.

'Oh dear. Displeasure? And so early in the morning?'

She normally melted with his blatantly disingenuous charm, but not this morning.

'The last few weeks, Harry, the samples have been rather unsatisfactory – to put it mildly. I've been able to conceal it from Dr Crowther, but quite honestly, it's not fair to the patients – the women who come week after week, you know...'

'I'm sorry, Liz...'

'You've really got to obey the rules. It won't be long before we see a definite drop in your success rate, and that'll be it, I'm afraid.'

He lowers his head and looks genuinely penitent. But today, he has an ace up his sleeve, or more precisely an ace sample in his pocket.

'This morning, we've matched you with a very nice lady who rang up yesterday, who will be coming in from Stilton Keynes. The poor woman is desperate. She's been attending faithfully for almost one year now – not missing one single month. Sadly, today will be her last attempt, and we're not that hopeful. As you probably know, Dr Crowther doesn't advise any more after twelve goes. So you see, she deserves the very best sample she can get today. You have been one of our very best donors, and pretty reliable until the last few months. Dare I look at this morning's offering?'

Harry stands in front of Liz, not able to speak for a moment. He feels genuine anguish and for once can actually visualise an anxious, distraught woman desperate to get pregnant.

He reaches into his jacket pocket, and with a theatrical flourish, rather like a magician who is about to dazzle his audience with his final trick, produces the second brown pot.

There! Take a look at that lot! He smiles smugly as he hands over the pot to Liz, not saying a word. She carefully removes the white cover.

'Uuuum. Uuuum. We have been a good little boy, haven't we?'

100

Carefully, she replaces the white cover.

'Harry, I'm proud of you. Dr Crowther, I am sure, will be delighted – Mrs X might even have a fighting chance with this.'

Harry stares at the floor impassively. Conscience again. Damn. It had never bothered him before. Still, there might be one or two aggressive sperms swimming around in the Lemon Barley, not quite drowned yet, just itching to explore a female reproductive tract. But his knowledge of reproductive physiology reminds him that the chances are remote, very remote. A sample from her husband, deemed infertile, may well contain millions of sperms which were, nevertheless, not enough. Although it was only one sperm that ultimately penetrated the egg, somewhere in the dark recesses of the fallopian tube, it required by some sort of mass action effect many, many millions, in fact above a well-defined minimum concentration of spermatozoa, to enable the one solitary sperm to achieve its goal. Harry supposed it was analogous to the salmon returning against all odds, swimming vast distances and jumping impossible rapids in order to spawn in their birthplace. Only one or two ever got through, but countless numbers were required to realise the fact. Oh well, *c'est la vie.*

'Liz, what if she fails this time? Is that really it?'

''Fraid so. It's a pretty strict policy of Dr Crowther's. Twelve goes only. It's pointless after that – from our experience, anyway. And don't forget, these people are paying a lot of money and some, if not most, are not rich. They've got mortgages like everybody else and are using their savings most of the time. They are so desperate that some even borrow on their houses and go further into debt. Of course, you never see that side of things, do you?'

'No, of course not,' he nods soberly. 'Oh well – maybe she'll get lucky this last time, eh?'

He is struggling now with his conscience. But does he really give a damn about Mrs X and whether she spawns a sprog or not? Sheer ego, that's all it was. And pandering to the selfish genes to perpetuate one's own line. Why bother? Why allow

101

the forces of nature to push you around so much and put you to so much trouble? What a nonsense! Goodness knows, the world was crowded enough with wretched, starving children. Forget it.

And who knows, by denying her the fleeting joys of pregnancy and childbirth, he might be saving her from a stressful lifetime of thankless commitment. But then who was he to deny her something nature compelled her to experience?

Sadly, for most of these blighted women it became an all-consuming obsession which took over their lives and those of their husbands. For him, the real would-be father, it meant nothing. It was totally devoid of any emotional element – the consequence of a mere flippant masturbatory act, where the normal highly emotive process of procreation was reduced to nothing more than a mechanical exercise. It was physiological fatherhood only. It could never be construed as anything more than that. It was as if the male contribution to the offspring had been effectively dehumanised and sanitised of its spiritual entity.

Could there ever be any empathy with the donor? Could the genes transfer emotions and patterns of innate recognition between progenitor and progeny without the nurturing process from the beginning, which started with the natural copulatory act, the union of flesh and the spirit together? Hardly likely! Artificial Insemination precluded any such initial bonding process.

And what about his own instincts to procreate and ensure genetic immortality? He was just as susceptible to the powerful forces of nature as anybody else. He would, no doubt, be just as vulnerable to the emotional commitment of reproduction. But didn't this business of anonymous sperm donation satisfy all the instincts of procreation without the worries of lifelong commitments? He could simply get on with his own life without domestic involvement, marriage and all the problems that could entail. And he would be safe in the assumption that he'd already satisfied the instruction of his genetic code and yet remain aloof from the inevitable emotional entanglements of the mating game.

102

'I know it's strictly against policy, Liz, and in all honesty, I never give it a second thought, but ... well, you know, this time, perhaps you'd let me know if she makes it?'

'Do you really care, Harry – really?'

'Sure.'

'Okay. Just this once. No names, of course. I'll simply say "yes" or "no" in around a month's time – but I'm sure you will have forgotten totally by then.'

'I appreciate that ... what's the time?'

'Just after a quarter to nine.'

'Oh shit. I'll be in real trouble if I don't get to the ward before Aubrey's round. I'm meant to allocate the new patients. He'll kill me. Got to run. Pay me next week – I'll ring for an appointment – bye.'

Harry takes off and sprints down Harley Street. He stops for a breather at the traffic lights, his mind racing almost as fast as his thumping heart. It wasn't for nothing that the select band of donors were known as the 'Harley Street Runners'. It was an apt if not derogatory title, and less offensive than some of the other adjectives applied to their trade.

Anyone would think they were selling their souls to the devil, instead of a few drops of milky grey fluid to an eternally grateful infertile couple desperate for a baby. A few measly drops of semen – how could that be equated with such a condemnation? His responsibility in the business ended when he'd delivered the pot. He would never have to know what happened to it – the final outcome, the joy or sorrow it might bring. It could not possibly affect him. And it would be a futile, sentimental exercise to speculate on the life it might initiate or the individual it might create. He is simply the facilitator, the source of a few potent cells, a *soupçon* of chromosomes, a sprinkling of genes which fused with some anonymous female egg and transformed into another anonymous genetic entity. It was a simple biological phenomenon, merely a manifestation of cellular biochemistry. How on earth could it be seen as something morally questionable?

The products of his cells, his chromosomes and genes, would join the infinitely large genetic pool (more like an ocean) of human life, and the individual produced would be none the wiser regarding their origin. Did that matter? Would they care anyway? Of course not! Only the ego and arrogance of the evolved human being fed such a desire, the compulsion to know from whence it came. It was as if evolution had created an emotional strait-jacket for itself.

This method of reproduction would stop that nonsense, at least for him. He would be free from any such emotional straitjacket, and at the same time he could refute any accusation that he might have ducked out of his biological responsibilities. His frequent errands to Harley Street through the morning rush hour ensured his contribution to the genetic pool. And a contribution of the highest quality, naturally. He would never have to compromise the rest of his life worrying about the offspring and go through the emotional trauma which that entailed. The vast majority of the human race played that energy-sapping game which drained their resources and ultimately sent them to an early grave.

The lights change. Harry runs across the road and down the steps leading to the underground.

When he emerges into the grey daylight 20 minutes later, he is still feeling clammy and uncomfortable from his exertions and the stifling stuffy atmosphere in the overcrowded train. He runs along Newgate Street, turning right into West Smithfield past the revolving ambulance platform of the Accident Department, and through the Henry VIII gate into the quadrangle of Barts Hospital.

The hospital site is the oldest in London. The little church of St Bartholomew-the-Less, which nestles comfortably inside the main gate, dates back to the 12th century. In the modern day hustle and bustle of the City of London square mile, the hospital quadrangle, constructed in the Georgian period of the 18th century, is a refuge and sanctuary, with its old wooden benches, ornate gardens and swaying silver birch trees. On warm days in the summer, patients would be wheeled out in their beds to bask in the sun.

Reaching the far side of the square, Harry turns sharp right and heads for the male students' clinical cloakroom, where he will pick up a white coat from his locker. The MSCR is subterranean, and the atmosphere is forever dusty and gloomy. He runs down the cold concrete steps and enters a labyrinth of hundreds of steel lockers. Today, it feels even more musty and damp than usual, and there is a pervasive smell of stale sweat. It is dungeon-like and austere. The few bare lightbulbs throw shadows between the rows of lockers, concealing decades of cobwebs and dust.

Harry opens his locker and snatches the white coat from the peg. It is a simple, standard white cotton coat, the same in fact, as the managers wore in the meat market opposite the hospital, clean, pristine and unsoiled. But from his coat, a stethoscope dangles conspicuously from one pocket, which together with the white-on-black name badge on one lapel, signal clearly what he and the rest of the medical students feel they personify in this hallowed place of healing – the darlings of the hospital, the very reason for its continued existence.

They are the fledgling doctors who, having completed their sterile pre-clinical module, have successfully graduated to the clinical phase of their training. The white coats are a mark of their new-found privilege, but the visible stethoscope served as a more potent symbol of their elitism. It ensures they are not mistaken for ordinary mortals in the vicinity (such as the meat market managers) who might also be wearing a white coat. Most hardly know one end from the other, but that doesn't matter.

Traipsing round the wards hard on the heels of a consultant, like a gaggle of goslings after a mother goose, put them centre stage for everyone to see. It could be role-play at drama school. Apart from the nitty-gritty of medicine, they were learning the moves, the attitude, the style, the 'feel' – the famous bedside manner necessary to convince a patient that they are a trustworthy expert in all matters concerned with health. Even at this stage Harry is aware that it is all a bit of a charade, a performance which highlighted and reinforced the importance and prestige of the doctors, whilst reminding the patients to submit totally to their ministrations.

He rushes out of the locker room and up the stone steps towards one corner of the square, which will take him to the ground floor surgical block and the wards. He barges through the rubber swing doors and runs helter-skelter along the corridor to Abernethy and Waring wards, where he was supposed to be in attendance half an hour earlier. The ward clerk can hear his rapidly echoing steps as he approaches the ward office, and she appears at the door to witness his breathless arrival.

'Hiya Trudi,' he gasps, 'have they started yet?'

'Certainly have, Harry. And what have you been doing this morning – oh, I see,' she says, reading the silent expression on his face, 'flogging your hide again.'

'Financial reality, my dear ... how else do you expect me to pay the rent? And besides, think about all those poor unfortunate women desperate for babies...'

'God help any of yours – anyway, young man, you'd better get a move on. Mr Aubrey-Taylor asked where you were, and whether the patients had been allocated or not. I said you'd gone to the dentist.'

'Very original. Thanks a million, Trudi, I'm sure he believed that.'

'They're on Abernethy. You'd better hurry.'

Harry adjusts his tie and wipes a bead of sweat from his forehead, trying to compose himself ready for the anticipated confrontation. He approaches the entrance to the female ward and can see a cluster of white coats halfway down, gathered around a patient's bed. An accompanying entourage of nursing staff stands motionless, like a bodyguard, to one side of a short stout figure with thinning grey hair and gold-rimmed half-moon spectacles balanced on the end of his nose. He is standing at the head of the bed, and when he hears Harry approaching he looks up slowly and deliberately, peering over his spectacles.

Harry has slowed down and takes positive deliberate steps, trying hard to instil a feeling of calm and order in his demeanour with a look of penitent concern on his face. It is a face which apologises but at the same time suggests that he has a worthy excuse. His first words are launched on a residual wave of breathlessness.

'I'm sorry I'm late, sir, but I've been . . .'

'Yes, we already know, Lester. In fact we were all a little late this morning, so you can count yourself lucky that you haven't missed much. This is the first patient, and you have arrived just in time to tell us to whom this lady has been allocated.'

Heads tilt down to the shiny lino floor. Some heads turn sideways to conceal a smile. The sister looks smug. She knows. One of the arrogant little pipsqueaks who thinks he knows everything about medicine, but in reality knew much less than one of her first-year nurses, is about to get his come-uppance.

'Lester, whose patient?'

'Well, sir, I'm not sure exactly . . .' Harry flounders.

Montague Aubrey-Taylor, already in his sixties, is of a previous generation. He is of the old school of traditional doctors who knew their place and everybody else's place in society. Their place was well-defined and set apart from other mere mortals. Within the hallowed shrine of their teaching hospital, they ruled unopposed. At best, they might be regarded as benevolent dictators, at worst, despised despots. Montague Aubrey-Taylor was probably somewhere in the middle of that range, oscillating from avuncular patronage to tyrannical tirade, depending on his mood. In the wave of permissive liberalism which was sweeping the Sixties, his generation was being swiftly replaced by young dynamic technocrats of the micro-chip era who, much less concerned with image and presentation, were unapologetic disciples of 'efficient functionality'. But his world was still firmly based on formal protocol and well-circumscribed patterns of behaviour and decorum which had stood the test of time. Such style formed the basis of all that was to be admired in Western civilisation. A threat to that order would be tantamount to blasphemy.

In his estimation, medical students, embryonic doctors, who one day would become pillars of the establishment, were, at best hopelessly misguided souls in their formative years, and at worst anarchic, amoral, even immoral beasts who needed firm handling. Their saving grace was that most of them had cavernous brains like huge unfilled sponges, which were primed ready to soak up all the information and ideas thrown at them. But it was vital to instil in them the correct ideas. The proper way of doing things. Otherwise, how could they call themselves civilised?

'Not sure? Lester. LESTER! Come here.'

The distinguished-looking consultant moves menacingly towards Harry, sensing his vulnerability, closing in for the kill. The sister at the end of the bed automatically moves her flock half a pace backwards into the centre of the ward. The circle of students, passive and apprehensive, widens as Mr Aubrey-Taylor comes within less than an arm's length of where Harry is standing.

'God forbid, man, you look as if you've been up half the night – and you haven't even shaved.'

'Well, sir . . .'

Sister Walker suppresses a smile, pursing her lips firmly downwards, and focuses on the brilliantly polished wheels at the end of the bed, which she always ensured were facing outwards for Mr Aubrey-Taylor's ward round with regimented precision.

'Good God, man, I can smell the alcohol from here. You're an absolute disgrace!'

'But sir, I can explain . . .'

'Don't answer me back. BE WARNED, Lester. You will see me after the ward round in my office.'

Harry looks down in silence, cursing Debbie in his mind as the root cause of this highly embarrassing confrontation.

'Now, Lester, tell me about the signs and symptoms of acute cholecystitis.'

CHAPTER 5

DELIVERY

Why did sex evolve at all? Until recently it was assumed that sex evolved as a means of repairing damaged genes, and of offering a variation in the resultant offspring which would enable the latter to cope with the unpredictable environmental changes. New theories suggest, however, that the natural gene mutations, certainly in multi-cellular organisms, would be adequate to provide for this environmental uncertainty without the necessity for sexual fusion and subsequent recombination. Sexual reproduction, it is argued, arose out of the necessity to cope with the micro-parasites, that is the viruses, bacteria, fungi or protozoans. These all have a smaller genome, and shorter generation time than their hosts. This explains the need for sexual recombination in the host, to enable it to keep ahead of its parasites, and to survive. Studies in the New Zealand freshwater snail (which reproduces both pathogenetically and sexually) and its trematode parasite have demonstrated that those individual snails infested by the parasite showed a much higher incidence of sexual reproduction to keep pace with the defence mechanisms of the parasite. This process of mutual interaction between host and parasite is referred to as 'co-evaluation'.

British Journal of Sexual Medicine, 1989

Stilton Keynes is a 'new town', purpose-built in an area of previously isolated rural serenity, yet only a short train journey from London and close to the main lines of communication linking the north and south of the country. It was designed not just to accommodate an expanding commuter population, but also to encourage expanding businesses to relocate away from the congested metropolis. The social architects of this brave new urban planning saw a vision of a medium-sized town with all that 20th-century amenities could provide, whilst maintaining the traditional qualities of life found in a pastoral setting.

Not unexpectedly, the critics of such carefully planned uniformity have tarnished the image. If you lived in Stilton Keynes you were likely to be categorised as the faceless, uniform urban commuter whose life profile fitted a well-defined conventional pattern:

Residence – a drab, modern-style three-bedroomed semi-detached house with integral garage and medium-sized garden (rose bushes in the front and a small goldfish pond in the back), situated in a quiet cul-de-sac within walking distance of the station.

Domestic profile – the standard family unit. A husband who is a medium-grade higher clerical officer in a commercial bank in the City of London, but with aspirations to higher things. A wife who works maximum part-time as an assistant manageress in a ladies' wear shop, even though she feels a woman's place is

111

in the home. Two children, one at junior school and one at high school, both perfectly disciplined and behaved with a keen sense of ambition.

Beacons of success and status – a quality secondhand car, possibly an ageing BMW, polished and kept pristine in the garage and used only at weekends. Membership of the local Rotary Club for him, and women's circle and church group for her. Short holidays twice a year, including an obligatory visit to one of the in-laws and a package deal to the Costa Brava.

The Browns, Roy and Doreen, almost fitted this classic stereotype to perfection. The 'almost' was the fact that they did not have the two children. And therein lay the central problem in their lives, the cause of inestimable anguish and stress, and the blight which cast a shadow on an otherwise idyllic existence.

About the same time Harry is receiving his come-uppance on the ward round at Barts Hospital, in the nicely fitted Formica kitchen in Stilton Keynes, Roy and Doreen are arguing again.

'Really Doreen, if I've told you once, I've told you a thousand times, it isn't necessary. You've – I mean we've suffered enough. Look, for God's sake, it's killing us, not to mention our marriage...'

'One more try, that's all, and that is it – I promise. I've just got to complete the programme. You never know, it might just work this last time.'

'But, you've been going for almost a year now – eleven months, to be exact – and not a thing. Face it, dear, if the Lord meant us to have a child he would have provided, I am sure. Even Dr Crowther was pessimistic the last time we spoke to him. And he did say if we really want children we can always adopt. Besides, dear, this AID business – you know I've never liked the idea of you getting pregnant from another man. It's just not right, not natural...'

'Please, Roy, we've been through all this so many times. You know in reality it would be your child. The donor would only be the mechanical – oh, what was the word he used – physiological father. But you would be the real one who brought him up, and no one, absolutely no one, could dispute that.'

'Well I would, my dear. It's just not natural. Why for God's sake are you so obsessed with having your own baby?'

'I have to. Something inside me cannot stop the desire – it's so strong, believe me.'

'All I can say is thank God it's your last time today. Quite frankly, I'll be relieved when we've put this madness behind us. We can still adopt, if you must...'

'It's not the same, and you know that, Roy.'

'Don't be silly. Just look at you. You're a nervous wreck. For what? This business has put a tremendous strain on our marriage and you know it, my dear.'

'Oh, for Christ's sake go to work and let me get myself ready.'

Doreen doesn't speak as Roy disappears into the hall. She follows menacingly and slams the door behind him with such force the glass could break. She turns and stand still in the centre of the room for a few moments as if paralysed by the thought of her final mission to the clinic, for which she must now prepare.

It is imperative that she goes through with it to the bitter end. She turns and flops into a comfy chair, letting out a long anguished sigh. She stretches for a light brown folder lying on the glass-topped table under the green alabaster lamp, pulls out an A4 sheet of paper and looks at it studiously. Plotted on the left-hand vertical column is a temperature scale in degrees fahrenheit and centigrade, and the horizontal line along the bottom of the page marks off the days of the month.

It is her twelfth temperature chart, and the clinic has made it clear that it will be the last. In the beginning it had frightened her. It had seemed so technical, plotting her daily temperature on a special chart. She'd always imagined such charts were the exclusive preserve of scientists and technocrats, not suburban housewives. But by the fourth month she'd felt confident in the daily routine, and precisely as instructed, she had taken her temperature at seven o'clock each morning and recorded it with a little cross on the chart for that particular day.

Dr Crowther and his assistant had explained the significance of her body temperature in relation to the menstrual cycle. Daily plotting of the temperature provided a simple and pretty reliable indicator of when she ovulated. When that happened, usually around mid-cycle in most women, it was accompanied by a temperature rise, small but definitely significant and unequivocally recordable. It only lasted 24–36 hours, but if during that time sperms were introduced into her reproductive tract, then there was a good chance (providing there were enough sperms of good enough quality) that fertilisation of a released ovum would occur – that is, she would conceive and a pregnancy would follow.

That was the theory, and for most fertile women it was born out by fact. Unfortunately, in Doreen's case her contribution to the biological process of procreation was intact whilst that of her husband's was not. Dr Crowther had said that Roy's sperm count was very low, almost nonexistent in most specimens he'd brought for analysis, and contained many abnormal forms with depressed motility – which in lay terms meant he was infertile.

This unforeseeable state of affairs had set the scene for almost irreversible marital disharmony. By the time they had gone for tests Doreen was absolutely desperate to get pregnant. And it had become an obsession when it was revealed that she was fine but Roy was lacking. It had been a terrible shock to them both, and had been hard for Roy to accept as the truth in the beginning. The numerous visits and tests had cost them a small fortune, and they'd had to raise the money by partially remortgaging the house.

Theirs had been such a perfect relationship ever since schooldays. She had been his first girlfriend and he her first boyfriend. They'd been inseparable at school, and it had seemed quite natural and entirely appropriate that they get engaged after he'd passed his intermediate bank exams and she'd finished her advanced secretarial and shorthand course at the commercial college.

Their marriage had been blissful. Perhaps too blissful to last. They had planned carefully not to start a family for five years

114

until the mortgage repayments were well-established and they'd saved a thousand pounds. When Doreen had stopped taking the pill, she hadn't expected to fall pregnant immediately. Her family doctor had told her that. It might take up to six months before normal fertility resumed. But after six months the concern and niggling doubts had started.

Their sex life, conventional and steady according to their doctor (although they themselves had not compared it to anyone else's), had always seemed satisfactory and as fulfilling as they'd imagined it should be. Copulation occurred at least three times per week. Her periods were always regular and very predictably every 28–30 days, so after six months had passed without any signs of pregnancy their doctor had advised 'making love' more times around the mid-cycle days, to increase the chances of conception. This they had dutifully done. In fact, from the twelfth to the nineteenth day of each cycle they'd had sexual intercourse every night, whether either of them felt like it or not.

After a further six months Doreen had gone to her doctor again. By this stage she had begun to feel anxiety, and every time she saw a mother with a newborn baby she'd found it hard to suppress a pang of envy.

'Don't worry,' he'd said, 'it happens all the time. You've been on the pill for six years, and it often takes a year to get back on track. Don't worry. Keep plugging away – I'm confident you'll fall pregnant sooner or later.'

She'd felt happier on leaving his office, but in the back of her mind the niggling doubts would not disappear. Roy hadn't shared or appreciated her concern. He wasn't really interested in children, anyway. He worshipped the ground that she walked on, and that was all that mattered. In a way, children coming along might even threaten her attentiveness and devotion to him. Besides, with his work and developing obsession with golf he suspected that children might curtail his freedom.

After 18 months her doubts had become daily concerns and a more than frequent topic of conversation. Why? Why them? she'd said to Roy every night when he came in tired and lifeless from a long day in the office and a stressful commuter trek home.

'Don't worry, my dear,' he'd said, echoing their doctor's words, 'maybe it's just not meant to happen. And besides, if the worse comes to the worse we can always adopt.'

When he'd said that she'd screamed she didn't want another woman's baby and locked herself in the bedroom in a fit of tears and anguish.

By the time two years had passed their doctor had agreed it was time they saw a specialist. But Stilton Keynes General Hospital Gynaecology Department didn't have an infertility clinic – it was still early days in this field. The consultant had given them two options – either one of the new specialist clinics in a London teaching hospital, which would inevitably mean up to a year at least on a waiting list, or a rapid referral to a private clinic in Harley Street.

'But look, my dear,' Roy had said, 'we can't afford it if we go private.'

'And what about all the money we've saved?' she'd snapped back.

'That won't be enough. And besides, we need new things for the house.'

For the first time in their lives, their relationship deteriorated. She became depressed. She was tearful nearly every single day, especially around menstruation, when the onset of her period heralded another failed conception.

'I've made my mind up,' she'd said firmly to Roy, 'I'm going to phone this number in London that the hospital gave me.'

Roy could see that it was hopeless. He knew he had to concede if only to save his marriage.

But when Dr Boris Crowther, the infertility specialist in London, had insisted on a semen sample from Roy after the first visit, an enormous row had developed. How the hell could he do it? When he had been given the small plastic pot with a blank label on it, he'd cringed in horror and embarrassment.

'No no,' he'd said, 'I won't do it. I won't. I can't.'

It had taken over a week of coaxing, and only when she had threatened to leave him had he reluctantly taken the pot.

When Dr Crowther saw them the next time, he'd not been prepared for the verdict.

'I'm sorry, Mr Brown, but you are most certainly infertile. We had better take another two specimens to confirm your status. I'd like you to refrain from all sexual activity for at least five days, to ensure the best sample possible.'

It had been a complete bombshell.

'As far as we can ascertain, Mrs Brown is fine. No problem at all. I'm afraid it looks as though the failure to conceive is a direct result of your deficient semen. But don't worry. We can do something.'

They'd walked down Harley Street to the underground at Oxford Circus in complete silence, numbed by the reality and the cold, sober certainty of the doctor's pronouncement. Roy had felt devastated – half a man. Doreen had had conflicting feelings. Yes, there had been anguish and utter disappointment, as if a heavy black cloud had cast a shadow across their perfect existence. But she had also felt a sense of relief. It explained the failure. And it wasn't her fault.

Two weeks later, when the initial shock had subsided, they'd sat passively opposite Dr Crowther.

'AID Mrs Brown. That is the only course open to you.'

'What on earth is AID?' Roy had questioned in a tone hostile and defensive, sensing it was something of which he might not approve.

'Artificial Insemination by Donor. We use a semen specimen from a fertile male and introduce it into the female at the appropriate time in her menstrual cycle, that is around ovulation time, and hopefully a conception follows. It really is quite simple.'

Roy's lower lip had quivered as he'd turned slowly to look for Doreen's reaction. She had sat there calmly, without so much as a flicker of change in her facial expression.

'You can't be serious,' he had said.

Dr Crowther had spoken in a quiet matter-of-fact manner. He'd seen the reaction and witnessed the shock many times.

'Well, it's an option worth considering. In fact, it's the only option other than adoption. I might say that no one will ever

117

know it is not your child. We even try to match physical characteristics – you know, height, hair and eye colour, etc., but that is not essential. The donors are selected very carefully. Physically, they are all good specimens of above-average intelligence and are indubitably responsible members of our community. Needless to say, there is strict anonymity, and I mean strict. Their identity will never be divulged. And of course, they themselves will never know the fate of their "donations", shall we say?'

'You've got to be kidding,' Roy had said with incredulity, 'who in God's name would carry on with that sort of business? I mean, how on earth do you get the samples?'

'Oh come on Mr Brown,' Dr Crowther had replied, 'you can't be that unimaginative. I can tell you that we draw our donors from a very carefully selected group of medical students at a London teaching hospital. Believe me, they are all of excellent calibre in every sense of the word.'

'Medical students!' Roy had exclaimed with disbelief.

'They're fine specimens, I assure you, Mr Brown, and their genes are of proven quality...'

'B-b-but, surely they're just a bunch of irresponsible students, if you know what I mean.'

'Yes, I know exactly what you mean, but I really don't think the image that you have...'

'With all due respect, Dr Crowther, I'm not sure I would want one of their type to be responsible for my wife getting pregnant.'

Doreen had continued to sit silently throughout this exchange, and then she'd spoken quietly and deliberately.

'Is it a difficult process?'

'Simplicity itself,' he'd replied, 'the only inconvenience is having to take your temperature each day so that we can spot the ovulatory period. It's then that you come into the clinic to receive the semen specimen from an anonymous donor. We have a steady reliable "bank" of donors who we can call upon at short notice.'

'But how is it – I mean, is it very...'

'It really is a straightforward procedure, I can promise. No

118

different to having a routine gynaecological examination – and I'm sure you've already had your fair share of those. I, or my nurse introduce a small plastic syringe, without a needle of course, and then inject the semen sample into the upper reaches of the vaginal tract, close to the cervical canal which leads into the womb. You then lie on your back for half an hour to let things settle – and that's it.'

'That's it?' Roy had shouted, 'You think you can put my wife through that sort of business – quite frankly it sounds disgusting to me.'

'Why, Mr Brown?'

'It's just not natural, that's all I can say. It's not natural.'

They'd left the office without agreeing to the procedure and argued for most of the way home. Doreen had known immediately, despite the initial revulsion from Roy, moral or otherwise, that she would do it. The instinct and desire within her compelled. Roy had eventually conceded, if only to save his marriage. But when she had returned from the first session looking thoroughly exhausted and emotionally drained after what had taken the best part of a day to get in and out of London, he was unable to hide his feelings and resentment. He had acted morose and irritable.

He hadn't been able to have sex, especially with another man's seed inside her. For a little while their marriage had faltered. But Doreen had been determined and persisted. After six months and as many visits to Harley Street for the treatment, Roy had grudgingly accepted the routine, although each time she menstruated, heralding another unsuccessful mission, there had been a bitter row. The intense disappointment she experienced contrasted with his thinly disguised relief that she would not be carrying another man's offspring.

By the eleventh month the trek to the clinic had become a trip filled with anguish and despair and almost insufferable mental turmoil at the thought of another failure, which, indeed, it had turned out to be. When she'd telephoned for the twelfth and final time to dutifully announce her temperature rise and book the very last appointment, she knew it signalled the end of her insemination programme.

119

'All right, Mrs Brown,' Liz had said cheerfully and confidently over the phone, 'come in tomorrow. I might let you know confidentially that I've made sure that we'll be using one of our most reliable and successful donors.'

And now, on this cold and damp grey November morning, it is the very last time and she knows it. Over the last week the tension had built up to an almost unbearable level as this day had approached. She has tried so hard to stay calm and dispel the fear of a final failure and the realisation that she would never have her own child.

Roy had certainly been edgy for the last few days, but he had made an extra effort to conceal his feelings with a contrived cheerfulness that she recognised all too well. He prays that this will be the last attempt to get pregnant by another man, although the relief he anticipates from such a last fruitless attempt is overshadowed by the fear of how such a failure will effect Doreen and their future together. The glass door opens slowly, and he reappears from the hallway. The message on his face is a little conciliatory, if not penitent. He forces a smile.

'Anyway dear, good luck today. I'll be keeping my fingers crossed,' he says cheerfully and unemotionally, as if the last desperate gamble she is about to take is a flutter on the horses or a game of bingo, rather than her very last chance to become a mother.

'I'll be off then, my dear ... bye ... and good luck ...'

She is hardly aware of his hollow good wishes as she disappears into the bathroom. Everything in her life – her past, the present, her future, hinges on this final visit to the infertility clinic. Despite the eleven previous failures and the hard-to-ignore logic that she is not destined to give birth, she still clings to a last desperate hope that a miracle of some sort will occur – that in some mysterious way, this final attempt could be auspicious after the persistent catalogue of failure and disappointment. She has never been superstitious but maybe, just this one time, fate will lend a hand ...

Liz had said it would be their very best donor, but today, she doesn't dare think of such a person. That would be chancing fate too much. In the first few months of visits she had

120

indulged in fantasy images of him. That he would be handsome, she had no doubt. Would he be dark or fair, have blue eyes or brown, or green like her own? Would he be tall and straight-backed, athletic and powerful? He was sure to be intelligent, with a sense of humour and a gentle, kind spirit. He would give all these qualities to her baby, and she would be eternally grateful. But these dreams and fantasies had faded as the months passed and the longed-for pregnancy hadn't come.

She sits on the edge of the bed and gazes out into the garden and the row of chattering sparrows on an empty clothesline – a clothesline that should be full of nappies and booties and...

'Oh please, please let it happen,' she whispers imploringly to herself.

Half an hour later she is on the London-bound train immersed in her thoughts. She prays she's got the temperature right. It is around mid-cycle, in fact it was the fifteenth day, but is that thermometer reliable, she wonders. Did she leave it too long in her mouth, willing it to register a temperature rise? BUT she is fertile, she is – the doctor told her – no question about it. There is an egg there today, there must be. Waiting eagerly. Oh please, PLEASE let it be fertilised.

From Baker Street Station she takes a taxi to Harley Street.

'Number 17 please,' she says wistfully to the cab driver.

'Hello, Mrs Brown. Lovely to see you again.'

Liz is deliberately over-cheerful and confident. She wants Mrs Brown to be as relaxed and submissive as possible, to facilitate an easy procedure. Alas, with the best will in the world it wasn't that easy to be relaxed and submissive, lying on the back with legs splayed upwards and outwards suspended in straps, so that a cold metal instrument could be thrust up into the very innards and a syringeful of sticky grey liquid squirted into the vagina.

'Cheer up. I know it's the last session, but we are always confident right up to the end of the programme. We must give it a hundred per cent every time.'

121

Doreen forces a weak half-smile.

'I know it has been a huge disappointment not to get pregnant, but today – well today, I can tell you confidentially that we're using one of our best, VERY best, if not THE best donor that we've got on the books. And what's more – and I really shouldn't tell you this – he's brought a first-rate sample. But please remember, whatever happens, Mrs Brown, you know this has to be the last time. It's Dr Crowther's absolute rule. He really does know best, I can promise you, he is a world authority in this technique and he wouldn't want any of his patients to suffer more anguish and psychological trauma than is absolutely necessary. Anyway, don't let's dwell on the negative side. We must be hopeful and optimistic. Shall we go next door and get started?'

Doreen undresses.

'There you are, up onto the couch. I'll just fix the stirrups. That's it. Legs up. Knees bend, you should be used to it by now.'

Doreen has never got used to being trussed up like a turkey about to be stuffed, but she does her best to cooperate in dignified silence. Liz stands back, checks the final position with a minor adjustment of the buttocks, and then turns towards the fridge.

'Now, where's that golden sample?'

She opens the fridge door. She has a 5 ml syringe in her hand. Normally, Dr Crowther injected only 1 ml, which was usually more than enough if the sample was good quality. If a donor's specimen was 5 ml or over, he assumed it was satisfactory without checking in the microscope, and he would use it for five patients. Business was business, and 1 ml from a fertile donor was infinitely better than 5 ml from an infertile husband.

'There! All done.' Liz had emptied the whole syringe, all 5 ml into the posterior fornix of her vagina.

'Dr Crowther will be none the wiser,' she mutters, more to herself.

Although she is just another patient, one of a large number that pass through the clinic, Liz has a particular feeling of compassion for Mrs Brown and wants success almost as much

122

as she, although her professional impartiality tells her that there isn't much of a chance.

'Now, Mrs Brown, you must relax, RELAX, RELAX. I'll unhook you from the stirrups and then you lie there for at least twenty minutes to let that magic stuff do its trick. I'll be back soon.'

Doreen lets out a long sigh as Liz leaves the room. The final act is done. Although there has been bitter disappointment, even resentment, there is a sensation of relief that it is all over. Whatever happens, she will never go through this ghastly business again. She thinks she doesn't care anymore. The risk of chancing fate no longer matters, and so she permits herself to indulge in fantasy. She dreams now of a baby, her very own baby – and she dreams of the donor, the mysterious father, tall, handsome, broad-shouldered, bright-eyed and intelligent.

'Oh please, PLEASE let it happen,' she whispers to herself, conceding that it does matter and always will.

The viscous pool of 99 per cent Lemon Barley cordial settles in the deep recess of the vagina.

Liz returns.

'You can get dressed now, and then there'll be a few forms to complete – you know the drill. You mustn't worry about anything, as it will do no good. Stay relaxed, go home and let nature take its course.'

Unfortunately, that is precisely what had happened over the last 11 months when she had menstruated bang on time two weeks after each insemination. There was no logical reason to suppose it wouldn't happen for a twelfth time – unless, of course, the sample proved to be something 'special'.

She looks pale and drained of energy as she slips behind the light green curtain. She picks up her panties from the neat pile of clothes on the couch and slowly steps into them, still dreaming of what it must be like – the sheer wonder, the absolute miracle of a baby. Her fantasy is given full rein. She throws all superstitious caution to the wind – it hadn't made any difference in the past 11 attempts, so why should she care now? As she dresses slowly, she imagines the beautiful little creature that could come forth from her womb. Will it be a boy, a girl – perhaps there will be one of each! Oh, how heavenly that would be...

'Are you ready, Mrs Brown?'

'Uuu-h, yes – of course – won't be a minute.'

She makes a final adjustment and swishes open the curtain.

'You really do look very elegant today, Mrs Brown – but then you always do. Cheer up. Be positive.'

'Thank you, Liz. Whatever happens – I wish I could share your optimism – I want you to know how grateful I am to you for always being so kind and considerate and...'

'Don't cry, Mrs Brown. It will all work out in the end, I'm sure. Here, dry your eyes. Your taxi will be here at any moment. Now – don't forget – you call in, whether your period starts or not.'

'I will – I promise. I promise.'

The doorbell rings.

'That'll be your taxi. Goodbye, Mrs Brown – and good luck.'

'You're very edgy this morning, dear. Have I said something to upset you?'

'No.'

'Sorry I asked. Period, I expect,' Roy says automatically, forgetting the significance of such an event in Doreen's life. He continues to munch on a piece of toast whilst reading the morning newspaper propped up against the teapot, oblivious of Doreen's reaction until she speaks.

'For Christ's sake, don't you have any feelings?'

'W-w-what, dear?'

Doreen leaps from her chair and runs out through the kitchen door into the entrance hall and up the stairs to their bedroom, slamming the door behind her. She sits sobbing on the edge of the bed for a full five minutes.

A muffled, distant voice calls out.

'I must be off, dear. See you tonight.'

Roy is less affected now by her unpredictable outbursts, which have increased over the last few months, and he has tended to play them down, hoping that when her visits to the

124

infertility clinic finally finished things would get back to normal. In his mind he accepted their fate of childlessness a long time ago, and if he admitted it, preferred it that way. They were certainly better off than most of their friends who had young families, and he might now be able to buy the brand-new BMW he'd always dreamed about with his new promotion and pay rise.

Doreen stops crying and reminds herself that she must stay calm and as relaxed as possible – that is what Liz had advised at the last visit.

There hasn't been a single speck of discharge – brown, red, yellow or anything. She has always been on time, an exact 28, occasionally 30-day cycle, which she was able to predict almost to the minute. But Dr Crowther had explained clearly how emotions and the hormones controlling them could fluctuate wildly and influence the regularity of her menstrual cycle. This could be expected if there was stress of any kind, particularly the sort of psychological stress associated with treatment at an infertility clinic. For that reason, she'd been well-counselled to be mentally prepared for false alarms, late periods and even pseudo-pregnancies. The latter phenomenon was not uncommon in a woman desperate for a child and was a clear illustration of how she could impose with her will, conscious or otherwise, the necessary hormonal conditions in her body to sustain a pregnancy, whether it be false or real. Such women ceased to menstruate and even put on considerable weight, but ultimately it was destined to end in bitter disappointment when the truth was revealed.

She didn't want that. It would be immeasurably more painful than no pregnancy at all. But how could she stop her emotions? Her desperate hopes, her fears, her desires? All these passions effected the hormonal balance. And how easy it might be to trigger off a false alarm or, heaven forbid, a miscarriage? That would be the ultimate ironic tragedy. A conception, a very precious unique conception squandered by the nervous tension engendered by the desperate desire to have one.

'I will not ring Liz,' she tells herself determinedly, 'just because I should have come on today. She said I must wait at least five days.'

'I'm home, dear.'

Roy comes into the lounge, throwing his beige Burberry and briefcase onto the sofa in his customary style.

'What's for dinner, then?' he says enthusiastically, 'I'm starving.'

She stares at her husband in silence.

'Cheer up, Doreen my love. C'mon, tell me what you've been doing all day. Uuum. Whatever it is, it smells delicious.'

Still she does not speak.

'Anything the matter, dear?'

'I'm five days late.'

'Oh.'

'I'm going to ring the clinic tomorrow. If they say I must go in for a test, then I'll be leaving early.'

'Right you are, dear. Fine,' he says matter-of-factly.

'Is that your total reaction?'

'What, dear?'

'Don't you realise what I've just said?'

'Yes, but...'

'For Christ's sake, man, this could be it.'

'All right, dear. But remember, it happened once before, don't you recall? About three years ago, before we ever went to the clinic.'

'That was different. I got my dates muddled up. This is absolutely accurate, I'm certain. My last period was November the 10th. I was due on December the 8th, at the latest on the 10th. Today is the 15th, and I haven't come on yet.'

'I don't want you to build up your hopes and then be disappointed – that's all, Doreen. Perhaps it's the anticipation of Christmas...'

'No. NO. NO.'

'All right, all right, dear. I won't say any more. You'd better ring the clinic tomorrow.'

126

* * *

'Yes, Mrs Brown, I understand. You're absolutely certain. You've checked the dates and rechecked carefully – no mistake – all right, all right ... good ... wait a minute, I'll fetch your file.'

Liz goes to the grey metal filing cabinet in one corner of her office and opens the top drawer where she knows Mrs Brown's file to be. It is jammed solid with case-note files. She flicks through quickly and sifts through the last few pages. She stops at the last entry.

'Yes. You appear to be correct, Mrs Brown, LMP is noted as November the 10th, so that makes you five days late on a twenty-eight-day cycle. But please, remember what Dr Crowther has told you. We wouldn't want you to get too excited with the certainty ... the disappointment would be shattering if you raised your hopes too much. I advise you to leave it for another week, and if you haven't come on by then, you can ring for an appointment to see Dr Crowther ... all right? Good. We'll be hearing from you ... bye now.'

It is the longest week in Doreen's life. Even though Christmas is approaching and there is an atmosphere of festivity everywhere, she cannot let herself be a part of the spirit that seems to envelop everyone. Roy has finished at the office for a few days and has been putting up the Christmas decorations. He is trying hard not to upset Doreen, and prays that it will be a happy time when they can put all the misery of the last year behind them.

Doreen is totally preoccupied. She couldn't give a damn about the festive season. In the circumstances, it has no meaning for her.

Each and every morning now, she awakes dreading that she might feel wet. She knows she is tempting fate, but she refuses to wear a tampon, which she has always done previously, in anticipation of the monthly event. If it happens, then she will soil the bed and won't give a damn. It would be the end.

On the seventh day after her call to Liz she awakens and

automatically puts her hand between the top of her legs, sweeping her fingers gently between the vulval lips.

Dry. DRY!

She has not allowed Roy to touch her for nearly four weeks. He doesn't really care. In fact, he is relieved. His sexual drive, never high, is on the wane, especially with Doreen's obsession to get pregnant, and it gives him a good excuse not to perform.

'Sit down, Mrs Brown. I'll get Liz to make some tea. Liz? A pot of tea for Mrs Brown and myself.'

'On its way.'

'Now let's go through your history again, and more importantly, the dates very carefully and precisely.'

Dr Crowther browses through her thick file.

'Uuuum – yes. It does look as if you are now nearly two weeks overdue. That would imply a pregnancy of around six weeks, and a pregnancy test should be positive. Did you bring an early morning specimen?'

'Yes. I gave it to Liz.'

'Good. She's probably testing it right now. Here, have some tea ... remember, Mrs Brown, not to expect too much. The body can play some wicked tricks.'

Liz appears at the door, her eyes avoiding Doreen's searching glare. She intends to maintain professional propriety.

'Can you come, Dr Crowther?'

'Why, of course.'

He gets up from his chair and follows Liz into the side room.

'Positive, very definitely positive – no question of it. This is not even the most sensitive test kit we use, so it really must be ... well, well, well. I must say, Liz, I'm surprised – we didn't expect it, did we? Who was the donor, as a matter of interest?'

'Harry Lester.'

'Ah yes. He must have heeded our warning to improve the quality of his samples. I just hope nothing goes wrong.'

Dr Crowther walks back through the connecting door to his office, where Doreen sits bolt upright in the chair in front of his desk. There is a desperate pleading expression in her eyes as she follows his every step, but his face gives nothing away until he sits down.

With a sense of carefully contrived drama, which he feels would not be inappropriate to the occasion, he places both hands together in the centre of the desk and leans slightly forward towards Mrs Brown. Her heart is thumping so hard it feels as if it is about to jump out of her chest.

'Yes, Mrs Brown. No doubt about it. The test is positive. Congratulations.'

As each day passes, Doreen's mood elevates by a notch. In the beginning, although ecstatic at Dr Crowther's pronouncement, she has been fearful of losing this priceless gift of pregnancy. But by three months a quiet confidence and serenity is beginning to take hold of her. She smiles constantly, and when she talks to Roy it is no longer in a harsh tone but is with affection and genuine warmth. He is not able to share her joy, but is careful to conceal any smouldering resentment he might have for another man's seed growing in his wife's womb. In fact, any discomfiture he might admit to because of this fact, is overshadowed by Doreen's undoubted happiness. She no longer snaps at him.

There has been a complete embargo on sexual intercourse, even though Dr Crowther had not insisted it was entirely necessary. But she has told Roy that she didn't want to take any chances. Yet ironically, her affections for him have increased and become more overtly physical than before as if he were the father-to-be.

Now it seems the pregnancy is advancing normally, her fears are becoming less and she cannot stop fantasies of the anonymous sperm donor, the real father. She is now fixed on the image that he is young, tall, strong, handsome and intelligent. In her imagination she stereotypes the ideal role model to the extreme. He combines all the elements of the perfect man with a flawless genetic blueprint. But what sort of personality, what sort of qualities, habits, interests does he have? She is confident he will be kind, considerate and humorous, with a twinkle in his eye and a devilish captivating smile, enough to make any woman swoon – the ultimate Prince Charming.

And then her fantasy ends and she reminds herself that she will never know his true spirit. Only perhaps vicariously, through the product of the union, the new human being to come, will she ever catch a glimpse of this very special 'fairy godfather'.

At around 20 weeks she awakes suddenly in the night.

'Roy ... ROY! I felt something! I definitely felt something!'

'Yes, dear.'

'I'm sure it's not the collywobbles – I've never felt anything like it before. It's moving. It's moving. My baby's moving, I'm sure Roy dear, I'm sure.'

Doreen hugs her husband. He remains passive, stifling a yawn.

'Of course, dear. Now go back to sleep.'

At 32 weeks she sees Dr Crowther.

'Everything is fine, Mrs Brown – all the blood tests, scans and your progress have been spot-on. We do not anticipate any problems and expect a normal delivery. I think you might just as well be confined at Stilton Keynes General Hospital. I know Mr Letchworth there. He is an ex-Barts man and a first-class obstetrician. I'll write to him and make an appointment for you in two weeks.'

'Push, Mrs Brown. Push. PUSH. Relax. RELAX. It's gone. The contraction's gone. Relax. That's it – slow deep breaths. Nice and easy. Save all your energy for the next one. They're coming every two minutes now – you're doing very well.'

'Oooh, but it hurts. I never thought it would be so difficult and painful – but I won't have any injections. Nothing must affect my baby. Nothing. Oooh – it's coming again ... aaaah! The pain.'

'Deep DEEP breathing now.'

Sister Francesca Chong, the senior midwife on the obstetric unit, places a hand on Doreen's abdomen.

'Now, deep breath – push. PUSH. PUSH. Right into your

130

bottom. Let me see. Yes. fair hair. I can see the head. It's coming. You're doing well Doreen. Rest. REST. Wait for the next one.'

Roy sits at the head of the bed, masked and gowned. He is silent. It is all too much for him. He holds Doreen's hand.

'Aaaaah – here it comes again.'

He whispers in a shaky voice, 'It's all right, dear. It's all right.'

'Deep breath. Push now. PUSH,' coaxes Sister Chong, 'one big long one and it's all over.'

Doreen takes a huge breath and her face turns purple with effort.

'Good. Good. We're nearly there. I think two more – a little episiotomy and it'll all be over.'

Sweat pours down from Doreen's brow.

'Uuuugh – it's coming. Oh God, it's coming...'

'There we are – a little local anaesthetic, and then a little snip.'

Sister Chong cuts boldly into the perineum, scything through flesh like a hot knife through butter. Bright red blood spurts all over the fresh green towels. Roy holds onto the other end of the bed with one hand and squeezes Doreen's hand with his other. He is determined not to faint.

'It's coming,' says the experienced midwife calmly and confidently, as she has done thousands of times before.

'Aaaaagh!'

'Push. PUSH. Here we are, it's crowned, the head's out. Pant. PANT. Relax, relax. The worst is over now.'

Deftly she manipulates the head, allowing it to adjust to the natural position of occiput-to-pubes before applying gentle traction. A shoulder slithers out easily followed swiftly by another, then the whole trunk and legs shoot out almost faster than she can catch it.

'There!'

A harsh slap is superfluous, as a high-pitched squall announces the arrival at three minutes past midnight.

'It's a boy, Mrs Brown. You've got a baby boy.'

131

CHAPTER 6

CONFESSION

Once let the public become sufficiently clean-minded to allow every adult access to all that is known about the psychology, physiology, hygiene and ethics of sex, and in two generations we will have a new humanity, with more health and joy, fewer wrecked nerves and almost no divorces. All morbid curiosity will then be dispelled, and thus the dealer in bawdy art and literature will become bankrupt. Our sanatoriums and insane asylums will become uninhabited by those thousands of inmates who are there because of compulsory ignorance of their own sexual nature. All these present evils are the outgrowth of that enforced sexual ignorance resulting from our legalised prudery, brought about by our general acquiescence in the 'obscene' superstition.

Theodore Schroder (1864–1935)

Sex has become one of the most discussed subjects of modern times. The Victorians pretended it did not exist; the moderns pretend that nothing else exists.

Fulton J. Sheen

Some things are better than sex, and some are worse, but there's nothing exactly like it.

W. C. Fields

'Banana flambé, Dottore?'

'Pardon? Oh yes – I'm sorry Romero, I was dreaming ... yes, yes please. Just one slice of banana and a little sauce.'

'It is delicious, Dottore – you are sure you won't have another?'

'Quite sure, Romero.'

'Go on, Harry, says Louise, 'how can you eat so little?'

'Too many calories by far,' he says, gently reminding her of calories she could well do without.

'I don't care. I've allowed at least eight pounds for this cruise. When I get home I'll diet and soon lose it. But in the meantime, I intend to enjoy.'

Despite the fact that it is the first meal with their host and in fact the first time they have met the doctor, his new guests have relaxed and developed a first-name intimacy in a way only Americans seem naturally to do. It is in such contrast to the inflexible starchiness of Edith Baxter, who despite being on the ship for a few weeks, is still uncomfortable with the informal familiarity that Harry prefers in his guests.

'Why not, indeed! Mind you, from the aroma of that liqueur, I think if you eat more than a couple of slices you'll be drunk.'

The Rosenthals attack their dessert in a thoroughly workman-like fashion, knowing that they will be first in line for the leftovers still sizzling in the copper pan.

Desmond throws a sly smile in Harry's direction. He has readily attuned to the casual bonhomie that Harry displays, having deciphered that it is a carefully erected façade behind which Harry conceals a distaste, if not contempt, for the ritual nightly performance at the table. The fleeting visual exchange between them, which the others do not notice, acknowledges this mutual understanding.

Louise has extinguished her fifth cigarette and is attacking the banana flambé with barely restrained gusto. Suddenly she cranes her head upwards and looks directly, almost menacingly into Harry's eyes, as if she is to reprimand him for something he has done wrong.

'So, Doctor – I mean Harry, you never did tell us if you have any children or not. But you seemed to hint there might be something.'

It would be so easy to simply say no, and make the standard cliché comment about the peripatetic seaman leaving his calling card all over the world – but Harry is in a benign and affable mood, and not reluctant to share a secret.

'Well, yes – and no. What I mean to say is...'

'That sure makes sense to me, Doc,' shouts Lulu derisively to everyone's surprise, none more than Harry's, who'd safely assumed the pre-senile errant dipsomaniac was present only in body.

'Well, let me explain...'

'I want some more bananas,' she screams petulantly, jerking her head around. Romero appears as if from thin air.

'Yes, Madame?'

'Give me some more of that flambé stuff – what's your name?'

'Romero, Madame. I am the Assistant Maitre d', and...'

'I know, I know. Just give me some more of those sickly bananas, will you?'

'Certainly, Madame.'

The others stare silently and not a little uncomfortably at Romero as he efficiently goes about his task of replenishing Lulu's dish. Harry follows his movements, and smiles. He is able to penetrate Romero's near-perfect disguise which has been elaborated, polished and refined over the years. It is one of appearing ever-calm, unruffled and exceedingly polite, no

136

matter how awfully the passenger behaves. The subtle tone in his fawning effusiveness (which Lulu would never detect) says clearly that he'd like to pour the remains of the liqueur sauce over her head and force the bananas into another orifice, followed by a hundred more of the same. But he must be content with the fantasy alone.

She straightens up as Romero places the dish brimming full of alcohol-soaked bananas in front of her. With her attention suitably distracted from the others and re-focused solely on the sickly dessert, Louise feels confident enough to push Harry for an answer to her question.

'You were about to tell us, Harry?'

'Yes. We'd all like to hear.' Even Edith Baxter's curiosity has been aroused by the suggestion that Harry might reveal some juicy secret from the past.

Desmond maintains a quiet dignity, sensing they might be putting Harry on the spot. Hal Van Dicky sits as impassively as ever and is likely to remain in that mode unless money or deals of any kind are mentioned.

Harry can see that they are ready to hear an interesting story, and he will not disappoint them. It is still too early to meet Janine for the final act of the day, so he is quite content to spend a little more time entertaining his table guests. They are quiet now, waiting for him to speak.

'Back in my student days, like many, I was struggling to work my way through medical school. The more entrepreneurial amongst us would grab at any chance that came along to make some ready extra cash. Now, around that time, in the mid Sixties, private clinics had begun to offer a rather revolutionary service to childless couples, that is, those couples who had been trying for a baby for some years without success. AID, that is, Artificial Insemination by Donor was the solution that these clinics offered.'

Harry pauses for a moment, more to catch his breath, but it acts as a dramatic pause and his guests remain silent and attentive anxious for him to continue. It sounds too interesting to interrupt.

'Of course, it had been done down on the farm for years...'

A smirk appears on Desmond's face, and Edith's cheeks flush instantly.

'...with relative simplicity and great success, you know, selective breeding and all that. I suppose such a thing would be a bit of a taboo in humans – but anyway, around this time the very same process started to be used in these infertility clinics in London. I'm talking about the situation where the husband is infertile and the wife fertile...'

'How do you know that?'

'Simple tests, Hal. Basically, a semen sample from the male will reveal any deficiency.'

'Oh, I see.'

'So, what happens then, is that a suitable donor provides a sample of fertile semen, which is then introduced into the woman at an appropriate time in her cycle, and bingo – she gets pregnant. Or at least, that is the theory. But in fact, it was born out in most cases in practice.'

'Suitable donor, Harry?'

'That's the point I'm coming to, Desmond. Suitable donors were naturally required for this process.'

Edith's flush deepens and Louise cranes her neck forward in anticipation of what Harry is about to say.

'Now, a convenient source of donors which would provide good-quality samples that were considered genetically acceptable, you know, physically and intellectually, happened to be medical students. They were taken on, rather casually in those days I'm afraid, after a semen sample and couple of blood tests were shown to be satisfactory, and thereafter continued to provide samples on a regular basis. In those early years the baby farming business, if you'll excuse the expression, took off in a big way ... and before you accuse me of sounding a bit cynical, I can tell you it brought a lot of happiness and fulfilment to many many childless couples...'

'You mentioned money.'

'Yes, Hal. That was the main motive – for us poor hard-up medical students anyway.'

For a moment, nobody speaks. Harry looks down at his napkin which he has folded and replaced, sensing that his

138

matter-of-fact description of 'baby farming' and pecuniary motive for being intimately involved in such a business may have offended. Desmond breaks the silence.

'So what you are saying, Harry, is that you've probably got many children – somewhere?'

'Correct. But you must realise, they are absolutely anonymous and unknown to me, and for that matter, I am unknown to them. In that sense they cannot be real to me. Face it, there is none of the emotional attachment you would associate with childbearing or nurturing done in the normal way. You could call it physiological fatherhood if you like – it's nothing more than that, quite honestly.'

Edith's curiosity overcomes her usual haughtiness to join in the conversation.

'How many babies do you think you have then?' she asks almost accusingly.

'Never really thought about it. Well, let's work it out. Firstly, you must remember that not every insemination resulted in a viable pregnancy. There were many variable factors. I would guess, conservatively, that it was about a thirty per cent success rate – say about three per month, that's thirty-six a year, which is...'

'Hundreds!' exclaims Edith incredulously. 'Oh, I just can't believe such a thing, hundreds of children ... oh my God.'

'As I said, it was all purely physiological. Now look – down on the farm they've got prize bulls who have technically sired tens of thousands of calves by exactly the same method.'

'Yes, but Harry – these are children you're talking about – your children – you can't deny it,' says Louise with an exaggerated sense of drama in her voice.

'How much a shot?' asks Hal.

'It varied from clinic to clinic, actually – and of course went up over the five years I was involved – but I would say on average, about £5 per specimen.'

'Let's see ... how many a week did you say?'

'On average, about three.'

'That's about £4000 over a five-year period,' says Hal with the speed of a mainframe computer.

'Can't say I've ever worked it out, Hal, but I know it was a lot to me in those days and made all the difference to completing my medical studies successfully without financial worries.'

'But Harry, I mean...' Louise cannot swallow his undetached and unemotional pragmatism, '...you're saying that you have absolutely no feeling for these children of yours?'

'They're not really mine, Louise, are they? Well, I suppose I am the biological father, but it ends there. Their emotional and bonded father is the adoptive one. How can they ever know any different? I'm pretty confident that if ever I had the extremely unlikely opportunity to meet such an individual, there would be absolutely no feeling for them from me, or for that matter, from them to me – if you see what I mean. I admit that the genes are there, but I don't believe that they can transmit such an automatic emotional bond. I would categorise that sort of effect as somewhat metaphysical.'

'Well, Harry, I tend to agree with Louise. Don't you think there might be something, uuum, I can't define exactly what, but you know, some sort of "spiritual" connection, shall we say, that might exist between such people?'

'That's a bit fanciful, I think, Desmond – but who knows. I think those feelings that you imply are naturally and automatically present in the "normal" situation are in fact rapidly introduced by the substitute adoptive father, and in reality it amounts to the same thing.'

'I disagree.' Melville says quietly, 'I think the real father would have the real deep feelings, and I'm pretty sure if I was not the real father then I couldn't have the same feelings.'

'Not so. It depends on the commitment. You can become emotionally involved with an infant as if it were really your own, especially if you assume full responsibility for it. Many people adopt, and they would tell you just that.'

'Maybe, but I just don't think it can be the same.'

'How on earth did you get the samples?' asks Hal, not realising the potential embarrassment of such a question.

'It was very straightforward, really. One simply masturbated into a plastic pot...'

140

Faces flush around the table. There is an awkward silence. Louise looked extremely uncomfortable. Edith's face is a mixture of embarrassment and revulsion. Desmond wants to explore the subject in more detail despite the overt embarrassment of the rest of the table.

'I imagine that wasn't always easy, was it?'

'Damn right, Desmond. There was a flourishing trade in porno mags – you know the sort of stuff...' Harry stops abruptly. The ladies cannot disguise their disgust and embarrassment. There is another tense silence.

'Really Doctor, you surprise me. I think you must agree, pornography is evil.'

'I don't actually agree with you, Edith. There are probably many worse things that you might view as acceptable practice in our society without a second thought because of your conditioning, but anything that smacks of sex is strictly taboo. It's a shame. Everyone gets so excited about anything that is remotely connected with sex – the forbidden fruit! In all truth, it really is a mundane everyday event which doesn't deserve so much attention. It's merely another physiological function, like evacuating your bowels and bladder. You can do it on your own or with someone else depending on...'

'Really, Doctor! I can't believe you're saying this!' says Louise, looking equally shocked as Edith who raises her eyebrows in horror whilst pursing her lips in a show of absolute disapproval.

Harry is more than comfortable with the subject. He has spent many years thinking about it and putting his philosophies into practice.

'You know, our social values are all wrong. We still view sex with, with – such ambivalence, such ambiguity and hypocrisy. It is as if it is something we must be wary of, an activity of questionable morality if it is not constrained to well-defined, inviolable limits. Sexual behaviour attracts such inordinate attention, so much more than it actually deserves, as if it were the most important human activity ... perhaps it is! You must agree, it is forever under the microscope – dissected, analysed, exaggerated in its importance and effects – indeed, exploited

141

by the media and entertainment industry as if it were the only relevant human experience. It gets far too much attention... And God, how people moralise about it continually ... venereal disease is still considered an affliction of irresponsible behaviour, the wages of sin, I suppose unlike any other disease.'

Louise fidgets as Harry's sermon intensifies. She plainly doesn't approve. It conflicts too much with her pattern of life and the way she views the world. She reaches for another cigarette, which is a cue for Harry.

'For goodness sake, Louise, smoking is a far more wicked and antisocial habit than the sexual permissiveness that you condemn. Drinking alcohol is just as bad – probably worse. Both practices are considered quite acceptable morally and encouraged by marketing and advertising on an unprecedented scale in our society – and happily sanctioned by the moral pillars of our establishment. But pictures of a couple having sexual intercourse – wow! That's a heinous crime.'

'It's disgusting...'

'I might agree when there is obvious perversity, shall we say – you know, bestiality and the like, or even perhaps homosexuality ... but honestly, there are so many other parameters of human abuse, usually more subtle and less easy to define, which escape our attention and are rarely under the spotlight. Exploitation of human resources like labour, thought, ideas, creativity ... or the crushing of the human spirit by the invisible forces of conformity and the all-pervading influences of the established hierarchy – I'm sorry if that sounds a bit pompous – but maybe these less obvious activities should be labelled pornography, if by that word, we mean an activity which abuses and degrades human beings without their consent. Quite frankly, pictures of couples having sex never did harm to anyone, I'm sure...'

'Doctor – Harry – I'm afraid we're on a different wavelength to you. I, for one, cannot understand the way you see things.'

'Fine, Louise – everyone to their own philosophy; that's democracy.'

Romero spots a natural pause in the conversation and darts in before anyone can speak.

142

'Coffee, ladies and gentlemen?'

Everyone opts except Lulu. She is snoring now. Harry nods to Romero and in a half-whisper says they will be finished soon and Miss Edwards might need some help back to her state-room.

Louise extinguishes her cigarette and looks directly at Harry.

'I wonder what they look like – I mean, I wonder whether they look like you?'

'I'm sorry?'

'You know – the children from your activities at medical school.'

'Oh sorry! – yes – well, what can I say? Who knows I suppose some of them must. But quite honestly, I've never given it a moment's thought.'

'They must be in their twenties now, I guess,' echoes Louise, 'surely you must think sometimes that you have a son or daughter somewhere just like you. Your looks. Your ways – and maybe even your personality...'

'Not really. Can't say I ever think of such a thing.'

Edith shakes her head as if Harry is beyond hope.

'Well, at least I can say one thing. If I never get married or never have children by the conventional method, then I've at least performed my biological role on earth.'

'Harry.'

'Yes, Hal?'

'Have you ever considered – well, ever imagined – I mean, what if you actually met one of these, these "offspring" in the street or anywhere, you know what I mean?'

'Millions to one chance.'

'But let's just say you did – would you know, I wonder?'

'Of course not! Why should I? – unless they were the spitting image of me.'

'But do you think there would be any feeling, you know, some sort of sensation?' says Desmond, excited by the idea thrown up by Hal.

'I don't think so.'

'Well, that's a great pity,' says Louise, 'I think there should

143

be – if they are really your children – and – and you're human like the rest of us.'

Harry laughs.

'Anyway, Hal, the likelihood of such a thing ever happening must be millions and millions to one against. Finding a needle in a haystack – as much chance as landing on the planet Mars...'

Hal's face screws up momentarily as he concentrates on the mathematical possibilities of such an eventuality.

'What's the population of Britain, Harry?'

'I can't say with any accuracy, but I guess around sixty million. In the mid Sixties it would have been around fifty-five million.'

'And how many visits per week did you make, and for how many years?'

'Don't be crazy Hal – what you're suggesting is impossible, a wasted exercise – you cannot calculate such a thing...'

'Harry, it may not be as fanciful as you think,' interrupts Desmond, 'Hal's maybe got a point. Remember, these off-spring are carrying your genes – with many of your characteristics. The probability of meeting by chance might be reduced if such children inherited the wanderlust spirit like yourself – if you don't mind me saying that. Just think – they might trail around the world, going quite naturally to the standard places that such people tend to visit on planes, trains and boats ... I really believe it could considerably increase the chances of such an occurrence, especially as you're still travelling around the world and continually visiting all these exotic places which appeal to young, adventurous travellers...'

'Really, Desmond, you can't possibly believe such a nonsensical idea. I admit it might have a certain logic, but there isn't even the remotest chance of me ever meeting one of these, these ... "ones off the production line" shall we say – sorry Edith – and if I did, heaven forbid, I'm pretty sure I wouldn't be aware of it. I'm certainly sceptical of any metaphysical or "spiritual" communication.'

The Rosenthals finish the last of their banana flambé. Sophie, who has been more absorbed with the sickly dessert

144

than the conversation, feels it appropriate to make a final comment.

'Sounds pretty disgusting to me, anyway, I'm sorry to say.'

Benjamin, who like Sophie appears to have been far more interested in the bananas, speaks.

'What you've been saying is pretty interesting, actually. I remember when I used to treat infertile men, mostly varicoceles – that's varicose veins in the testicles, Louise – must have operated on thousands in my career – quite honestly, it hardly ever made any difference, except to my bank balance of course – but wish I'd got into the AID business in the Seventies – that was big big money...'

Harry steals a glance at his watch. Christ! 10.45. He has to meet Janine in the Theatre Bar. Time to extricate himself. The lull in conversation gives him an opportunity.

'It's been a pleasure, everybody – really. You must excuse me now, I have to make the last round of the sick bay before turning in, and I'm sure you're all anxious to see the late show...'

Before anyone can speak, Harry has stood up, placing his folded napkin on the side plate and turned ready to make a quick exit. Desmond attempts to speak but Harry swivels round swiftly, at the same time fastening the brass button of his mess jacket and nodding to Romero, who still stands patiently by the dumb waiter.

'Thank you, Romero – and good night, everyone. See you all tomorrow night.'

He moves fast as he threads his way through the tables, which are now emptying and being rapidly cleared by the waiters. He is trying to clear his brain of the conversation at the table so he can begin to concentrate on the job in hand – Janine. She must be the focus of his undivided attention for the next few hours. He reaches the main stairway to the upper lounge. His mind will not clear. Uninvited thoughts muscle in on his consciousness ... offspring, offspring. How strange. They must be in their late teens now, the first batch. What on earth would they be like?

145

CHAPTER 7

VAPOUR TRAILS

'Father, father, where are you going?
O do not walk so fast.
Speak father, speak to your little boy,
Or else I shall be lost.'

'The little boy lost', William Blake (1750–1827)

'And look at the money we've spent on him – he's taken every spare penny we've ever had. Face it dear, we could have had extra holidays, a new car every year – even a new house. But no – you insisted he had everything, absolutely everything right from the moment he was born. Spoilt, that's what he's been – absolutely spoilt. And for what? The best private education money can buy so that he can run off and become a sailor? Is that what we sacrificed for – well, is it?'

'Oh shut up. If that is what he wants to do, then as long as it makes him happy I don't care. Besides, he's only doing it for experience. When he's got it out of his system I'm sure he'll go to university. You know his school qualifications are more than adequate...'

'Wasted. That's what they are – bloody wasted. And MY money...'

'OUR money, my dear. OURS. It's always been "my" "my" – you really are a selfish...'

'Aarrrrh – you should never have done it. Never. NEVER.'

'Never done what?'

'Don't pretend, for God's sake – you know – that awful business. That, that artificial insemination business. If you could have only been satisfied with what we had. But oh no – you had to...'

'You bastard. You, you BASTARD!'

'I said then it was a mistake. But no, you had to go through with it – and now look what we've got – a wayward son, with an

149

uncontrollable wanderlust and a wild, wicked nature who is spurning all that we've sacrificed for him.'

'For Christ's sake, he'll only be at sea for a while. His teacher advised him not to go straight up to university. Remember, he took his A levels one year early, and even the Headmaster advised going out into the world to mature a bit.'

'Yeah, yeah. And here we are over eighteen months on, and he's still a damned seaman. He has developed a taste for it no doubt. Damn degenerate, that's what I call it.'

'I think your attitude is making him rebel. If you could have only been a more sympathetic and understanding father. You've never been warm or shown any real emotion to him – except that is, to shout.'

'I said right at the very beginning it was a damn mistake – I mean, just look at him now.'

'But he's our son, for better or worse.'

'Correction. He's YOUR son. YOURS and yours alone. Certainly not mine, and you know it. If he were mine he'd be damn more obedient and sensible about the future, I can tell you.'

'Well, I love him for his wildness. I imagine his real father must have been just as wild. He couldn't have been a bank manager, that's for sure.'

'That's cruel, Doreen. You had no right saying such a thing. I've been a good father. He's not wanted for anything.'

'Except your love and understanding.'

Doreen looks away, focusing through the window into the distance as if distracted by her own description of the mysterious progenitor of her son. Her mind creates a perfect image. Her eyes are glazed as tears form and threaten to run in a torrent down her cheeks.

'A filthy medical student masturbating into a pot – that's what his father is – yes, a potful of, of – of semen.'

'Hello Mother, Father. What were you saying about a potful of cement?'

The quietly opening door heralds the arrival of a slender youth, a shade over six feet, whose gangly growth spurt of

adolescence is maturing fast into the firm definition of muscula-
ture and confident stature of a young adult male. Solid broad
shoulders taper to a narrow waist and boardlike abdomen. The
biceps have gained definition and the taut small buttocks and
well shaped thighs are testament to his genetic inheritance and
the fact that he works out most days either on the playing field
or in the gymnasium. His light brown hair cropped short at the
sides has generous streaks of blond, even white, a natural gift
from the sun which gives him a head start in the fashion stakes
and an unchallengeable superiority over the synthetically
acquired equivalent. Sharp grey blue eyes which do not deviate
when he engages in conversation strip the recipient of all
defences.

He stands at the door passively but with the proud demeanour of an individual who is disciplined and strongwilled. A
prize specimen whose future promised everything. Despite
the stance of barely subdued aggression, there is an open
honesty in his face engaging and inviting. From such a face
radiates the boundless enthusiasm and limitless vigour of
youthful optimism. The world is to be his oyster and he will
settle for nothing less.

His slightly angulated broadening nose is a casualty of the
rugby field and although the septal deviation has been nicely
realigned by the local specialist it still represents a beacon of
the young warrior in the making, a battle trophy, a duelling
scar which carves the early face of maturity on the softness
of youth. Missing are the lines and creases of character that
only adult life and all its vicissitudes will bring. But it is
undeniably a strong face. With the superfluous tissue of
youth now absorbed, his cheek bones are prominent and jaw
square and solid looking. He has a healthy well-weathered
outdoor complexion, and could well be the universal expression of any other culture of this, or bygone ages – an emerging
Aztec brave or a young Masai warrior expecting soon to kill
his first lion – the unyielding and unconquerable energy of
fresh new blood.

He is no longer a fledgling and his flight from the family nest
is more or less complete. He is ready to take on the world, seize

it by the scruff of the neck, shake it and establish unambiguously his ascendant position in its hierarchy.

His mother adores him. It is a different matter with his father.

'Where the hell have you been? Down the pub, I expect. Drinking again. What have I told you? Don't come home if you're drunk. Look at you ...'

'For Christ's sake, father, I'm not drunk – I've only had a couple of pints ...'

'You'll make nothing. You'll end up being a nobody. All our effort and expense wasted on you. Some gratitude.'

'Roy, leave the boy alone, will you?'

'That's right, you side with him. He's yours. Go on. I've had just about enough.'

The door slams.

'I'm sorry, Mother. I really did only have a couple of pints. I met some friends in the pub and we got into a very interesting conversation. I had no idea of the time. I do wish Father wasn't so much against me. You know I've always tried to get on with him. But there seems to be some sort of block as if he doesn't want to. God, you know how I've tried. I wish I could have pleased him more in some way. Quite frankly, I don't care now. I suppose in a way I'm annoying him by staying at sea and wasting what he calls an expensive education. Well, he deserves to be bloody annoyed. And I'll stay at sea for as long as I want. Anyway, what on earth was he talking about a "potful of cement"? Sounds a bit bizarre.'

'Oh, it was nothing, Jason, nothing at all.'

'C'mon, you can tell me. I promise I won't say anything or interfere.'

'I can't.'

'Go on, tell me. You've fired my curiosity now.'

'It's very difficult, believe me. It's too sensitive and private a matter between your father and I ... it's just too painful.'

'Please, what did he mean?'

Doreen is silent. She looks at Jason with the love in her eyes that only a mother can show for her son. And then she speaks. Her voice is almost a whisper and tinged with a wistful lilt of pathos.

'Sit down, Jason. It's quite an involved story. Don't interrupt. Just listen. But I warn you – you'll be upset…'

'And so you were born. I can recall it as if it were only yesterday. It was the most wonderful moment of my life, and still is for that matter. Unfortunately, I don't think the sentiment was quite shared by your father.'

'B-but Mother, he isn't…'

'Not in a strictly natural sense, but he has provided for you all your life and given…'

'But what about my true father? What does he do? Where is he?'

'Don't be silly. We can never know that – I don't think it would be right anyway.'

'Surely there are times when you…'

'Yes, of course. I do think sometimes, just what he would be like. But those thoughts are much less frequent now than they used to be in the beginning.'

Doreen's eyes glaze over again as she stares into the distance.

'Can we ever know? Surely we can? It is my right. WE can find out, can't we? We CAN.'

'It's impossible. Absolutely impossible. And I don't think it would be a wise or…'

'Yes, yes we could. We should. I want to know. I need to know. I MUST know where I come from.'

'Half of you certainly comes from me, that's for sure.'

Jason gets up, walks slowly to her chair and bending over, kisses his mother on the forehead.

'I love you so much, Mother – but the other half, my real father – God, I must find out, I must.'

'Jason, it wouldn't be wise. It wouldn't be proper. Please put such a ridiculous idea out of your head.'

Doreen knows that it would be wrong to even contemplate such a thing, but her own fateful fascination, curiosity and long-smouldering desire to know temper the force of her objection and only serve to catalyse Jason's fast-accelerating resolve to pursue the matter.

153

He stands still for a few moments in silent thought before speaking.

'So you say a Harley Street private clinic? What was the doctor's name? That would be a starting point.'

'For God's sake, put it out of your mind. He – he must be retired now, or probably even dead. He was in his fifties, then.'

'Go on, you can tell me his name.'

'I can't remember – truly. I just cannot remember, isn't that strange? It was a strange thing. Not many months after you were born my mind seemed to blank out all of the unpleasant details associated with getting pregnant. Perhaps it was that I simply didn't want to believe that my husband was not your true father. Or maybe I subconsciously feared that one day this very conversation would happen and it would be too painful to resurrect the truth. I really don't know. The mind can play funny tricks. But I promise you with all my heart, I cannot remember his name. It is as if it has been wiped from my memory for ever. It's funny, but I do have a definite picture of the nurse. She was so gentle and understanding, and so very professional. I think it was she who kept my spirits up and determination to see the whole business right through to the end.'

'What was her name?'

'Oh dear. Now you're asking ... let me see – Lisa, no – Libby. Could be. Uuuum. Now what was it? It's on the tip of my tongue. LIZ! That's it. Definitely Liz. NOW I can see her clearly. She was lovely. So understanding and sympathetic. I wonder where she is now? Probably married with a family of her own – I hope so.'

Jason's face is a mixture of incredulity and anguish.

'All I can say is that he must have been a medical student, as Liz told me that most of the donors were medical students. It meant that they were good quality, so to speak, reliable, and could be trusted.'

'So he could have be a medical student then!'

'Honestly, I really cannot say for certain. The memory is hazy.'

'He would be a doctor by now, of course, that's for sure – wouldn't he?'

'I don't know. This is becoming stupid. The whole thing is foolish speculation. It will only make you more upset in the long run.'

'I wonder where he is now – and what is he doing?'

'He'll be married with a family of his own, and the last thing he'd want is you "discovering" him in some way. Such a thing could cause untold anguish. It's silly. Just accept, it's history and so long ago...'

Jason's eyes are moist. The corners of his mouth tighten and he winces involuntarily. His mouth opens and the lower lip quivers. He takes a deep breath and speaks, trying to control the shakiness in his voice.

'I know I can find out what happened to that clinic doctor. I KNOW I can.'

Doreen face takes on a pained expression as she looks directly into his eyes.

'But even if you could – and I'm sure it is totally out of the question – he, the doctor, could not tell you anything. He can't. He is sworn to complete confidentiality. Absolute secrecy. He wouldn't dare or even contemplate such a thing. It would be unprofessional, if not illegal to divulge such information.'

'Who cares about that? This is too important to sweep under the carpet. It's too late – you have told me now. It is vital I find out. I must know. I cannot even say why. It is something inside that is telling me.'

'Oh I wish to God I hadn't said anything.'

'Thank God I've found out, Mother. I feel as if there is a missing piece of jigsaw in my life.'

'But Jason, you promised. It's time to take up your place at university. You cannot possibly delay any longer. It would be such a terrible waste of a wonderful privilege – and just remember how hard you studied – and for that matter how much your father and I have sacrificed ... no, NO. You simply cannot pack your bags now and leave. You mustn't!'

'I'm sorry. If I don't find out – or at least make an effort to

155

find out – then I will be tortured for the rest of my life. I'm going to pack my bag – I'll be leaving tomorrow...'

In his room Jason is efficient in his task. Having been at sea for 18 months, he is well-practiced at packing all he needs into one medium-sized suitcase.

He is troubled. He thinks of what he should do and how he will set about the seemingly impossible quest that he feels compelled to undertake. As he starts gathering a varied assortment of clothes and personal items, his mind racing ahead with a jumble of thoughts and ideas, an uninvited and inexplicable memory trace is evoked which jostles for space in his consciousness.

Manila. Manila. It is only for a few seconds. But how strange and unnerving it is. Surely it must be as a result of the emotional state he has been put in from the conversation with his mother. It is sheer nonsense to attach any significance to such a haphazard, uninvited thought. His mind must be playing tricks on him. It would be a millions-to-one chance of such a thing. It is plainly stupid and obviously emotionally driven to even think of such a fantastic notion. But then he hadn't consciously thought of it. It had appeared with no previous related train of thought, as he had opened the top drawer to find the keys to his trunk.

The thought and the accompanying sensation pass. He stops for a moment and tries to analyse what it could mean. He tries to concentrate on the face and the figure, fleeting as it was. But the face is blank. It was simply an apparition in the darkness of the night which had only momentarily distracted him from his pursuit of carnal pleasure. But then, he can definitely remember the broad shoulders, not unlike his own, and the athletic figure. And there were the beautiful Filipina companions clinging firmly on either side.

In fact, he had been more distracted by the rich aroma of the sizzling chicken and chunks of sate at the vendor's stall. He had not eaten for days, and had been wandering around drunk from bar to bar in an almost perpetual alcoholic haze. It was a

156

wonder he could recall anything at all of that time in Manila. But then he can remember signing on at the shipping office in Arquiza Street (for some strange reason he can see the name clearly) in the red-light district of Ermita, not far from the Manila docks. He had been in such a state of abject drunkenness that he hadn't known what to do or where to go. Ideas of returning to England and university had seemed eons away. At the time he had reached a real low point, and in his alcoholic stupor he'd not really cared whether he'd lived or died.

But in some strangely powerful way, the apparition he'd passed briefly in the street had momentarily pierced the fog of confusion. At the time it had been difficult to be rational about anything, but later, when he had recovered sufficiently from his chronic hangover, he'd simply put the experience down to alcoholic hallucination and had soon dispelled it from his thoughts completely.

And now it reappears after all this time – unsolicited, unprovoked and seemingly totally unrelated to current events – as a memory trace surfacing above the collage of muddled and confused thoughts brought on by his mother's incredible secret.

Is it not simply an hysterical reaction fuelled by a desperate desire to seek and find something he is not yet able to define? A frantic search in his conscious and subconscious memory for any symbolic event that might yield clues to his true origins? Any random occurrence, no matter how far-fetched it might seem?

Of course, he should dismiss such absolute nonsense. Such metaphysical twaddle! There could not have been any reality or meaning to such an event. His mind, emotionally charged, is simply playing tricks on him.

He throw the last items of clothing into the battered suitcase and looks around the room. The soft green curtains. The thick pile carpet and the Gulliver's Travels rug with the picture of Gulliver towing the small boats of the Lilliputians. The comfortable bed. The ornaments. Pictures. Photos. Memorabilia. A room lovingly arranged and kept intact and undisturbed by a devoted mother for her only son when he was away at sea.

But she is so upset!

157

His mind wavers. Is he not being unnecessarily cruel to his dear mother? She has confided her darkest secret, and this is how he will repay her. He shouldn't have forced her to tell him. Now she will fret and be desperately sad when he goes away for goodness knows how long.

He sits down in the comfy leather chair and heaves a loud sigh and buries his head in his hands. He is distraught and confused. What can he do? Where can he go? He falls back in the seat and soon his eyes are closed. He dreams. But his dreams are not arbitrary. They tell him what to do.

After a couple of hours he stirs. His fretfulness has gone. His mind is cool and calculating. Harley Street. The AID clinics. Medical schools. Students. And a nurse called Liz. There is nothing tangible, but there must be some starting point and a definite direction in which to aim.

He is now in London, staying at the seaman's mission in Whitechapel. His goodbye to his mother had been tearful and brief. He has now put it behind him to concentrate fully on the seemingly impossible task.

The attendant at the mission had told him where to find the local library. It is an old Victorian building tucked away in a side street, and is more or less empty when he enters through the glass-panelled door. At the enquiry desk he asks the young assistant where he can find any sort of Medical Directory. In a quiet gloomy alcove as far away from the enquiry desk as possible, under a grey window, dust-covered and engrimed from decades of city pollution, he sets about his seemingly insurmountable quest.

There are two volumes – two large very thick red books which list every doctor in the United Kingdom, each entry with a short description of their interests and their particular field of medicine. He sits facing both volumes for a moment, not moving and simply thinking what a daunting task he has set himself. How on earth can he find out anything about infertility clinics 20 years ago, and even more difficult, the doctors who ran them?

As his resolve wavers, the feverishly intense sensation compelling him in a way he cannot resist, makes him reach for the first book. There is only one place to start – at the very beginning. He opens the preface pages to the first page of 'A'. He will have to work his way painstakingly through every single entry to see if anything to do with infertility is listed with the particular doctor. It will be time-consuming, there is no doubt. It may be entirely a wasted effort which will yield few, if any, clues. But his motivation is all-consuming.

For the whole of the first day in the dingy library in Whitechapel that seems so far away from his purpose, he remains hunched over the first directory. Initially it seems to be so slow as each and every page is scoured. When the librarian comes over and politely tells him they are closing, he has only managed to go through the first 30 pages. He calculates it will take him a couple of weeks at least. But he is determined and committed.

The next day he is waiting outside the library when it opens. He is soon sitting in the same alcove in the same seat, and with a feverish intensity is devouring every word of every entry on every page. Any that is remotely connected with fertility he records.

For the next two weeks he repeats this pattern with patient diligence. His eyes ache, but now he has a list of 89 doctors who have the word 'fertility' or 'infertility' in their medical entry. Daunting as the prospects seem, he is now spurred on to consider the next stage in his strategy. The doctors on the list are from every part of the country. He decides, therefore, to limit his telephone calls to the London area. He knows that his mother attended a Harley Street clinic, but whether there are any of the same personnel still working, or indeed, whether the clinic is still in existence, is in doubt.

He begins to call from the only convenient telephone available to him, the public pay phone on the heavily smoke-stained yellow wall in the annexe at the Seaman's Mission. Fortunately, he still has a little money left from his last pay-off at sea.

'Yes – uh, hello, good morning. I'm writing an article for a

159

journal about infertility clinics. Could I speak to the doctor, please?' He had thought carefully on the best approach to avoid any suspicion or hostility.

'I'm sorry, that wouldn't be possible to arrange over the phone, but perhaps you would write giving full details and request an appointment...' 'I'm sorry, this is no longer an infertility clinic, but if you are interested in weight reduction or hair restoration...' 'But the entry in the medical directory?' 'Obviously not been updated – sorry.' 'Our doctors really are too busy...' 'Yes, we have six doctors in the practice. I suggest you make an appointment with the senior...' 'Our rooms are in Devonshire Place...' 'Wimpole Street...' 'Weymouth Mews...'

By the end of five days Jason has a list of nine clinics in Harley Street alone. There are others in the immediate vicinity, Wimpole Street, Devonshire Place, and a few of the lesser-known sidestreets that share the same prestigious mantle of Harley Street. He excludes those clinics not actually in the street. His mother had been quite definite. It was Harley Street.

He will start early. There is no time to waste. He feels tremulous at the prospect of knocking on clinic doors, but as he emerges from Oxford Circus underground station his anxiety is modulated by the relief that the difficulty and drudgery of telephoning is over.

The map in the station concourse details clearly that his destination is only a couple of blocks away. He takes a left turn off Upper Regent Street, along Cavendish Place into Cavendish Square, and right at the traffic lights into the lower end of Harley Street. He walks the whole length of the street to its northern end where it joins Marylebone Road, convincing himself that it was a more logical exercise to start at the far end and work his way back down the street, rather than a nervous reticence to commence knocking on doors. At the junction with Marylebone Road he stops and retrieves the piece of paper with the list of clinics he must visit from his coat pocket.

109 is the first, a little way down on the right-hand side. After a few minutes of slow, deliberate walking, he arrives at the doorstep. He looks up at the huge brass knocker standing out like an icy cold beacon on the black-gloss door. His face is only a few inches away and his heavy fast breathing vaporises in plumes, dulling the shine. It is February in England, and the days are cold, damp and gloomy. Today, there is even a slight frost.

He stands facing the door for a moment. His heart is heavy. The initial optimism has dampened in the dull grey reality of a winter morning. But there is something burning inside him that compels. His hand reaches up slowly and grasps the door knocker firmly. How cold it feels! Without further hesitation he pulls it back and strikes two times in rapid succession, hard and deliberate to counter any faltering resolve in his purpose.

After a few seconds he can hear the clip of footsteps on a tiled floor approaching. The white plumes of vapour increase as his pulse and breathing accelerate.

'Good morning. Can I help you?'

'Yes. I wonder if I could speak to Dr Simmonds, please?'

'Do you have an appointment?'

'Well – not exactly, but . . .'

'I'm afraid you will need an appointment. He is a very busy man.'

'Actually it's not a medical matter.'

'Maybe I can help you then. I am his personal secretary.'

'Can I come in for a moment?'

The heavy door closes stiffly and Jason follows the matronly grey-haired secretary.

'Come into my office please, Mr – ?'

'Brown. The name is Jason Brown.'

'Please sit down, Mr Brown, and tell me how I might help.'

Jason tries to be brief, but starts at the beginning with the conversation he overheard between his mother and father. The secretary sits attentively with little emotional reaction despite the rising tension in Jason's voice as he reveals his anguish.

'And so you see I've got to know. I must find the truth. I can never rest until I know. It is my right.'

Her response is measured. Although she can see clearly Jason's agony, she knows that there is very little she can do to help.

'I have every sympathy for you, Mr Brown, but I'm afraid it would be absolutely impossible. Totally impossible. Dr Simmonds, I know, would not even agree to see you with such a request, believe me – and if he did, I am more than confident that he could not help you any more than myself. We're talking about a very sensitive and confidential business, and it would be more than any doctor would dare reveal.'

'I promise I wouldn't divulge where I got the information from if there was any . . .'

'I'm truly sorry, Mr Brown. No doubt you will try other clinics, but I'm pretty sure you'll get the same response from all of them.'

Jason stands up silently, not able to conceal his bitter disappointment. If this is going to be the pattern of response to his enquiry from the other clinics, then he might as well pack up right now.

'Thank you anyway. You have been most kind.'

At 93 there is an even larger brass plate with at least half a dozen names on it. He scans quickly. There – halfway down – 'Dr Harvey Wagstaff'. Again, he hesitates before knocking. This time his knock is less forceful, as if his confidence and determination have already been seriously undermined.

'Can I see Dr Wagstaff, please?'

'Do you have an appointment?'

'No – but . . .'

After leaving 93, where again a secretary prevented him seeing the doctor in question, he looks at his list to remind himself how many are left. He feels even more dejected. He bites his bottom lip as he attempts to rekindle his faltering determination. He mustn't give up. Crazy as the idea is now beginning to seem, he has a right to know. It is the undeniable birthright of every human being to know – it is HIS birthright to know.

He walks faster, having crossed the road to follow the even numbers on the other side. His breathing is noisy and from his half-open mouth come rapid puffs of vapour in bursts into the cold atmosphere, like a steam train labouring under its load.

'Good morning. I wonder if I could see Dr Reginald Bodkins?'

'I'm sorry, but he died several years ago. His son, Dr Alistair Bodkins, took over his rooms if you are interested in making an appointment...'

'No – no thank you.'

When the door closes at 52, Jason pulls out the crumpled piece of paper and draws a line through the name of Dr Bodkins.

There are four more names. Two on either side of the street. At 46, an old woman with a heavy foreign accent is suspicious.

'Dr Spacek is dead. This is a private house.'

Numbers 35 and 28 are equally fruitless. Turning from the doorstep of 28 he can see the traffic lights at the junction of Harley Street with Cavendish Square just a hundred yards along. The doubts and fears which had threatened to dissipate his resolve since the very beginning of his quest look as if they will now triumph. He crosses back to the odd number side of the street, his head down and the spring in his step all but gone. Number 17 is the last on his list – 'Dr Boris Crowther'.

He lifts his head slowly and scans the brass plates on either side of the door of the four-storied terraced building. No Boris Crowther!

That's it! There was no point in torturing himself anymore. He stands passively for a moment, in abject defeat. His head flops down and forward in a final gesture of submission and hopelessness. His forehead nudges the door inadvertently and with a force he might not have intended. Within seconds it opens.

'Can I help you?'

'Oh. Oh. I – I'm very sorry – I didn't mean to knock.'

163

'So you don't wish to see any of the doctors here?'

'No – no thank you.'

Jason stands passive and mute for a moment, as if suspended in time, unable to react in an appropriate manner. The young receptionist's initial politeness transforms rapidly to impatience.

'I'll close the door then, if you don't mind.'

The harsher tone jolts Jason from his semi-stupor and prickles an immediate response.

'Actually, I am looking for a Dr Crowther. I know his plate is not up here, but perhaps...'

'I've only been working here for a couple of weeks, so I really wouldn't know – sorry, I can't help you.'

The tone in her voice is irritable and vaguely hostile. Perhaps if she had remained polite and considerate he would have readily left and accepted defeat gracefully. This was the end of the trail as far as he was concerned, and it looked pretty certain that it was a trail long dead and buried. His excursion to London had been painful and unrewarding, and now it seemed his mother had been right. Perhaps now his mind would be ready to accept the reality.

But the flippant, offhand manner of this young girl, only marginally polite in the beginning, has upset him. If nothing else, it is a challenge.

'Uuuuh, excuse me, but is there anyone else who might know?'

She doesn't reply immediately, but rolls her lips inside tightly and makes a facial expression that signals clearly that she is deciding whether to be of further help or to close the conversation and send him on his way.

'Eileen has been here for years. She's the other receptionist.'

'Please, please – could you ask her?'

'All right,' she says, as if the concession is an enormous favour, 'I'll see what she says.'

She turns and walks back along the lush-carpeted hallway, goes behind the reception desk and disappears through an open door into a back room. After what seems an eternity, she returns. She is tight-lipped until she reaches him.

Jason prompts her to speak, impatient that she is making such a meal of it.

'Dr Crowther?'

'Yes. Apparently he did operate this clinic ten years ago. But he is dead now.'

A look of extreme anguish and bitter disappointment returns to Jason's face.

'Oh well, that's it, I guess.'

He cups his hands over his face as the final submissive gesture. And then he looks at her. She is stony-faced.

'You are sure ... ?'

'That's what Eileen has just told me, so it must be true.'

'I see. I see. All right then. All right. Thank you. You've been most kind...'

She moves towards the door and Jason steps back in anticipation of being shown out. He turns and sidesteps to allow her to swing the door open fully. He then descends the cold concrete outside steps. She pushes the heavy door and it starts to close behind him. It is almost shut tight when he turns impulsively and blurts out, 'Could I speak to Eileen – only a second, I promise?'

'We are really very very busy and I have given you all the information that we have ... so please, I must close the door.'

In the dim light of the far end of the corridor he sees an older woman emerge from the office. In one enormous leap he straddles the steps and strides aggressively past the frightened-looking receptionist, shouting at the same time to the older woman, whose back is disappearing into the office.

'Excuse me ... EXCUSE ME...'

The figure stops and turns with an expression of faint alarm at this unsuspected outburst. Jason walks a few steps forward, trying not to appear too agitated.

'I'm sorry for shouting ... but is it Eileen?'

'Yes – what do you want?' She says in a manner which implies it ought to be important enough to justify his brusque intrusion.

165

'I'm sorry, I really am. I know I shouldn't, but you see, I'm looking for Dr Crowther, and, and...'

'He's dead. I believe the receptionist has already told you.'

'Oh – I see ... but, but did you know him – I mean – did you keep his old files ... could I possibly look?'

'Look young man, I'm afraid you are behaving in a very forward manner. We don't know who you are, and you are asking questions which...'

'Please, I beg you ... can you listen to me for just a minute while I explain everything?'

Jason relates as quickly and as succinctly as he can in the circumstances in a pleading voice which begs her compassion.

'Impossible. Quite impossible, young man. Totally out of the question. I can sympathise with you – I'm sorry – but if I were you, I'd forget it.'

'Could I at least speak to the doctor who is here now? Did he take over the practice from Dr Crowther after he died?'

'Dr Templeton is an extremely busy man and couldn't possibly see anyone without an appointment. I can't see that he can help you anyhow, Mr – I'm sorry, Mr – ?'

'Brown. Jason Brown.'

'Mr Brown. Well, I'm truly sorry, but now you really must leave. We have an extremely busy clinic to run...'

'It would take just two minutes of the doctor's time, that's all. Please. PLEASE ... I have the right ... you cannot stop me...'

Jason's voice is loud and desperate.

'Young man, you had better leave now or ... or – we'll have to fetch the police and...'

An elegantly dressed woman in her mid-forties emerges from another door opposite the reception desk.

'What is it, Eileen? Is there a problem?'

'Yes, Mrs Beckett. This rather objectionable young man won't leave. I've told him that we will call the police if he doesn't.'

'I'm sure that won't be necessary, Eileen. What does he want?'

The woman looks at Jason. For a split second there is a flicker in her reaction as if the face is familiar, but any conscious appreciation of recognition is lost in the tension of the moment.

'He won't go, Liz,' repeats Eileen forcefully, 'we should call the police.'

'Wait a minute, Eileen. Let's not get too excited.'

She turns to face Jason squarely.

'What do you want?'

'My father.'

'Your father? What on earth are you talking about?'

'I know my mother came to a fertility clinic before I was born and I know that my father was ... was ... was a sperm donor...'

'Young man, come this way.'

'What did you say your name was?'

'Jason. Jason Brown.'

'Sit down please, Jason. How old are you?'

'Nineteen – well, nineteen and a half.'

'The early days.'

Her face softens, and her eyes focus on the distant wall as if she is scanning the years and being transported back to a time of fond nostalgia. Finally she speaks, more to herself than Jason.

'Oh those days, those days. They were exciting ... a lot of heartache, mind you! Of course, it's all advanced so much now ... in-vitro stuff – you know, test-tube babies and all that ... but in all modesty, we were just as successful in those days, even with the most difficult of cases. In some ways, it was simpler and less things could go wrong. And we only used donors – anonymous, of course – none of this cold test-tube nonsense then...'

'Excuse me for interrupting ... you say "donors". Anonymous and ...'

'Well – I mean we knew who they were, of course, but they themselves would never be aware of the recipients, you know,

167

the would-be mothers – those poor women who were so desperate to get pregnant at almost any price. And of course, the infertile couple would never know the donor – strictly forbidden that was, even if they asked. It's funny. It seems so crude now – what we used to do ... but I can tell you, it made many, many women – I should say couples, very happy.'

'Well, it didn't make BOTH of my parents happy. My father has never accepted me. And now I know why ... please, PLEASE, if you can only help me, help me to find my true father ... if you know anything?'

'So you think you are one of these babies, do you? How do you know?'

'My mother. There was a family argument.'

'And why have you come to this clinic?'

'I've been to all the others I know about in Harley Street, and this is the last one ... if only you can help me ...'

Jason's voice cracks and his eyes are moist.

'And so your mother told you everything, then?'

'Not everything. She couldn't remember the exact address, and she swore that she could not remember the doctor's name – only the nurse's name, "Liz" – and the clinic was in Harley Street, that was all.'

Liz's eyes fix on Jason. A distant bell rings in her memory. There is recognition, but she cannot match a name with the face.

'Jason, it's a long time ago that we're talking about – almost twenty years – and even if the records are available somewhere, it is absolutely forbidden to reveal to you, or anyone else for that matter, confidential information. Besides, as Eileen told you, the doctor who was involved at that time is dead now. I know that he kept all his original records locked in a safe. We only had temporary copies, many of which are cleared out at regular intervals. Although Dr Templeton was his partner in the last few years before he died, I doubt whether he would have kept those records of so long ago.

'I think there are some pretty old records still stored in the basement, but I don't think it would help ... and as I say, they would be strictly and legally confidential ... really, Jason, I can sympathise with you – I know how you must feel – but I think you have to accept that it is a hopeless search, which I believe can only result in unhappiness for you. You are torturing yourself, and you should also think of your parents, your mother and father...'

'But he's not my real father, is he?'

'Not exactly, but I'm sure he's been everything a real father would be, except biologically...'

'EXACTLY. He's not my biological father.'

'Is that so important for you to know?'

'Yes. YES. YES. I must know. I MUST.'

'Jason, you oughtn't punish yourself anymore. And to be frank, it's probably hurting your parents deeply.'

Jason sits quietly. He is calmer now. His self-control returns and with it his natural charm. He tells Liz about his family and his life, and what plans they had had for him in the future. This business had interrupted everything, although he had already passed his school certificate with credits, which would qualify him for a place in law school.

'Did you work with Dr Crowther, then – twenty years ago?'

Before Liz answers, she stares long and hard at Jason, taking in every line and contour of his features. After an interminably long silence she nods knowingly. A warm sentimental gleam appears in her eyes.

'Uuuuum. Uuuuum – yes. Yes, I can see clearly now. Of course, I should have known as soon as I saw you. Jason Brown. What did you say your mother's name was?'

'I didn't – but it was Doreen.'

'Aaah, yes. I remember her well. Poor lady. She went through hell for a year – made worse, I seem to remember, because Mr Brown hadn't shared her enthusiasm. He didn't make it easy for her, but despite all that, she was deliriously happy when she became pregnant with you.'

Jason's eyes open wide and sparkle like dying embers ignited by a blast of air from a bellows.

'You remember! You know! You KNOW!'

Liz says nothing but stares into the distance. There is a mixture of serenity and pathos on her face as she invokes long-lost memories. She can see now a clear image of Harry Lester and his features, which she so unmistakably recognises in the young man sitting in front of her.

'Tell me – please!'

She is jolted back to the present.

'I can't, Jason. I simply cannot, must not do it. It would be wrong. So wrong.

'Please tell me. Why did my mother go through such hell, why, why?'

'I can only tell you certain things. It is only fair to your parents that I do not betray their trust in our confidentiality. With your mother, every treatment had failed until the very last one. I can remember clearly that last day she came. She was so nervous and distraught at the thought of failure after completing the full twelve-month course of treatment. I had made sure that we used one of our prize donors on that occasion – but even then, we didn't expect success. Quite frankly, we all thought you were a bit of a miracle. Your mother was so thrilled when she got pregnant from that very last session. It was her last chance. But sadly, your father was not so enthusiastic.'

Jason leans back in the chair and lets go a heavy sigh. He leans forward abruptly.

'You do remember the donor, then? His name? What he did?'

'Yes of course, but I cannot possibly reveal it. That would be entirely out of the question. Can you imagine the problems and anxiety it might cause – apart from being a breach of confidentiality.'

'But you can see how important it is to me. I can hardly live my life anymore without knowing. Really, it is torturing me...'

'I do feel so sorry for you, Jason, I really do.'

'Do I look like him?'

Liz smiles.

'Yes, you do, you most certainly do – no mistake about that. And you have an air about you – oh yes, I can see clearly,' she says softly, not realising she is compounding the agony.

170

'It's funny, you know, there have been thousands through this clinic over the years, but there are only a handful that I can remember so clearly – all the details as if it were only yesterday. Quite honestly, I never thought I would stay here for so long – in fact, I had left to get married not long after you were born – but after my divorce, Dr Crowther took me back as office manager. I hadn't wanted to get involved any more with the clinical side – it could be so stressful.

'And as you can see, I'm still here after all these years. When Dr Crowther died, it was as if all those earlier cases had died with him. You know? But you, Jason – it was not difficult to remember – the resemblance is so clear – I'm sorry, this is hard for you . . .'

'You have to tell me . . . no one will ever know, I promise . . . I have a right to know, I do . . .'

'I cannot. I AM sorry – TRULY – but it would wreck so many lives . . . and I am forbidden, in law as well.'

'Just a little hint, then. A clue that could never be traced to you or this clinic,' pleads Jason desperately.

Liz lifts up her chin in a matronly fashion and her face takes on a serious expression to make a final pronouncement.

'Jason, go home to your mother and father. Be satisfied that you know this much. Remember that your father at home is the one who has brought you up in this world – the one who, with your mother, has nurtured you from the very beginning. Go home – please – and forget this.'

He is silent. His face shows sadness and despair again. It is a dead end. The final word in the final chapter.

'Look, I'm sorry, Jason, but you must go now. We really do have an incredibly busy clinic today, and I think you will understand just what that means to everybody concerned – I am sorry, but I cannot help you any more.'

Tears of frustration appear in Jason's eyes. He stands up and slowly extends a hand towards Liz.

'It's been a pleasure meeting you.'

Silently she walks down the passage. He follows meekly behind. At the front door he pauses before going down the steps, hesitating half-heartedly, and turns as if to say

171

something. Liz can see now the full extent of heartrending disappointment written on his face. For a second her expression softens as she places a hand on his arm. It prompts a parting shot from Jason.

'Can't you even tell me what he did?'

Liz concedes.

'Well, I guess that wouldn't be divulging anything of any consequence – yes Jason, as your father quite rightly said, he WAS a medical student.'

'So he must be a doctor now, after all these years.'

'I didn't say that, Jason – look, you must go.'

Jason hovers on the step, puffing out plumes of cold vapour. Liz shivers – and calculates.

'All I know, Jason – and I really mean this has got to be the very last thing I tell you – I believe, but I am not certain, that he went to sea for a while as a ship's doctor ... but then, that would be so many years ago, and I've already said too much. Goodbye.'

The door closes. Jason stands for a moment, his mind swimming with a mixture of emotions. The overburdening feeling of utter misery and hopelessness that he'd felt initially when Liz had steadfastly refused to tell him anything is compensated by a glimmer of hope. A faint lead, small as it might seem, gives him the strength and purpose to go on. But then doubts. The flimsy piece of evidence that he might have been a ship's doctor many years ago is hardly substantial enough to facilitate a continued search. Perhaps it would have been better, painful as it had seemed, to have closed the matter once and for all at number 17 Harley Street.

He starts walking back towards the underground station at Oxford Circus. His mind clears in the cold air, and he walks in a purposeful and determined step which gives him his answer – his natural father was indeed a medical student and he became a doctor – that could be the end, the dead end of his quest, but there is one vital gratuitous clue thrown out not so much as a scrap of worthless information, but more as a fleeting gesture of compassion – he may have been a ship's doctor at some time in his career. It isn't much to

172

go on, but it gives Jason a direction in which to focus his energies.

But then another wave of doubt and pessimism washes over his new-found optimism. It was so many years ago, a generation, in fact. The trail must be stone cold, if not completely dead and buried.

He descends the cold, grey cigarette-littered steps into the large rotunda ticket hall of the station, fumbling for coins to put in the ticket machine. Ship's doctor. Ship's doctor. Ship's doctor ... he recites to himself under his breath as if to strengthen his wavering doubts and flagging resolve.

Back at the Seaman's Mission he unlocks the door to his cubicle. The room is tiny, stark and sparsely furnished. Brown lino, cracked and curling up at the edges, covers the floor. There is a rickety old single bed, with rusty and broken springs, of minimal width to accommodate a small-sized man. Young men of this generation are bigger, heavier, taller and broader than those of the era that this battered old bedstead was made for. A small wormholed cabinet, varnish peeling, drawers musty and lined with sheets of faded and stained wallpaper, stands on one side of the bed. A spindly chair with one leg shorter than the others, almost too fragile to sit on, completes the furnishing. There is a faded reproduction of the Virgin Mary framed in black plastic hanging skew-whiff on the smoke-stained yellow wall over the head of the bed. It is seedy, to say the least.

But the room is warm – and Jason has hope. He pulls off his boots and flops onto the bed, folding his arms behind his head. He stares up at the ceiling and fixes his gaze on the low-wattage lightbulb and the faded green lampshade frayed at the edges. It is not exactly home, but it will do until he can find direction and a positive lead.

He will not allow himself to falter. He strives now, to consolidate his resolve by reciting aloud, as if to convince himself:

'I must. I will find him. I will not give up. It is my chosen purpose, and it must take priority over everything in my life. It is my right, and nobody can stop me ... I will ... I must ... I CAN.'

His consciousness clouds as he is falls under a self-induced hypnotic spell. He is rooting his objective deep into his psyche so that he will not falter in his resolve or be deterred by the obstacles and forces which will be undoubtedly acting against him. And finally he falls asleep.

He awakes feeling refreshed. His mind seems now to be completely cleared of all doubts. Whatever mental processes he'd induced in himself seemed to have worked, and he senses a cool determination to get to grips with the immense task of finding his true father.

He gets off the bed and sits carefully on the rickety chair, which lurches threateningly to one side. Strategy. Strategy. A definite plan of action. A starting point. What? How? Where? His mind concentrates. Ship's doctor. Ship's doctor. Of course! Quite simple – the only logical starting point, shipping companies – how very simple! But then the realisation of the enormity of such a line of inquiry dawns on him and he leans forward, burying his face in his hands.

Christ! How many shipping companies are there in the world? He has been at sea now himself for a couple of years, and during that time he had signed on numerous ships flying under the flags of different companies and nationalities – and he is aware that he had only worked for a fraction of the total around the world. It would take a lifetime to search them all out. Needle in a haystack – that's what it was – but it is the only possible lead, and he has no other choice. There must be a way. He needs to narrow the field down. Logical exclusion – that's it.

God knows how many British companies, let alone foreign – but hang on, foreign companies? They don't speak English – or at least are unlikely to recruit English doctors. That reduces the field considerably at a stroke. It must be English-speaking, and so the likelihood is a British company.

Company? But it may not be a company. Liz only said he was a doctor at sea. What about the military – the Royal

174

Navy? Perhaps he had joined the armed service? But then she said 'ship's doctor'. Most people naturally think of a civilian doctor, not a military one. Surely she would have said 'Royal Navy' if he had joined the armed services. So, exclude the Royal Navy.

The merchant marine. A doctor in the merchant marine. Tankers. Cargo ships. Containers. Thousands and thousands. God! How many doctors? But they don't have doctors on all the ships these days. Most are fully automated and run efficiently on small crews and computers. Gone are the days of sheer unlimited manpower. He knows that international law only requires a suitably qualified practitioner on board if the total of the ship's company with or without passengers is over 90.

Of course! Why hadn't he thought of it immediately? Cruise liners! That's it! Passenger ships, plain and simple. It must be. With another stroke he could cut out the thousands of merchant ships which weren't involved in the cruising business. And everybody had heard of the famous doctor at sea and the traditional life on board the luxury cruise liners. So it had to be shipping companies with cruise liners in their fleet. English-speaking ... the field was getting narrower and Jason's spirits were buoyant.

But where? How? How could he investigate these ships – there would be so many?

Cruise ships. If he wanted to go on a cruise ship, how would he go about arranging it? Why of course – a travel agent! His spirits rise even higher. This isn't so bad as he'd thought. With the slim lead he'd been given from the clinic by the lady who had known his mother all those years ago, there is now a definite direction in which to aim himself and all his energies.

And then a negative thought. It is so long ago. What chances are there, realistically, of ever finding a ship that his father could have worked on – assuming that it was a cruise ship? With this last thought swimming in his head he moves back to the bed, already feeling exhausted after the initial exhilaration followed by the feeling of doubtfulness. Soon he has drifted into a deep sleep.

The next day his resolve has reappeared as strong as ever and he takes a bus from the East End up West to the Thomas Cook office in the Strand.

Although there is a desk free with a male assistant sitting behind it, Jason waits a few minutes, pretending to browse through the catalogues and brochures on the shelf. And then a vivacious-looking brunette becomes vacant and he casually saunters over.

'Yes sir, how can I help you?' she says cheerfully, beckoning him to sit down.

He says he is vaguely interested in a cruise holiday – how many cruise companies are there? She says there are so many to choose from, but in her experience she can recommend a short list of favourites. But he would appreciate an exhaustive list, if she didn't mind. She is perplexed and doubts if he will buy a package, which is always the easiest thing to arrange. And then he confesses. He only really wants a list of the names of all the cruise line companies who operate.

She is less helpful when she realises he does not wish to buy a cruise. Jason presses her. She wants to get rid of him, and so she advises in a decidedly unfriendly tone that he can get a full list from the Shipping Federation. Naturally! He really should have thought of that before. No, she hasn't got the telephone number or address. Now could he please excuse her, as there are many other clients to attend to?

Directory enquiries. In the first public phone booth he comes to, he obtains the number from the operator and calls.

'If you send a self-addressed envelope and a three-pound postal order, sir, we will send you a complete list,' answers the grey computer-like voice.

'Actually, I just want cruise line companies – oh, and just English-speaking...'

'I'm afraid we don't differentiate, sir – and it will still be three pounds.'

'Fine. That's fine. What's the address, please?'

'I might advise you, sir, that most cruise ships operate in the English language, even the Russian ones...'

'Thank you. Thank you indeed. I am most grateful.'

* * *

Jason receives a thick brown package a few days after sending his £3 to the Shipping Federation. He can hardly believe the number of companies there are with cruise ships around the world – apart from British, there are American, Russian, German, Dutch, Norwegian, Japanese and even Chinese. The list seems endless. But he should be able to exclude most of the companies and choose those lines which an English doctor would be most likely to join. Russian, Chinese and Japanese he can exclude confidently.

The next day he goes to the bank and gets £20 worth of coins for the public telephone in the Mission. And the grind starts.

'...that's right – doctors who work for you. Do you have a list of their names and addresses?'

He is initially incredibly naïve about such requests on personnel information from companies.

'I'm sorry, sir, we cannot possibly give out that sort of information about our employees. If you are a doctor yourself and looking for a job, I'm afraid there are no posts available.'

'No no – it's just that I was looking for a long-lost uncle and was told he had a job with your line some years ago.'

'What was his name, sir?'

'Oh ... would you believe, my mind has gone completely blank and I cannot remember – I'm sorry...'

'"Long lost uncle"? I regret we are unable to help you, sir.'

It is a random process. Jason has listed all of what he thinks are the English-speaking lines, including American and Scandinavian companies, and is simply working his way down the list. By the tenth call he is beginning to recognise a monotonously uniform pattern from each number he has called. Soon he has exhausted what he thinks are the strictly English-speaking companies and has started to call the foreign lines. In the international cruise market, English would still be the working language, he rationalises. But the replies are in the same vein:

'No sir, I'm afraid we cannot help you, even if he is a relative.'

'I'm afraid we only employ Italian doctors...'

'We only employ Greek doctors...'

'...only Russian doctors.'

The list is getting smaller and smaller.

'Yes sir, we have employed one or two English doctors in the past, but in the main, we use Norwegian ... and I'm sorry, we cannot possibly give out that sort of personal data over the phone...'

It is hopeless. He had started off with such eagerness and enthusiasm almost as if it were some game, confident that the next stage in his search would be successful. But now, a feeling of hopelessness strikes him to the very core. It is late afternoon and the gloomy cold corridor in the Mission, where he has spent most of the day hunched over the public telephone, is stark and depressing. This could be it. It seems the trail is cold. The only possible source of information which might corroborate the slim clue from the clinic has drawn a complete blank.

He had just better face up to the reality. He will have to admit failure and bury once and for all this stupid obsession. Why the hell does it matter anyway? Does he really give a damn who his real father might be? Liz in the clinic was right. He remembers her words clearly. 'Only the physiological father ... your father at home is your true father, the one who has brought you up from the cradle...'

Jason calls his mother.

'Jason! For God's sake, where on earth have you been? We didn't know if you had signed on with another ship and we have been worried stiff, your father and I...'

'I'm truly sorry. I've been staying in London for a little while and thinking about everything. I think I'm OK now ... I'll come home tomorrow...'

The next day, Jason embraces his tearful mother at the station.

'Jason, you must never do anything like that again – promise me?'

'I promise.'

'It was so hurtful to your father and I. If only you had told us where you were going. I'm afraid your father has reached the end of his tether. He says he wants nothing more to do with you. He's given you up, son. He says you can do what you like and go where you like. Oh, Jason, why? WHY?'

She is crying now. Jason grimaces and holds back the tears.

'It's not too late. You can still go to university – just as we always planned. Your father would be so pleased, and I know everything would turn out fine.'

'No, Mother, it is too late for me now. I have lost interest. I will come home for a few days until I can arrange a ship. I'm going back to sea.'

It is a beautiful spring morning. There is warmth and bright-ness in the sun's rays after the long winter. The grass has begun to grow a rich dark green. Buds are beginning to sprout on the trees in the garden. There is a profusion of yellow daffodils everywhere. The sky is a soft pale blue with hardly a trace of cloud. As Jason walks in his parents' garden he feels a certain harmony and peace with his world, as if the birth of spring heralds a new and hopeful chapter in his life.

After 18 months back at sea, he has been home now for three weeks and settled back into a relaxed routine, with no thoughts of the future. The initial tension felt between he and his father, if not resolved, has eased considerably by a sort of tacit mutual understanding that they will both politely acknowledge each other, but nothing more. His mother is sad but feels there is little she can do. She makes a brave face and looks on the bright side, ever-hopeful that her son will somehow begin to see sense and return to the fold.

Jason's thoughts as he ambles aimlessly in the garden are random and disconnected. He is savouring this beautiful spring morning. The future can take care of itself. Images from all round the world appear in his mind's eye. He chuckles to

179

himself and indulges in the cascade of memories which are flooding his consciousness.

Manila! Manila! Of course! MANILA! Why the hell hadn't he thought of it before? Damn fool that he was! All that wasted time. It had to mean something, otherwise, why the hell would he have thought of it in the first place? Wait a minute. Is his mind playing tricks again? His pace accelerates. He is walking round and round the garden in circles. His mind is swirling and he can feel his heart thumping in excitement. His mood has suddenly elevated as if something in the deep recesses of his subconscious mind has stirred and bubbled to the surface unexpectedly, without prompting.

Manila. It has to be. Cruise ships in Manila. Of course!

He is clear what has to be done. He hurries inside the house and finds his mother, who his busy ironing a pile of his clothes.

'Hello, is that the Shipping Federation?'

'Yes, sir. How can I help you?'

'Yes – uuh, yes. I wonder if you could – uuh, what I mean to say is – well, I need to know...'

Jason finds it difficult to formulate a specific question for information of a vague, uncertain nature based on tenuous and unreliable memories of an incident lasting but a few fleeting seconds in a Far Eastern port some three years ago – especially as he had been drunk enough to confuse or obliterate all recall of such a memory.

'You were saying, sir?'

'Uuum – well – do you keep records of ships and where, uuh where...?'

'In what context do you mean, sir?'

'Well, I mean – if I say, for instance there was a cruise ship, in shall we say Manila, about three years ago, then would you have a record of it?'

'Most certainly, sir. We pride ourselves in having the most comprehensive records of all registered shipping in the world. We could give you a complete record of every ship's movement, ports of call, time of arrival, departure, tonnage, cargo, etc. etc. for all British and in fact all foreign-registered ships going right back to the turn of the century, when these records began. Of course now, it is much easier and quicker with all the information computerised...'

'Yes, yes, I appreciate that Mr – ?'

'Dodds. I have been the senior clerk in the records office for the last twenty-eight years and...'

'Thank you, thank you, Mr Dodds, I am most grateful ... can I call you back shortly?'

'Are you connected with shipping, sir?'

'I'm a seaman and a fully paid-up member of the Union.'

'Ah, well, that's all right, sir – we get some funny calls from some very funny people sometimes, and we have to be careful...'

'Of course, of course. I understand, Mr Dodds. I'll call you back when I've just looked up some information.'

'Right you are, sir.'

Jason puts the phone down. He sits motionless his mind in turmoil. If only his brain would clear, he tells himself. Think. THINK.

He picks up a pen and scribbles dates on a piece of paper. It must have been July or August – it was definitely the rainy season in the Philippines, and every day he can remember there was a torrential downpour, although on the particular night in question the rain had stopped and it had been particularly humid and hot.

He rings back.

'Can I help you? Mr Dodds speaking.'

'Oh thank goodness, Mr Dodds. It's me again.'

'I'm sorry, sir – who is that exactly?'

'We were talking about ship records and...'

'Oh yes, sir. You said you would call back. Now what is it you want to know exactly?'

'I was a deckhand on a large container that was docked in Manila – about three years ago – it must have been around July, August, September I think – around that time – it was the wet season, I remember. Anyway, I had a close friend who was working on a cruise ship that happened to be in Manila at the

181

same time. I haven't seen him since that time, and it is vital I find him ... if only I could remember the name of the cruise ship he was on, then I could contact the line and maybe locate him through them.'

'That sounds quite possible, sir. So what you are asking is the record of any cruise ships that were in Manila around that time – am I correct, sir?'

'Precisely, Mr Dodds. Precisely.'

'Could you be a little more specific, sir, as to the date. It covers a three-month period, and as you might well remember, Manila is a very busy port. The number of individual ships going in and out over three months is enormous – and that includes a lot of cruise ships flying with many different flags.'

'I'm sure it would have been a British-registered ship – perhaps that reduces the number.'

'Perhaps, sir. Perhaps.'

'Would it help if I came in to see you, Mr Dodds?'

'Not really, sir. That is not necessary, I assure you – if you bear with me for a moment I'll flash up July and see what we've got ... let me see ... a couple of Russian ... that's Greek ... Italian ... Chinese from Taiwan ... and the *Lagarfiord* – that's Norwegian. There's nothing British, I'm afraid.'

'Norwegian companies employ English crews at times, do they not?'

'That I couldn't answer, sir, really. Would you like me to go through August?'

'Yes please.'

'Let me see ... Dutch – they might have some English crew sir, don't you think – it was an Englishman, your friend, I take it, sir?'

'Yes, yes – of course.'

'... Russian again. German. Russian. They seem to call pretty frequently, I think, sir – Far Eastern cruises out of Vladivostok, I believe ...'

'Yes, yes ... any more, Mr Dodds?'

'No – that's about it, sir. Do you still want me to go through September?'

'I don't think that will be necessary, Mr Dodds – thank you –

you have been very helpful. I appreciate it very much. Goodbye and thank you.'

'Goodbye sir – and good luck.'

Jason replaces the receiver and grimaces. What on earth can he do now? Not even one British ship. Why bother anymore? He thought he had got it out of his system in the last 18 months at sea, but clearly he is still affected. It is a veritable curse!

Norwegian ships. He knows the Norwegian cruise liners were very international and sailed worldwide. He had seen such ships in all sorts of exotic locations around the world – and come to think of it, he had noticed lots of English-speaking passengers when he had gone ashore and the cruisers had flooded the port. They must have recruited some of their crew from Britain – and maybe, maybe even a doctor! Maybe. He can only try. It's a slim chance, but he cannot help himself. He is compelled by whatever mysterious force is driving him. It seems the only plausible avenue left. Norwegian ships – that's it. Oh God! Where to start?

The *Lagarfiord*! That was the cruise liner that Mr Dodds had said was in Manila around the time Jason may have been there himself. He'll have to call him back to get the address of the shipping company.

'Are you sure, Mr Dodds – Oslo you say – the head office – all the recruiting done there – I see. Thank you – thank you again.'

Oslo! How can he go there? His money has almost run out. His mother has already been too generous, and he would never dream of asking his father. He'll just have to sell the car. He hardly uses it anyway. He won't get much for it, but it should be enough to finance his trip to Norway. And then the doubts again. Is it not a waste of time and effort and not inconsiderable expense? Surely it is a wild goose chase now? Chasing a dream, a fantasy, an emotion-driven obsession with little basis of reality. But he must. He must see it through to the bitter end.

* * *

183

One week later Jason hauls his canvas kitbag from the slow-moving carousel at Oslo airport and looks for a sign to the taxi rank. He will ask the cab driver to take him to the Seaman's Mission, which should be cheap and comfortable. He has the address of the shipping company which owns the *Lagarfiord* – Norsk International, which has its main office in the dock area.

In the taxi he reflects on the purpose of his life. He has relegated to the very depths of his consciousness all thoughts of ambition or career. The painful quest he had embarked upon has dominated his thinking since that astonishing conversation with his mother when she had told him of his unusual origin. It is a quest to find his true identity, his very being.

The next day, after a short walk through the old part of Oslo Docks, pungent with the smell of fish, he locates the shipping office of Norsk International.

With its pristine newness, the large white concrete office block looks strangely out of place in the quaint dockland area – sandwiched as it is between old 19th-century traditional houses and the sprawling fish markets.

As he approaches the main entrance he feels nervous, but there is a guarded optimism, as much as he dares, tempered by the thought that this will probably be the very last chance, slim as it may seem, of ever finding out. He steps closer. The sliding doors open automatically startling him. He sees an enquiry desk on the other side of the spacious foyer. Behind it sits a woman. He strides purposefully towards the desk.

'Good morning. I am sorry, but I do not speak Norwegian...'

'That's quite all right. We all speak English in this office. It is very necessary with so many foreigners who come to work for the company – now, what can I do for you?'

'I am looking for a doct – I mean, I am looking for a job. Do you have any vacancies for seamen?'

'I am sorry, I do not know. You will have to go to our recruitment office. It is just around the corner. Have you been a seaman?'

'Oh yes,' answers Jason confidently, but in a distracted

184

manner as he stares at the pictures on the wall directly behind the receptionist.

There is a pause, as if she is waiting for him to elaborate details of his previous work experience.

'You wanted to say?'

'Aren't those British ships on the wall? Sorry, if you don't mind me asking.'

'Yes, they are. Up until five years ago, we, that is the original Norwegian shipping line, were in a sort of loose arrangement – or you call it a "consortium" I think – with a British company. But around that time I'm afraid they, the British shipping line that is, got into financial difficulties, and so the Norwegian Line bought them out. It used to be the old Cunedin Line I think, based in London and Southampton. Anyway, their ships became our ships and changed their names, or at least most of them did – and flew under the new flag of the newly named company, Norsk International.'

'So, what you are saying, is that the present fleet is a mixture of Norwegian and old British ships?'

'Yes – that is correct.'

Jason is aware of his heart thumping against the wall of his chest. This is a startling piece of good luck, and he feels it must be auspicious. He trys to remain calm and modulate the excitement in his voice.

'And I suppose all of the British crews were replaced by Norwegian?'

'Yes. The vast majority – but not entirely. Quite a lot of the British sailors came over to work for us – especially the officers.'

Suddenly, Jason is aware of the butterflies in his stomach.

'And you still employ British crew, then?'

'Of course! Otherwise I wouldn't be sending you round the corner to our recruitment office, would I?'

'No, of course not – how silly of me.'

Jason blushes.

'What about doctors, then – I mean – are there...?'

He can hardly contain his excitement.

'Why do you ask? You are not a doctor, I think? You look much too young!'

185

'No no – of course not! I am a seaman – a simple deckhand ... but, but – I had a friend who was a doctor who worked for a cruise line – I think it was – yes, I am sure it was your company...'

'What was his name?'

'How many doctors does the company employ?'

'Oh, hundreds I think. Well, maybe not hundreds, but you know what I mean. All the cruise ships have at least one doctor, depending on how big the ship – sometimes they carry a sort of second junior one as well – and there is a generous leave allowance – so you see, the company needs to have many doctors on its books. In fact, there are about twelve permanent doctors who rotate around the cruise fleet – and quite a few more temporary doctors who relieve. Maybe your friend is one of them?'

'Maybe ... perhaps...'

'When did he start with the company – and you haven't even told me his name!'

Jason blushes again.

'I'm afraid I can't remember his name – it was quite some time ago.'

'I see – well – very few of even our permanent doctors stay more than three or four years, so if it is before that then it is very unlikely that he is still with the company.'

Jason's hopes flounder again. She observes his meteoric mood swing from his rapidly changed facial expression.

'Are you all right?'

'Y – yes – thank you.'

'As I was saying, very few doctors stay more than a few years. Most are pretty young – in their late twenties or early thirties – you know – having some fun before they settle down ashore in serious jobs ... but in fact, come to think of it, there are one or two who are quite a bit older.'

Jason nods in acknowledgment and gratitude and suppresses a deep sigh.

'You really have been very helpful.'

She can see he is a little perturbed.

'Can I get you a coffee, perhaps?'

'No – no thanks. The recruitment office – round the corner, first to the right, you say?'

'Yes.'

'Thank you – thank you very much. I am very grateful.'

He finds the office without any trouble in a much older building, the sort one would expect to find in the port area of Oslo. He enters through a ripple-glassed door into a small, drab reception area reeking of stale tobacco smoke. The ceiling is a dirty stained yellow with the wallpaper peeling in the corners. There is a man behind a solid-looking dark brown wooden counter who looks as old, although less well-preserved, as the wood itself. He looks up as Jason enters and speaks first, anticipating Jason's enquiry.

'First door on the left,' he says in heavily accented English, assuming that Jason is a foreigner.

Jason nods obediently as if he knows the drill and turns left and goes through a door with the word 'Recruitment' in large white letters stencilled prominently across it. It is a small office, more of an anteroom, and the reek of fish, combined with stale smoke and body odour, hits Jason's nostrils immediately – although it is not unpleasant and seems appropriate.

A short man with a hugely protuberant abdomen appears through a glass door leading to yet another office. Without speaking, he gestures with a sudden wave of the hand for Jason to sit down on one of the ancient looking chairs lined up against one wall. From this brief contact he has already categorised Jason, assuming he is a foreign sailor looking for a ship.

'You are a seaman – no?'

'Yes. I am a deckhand, second class.'

'Do you have your seaman's discharge book and union card?'

'Yes. Here you are.'

Jason reaches into his breast pocket.

The clerk flicks efficiently through the book in seconds.

'You have served on quite a few ships, have you not, in your short time at sea?'

'Yes – I get bored easily if I stay on one ship for too long.'

187

The clerk looks up abruptly and sends Jason a quizzical look as if getting bored at sea is an unusual emotion to complain about.

'Well Mr Brown, that all seems in order. Any references?'

'Yes – I have a testimonial here from ACTA Line, from the chief officer of one of their giant container ships.'

'Let me see ... uuuum yes, that seems to be satisfactory. Now – do you have any preference for the ship you would like?'

'As you can see, I've worked only on cargo ships before – so I am thinking it might be a change to get a job on a passenger ship – you know – cruise liners – I'm sure the work is much the same.'

'It is quite a bit different to cargo, I can tell you, my friend. It doesn't suit all seamen. Sure, the job is basically the same – but the environment and the voyage schedules are very much different. As I say, it doesn't suit all ... anyway, we will see what we can do, if that is what you really want. At the moment we have many vacancies in the cargo fleet, but there are not many in the passenger ships ... are you sure?'

'No – no. I mean it must be a passenger ship – and, and ... if possible, the *Lagarfiord* please.'

The clerk looks up quizzically again, but cannot be bothered to comment.

'OK, OK. But I have to check the files. We only have twelve passenger ships and the jobs do not become vacant so frequently these days. Sailors have a much better life at sea than before, and so they are staying on the ships longer ... you will have to take what is available. Please wait a moment.'

The clerk has been in the back office for at least ten minutes, and Jason is becoming anxious and doubtful again. He sits motionless, focusing on the old black and white prints of early company ships which cover the wall opposite.

The glass door opens and the clerk re-emerges.

'You are lucky, Mr Brown. An unexpected vacancy for a deckhand has just come up on one of our smaller passenger vessels – it is not the *Lagarfiord*, I'm afraid – and you will have to fly out to join her with minimal notice.'

188

'That's fine. I'm ready to go without delay.'

'That is good, then. It is settled. You will join the *Bergenfiord* as soon as we can arrange your flight to Athens.'

'Is it easy to get transfers within the passenger fleet?'

The clerk fixes his gaze on Jason and delays his answer for a couple of seconds.

'Once you have completed three months satisfactory service on your assigned ship, then you are free to apply for another ship. But I advise you that three months is the minimum contract and most crew are expected to stay on one ship for much longer periods.' There is another quizzical look which Jason ignores.

'I see. I see. So if a vacancy comes up on the *Lagarfiord*, I can apply for it?'

'Yes you can. But as I have already advised you, only if you have completed at least three months satisfactory service on your previous vessel.'

'Thank you.'

'Don't mention it – we will arrange for all of the necessary instructions and tickets to be sent to the Mission – I take it you are staying there?'

'Yes.'

'But please be ready on Friday morning.'

'I will – I assure you.'

'You sound too educated to be a seaman,' the Bosun on the *Bergenfiord* spits out in mild contempt, thinly disguised enough only to prevent a confrontation.

He is a Geordie with an unmistakable accent, tough and uncompromising, hard as nails and very few dare to cross him. What he doesn't know about being a sailor is not worth knowing. He started as a deck boy when he was only 15, and now he has reached the pinnacle of his ambitions as Chief Bosun on a luxury cruise liner.

'Do you really think so, Tom?'

'You sound a bit too clever for me, fellah.'

Jason misses the thinly veiled facetiousness and answers in a

189

genuine manner. He has only been on the ship two days, and for most of that time has been with the Bosun, big Tom McGarvey, whom the men fear more than they respect. Although he was considered a fair and straightforward man, woe betide any of his crew who crossed him. Jason had already heard stories in the 'pig' of his legendary temper and aggression.

'Yes – well, Tom, I took my A levels at school and had planned to go to university. I was lucky to get a job for a year on an old banana boat sailing out of St Lucia ... I felt I was too young to go straight up to uni ... anyway, the thing is, I got a taste for the sea and decided to become a fully-fledged deck-hand ... so here I am, three years on.

'It don't make sense to me – you being educated and an ordinary seaman, like – with all those qualifications. If you like the sea so much, why don't you become a merchant officer?'

'Good point. It's just that I wasn't so sure in the beginning and didn't want to commit myself to – and...'

'Well fellah, you're taking more time than a virgin to decide. Seems a funny way of doin' things to me.'

Jason cannot think of a suitable reply and tightens his lips.

'And another thing, lad, a nice brought-up boy like you meets a lot of rough and ready characters below decks – you know what ah mean?'

'Oh, I don't mind – all part of life's rich experience.'

Tom could not possibly engage Jason's philosophy. They are from entirely different social orbits. But on this ship, a world away from the world he had been brought up in, Tom is his immediate boss and he must do his bidding.

'Anyway, you seem to know your job well enough, fellah. That's all that matters to me.'

There is a prolonged silence as they continue painting the outside railing a brilliant white. Without interrupting his concentrated brushstrokes to the angle between a sturdy upright and its joint with a more delicate cross-strut, Jason speaks.

'Can I ask you a question, Tom?'

'Aye lad, go ahead – as long as it's not one of those fancy questions I canna answer.'

'No no no … nothing complicated. It's just that, well, what I wanted to ask is, what are the doctors like on the ships?'

'That's a queer question to start with, lad.'

'What I mean to say is…'

'I can tell you, a rum bunch they are, that's for sure.'

'What do you mean?'

'Well, fellah, I've seen some strange characters over the years, I can tell you.'

Tom McGarvey, the tough-as-nails Geordie who had fought hard and long over the years to attain his position as a bosun on a big ship, had always been contemptuously unrestrained in his descriptions of officers. Perhaps this natural aversion for many he considered undeservedly privileged in the hierarchy of the merchant marine, had slowed his promotion in the company. It doesn't matter a damn now what he says or to whom he says it. Besides, Jason is only a deckhand and there are hardly likely to be any repercussions from what he says to him.

'Alcoholics, bloody alcoholics, most of 'em … lazy and arrogant … snobs … everything but decent doctors – most certainly the ones I've come across anyway. Take the present one on this ship. He's even worse, if you can believe it – a raving poof, that's what he is – a bloody queer … queer as a coot, that one. Steer clear o' 'im, tha's my advice, lad.'

'Funny you should mention it, Tom. I've got to see him tomorrow to have my joining medical. I was going to ask you for the time off around ten o'clock, if that's OK?'

'That'll be all right with me – you've got to have it done, I know – but just you make sure to keep your back to the wall – and keep your pants on.'

'How old is he?'

'Not too old. A youngster really for a doctor – I'd say in his early thirties … a right fairy 'e is … you watch him, m'lad.'

Tom winks, but his expression is serious.

191

'He's usually half-cut as well. The sick bay stinks o' liquor. And to think we have to call him "sir". I tell you, Jason, if he ever tries it on with one o' my lads I'll bleedin' kill 'im, God 'elp me.'

'I understand.'

'How long are you on for, Jason lad?'

'I've signed on for three months. After that I don't know. I might apply for another ship – I really cannot say. I'd like to try some of the other cruise ships in the fleet.'

'Let's get this job finished, lad, before that squall hits us, and then we can break for smoko.'

Three months have passed surprising quickly. Jason had soon fitted into the routine and become an accepted and respected member of the stalwart sailors' fraternity. His previous experience on cargo ships had made the task easier. Work on a passenger ship wasn't so different from a cargo vessel, except that it had taken a little getting used to passengers walking around the decks and occasionally striking up a conversation. Like the rest of the sailors, he resented clearing up the huge mess of litter and broken bottles after a wild deck party for the passengers, but enjoyed anchor port days when the seamen supervised the shuttling of passengers ashore in the ship's tenders.

Tomorrow the ship will dock in Venice at the end of a ten-day Mediterranean cruise. It is the end of his first three months, and he is to return to England for leave. He has already decided he will not be coming back to this ship. Although it has been a pleasant enough job, he cannot stifle the desire to move on until he finds what he is looking for. Oh God! If only he had more concrete clues to direct him. But if he is honest to himself, he is wasting his time. Perhaps wasting his life – hell-bent on a mission that was doomed to failure almost before it began.

It is late afternoon, and he is alone on the anchor deck leaning on the rail, looking aft at the turbulent wake of the ship and the gulls as they swoop down and shoot up again on the violent updraft of spray and foam. He is in a pensive mood. He thoughts turn to his future plans. If only he could resolve his dilemma!

He gazes randomly skywards and sees the glinting speck of a plane at high altitude moving steadily across the clear blue sky, its steady progress marked by the vapour trails which etch two straight white lines as far as the eye can see. But the lines, clean and distinct at first, gradually become blurred and more blurred and eventually so vague that they could be mistaken for wisps of cloud.

Jason cannot fail to see the poignancy of what he sees in relation to his own chosen objective and sense of purpose. For him, the trail has become blurred and indistinct as life's events took control of his destiny. Now, he is confused and not sure what he wants or where he is going. Like the vapour trails in the clear blue sky his early well-defined incisiveness is blunting, his determined motivation clouding over with doubts. He is in danger of losing control completely and becoming irretrievably lost to the whims of fate forever.

The next day Jason turns round at the bottom of the gangway and looks up at the liner. He consoles himself, despite the empty feeling inside. It hasn't been too bad, he thinks. But why doesn't he give up this dream, a blighted dream, a dream that might cause him to drift aimlessly for the rest of his life? Slowly, although in the beginning painfully, he has been able to sublimate his agony and frustration by throwing himself into the immediate demands of labour. So why not simply continue to work on the ships until the impossible dream is buried once and for all under the impenetrable thickness of life's perpetual distractions?

It was funny. He was going to ask the doctor about other doctors who worked in the fleet, but after Tom's warning, he had been reluctant, if not a little apprehensive, to open up any social discourse during his medical. In fact, the doctor's overt homosexuality had alarmed him, and he'd breathed a sigh of relief when it was over. He couldn't believe how blatantly the homosexual characters disported themselves on cruise ships – something he'd rarely witnessed on the cargo boats. But now he is putting it all behind him, and cannot wait to get home to see his mother.

She embraces him fiercely as if she is desperate to restrain his wandering spirit, his restless soul.

Her tears of joy are unrestrained. Jason shares her joy and kisses her repeatedly on the face. The physical affection between them has always been strong and demonstrative in a way he has not been able to develop with his father. It is the afternoon, and he is still at work. When he returns in the evening, he and Jason exchange a polite acknowledgment and that is all. It is a sad state of affairs for his mother, who loves them both, but if she would ever dare admit it, her fierce loyalty to her son overrides all other considerations.

Over the next few weeks Jason relaxes, spending most of his time walking for miles and miles along the myriad of footpaths and trails in the countryside which he can reach from his home by a short bus ride to the edge of town. Every day when he returns in the late afternoon, he has long conversations with his mother about anything and everything, but these invariably turn to a discussion about his future plans.

She implores him desperately to give up the sea – 'running away from reality' she calls it – and get on with a worthwhile career at home. They might become a happy family once more. All would soon be forgotten, and his father could be proud of his son. It wasn't too late. If only he could see sense.

But it is no use. His mother cannot persuade him, even though he knows it is breaking her heart. The compulsion that seems so indelibly printed in his psyche might destroy him eventually, and he knows it. But this awareness of the self-destructive process doesn't help matters.

After one month at home an offer comes of a job on the *Laconia*, one of the old British ships still sailing in the passenger fleet. He takes it and bids farewell again to his mother for another voyage of three months. After that, there is another short spell at home before he joins another passenger ship, the *Stavangerfiord* for another three-month tour of duty. By the time he joins yet a third ship, he has proved his worth to the company and they seem quite agreeable to accede to his frequent requests to change ships within the passenger fleet, although they would prefer him to stay longer on the same ship.

The pattern becomes established. By the time he joins the fifth cruise ship he doesn't seem to care any more about anything. His senses seem blunted, and the routine of three months on and one month off suits him. He is only vaguely aware that he is drifting further and further down a path dictated more by fate than deliberate choice. And he is becoming resigned to it. Each new ship he joins is the arbitrary choice of the company depending on vacancies for seamen at any particular time, and he goes willingly without question. There is no longer any sort of strategy which might relate to his initial quest. There are no new leads to reinforce the compulsion that drove him back to sea in the first place, and it slowly begins to dawn on him that he is becoming less concerned with any original objective and simply content to stay at sea because the lifestyle suits him.

After three years he has worked on almost every passenger ship in the fleet – 11 of the 12 fact. All of them except the flagship, which was one of the original old cruise liners with the Cunedin line.

Not one of the doctors he had seen on these ships fitted anywhere near the idealised image he had in his mind of the man he was searching for. Each new ship and each new doctor reinforced his gradual acceptance that the trail was cold. It was all too long ago. They were all either too young, too old, too drunk or just too degenerate and unsavoury in their character. He can admit to himself now that in the beginning he had desperately wanted to find the man who was his real father, the true source of the male force which he had inherited. But the harsh face of reality and the passage of time had clouded that vision, and when he returns home after a three-month spell on the *Arcadia*, the original purpose and compulsion have dissipated almost completely.

195

As usual, his mother is overjoyed to see him. She has stopped telling him now that he is wasting his life, but secretly she has not given up hope and still prays that he will somehow miraculously snap out of it and come to his senses. She is aware of the change in Jason. She looks at him and can see that his outer cheerfulness hides a deep-seated sadness that is like a dagger in her heart. He would never admit it, but she knows deep down, he is suffering. But she remains silent and prays that his ultimate salvation will come.

'There's a letter for you, Jason – from the company, I think.'

'It must be my new ship. I'll open it later – thanks. I was just on my way out. I'll be back for supper.'

He gets a bus to the outskirts and then sets off along the little footpath which takes him through a heavily wooded area, which in the summer is a profusion of green trees and dense undergrowth and seems a world away from the town. It has always been for Jason the ideal setting to be able to walk alone, without distraction, free of noise and people, where he can think and meditate on matters that are important to him. In the winter, the trees, divested of their foliage, are grey and skeletal in appearance, and the labyrinth of pathways through the wood is often muddy or on occasion under snow. But he walks there come rain or shine, and it rarely fails to lift his spirits.

Today it is clear and dry, and though cold enough to warrant a jacket, the winter is all but over, signalled clearly by the few small buds which are appearing in the trees and bushes. His thoughts are random and evade any concentrated analysis of his life. Ideas of getting a job ashore or even going to university appear uninvited in his mind.

University? Surely it is too late to consider such a move – and would it not be too difficult to cope with such a contrast to the lifestyle he had now got used to? And more importantly, has he rested once and for all the demon that has driven him for the last three years? Perhaps. Perhaps. He is still not a hundred per cent sure. Time will tell. His ruminations continue as he walks, and by the time he returns hours later he is very tired, but is

aware that something has happened – there has been a transformation – he feels confident for the first time that the
demon may have finally been cast out. It is as if he has been
reborn and can seriously think about starting afresh. As impulsive as ever, he cannot wait to tell his mother the good news,
dispelling the self-doubt that it might simply be a transient
state of mind.

She greets him cheerfully as always.

'Cup of tea?'

'Thank you.'

'Jason – did they tell you which ship you will be joining
next?'

'Oh yes – I forgot to open the letter. I left it on the dressing
table in my bedroom – won't be minute.'

He returns with the envelope torn half-open.

'Here, use the bread knife, it's easier.'

He slits open the rest of the envelope and pulls out the
single sheet of paper folded in four. He opens it slowly and
scans down the page.

'Go on then, tell me. What is the name of the ship to which I
have to address your mail?'

'Well, well, it's about time I got the chance to go on the
biggest and grandest of them all – the real daddy of the fleet.
Wow! Honolulu! They're expecting me to fly out to Honolulu
of all places to join it. I guess it'll be halfway into the world
cruise it does every year and should be back in Europe in three
months.'

'That's an awfully long flight, my dear. It will be very tiring.'

'Well you needn't worry – I've been giving the matter a great
deal of thought lately – and – and I've made up my mind finally
– to leave – to leave the sea once and for all ... truly ... I'm
sure this time.'

'Oh do you really mean it? Promise me, promise me you
mean it...'

'Yes, Mother – I promise. I am definitely leaving the ships.'

'And – and you can still go to university – can't you?'

'Just hold on a minute. I haven't said what I plan to do yet ...
but it's a possibility – yes.'

197

'Oh, please say you will. It would make me so happy ... and I know your father would be ... please son.'

'I'll need to do another two or three trips to get enough money so I can plan...'

'Don't worry, your father and I will be only too happy to help. You won't have to worry about money, I promise.'

Doreen can suppress her tears no longer. She cries openly, but hers are tears of joy and her eyes shine bright with a renewed sparkle of hope and optimism for her son's future.

Jason takes his mother in his arms and pulls her close. He feels her gentle heave as she rests her head against his chest. There is a lump in his throat and his eyes are moist. He is pleased he has made his choice, and feels confident that his mind is settled.

She pulls away.

'No more than one or two trips, that's all Jason – now promise me, promise!'

'I promise.'

'What did you say the name of the ship was so that I know where to write?'

'I didn't – but it's the grand old flagship of the fleet ... the the only company ship that I haven't sailed on yet ... well, I guess it'll probably be my last opportunity to sail on the *Empress of the Seas*.'

CHAPTER 8

SHIP'S NURSE

With Cupid's arrow; she hath Dian's wit;
And in strong proof of chastity well armed,
She will not stage the siege of loving terms,
Nor bide the encounter of assailing eyes,
Nor ope her lap to saint-seducing gold:
O! She is rich in beauty;

       Romeo and Juliet, William Shakespeare (1564–1616)

'Staff Nurse Reeves, have you given Mr Davies his bed bath yet?'

'Yes, Sister. He says he feels very comfortable now. I've changed his sheets and checked his fluid chart. Doctor has altered the volume of intake from three litres to two in each twenty-four hours and says we can start him on oral intake at thirty ml an hour.'

'Good. Well done.'

'Oh, Sister – and the houseman is coming back to change his catheter.'

'That's fine, Miss Reeves. Now, before report, could you please check on the drips of our prostate cases – make sure their catheters are not blocked – and then you can help Nurse Andrews set up the trolley for the drug round, all right?'

'Yes, Sister.'

Penelope Reeves, Penny to everyone except her mother, positively glows at being addressed 'Staff Nurse'. She has been at St Thomas's hospital in London for nearly three and a half years. Even though it is almost six months since she passed her Registered Nurse exams (winning the coveted Gold Medal) and 'belted' on Scutari Ward (Florence Nightingale, the Crimean War heroine, trained at St Thomas's in the 1850s), she still feels tremendous satisfaction at being called 'Staff Nurse' instead of simply 'nurse' or 'lovey' or 'my dear'. She proudly displays her black belt of rank with its individual silver buckle, the only symbol of personal choice in the starchy stiff traditional nurse's uniform. Most hospitals in the country had long since introduced the standard simple uniform, which was described by traditionalists as characterless and too much like that of a cafeteria waitress. But the illustrious London teaching hospitals displayed a certain contempt for this standardisation, and continued to wear proudly their nineteenth century nurse's apparel – including the picturesque hats and well-below-the-knee dresses.

When she goes off duty and has reached the sanctuary of her room in the nurses' residence the first thing she does in a gesture of private defiance is to rip out the tight stud from the stiffened collar as if it represents the straitjacketed conformity, the very apotheosis of her chosen profession. And then she swiftly undoes her hair with a liberating gesture of exaggerated flourish letting the silky natural blond tresses cascade freely down her back. Briskly, she unfastens and steps out of the starched restraint of her nurse's uniform. In one economical action, cocking a subliminal snook at the depersonalisation of uniforms, she sheds the constricting high collar and the tight fitting tunic with prissy apron all in one piece and it drops unceremoniously to the floor. The only concession to her womanly configuration is the silver buckled black belt drawn in tightly at the waist. Starched to the point of unyielding rigidity, the style of the garment, including the carefully positioned small white hat hasn't changed in a century. Only by the end of a long strenuous shift has it softened up enough to crumple to the floor as it was let loose.

The message intended from this carefully constructed sartorial statement is one of absolute discipline and control. Emotions are not encouraged if at all permitted.

Penny has a perfectly straight back and utilises all of her five feet five inches to maximum effect. Even the carefully designed neutrality of the nurses' uniform cannot disguise her athletic shape. Wide, square shoulders with long graceful arms and a generous bust (firmly compressed by the starch) taper down to a small, rock solid waistline and then gently slope out to the perfect hips and rounded pelvic contours of a woman in her reproductive prime. At a glance, she is guaranteed to attract

202

the attention of the most disinterested male observer – whether they are sick or not and in spite of the quaint uniform. Her long slender legs are well developed but shapely, and not brutally, uncompromisingly athletic. Indeed she walks miles on the wards as a nurse but the muscle definition of her calves tapering down to slim ankles is more the result of years of running at school and long hours in the gym.

She is the perfect specimen of young womanhood impatient to jump into the hectic whirligig of life and fly as far and wide as she dares – far away from the rigid routine of her nursing training which has kept her occupied for precisely the last three years and six months.

Although naturally modest and unassuming, and a little self-deprecating at times, she is realistically aware of her natural talents and although she mightn't flaunt such a powerful biological weapon, it is held barely in check, simmering gently just beneath the surface, but threatening to boil over once she has made the jump.

It had been a dream for as long as she could remember to become a nurse. She couldn't think why. Neither parent, in fact no one in the family, was remotely connected to the health care profession. Her father is a solicitor and her mother a librarian.

Her lifelong ambition to become a nurse was equalled only by her desire to travel, 'as far and wide as possible' she has said so many times to her parents. They could never understand this innate wanderlust. Ever since she was a toddler, she'd run off and been lost so many times they'd aged considerably by the time she'd gone to infant school.

They had been able to tame her adventurous spirit to a manageable degree as she grew older, but it had only served to strengthen her resolve to achieve her ambition in the nursing profession and then utilise her skills to travel the world.

At St Thomas's she excelled. The three years training to become a registered nurse flew by. And in that short time her parents marvelled at the transformation they witnessed in their young daughter. They were able to see her every three to four weeks when she got a free weekend and travelled dutifully back to Broadstairs on the Kent coast. In an astonishingly short period she developed a maturity and self-confident assuredness, which gave them ambivalent feelings. They were delighted to see their daughter mature so quickly and in the way they had always wanted, but at the same time they realised that they would be losing the child that had depended so much on them.

Winning the Gold Medal at the end of her training had been the absolute pinnacle, and she'd had her picture in the local paper. Her tutors and her parents had prompted her to continue her postgraduate studies and aim for higher things.

But she knew exactly what she wanted. Her sights had been set over the distant horizon for as long as she could remember. She simply had to travel. The initial disappointment of her parents and her tutors faded as they saw how happy and excited she was about her future. Her six-month 'belting period', the minimum registration time necessary in a major hospital is almost finished and now she can hardly contain her excitement with what is in store.

The success in the exams, the immense satisfaction and privilege she felt working at St Thomas's, not to mention the strong persistent advice she'd received from so many quarters, had almost persuaded her to continue her hospital career straight after registration. She'd definitely wavered for a while, but when the letter from the shipping company had arrived, the die had been cast.

Norsk International had been on a long list of companies all over the world that she'd written to for a job as a ship's nurse. She'd had an incredible response, probably because of her winning the coveted Gold Medal, but also because of the prestige of her parent hospital. There were numerous offers from many cruise lines, and it had not been an easy choice. She'd no experience of the sea or in fact work anywhere else, and so had nothing to compare. Only Mr O'Rourke, the elderly patient who'd recently had a prostatectomy, could give her any information about the lifestyle she might expect.

He'd been a seafarer all his life, and had even worked as a deck boy on sailing ships, over 60 years ago. After his operation she'd spent hours at his bedside as he reminisced his long nautical career. It only served to galvanise her excitement and expectations.

She had been vaguely aware of Norsk International and its reputation as one of the oldest most traditional cruise fleets in the merchant service, and had even heard of some of its more famous liners. The future possibility of joining the flagship of the fleet at some time had been the clincher. After her acceptance letter they had told her that there would be a week of induction in the Southampton medical office, prior to being sent to one of the smaller ships in the fleet. This had all been scheduled to take place one month after leaving St Thomas's, so when the registered letter had arrived requesting urgently if it could be arranged she join a ship the following week in Singapore, she had positively trembled.

In fact, she'd still had a week left at St Thomas's so the chief personnel officer at Norsk International had himself telephoned the senior nursing officer, explaining the urgency of the circumstances, and gratefully requesting she be allowed to leave a few days earlier than planned so that she could receive a cram induction of two days before flying out.

He had explained how an urgent staffing problem had arisen in the company because of sudden illness of several of the regular nursing staff, together with the unexpected abrupt resignation of two key figures. It had left one of their ships in desperate need for a nurse at short notice, and that was the one she was being asked to join.

It will all come as a bit of a shock to her parents. Although they know about the job, they will not know until she travels home on the weekend that she will be starting prematurely. Their reaction will be a mixture of sadness and joy. Sadness at her unexpected hasty departure, but still joy with her undoubted happiness.

Her father is affected more than her mother. They are very close. Strangely, people said that she looked much more like her mother and not at all like her father. But that didn't matter to her. The physical similarity or lack of it was not important, for she worshipped her father, and throughout her life she had confided in him more than a girl might her mother. All in all, they are a closely-knit family – although at times there was a strange invisible veil which stopped her getting too close to her mother, as if she were hiding some dark unmentionable secret from her daughter.

Her relationship with her brother Mark is like any other between a sister and a brother who is three years younger. They are completely unalike, physically and in personality. As children they squabbled endlessly, and in their teens this developed into a healthy sibling rivalry which saw Mark being mother's favourite and Penny the apple of her father's eye.

It is Friday now and for Penny the last day on the ward at St Thomas's. The stiff starchy uniforms, unchanged in design since the days of Florence Nightingale, not to mention the strict hierarchies of seniority symbolised by slight variations in the colour and style of hat, will all soon be behind her. She pretends total ignorance on this last day on the ward, but she knows they have arranged a little surprise tea party for her in Sister's office.

Report is finished, and the circle of nurses surrounding Sister Walker at her desk wait for her to begin. Even though it is an agreeable social occasion, it must be performed in the correct and proper manner. Penny sits passively, feeling a little self-conscious.

'Staff Nurse Reeves – I should say "Penny" – we are all sad to see you leave today – but we are happy that you will be moving on to something so, so – exciting and far away. You are a very good nurse, and we had hoped you might stay at St Thomas's a little longer – but you always had your eye on the horizon – though we hope that one day in the not-too-distant future you will come back and share with us all of your experiences. We pray for your success and happiness ... and, and would like you to accept this little token of our good wishes.'

Sister Walker hands her a small, perfectly wrapped package. Penny has a lump in her throat. She sits paralysed by the emotion of the moment, barely able to hold back the tears. They are waiting for her to say something, but she cannot speak. Her friend Angela saves her.

'Go on then, Penny – open it!'

She rips open the silver wrapping paper. It reveals an oblong leather case with a gold clasp. Slowly, almost tentatively, subconsciously playing the part, she opens it.

'Pearls! Oh, they're so beautiful – I really don't know what to say ... oh, thank you – thank you all so much...'

The tears are now rolling down her cheek, and she bites her bottom lip.

'Come on, young lady,' marshals Sister Walker, not unlike a mother hen, 'have another cup of tea and just think of all that sunshine you are going to get.'

The last weekend at home is special, and everyone seems anxious to help. She is not flying out to Singapore until Tuesday evening, and she must spend Monday and Tuesday in the cruise line offices in Southampton, getting a crammed briefing and trying to learn all there is to know about working on a passenger ship. There will only be one last brief meal with the family on Tuesday evening before her father takes her to the airport.

Even Mark is subdued and less hostile than usual. He knows that he will inherit the larger bedroom when she has gone and will not have to compete for his parents' attention. But she will not be coming home at weekends anymore, at least not for a long time, and he admits to himself that he will miss her.

Although her parents had got used to the idea of her going away to work on a cruise liner, it had been a bit of a shock when she came home and told them of the sudden departure next week. Now they appear ruffled.

'I do wish you had more time to relax and prepare properly rather than this big rush, dear.'

'It will be all right. I can easily cope with it – honestly.'

She has the fresh enthusiasm and energetic optimism of youth. All she can see in front of her is excitement and adventure, and nothing can put her off.

'Now if you'll excuse me, I must get on with my packing!'

In her room her mind will not clear as she opens drawers. Packing and unpacking. It is not as easy as she thought. How many formal dresses should she take – and how many casual clothes – going ashore in all those exotic places! And the different climates! She has had so little experience.

And then she remembers that she has yet to say goodbye to her boyfriend. She can do that tomorrow, Sunday. It will not be too difficult or emotional. It was never a serious relationship, more a continuation of an innocent school romance. In reality, they were more like brother and sister. He represented her total experience with men. In that respect she had led a fairly sheltered and protected life, where study and hobbies had taken precedence. But now her mind is filled with romantic dreams – of sailing to exotic places and meeting people from so many countries – and in the deeper recesses of her sub-conscious, although she would never openly admit it, perhaps meeting the man of her dreams.

She can hardly contain her excitement as the images crowd her thoughts with fantasy upon fantasy. But then the doubts. The reality. Won't she be homesick? How easy will it be to adapt to new friends? How will she cope in a new environment that promises to be so completely different to her hospital experience in England?

The train slowly creaks to a halt in Southampton station. Penny is nervous now for the first time as she waits by the taxi rank just outside the station. She knows that two days of concentrated induction, a process which she was told normally took a week, could be stressful.

It is only a short taxi ride, and within five minutes she is standing outside the main entrance of Norsk International's offices, close to dock gate four.

'Medical department, Miss? Lift to the third floor, turn left and then it's first on your right,' says the man who opened the huge glass-fronted door leading into the grand foyer.

'Medical Department – that's it,' she mutters to herself, trying to control her intensifying nervousness. She approaches the enquiry desk.

'Good morning. My name is Miss . . .'

208

'Ah, you must be Miss Reeves. Good morning and welcome. We were expecting you. Please follow me and I'll take you to Miss Yetton's office. She is the principal nursing officer. She'll be able to tell you everything you'll need to know.'

By lunchtime, Penny's head is swimming – so many facts to digest, rules to remember, regulations, instructions, counter-instructions, procedures ... things to do and not to do, pre-cautions, suggestions, warnings ... it is all so much that she is positively bewildered and her confidence and eagerness to start the job visibly wavers. Miss Yetton, who had been at sea for years, recognises the expected confusion and self-doubt.

'Don't worry, Miss Reeves, by necessity we're cramming in what seems to be a never-ending list of do's and don'ts – but it all falls into place, I promise, once you get onto the ship and start work. And remember, you've done it all before only in a different setting. Admittedly, there may well be a little more paperwork to deal with on a voyage-by-voyage basis than you're used to in a land-based hospital – but it will become easier after a while. Don't forget, we're covering everything today and tomorrow which takes a week to complete in the in the normal circumstances – so don't panic.'

'But – but, what if I forget something – or – or, I've forgotten how to ...'

'Don't worry. There are two very experienced nurses already on board – not to mention a doctor who has been with the company for many years. They'll be only too happy to guide you ... everything will be all right – I promise.'

In the afternoon, there are still more facts and procedures to assimilate, and by five o'clock, tired and not a little confused, she breaths a long sigh of relief, wondering how she is possibly going to remember everything.

Miss Yetton accompanies her to the lift.

'You've done really well today,' she says cheerfully in a plain attempt to boost her confidence, 'we're actually ahead of ourselves, so to speak, and tomorrow morning we'll have lots of time to go through procedures for landing very ill pas-sengers and crew, or dead ones ... oh – and we mustn't forget stores requisitioning, medical supplies, etc. etc. It should be easier than today. It will also be your opportunity to meet our medical director, Dr Oliver O. Peters, otherwise known as "OOPS" – but forget I told you that – and don't ask what the "O" stands for, because nobody knows. Now, go to your hotel and get a good night's sleep – and don't worry about anything.'

The next morning she arrives ten minutes early. The receptionist greets her warmly with a friendly smile and waves her down the corridor to Miss Yetton's office. The door is slightly ajar and she can see the principal nursing officer busily writing at her desk.

'Ah, Miss Reeves, come in – nice to see you so early. Sleep well, I trust?'

'Yes, thank you.'

In fact she hadn't slept a wink all night, despite her tiredness, but fortunately the excitement and expectation of the flight to Singapore that evening has primed her ready for the final induction session.

'We'll say hello to Dr Peters first before completing our list – he has no appointments at this time of the morning. Follow me – he's only in the office next door.'

'Come in, come in. You must be Miss Reeves. Take a seat. I trust Miss Yetton has so thoroughly drilled you with our system that you don't know whether you're coming or going?'

Before she can answer, he continues.

'Of course, we're sorry it all had to be so rushed. Normally it takes a week and is far more leisurely. But as we explained in the letter, there has been a staffing crisis in the fleet and we needed to get you out as soon as possible. In fact, I should say to you that you are pretty lucky, because we are sending you directly to our flagship for your very first assignment. Normally we would expect our new nurses to work on one of the smaller ships in the fleet until they are familiar with the routine, before transferring them over to the "Grand Old Lady". It would be at least a year, in normal circumstances, before you get on to that ship – and in truth, my dear, that's the one that everybody wants to get on – so in reality you can look on this rushed induction as a bit of a bonus, if you see what I mean.'

'Thank you, Dr Peters. I am most grateful.'

210

He is friendly, and has a bluff, no-nonsense manner which puts Penny at her ease. He is older than her father, probably in his mid-sixties, and with his grey-white hair and rimless bifocal specs, has a decidedly avuncular air.

'We really should thank you, young lady, for making yourself available at such short notice. Now, are there any questions you would like to ask me – about anything?'

She'd had lots of questions saved up, but now her mind has gone blank. And then she thinks of asking about the doctor she must work with on the ship, but something tells her that it might not be an appropriate question.

'All right – go along with Miss Yetton and finish your induction. I'm sure we will be seeing you again in the future, but in the meantime, good luck, have a safe journey to Singapore and – and bon voyage.'

By lunchtime they had finished.

'That's it, Miss Reeves. I must say, you have done extremely well in the circumstances. I'm very confident that everything will go smoothly once you get on board.'

'On board'! It sounds so imminent now that she feels a transitory flutter of butterflies in her stomach.

'Personnel on the second floor will issue you with your tickets and the necessary instructions, so I suggest you make your way down there in a minute, as they are expecting you. Remember, the flight is 2200 hours – you'll get used to the 24-hour clock – and you should have plenty of time to get back home to Broadstairs and say your goodbyes.'

Penny slumps back in the chair in an exaggerated gesture of fatigue.

'Yes, Miss Reeves, you've done very well – truly. We've covered much more than I thought possible, to be quite honest...'

'I'll never remember it all, I really won't. I'm sure I'll make so many mistakes...'

'You'll be okay, I promise – we have the fullest confidence in you and your abilities. It will be easier than you imagine. Now – final things – as personnel will tell you in detail, you are booked on the night flight – I think it's British Airways – from

211

Heathrow. They've booked you in the Penta hotel in Singapore for one night, and then you will join the ship the next day when it docks. It's usually all as smooth as clockwork, believe me. An agent will meet you at the airport to take you to the hotel, and he will collect you the next morning to take you to the ship – so don't worry, you're unlikely to get lost.'

'Where is the ship going – from Singapore, I mean?'

'Well, as you know, it's on a world cruise and the next port of call, if I remember rightly, should be Pattaya in Thailand, where it anchors out in the bay for a couple of days – that's fun, I can tell you! – you'll be busy after that port! And then it sails up to China, Hong Kong first and then Shanghai I think, before going on to Japan – Tokyo and Yokohama, to be exact. After a few days in Japan it sails across the Pacific to Hawaii, where it sails around the islands for a couple of days and then it's on to the West Coast of America, San Francisco and Los Angeles etc. – you will have to study the exact itinerary after that, because I'm not sure.'

Penny is no longer able to contain herself.

'Oh, it sounds so exciting. I can't wait...'

'By the time you get to Hong Kong you should have found your sea legs and should be well and truly acclimatised. The biggest adjustment is the first week, especially after a long flight. It's all a bit different to what you've been used to in the National Health Service. To start with, all the patients, except the crew of course, are private patients and must pay for everything. But don't worry, you'll soon get used to that. As you've seen, we've spent a lot of time on the accounting procedures, and you'll realise soon enough how necessary that was. You will have much more responsibility and do more than simply nurse the patients, although of course, that should be the bulk of your work. Remember, it's just you, the doctor and two other nurses who will be looking after nearly three thousand people. There is, in fact, also a technician–dispenser who's pretty invaluable, as well as two orderlies who should help you a lot ... so, Penny, you are to become an important part of a small medical team attending to all the health-care needs of everyone on board at all times. If you remember that, then you cannot go far wrong. All in all, I think it might be more satisfying than what you've done before. And a final word – social life. You're a new face – and a pretty one at that...'

Penny blushes profusely and looks down at the floor.

'... it's a shipful of hundreds of men, a small tight community where privacy is a bit of a luxury – even for the passengers. I'm pretty sure you will be made an enormous fuss of – and I can tell you quite frankly, the wolves will be prowling from the very moment you walk up that gangway and step on board ... so, please please, Miss Reeves, don't let it go to your head. Take it all in your stride and maintain a sense of proportion. You will be fêted, I am sure of that – but stay cool, and for God's sake don't have too many late nights or drink too much. Remember, you are on duty seven days a week. Now, having said all that, enjoy your first voyage at sea as a ship's nurse – and welcome aboard!'

At dinner there is a tension which Penny senses but tries to counter with cheerful banter, but it barely works. Her parents and brother Mark are subdued. Their conversation is stilted and superficial and almost too polite for family talk.

'Now you be careful, my girl. Keep your wits about you at all times. And don't be too impressed by some of the characters – and I mean especially of the male variety – who undoubtedly will offer their undivided attention...'

The clichés that anxious parents heap upon their offspring as they are about to spread their wings come thick and fast.

'... but above all, my dear – enjoy yourself. Look on it as an enjoyable experience for a few months – get it out of your system and then come back refreshed so you can continue your career at home. Don't forget what they told you at St Thomas's – there's always a place for you, and they expect you to go a lot further in your profession.'

The words hardly register. Her mind is already transported. It has taken off and is on its way to Singapore and threatens never to return again.

'Seven-thirty. Come on, young lady, we'd better get you to the airport, otherwise the plane might go without you.'

Three hours later Penny passes through passport control. She turns one more time to wave before she disappears behind the partition. She cannot stop the tears coming. The last image is of her mother, father and brother gesticulating furiously at the barrier and blowing kisses. But now she feels she is finally on her way.

The total flying time to Singapore will be approximately 17 hours. She soon loses track of the time after following the advice of the first officer to change her watch to accommodate the next time zone.

At Bahrain she takes a plastic boarding card from the swarthy, heavily-armed security guard at the entrance to the transit area and saunters along the arcade of duty-free shops, relieved, like other passengers, to stretch her legs.

After a timeless period, like an automaton, she senses the passengers are drifting back to the boarding gate, and she dutifully joins the line, anticipating the relief of settling into her seat again and falling asleep.

'Fasten your seat belt please, make sure your seat back is upright and all cigarettes are extinguished...'

Over the next eight hours she drifts in and out of sleep, barely watching the film and not caring to eat much of the meal provided. She changes the time on her watch again and is now totally confused as to the real time of day. By the time the pre-landing announcement is made, the sky is dark again and her sense of diurnal reality is hopelessly lost.

Her tiredness and the darkness blunt the thrill she was certain she would experience on the approach to Singapore. Looking out of the window, all she can see as the plane gets lower is a gaudy kaleidoscope of neon below. It doesn't induce any significant emotion except relief that the long journey is about to end.

It seems like hours waiting in the immigration line before it is her turn to stand behind the yellow line in front of the glass immigration box. And then the middle-aged Chinese lady in uniform who sits behind the panel with just the top of her head visible, looks up momentarily and beckons with her hand. She moves forward, placing her bag on the shelf in front of the desk, passport in hand.

'How long you stay in Singapore?'

'Only for one day. I will be joining a ship tomorrow which leaves...'

'Okay, Okay.'

Stamp. Stamp. She is through.

By the time she is through the narrow exit and into the main outside hall, she is beginning to feel intimidated. The excitement and anticipation she'd felt in London had long disappeared and had now been replaced by a feeling of vulnerability and anxiety.

She looks around at the sea of faces – hundreds of them – all apparently staring at her. In between the faces, cardboard signs with names scrawled thrust in the air. It is confusing. Bewildering. And then, in the blur of signs and faces her eyes alight by sheer chance upon her name spelt out in big black letters, 'Miss Reves'. The spelling is not quite correct, but it must be her. Yes, just underneath in smaller letters the words 'Norsk Int'. She stares at it for a few seconds without moving. It is enough for the agent to approach her.

'Missy Reeves?'

'Yes.'

'Ah. So good. You are welcome to Singapore. I am Lee, agent for shipping company. You come with me. I take you to hotel, please. You give me bag.'

He is much shorter than Penny, thickset with a short neck and a head of close-cropped jet-black hair. His manner is more deferential than polite. He smiles as he scoops up her case without apparent difficulty, and his broad grin exposes a mass of unconvincing dental work which is more gold than ivory.

It wouldn't have mattered if he'd had two heads – he is warm and friendly, and is carrying her heavy case and taking her to the sanctuary of a luxury hotel.

215

'Thank you, Mr Lee.'

'This way, missy.'

The diminutive man weaves a course through the crowd at such an unbelievable speed that Penny can hardly keep up and at one point is in danger of losing sight of him altogether. She follows like a faithful dog, blind to the distractions around her.

By the kerb in the 'No waiting' area he stops by a gleaming black Toyota sedan.

'This car, missy. I put case in back.'

Penny nods in automatic approval and opens the door to the front passenger seat, feeling it would be impolite or unfriendly to sit in the rear. She sinks into the heavily padded seat as Lee gets in on the other side, now a little breathless from his exertion. He looks into the rear mirror.

'We okay now. No police. Me always lucky.'

Reclining back in the seat, Penny realises how exhausted she feels. The drive to the hotel is a blur of noise and lights from heavily congested traffic against a dense background of high buildings – concrete monoliths of starkly simple and uniform design.

'You been Singapore before, missy?' asks Lee as matter-of-factly as if he is asking Penny whether she'd ever been to Brighton.

'No. This is my first time,' she answers in a quiet and unemotional tone which might suggest she was a well-seasoned jet-set traveller rather than a raw novice who is simply extremely tired.

The hotel has 40 floors. To Penny it seems to go up into the sky forever. Lee stops outside the main entrance. A doorman appears. In a split second he has opened her door and gone to the trunk at the back. Lee gets out.

'Bellboy take your bag, missy. You okay now.'

She nods in appreciation, standing next to the revolving door.

'You have been so kind, Mr Lee. I am very grateful,' she says slowly, unconsciously enunciating each syllable of every word.

'I come nine o'clock in morning. Take you to ship.'
'Thank you. Thank you.'

The next morning Lee is prompt. At 8.55 he greets her in the lobby as she finishes checking out. Signing the chit that the desk clerk gives her makes her feel important. It is all so smooth and easy.

'Morning, Missy Reeves – you sleep well?'
'Yes thank you, Mr Lee.'
'You ready come now?'
'Yes, all packed.'
'Where your case?'
'Over there by the entrance.'
'We go now.'

Lee picks up her case and is swept through the revolving door by the immaculately turned-out doorman who beckons from the other side. A departing guest. Another cue for pay-off – and something substantial by a satisfied and rich customer. The senior doorman who facilitates their exit and opens the car door for Penny is the ultimate expert and a formidable challenge to the non-tipper. Penny is mindful of the mercenary reality and has some change which she scrambles for in her bag. Seasoned travellers of the sort who commonly frequent such expensive hotels invariably off-load a generous gratuity to the doorman as they climb into their luxury transport. They are used to good-sized tips, in the sort of range that she would hardly be expected to contemplate. She isn't well-travelled enough to be sensitive to the silent admonishment impugning her meanness with the dollar tip she believes is more than generous. The over-slamming of the car door by the vexed vulture confirms the subtle display of disapproval.

The Toyota has been standing long enough with the engine switched off for the interior to get uncomfortably warm, and it takes a few minutes to cool down after they have driven away. On her arrival the night before, she couldn't remember being aware of the humidity and heat. But then, in her transit to the hotel, she'd only spent a few brief moments in the open air, and for the rest of the time she'd been cocooned in air-conditioning. Now, as the sun is getting up quickly she is conscious of the oppressive atmosphere.

At the dock gates Lee shows his ID and is waved through into the huge container depot. The car is soon lost in a mountainous sea of steel. Stack upon stack of gigantic containers rise up immediately about them and stretch for as far as the eye can see. The way through seems impossible. It appears to Penny as a never-ending maze of complexity which Mr Lee must successfully negotiate if she is ever to reach the ship. Apart from giant cranes extending along the horizon beyond the mountains of containers, there is no sign or even suggestion of where the actual dockside is, let alone ships.

Lee seems unperturbed and, sensing Penny's apprehension, smiles and nods confidently as he steers the car around block after block of containers. Finally, he pulls the steering wheel over hard to the right and squeezes the car through a seemingly impossible space. There! Ships! And so many! Penny feels her pulse racing again as Lee straightens up and cruises slowly along the quayside parallel to the vessels, all of which appear to be container cargo ships, loading and unloading from the huge cranes hovering above them. It seems to go on forever as Penny concentrates her vision well ahead. All the ships look much the same, and there is nothing remotely resembling a passenger liner.

And then, in a split second, it appears, standing so high above all the others. She is awestruck. The veteran cruise liner displays a dimension of enormity she hadn't dared imagine as it looms up high and graceful against a scrambled horizon of cranes and high-rise buildings and a clear blue sky. Mr Lee is unaffected, it seems.

'We stop crew gangway, Missy Reeves – aft end ship.'

Penny cannot answer. She is indulging the reality of the moment as it more than matches her previous visions of fantasy. The Toyota comes slowly to a stop opposite a decidedly rickety-looking platform spanning the small gap of water between the dock and a large opening in the side of the ship. Before she gets out, Penny cannot resist straining her neck to gain a glimpse inside this huge metal monster, although from her vantage point she is only aware of blurred shapes moving in a gloomy cavernous space. It faintly alarms her.

'You get out her, Missy,' Lee says cheerfully, as if sensing her foreboding. 'Mr Venning, big boss security on gangway – he very nice man.'

She opens the door and steps out into the hot, humid atmosphere. She feels wet under her arms almost instantaneously. Lee, who has lifted her case from the trunk, drops it by the gangway.

Bob Venning, in tropical whites and displaying two and a half gold bars of rank on his epaulettes, acknowledges Lee. He has been at sea for over 35 years, most of which had been spent in the Royal Navy.

'Everything all right with you today, Lee?'

'Me okay, Mr Venning. This new nurse for ship – Missy Reeves. She come long way.'

'Nice to meet you, young lady – welcome aboard. I'll get someone to take your case to your quarters.'

'That's all right – I can manage...'

The distinguished-looking security officer winks at Mr Lee, who responds with his gold toothy grin.

'You can see she's never been on a ship this size, Lee – eh? Believe me, Miss – I'm sorry, what was your first name?'

'Penny.'

'Penny, believe me, the officers' quarters, apart from being impossible to find, would be such an obstacle for you to reach, along all the intricate little stairs and passageways, I guarantee, we would have to send out a search party to find you.'

Penny looks down sheepishly as if she has just been given her first lesson.

'Don't worry, young lady, it doesn't take that long to get your bearings – but you'd better hurry on board – otherwise the old *Empress o' the Seas* will sail without you.'

CHAPTER 9

BREAKING THE RULE

Sexual pleasure, widely used and not abused, may prove the stimulus and liberator of our finest and most exalted activities...

I regard sex as the central problem of life.

Havelock Ellis (1859–1939)

I don't pretend to understand the Universe – it's a great deal bigger than I am ... people ought to be modester.

Thomas Carlyle (1795–1881)

CHAPTER 6

BREAKING THE RULE

'This is the Purser's office. Could I have your attention please, ladies and gentlemen. Those passengers holding green cards are now free to disembark on two deck gangway, G stairway, starb'd side ... I repeat...'

Harry takes the D stairway down to 5 deck, which is the lowest passenger deck, and then walks forward to C stairway, which will take him down to the ship's hospital on 6 deck. The hospital is quiet and apparently deserted. He opens the door to the nursing station.

'Good morning, Suzanne.'

The senior sister is bent over the sink, washing instruments and talking to a girl sitting at the desk who, it appears, is hanging onto her every word.

'...so you see, Penny, if you feel the situation warrants it, even at three a.m., then don't hesitate to call the ... well, talk of the devil – here he is now – our doctor. Let me introduce you. Penny, this is Dr Lester. Dr Lester, this is Penny, Penny Reeves, our new nurse, just arrived from England.'

'How do you do, Doctor.'

'Pleased to meet you, Penny. Pleasant flight from England, I hope?'

'Yes, thank you.'

She looks directly at Harry. Their eyes meet, and for a second there is a fusion of visual pathways. He notes that she is certainly very attractive, a slim blond with fine angular features, medium height, around five feet five inches and a smooth flawless complexion free of make-up. Her thick golden hair is swept back and tied up neatly at the back with a simple white band. He takes this all in at the first glance, as he normally would react to seeing a female for the first time, but his usual predatory perception of a young attractive woman seems strangely, if only slightly, different for once.

'Suzanne has shown me round already, but I'm afraid I will get lost very easily. I cannot even remember how to get back to my cabin.'

She smiles diffidently and again looks at Harry in a way that makes him feel slightly uncomfortable, even though he feels an undeniable arousal. He laughs.

'Don't worry – it's the same for everyone. It'll take you at least a month to find your way around. There are only three places you need to find at the moment – the hospital, the officer's dining room and, of course, your cabin. The rest will come to you in time, I promise.'

'What about emergency cabin calls?'

'Don't worry. The numbers on each deck are in logical sequence, even on one side and odd on the other. If you have any trouble, then Derek or Malcolm, the hospital attendants, can take you.'

Once again, her eyes fix on Harry's and seem to bore into him with the penetration of an armour-piercing shell, impacting on the inner sanctum of his psyche. It makes him feel slightly uncomfortable and puzzled. It is most unlike his usual reaction to a beautiful young woman. Although he recognises clearly her beauty and sexuality, the feeling he experiences is not like his usual well-grooved sexual response. He deflects his gaze and turns his attention to Suzanne.

'Tea, Suzanne?'

'Oh my dear Penny, I forgot to mention the most important function of the nurse – making the tea for doctor.'

Penny hesitates for a moment and then, seeing a smile appear on Harry's face, she giggles nervously and blushes. For a second her guard is down, and there is revealed an innocent beauty which rivets Harry's attention.

'Very important, Penny,' he says with mock pomposity, 'and don't forget the biscuits.'

This time she laughs naturally and unaffectedly. Her smile is captivating, as far as Harry is concerned. She has an angular face with high cheekbones and a small, slightly upturned nose. Her chin is square and softened with the suggestion of a dimple. She feels their eyes on her, and that they are expecting her to say something.

'Have you – uuum – how long have you been at sea – uuum, I mean – how long have you been on the ship, Doctor – I mean...'

'Forever,' quips Suzanne caustically, before Harry can answer.

'A few years, Penny. Quite a few years, I must confess.'

'I didn't mean to – I mean, Doctor...'

'Don't worry, Penny. Don't worry ... now listen, let's get our protocols in order. It's first names except for formal situations in the clinic. Is that all right with you?'

'Yes.'

'Good. Now, down to business. I don't know whether Suzanne has gone through the timetable yet?'

'No.'

'Right. We meet in the ship's hospital at eight thirty every morning for the report. You've probably not met Libby yet. She's on nights. You'll meet her later, I'm sure. Anyway, I start the clinic at around nine o'clock. Crew attend until nine forty-five, and at ten o'clock we start to see passengers. There's no appointment system. It's first come, first served. Some mornings we are deathly quiet. Others, well – it's a madhouse, especially if the weather is bad on the first day out and we've got a lot of *mal de mer* – seasickness, that is.'

'Is it really that bad?'

'You mean seasickness? God, I should think so. People want to die. Down here, there are endless lines of passengers turning various shades of green who are desperate. But the injection works like a miracle, believe me...'

'What is it?'

'Good old-fashioned Phenergan – or promethazine – 37.5mg,

225

adjusted for age and size of course. Occasionally it doesn't do the trick or someone claims an allergy, so we use an alternative – Stemetil – prochlorperazine. If that fails then I'll use Largactil, you know, chlorpromazine in large doses – it never fails to knock them out.'

'How long does it last?'

'Most people only need one injection as they acclimatise by the time the drug affect has worn off. I just hope you don't get seasick yourself...'

'I've always been a good traveller.'

Her large saucer eyes fix on Harry and strip him of his defences so completely that he is almost mesmerised.

His reaction doesn't pass unnoticed by Suzanne. She has, in her more acerbic moods, described Harry as a 'bitch on heat' whenever attractive females were in the vicinity. He would invariably reply that he was in fact a dog and the male of the canine species didn't appear to exhibit any cyclical variations in sexual arousal as it was, quite naturally, the prevailing thought uppermost in his consciousness.

In fact, Suzanne was feeling a faint alarm at the effect Penny seemed to be having on Harry. She knew pretty confidently that he never ventured into the nursing staff. It might just as well have been etched on some holy tablet that sexual liaisons between departmental staff was a crime punishable by death. It was accepted tacitly by everyone that such romances could jeopardise the smooth running and harmony of such a small department.

'What are the plans today, Harry?' she says cheerfully, dismissing the unpalatable thought.

'It depends. When do we sail?'

'Midnight.'

'Good. Everybody will be off the ship all day, so it should be quiet. You can lock up and carry the bleeper. I'll call in at five o'clock to see if there are any emergencies. Can you show Penny the ropes?'

'Of course. Libby has two more nights and then she'll come on to days, but I think Penny should stay on days for a while until she's found her feet. She can start helping you in the clinic tomorrow.'

'Sounds fine by me.'

The thought fills Harry with a mixture of expectation and apprehension. Penny has already made a strong impression on him. But it is strange and rather unnerving, and different from the usual effect a female has on him. It is not even necessarily sexual in nature. It is as if there is some sort of magnetic force which he cannot resist.

The ship sails at midnight. Hundreds of passengers, many leaning perilously over the ship's rails, crowd the promenade deck, throwing rolls of streamers at the throng of people waving goodbye on the dockside 60 feet below. There is a local brass band playing – or attempting to play – a medley of nautical tunes as the huge ship slowly eases itself from the dockside. Strains of 'Auld Lang Syne' drift up on the stiffening breeze as the dock and the crowds slowly recede. The still water at the stern is churned up into a maelstrom of violent turbulence as the pitch of the propellers is altered to pull the bow of the ship round and aim it in the right direction out into the navigation channel and the open sea.

Harry has witnessed it all before, yet despite his cynicism for such contrived sentiment he cannot suppress a slight feeling of nostalgia. When at last he can no longer hear the band he turns his back on Singapore and heads for the stairway which will take him back into the bowels of the great liner and the Midship's cocktail lounge.

He is dressed in pristine white 'number tens', with the high collar tunic and epaulette insignia of the traditional Merchant Navy officer uniform worn in the tropics. Most shipping lines had discontinued the style and replaced it with a more utilitarian safari-type suit and conventional tie, but the officers of the Cunedin Line, once the take-over by Norsk International had been confirmed, had been unanimous in their determination to keep their traditional 'number tens'. For them, it was a determined gesture to preserve at least one symbol of the old seafaring traditions, traditions which they felt were being swept away by the strictly business pragmatism of the new-look shipping companies.

The Midship lounge is deserted except for the barman.

'Evening, George.'

'Good evening. Doctor. What can I get you?'

'Spritzer, please. I don't think I could take anything stronger before dinner.'

Bee-bee-bee-bee-bee-beep!

'Oh hell, that's the emergency bleep – sling over the phone please, George.'

Before the barman reaches the phone the ship's tannoy system blares out:

'Starlight! Starlight! Starlight! Cabin 8001. Cabin 8001. Starlight! Starlight! Starlight! Cabin 8001.'

Harry stands up unhurriedly, disguising any natural alarm, knowing that ninety per cent of the emergency Starlight calls turn out to be nothing more serious than a faint.

Once outside the door, he cannot suppress a sense of rising trepidation and he begins to walk rapidly, breaking into a half-trot by the time he gets to the stairs, as his conditioning tells him that there is always an outside chance of a cardiac arrest. The Starlight code over the ship's public address system is the rarely used call sign to mobilise the whole medical team on board to respond immediately to any perceived emergency. More often than not it turned out to be a simple faint brought on by over-indulgence of food and alcohol and the heat of the restaurant. But this call was from a cabin, and it makes him slightly more heedful.

By the time he has reached the Queen's Grill bar lounge he has broken into a run. At the far end he turns right, through a glass door which opens to a plush-carpeted stairway that leads up to the exclusive penthouse suites.

'Hello, Geoffrey.'

'This way, Doctor – it's one of our new joining passengers, a Mr Oldenburg. He's very elderly and – and ... oh dear, Doctor, oh dear ...'

'All right Geoffrey, calm down. Don't fret. Lead the way.'

Harry deliberately slows his pace to both galvanise himself

ready for the unexpected and to counteract the rising panic of the near-hysterical bedroom steward.

'This way please, Doctor.'

Geoffrey opens the main door to the suite. It opens into the day room.

'In the bedroom,' he says in a quivering voice, pointing through the open door. Harry walks in. It seems crowded. There are distraught-looking strangers and an old woman shrieking uncontrollably, who is most likely the wife of the prostrate figure of a man on the bed. Every member of the hospital is present. Suzanne is applying cardiac massage. Harry's mind switches into gear.

'Cardiac arrest, Suzanne?'

She is breathless and perspiring heavily. She nods without interrupting her rhythmic action. The old woman who is shrieking turns to Harry as he approaches the side of the bed.

'Are you the doctor?'

'Yes.'

'Oh please, Doctor, do something quickly ... please. I don't want him to die ... please Doctor, help him ...'

She is wailing now and cannot be consoled. Harry tilts his head towards her in an affirmative gesture and then turns towards the unconscious man. He bends over to feel the carotid pulse and gently opens an eyelid to assess the state of the man's pupils. Libby speaks.

'Apparently he collapsed onto the bed after coming out of the toilet ... he's had coronary by-pass ... oh, and three heart attacks in the past ...'

'Let's get him onto the floor – the cardiac massage will be easier and more effective. Libby, take over from Suzanne ... Brian, give me a size '8' endotracheal tube, please ... nobody attempted mouth-to-mouth, I take it?'

'No, Doctor. We all just literally arrived a few seconds before you, and ...'

'Right, Derek, bring the oxygen cylinder over here ... good. Can you – uuuuh Penny, can you attach the tube?'

Harry looks up towards Penny. Her face is serious with a

229

look of concentrated concern. But even in these circumstances – the intense distraction of the situation – Harry recognises how beautiful she looks, although any lingering indulgence of her striking features is quickly aborted by the immediacy of the events unfurling before him. She swiftly attaches the connecting piece to the oxygen cylinder. Libby is momentarily occupied with the suction machine, so Harry addresses Penny again.

'Penny, can you get a green Venflon and ampoules of adrenaline and calcium – and a bottle of soda bic'?'

'Laryngoscope please, somebody.'

Libby hands Harry the cold steel instrument that will allow him to look down into the unconscious man's throat and hopefully into his larynx. It is not an easy manoeuvre on the floor. Harry crouches over the man's head, and putting his right hand under the back of the man's neck, yanks it upwards so the chin juts out forwards. He prises open his mouth.

'No teeth,' he mutters more to himself, 'good.'

He slips the blade of the instrument over the lolling tongue. It is swollen and frothy. The strong light shines down into the back of the unconscious man's throat. Froth, froth and more froth. It is impossible to see the vocal cords through which he must aim the breathing tube.

'Sucker, please … sucker. SUCKER … anybody … Penny, PENNY – SUCKER PLEASE.'

Libby moves forward carrying the suction box and hands Penny the suction catheter.

'Quick Penny, down there in all that froth … good, good.'

Penny tentatively inserts the thin plastic tube into the man's mouth.

'Good, good, but deeper – go on, don't be frightened. Good, that's it. Well done. It's clearing now, you see …'

Harry jerks the man's head forward again more violently than before as he pushes the blade further down the laryngeal recess.

'Aaaah – good – cords. I can see the vocal cords. Quick Suzanne – tube please.'

Harry hunches over the unconscious man, who is rapidly assuming the blue-grey duskiness of death. Harry is breathing heavily now as he contorts his posture in order to peer down the thin beam of light and maintain for as long as possible the fleeting view of the dark space which appears momentarily between the vocal cords.

Now!

He thrusts boldly with the stiff plastic tube towards the gap between the cords, hoping it will not deflect and go down the oesophagus just behind. It slips down easily.

'Stethoscope please, anybody ... and attach the end of the tube, Derek, to the oxygen cylinder ... quick, please ... switch on ... let me listen ... see if we're in ... no. Damn it. Must be in the oesophagus. Let's try again. Quick. QUICKLY. PLEASE. Sucker. SUCKER. Quickly.'

Froth. Froth. Froth. Time is running out. The wailing continues in the background, but Harry is only vaguely aware of it. He pulls the neck upwards again and plunges almost wildly and not a little desperately with the tube. This time its passage seems smoother.

'Attach please, Derek ... full on. Pump the bag. Stethoscope, please ... good. Yes. Air entry both sides. Fine. Right Penny, you squeeze the bag, please – you know, two squeezes for every five chest compressions ... let me listen again, Libby.'

Libby is still kneeling over the man's chest. She is breathless and visibly sweating from her exertions.

'Suzanne, can you take over from Libby again, please? Let's see if we've got a pulse ... nothing. Adrenaline, please. Intracardiac. Paddles ... Derek, the fibrillator, please...'

Harry looks at the trace on the screen. It is a flat line. Asystole, but it could be fine VF.

'We'll try shock. Stand back everyone. 200 joules please, Derek ... stand back...'

Wham!

The body jerks violently. Harry looks at the trace. Unequivocal ventricular fibrillation.

'Shock again – 200 joules please – stand back. Stand back.'

Wham!

Ventricular fibrillation persists.

Third shock, this time 400 joules.

Wham!

Nothing.

Acidosis. Acidosis. Venflon. Where's the Venflon?

'Penny, the Venflon catheter please. Continue massage, somebody else. No veins. Sphyg please, somebody.'

There is but a suggestion of the distal cephalic vein in the forearm. Harry misses with his first attempt to insert the thick needle. Time is running out. No more veins apparent. Maybe a cut down? No time. Try the vein higher up. No good. Collapsed. Impossible. Maybe a cut down? No time. Try the ante-cubital fossa at the elbow ... success, third time lucky. Dark mauve blood slowly appears in the catheter.

'Quick. the soda bic' – switch on ... good, it seems to be running all right.'

Harry leans back on his haunches for a moment. He is aware of a mild stinging in his eyes as the sweat runs down from his forehead. He leans forward and retracts an eyelid. Pupils fixed and dilated. He's a goner. But he knows they must continue for a while longer if only for the wife, who is observing there desperate efforts in a state of utter shock and bewilderment.

'Let's try Calcium Gluconate, Penny.'

Penny hands him a syringe. For a brief moment their eyes meet, and even in the midst of this nightmarish scene Harry takes in her striking beauty and can feel a strong physical presence – as if she emits some sort of metaphysical force, a force powerful enough even to overcome the compelling distraction of the man dying at their very feet.

Kneeling awkwardly, Harry estimates the left fifth intercostal space just lateral to the lower end of the sternum. He plunges the needle down to the hilt and draws back. Nothing. He withdraws and moves the needle an inch to the right. Plunge again. Withdraw. Blood! Push down the plunger. A full ten ml of Calcium Gluconate.

'Paddles please. Let's see the trace.'

Nothing.

'Continue massage please, Suzanne. Penny, some ribbon gauze please – I'll fix the tube.'

Harry's words have a hollow ring to them, as if he has

announced in a cryptic message only appreciated by the medical personnel that it is hopeless and now they were simply going through the motions for the sake of the wife.

'Is he all right doctor? Is he all right? Doctor? DOCTOR? IS HE ALL RIGHT?'

The third plea reaches Harry's consciousness. He swivels round still on his knees and stares up at the crinkly-faced old woman.

'I'm afraid Mrs...'

Derek is standing next to her.

'...Derek, can you please take this lady next door? I'll be with you in a minute.'

The medical attendant grasps her arm firmly and leads her away into the dayroom. Harry is free to voice his impression out loud.

'Hopeless, I think, ladies, isn't it?'

'Looks like it, Harry,' Suzanne agrees, 'we've tried, at least – and pretty hard too ... and face it, we were all here quickly...'

It is self-consolation. And now they can relax. The emergency is over, and they can forget about it soon enough once the immediacy of the moment has passed. Harry ponders. For the woman next door with whom he must temporarily grieve it is the beginning of her widowhood, and she can never forget. He lets out an exaggerated sigh and looks up towards Penny. Her hair has fallen carelessly across her face. She is ruffled, and her slightly unkempt appearance only serves to make her more devastatingly attractive to him.

'Baptism of fire, eh, Penny?'

'I just cannot believe it – I mean – I had no idea...'

'"Luxury cruising", eh? You thought it was going to be one continuous cocktail party, no doubt, ha ha. Well, unfortunately people do get ill on luxury cruise liners as much as anywhere else – and some even die. But I'm sorry it had to happen so soon after you arrived. You've done very well – you'll be mentioned in dispatches.'

Penny forces an uneasy smile to acknowledge Harry's reassuring compliment, facetious as it might have seemed.

'Right,' he says, standing up and arching an aching back, 'I'd better do my duty and have a word with the lady next door. Derek, Malcolm – you'll bring the stretcher – it's not going to be easy getting him down all the stairs to 6 deck, but I'm sure you'll manage it.'

'You're not kidding, Doctor. Maybe if we prop him up in a wheelchair it would be easier?'

'Yes, that sounds a good idea. Then you can take him down D lift to 5 deck and along to C and down to 6. Hopefully there won't be too many passengers around, as they should all be at dinner. Suzanne? Can you stay with the lady after I've had a word with her? For a while, at least. It looks as though she has some friends, which will be useful ... I'll have a word with dear Geoffrey – God, he's going to be rather distraught as well ... I'll join you all in the hospital shortly after I've seen Mrs ...?'

'Oldenburg, Harry.'

'Thank you all. Everyone worked pretty hard. You did your best.'

Penny and Libby leave. Harry casually looks up to watch them go through the door. He looks away into the room, seemingly with a face of preoccupied concern with the task he is about to perform, but his thoughts and feelings are in a whirl of conflict as they disappear down the passage. A strange feeling comes over him. Perhaps it is the adrenaline of the performance which has just taken place. He is unsure – but he cannot suppress a sensation that he wants her. But it is different to the simple lustful desire he normally feels for a woman. There is another dimension to his desire. It is as if he wants to be a part of her and her to be a part of him. Possess her totally and be possessed by her. It is as if, in the short time since they met, there is already established a connecting thread that binds them.

But he is tired. It is late. Perhaps his imagination is playing tricks on him. Why should she be any different to the countless other 'pieces of arse' that he'd encountered over the years? But he cannot dispel the strange emotion he feels, which is faintly disturbing. It is compelling. He cannot recall from his repertoire of emotions ever experiencing such a response to a female. How utterly puzzling. He leans against the door frame

234

and ponders until the loud shriek from next door brings him back to the reality of the moment. God, she knows. Her friends must have realised. He gathers himself and goes through the door to perform the painful task of confirmation.

Over the next few days there are no more nerve-jangling emergencies. Routine work dominates. Clinics, the usual minor accidents, health and hygiene lectures to the crew. Social functions. Officer cocktail parties and hosting the table in the First Class restaurant – if Harry makes the effort to turn up.

Harry observes that Penny adjusts very quickly. After her baptism of fire on the first day, she appears able to take each new task in her stride. She is efficient and courteous, and soon the favourable comments from crew and passengers begin to multiply. She exudes a calm and caring professionalism in her general demeanour, and this, combined with her unquestionable ravishingly good looks, does not fail to melt the hearts of even the most cynical.

His desire for her,. not just sexual, but also the strange emotion he'd felt on the first night, has amplified considerably. But such desire engenders an uneasy conflict between emotion and logic. The golden rule echoes clearly in his mind: 'Don't tamper with the staff.'

Today, the sea is calm. The sky is a strikingly clear blue, with not a cloud in sight, and the temperature around 85 degrees. The ship is cruising leisurely in the Gulf of Thailand on its way to the coastal resort of Pattaya. Harry is wandering aimlessly around the top decks, taking the fresh air. He idly looks down from his vantage point on the helicopter deck onto the tennis court below as two girls come to join the two young officers who are already playing. Penny!

She is dressed in a white one-piece tennis outfit. It is close-fitting, and the hem barely reaches down to her upper thighs. He can see that she is already developing a healthy-looking tan. Her legs are a perfect shape. And that arse!

They cannot see him as he observes. They play. His attention is polarised to her every movement. She is very agile and athletic. Her laughter floats up and reinforces his attraction. Now she is by the net. She bends over to pick up the ball. She makes a gesture to modesty by bending at the knees, but cannot be aware that he can see her white panties and the smooth curvature of her buttocks. Perfection. Absolute perfection!

Like a salivating dog eying a juicy bone Harry allows himself the full expression of his indulgence. But then suddenly he recoils. It should not be. It must not be. He must not give in to the superficiality and transience of lust. It could cause unending problems if or when the lust was satiated and he lost interest. And then this overwhelming sexual desire for her takes on a different hue. There reappears the strange inexplicable sensation that he wants her, and feels for her in a different way – which is not sexual. It is disturbing to Harry, and he cannot recall in his emotional repertoire such feelings before. He tries to dispel it from his mind as he turns away and consciously thinks on other matters. But already his subconscious is scheming.

After the evening clinic has finished Harry announces to everyone that they are invited to his cabin the next day for pre-dinner drinks. It is not an unusual invitation and one of many which repeat at random intervals on most of the long cruises when the medical team get together socially. Only this time for Harry, there is self-deception. He is deluding himself. He will not recognise that his main purpose is to see Penny in a social setting. He knows she will be stunning and irresistible, but he cannot step off the hazardous path he appears to be taking.

The next evening Derek and Malcolm arrive first, and shortly after, Brian the dispenser appears.

'Beers all round, boys?'

'Thank you, Doctor. A Beck's will be fine,' says Brian, as the other two nod in approval.

'Where are the girls tonight?' says Harry.

'Libby says she cannot come because she's been invited to a passenger's private cocktail party – you know, Doctor, that family of rich Saudis who took over the waiting room when you saw their old man...'

'Oh yes, I remember. We must bill accordingly, ha ha.'

'Suzanne should be here shortly ... and Penny said she'd be late because of aerobics.'

'Fine.'

Aerobics! An image of Penny's perfect torso in a slinky leotard looms irrepressibly in Harry's mind. He masks any reaction.

'Good for her. Health and efficiency and all that – marvellous ... aah, here's Suzanne. Triple G and T for you, I suppose, Miss Richards?'

'That'll do nicely, thank you, Doctor.'

They talk aimlessly for a while. Harry hides his mild anxiety and impatience at Penny's non-appearance. He steals a glance at his watch. 8.25. Must go to dinner in 20 minutes, and still no sign of her. The conversation is dull. Harry is unable to play the host and breathe some fire into it, because of his preoccupation. And then there is a faint knock at the door. Harry feels flutterings in his stomach. He goes to the door and opens it slowly, hesitantly. It is Penny. His imagination and expectation are surpassed by the apparition standing before him. Dazzling. Breathtaking. Words and descriptions wait to spring forth, but everyone simply stares in silent admiration.

She is a stunning beauty. That is unquestioned. But she effuses an additional, less easily definable, quality of beauty that is in the possession of a rare few individuals. It is as if she radiates some sort of metaphysical aura which, Harry convinces himself, he is particularly attuned to, and in complete empathy with. He cannot say if the others feel the same way, but their response undeniably displays the effect she has made on them before she has even entered the room.

Harry comes down to earth and plays the host.

'Penny – lovely to see you – so glad you could make it.'

His tone and inflection gently admonish her, thinly disguising his disappointment that it is almost time to leave for dinner.

'What can I get you?'

'Something soft. I don't drink – alcohol, that is.'

She is radiant. Virginal in the purity she effervesces. Harry is pleased she doesn't drink. It only reinforces his fast-growing infatuation for her as a seemingly untainted spirit.

'Here you are – tonic with ice and lemon.'

'That's fine. Thanks.'

Derek, Malcolm and Brian get up to leave.

'Thank you, Doctor. We have got to get to the galley, otherwise we won't get any supper tonight.'

'See you tomorrow, fellahs.'

After ushering the three men out, Harry turns to face the two women.

'Girls, I'm tempted to join you in the Officers' Mess tonight.'

'Your table in the restaurant would miss you, Harry,' provokes Suzanne with a glint in her eye. She knows he finds it a chore, a forced social commitment, an unwritten expectation and a code of practice indelibly etched into the traditions of the Cruise Lifestyle.

'Actually, they're not too bad a bunch at the moment – except perhaps silly old Lulu – you know, the Camel heiress. She's always drunk. Fortunately she hasn't wet herself yet, not at the table anyway, and hasn't insulted anyone.'

'But honestly, Harry, do you ever talk about anything interesting – you know, sex, drugs – crime, that sort of thing – it might at least help the time pass quicker?'

'Yes Suzanne, occasionally we do. I remember recently, when I suggested that drugs should be legalised and all arms dealers strung up from the nearest lamppost, it didn't exactly go down too well. It didn't really fit with their neat philosophy of how the world should be run.'

'Do they ask lots of silly questions, Doctor, I mean, Harry?'

Penny is self-conscious and blushes furiously. To Harry, it is exquisite.

'Questions! Questions! God. So many questions! And always the same, week after week – from the newly joining passengers, as if from a script the travel agent gives them. Same lines, only different people. It drives me barmy.'

'You love all the attention, I'm sure, Harry,' says Suzanne caustically.

'Actually, things got a little embarrassing when they asked me whether I had any children, and I said – not being married, of course I didn't have any, but then – as an afterthought, I confessed that I probably had one or two somewhere around the world...'

'Yes, I bet you've left your calling card in a few places – it's called wild oats, I believe.'

'Seriously, things got very uncomfortable when I told them about my activities as a sperm donor when I was a medical student – God, I dread to think ... it must be well over twenty years ago now ... most of them thought it was disgusting and couldn't believe what I was telling them, especially when we worked out how many potential offspring I might have sired.'

'Yes, Harry, I agree with your table guests. What a terrible thought. One of you is enough!'

Penny is not able to contribute much to this frivolous banter between Suzanne and Harry, and looks decidedly uncomfortable. Harry is aware.

'Take no notice of her, Penny,' he says.

He looks at his watch.

'It's five minutes before nine. You'd better get to the mess or you'll miss dinner ... listen, why don't we meet after dinner – say around eleven o'clock in the Lido? Who knows, you might even get me on the dance floor.'

'Fat chance,' sneers Suzanne.

They drain the last drops from their glasses and move towards the door.

'It's agreed, then? The Lido club at eleven?'

At the table Harry is as unpredictably quiet as he was voluble the last time he attended.

'Where have you been, Harry?' Hal and Desmond and Louise say almost simultaneously.

'I thought you knew, quite honestly. The entertaining officers never come down in port or the night before arrival – and unfortunately, the other nights I was pretty busy. I'm sorry. Did you all miss me?'

239

'Sure did,' quips Desmond with a highly suggestive twinkle in his eye. Harry is undecided whether to entice him or not. Another night maybe, when he is more in the mood and not distracted by thoughts of Penny.

'I hear you had a serious emergency on the night of our departure from Singapore. Is that right?' says Melville cheerfully, expecting a full report.

'Yes, tell us all about it,' chips in Hal enthusiastically, more anxious to hear any gory detail than express concern for a fellow passenger. He probably already knows the full story inside out and backwards, but wants to hear it from the horse's mouth. Harry is reluctant to nourish his morbid trait and will not elaborate more than the minimum.

'He was an elderly chap – advanced heart disease, I'm afraid. We did our best, but we couldn't save him.'

'I believe he'd had a coronary by-pass, hadn't he?'

'Yes.'

'High-risk factor, I guess then?'

'Yes. Is there anything good on the menu tonight?'

They can see that Harry is not in the mood for conversation, and there is a prolonged silence. Desmond decides to liven up the proceedings.

'You know the other night we were talking about AID, you know that baby farming business...'

'Yes.'

'Well, I saw this picture in a veterinary magazine...'

'Yes, Desmond,' says Harry tightly, with a suitable inflection to caution him not to embarrass the table.

'...it was an article on artificial insemination in the cattle industry, and they showed this prize bull which had sired over ten thousand calves.'

'That's truly mind-boggling,' says Harry in thinly disguised sarcasm.

'I just thought I'd mention it so it put into perspective your own modest contribution to animal husbandry.'

'I appreciate that very much, Desmond,' says Harry, hoping that will be the end of the subject.

'But the fascinating thing was this picture of the contraption

240

they used to get the bull's samples, so to speak . . .'

'I don't want to hear,' interjects Edith Baxter forcibly, 'I was disgusted with the conversation the other night.'

But Desmond is going to tell Edith, whether she likes it or not. He hesitates before continuing, sensing that the table is not particularly enthusiastic. The Rosenthals divert to their roll and butter and are already signalling to the busboy for more. Louise and Melville appear decidedly uncomfortable and not eager to hear details about a contraption that milks semen samples from a prize bull. Hal Van Dicky's square jaw juts out and his face is noncommittal. There is one empty chair because Lulu hasn't turned up.

Edith seems to be in the process of transferring the vitriol she'd formulated and carefully nurtured for the Rosenthals to Desmond, who is beginning to represent something far more threatening and hideous to her sensibilities. Harry feels it expedient to mediate before a minor war erupts.

'All right Desmond, describe for us, if you must, what you've seen in the veterinary magazine – and then I suggest we drop the subject.'

Desmond's eyes are positively gleaming now, and his cheeks are flushed.

'Well, it's like this. There's a wooden frame structure, a bit like a wooden horse, I guess – or I should say cow, of course – ha ha – and there is a cowhide stretched over it – and at the back end, so to speak, there's a sort of – well – I guess it is an artificial rump with a large hole in the middle which the bull mounts. It looks as if the hole is lined with a sort of rubber seal, and it leads quite a distance down into a glass container. When the bull gets excited – I really don't know if the contraption makes him excited – anyway, when he gets excited, he is encouraged to mount this rather docile cow and, and . . .'

As the beads of sweat run down his forehead and his voice takes on a tremulous quality, it is plain to see that Desmond is in danger of revealing unashamedly the sexual excitement he is inducing in himself.

'. . . and he pushes his . . . his . . .'

'Penis,' says Harry.

'Yes ... uuuh, thank you Harry ... his, uuuh – penis into the hole and then ...'

'Thank you, Desmond. I think we all get the picture,' interrupts Harry, to prevent Edith throwing her roll at him.

Desmond purses his lips and nods his head, expecting some sort of response, but there is nothing but stunned silence.

Harry looks at the wall clock on the opposite pillar. 9.15 – and they haven't even begun the main course. The thought of another hour at least in a situation deteriorating by the second fills him with anguish. He cannot even bother to introduce a fresh topic agreeable to all. Instead, he will plan his hasty exit. Soup and then auto-activate his bleeper surreptitiously. That was always his last-ditch lifeline when social circumstances became really intolerable. He can then go to the library before meeting the girls at the Lido bar at eleven o'clock. But he'll make an extra effort for a few minutes until the timing is right, so nobody will suspect anything.

'Everybody enjoy Singapore?'

'Great shopping,' says Louise cheerfully, happy to take the initiative.

'Did you think it was cheap?' enquires Harry.

'Some things, I guess.'

'I got some great new golf clubs,' says Melville gleefully, like a child with a new toy, 'much cheaper than at home.'

'They must be cheap, then,' Harry states with earnest conviction. 'How about you, Hal? Any unbelievable bargains?'

'Wasn't too happy. They were too tough in the hi-fi and camera shops – although I did manage to beat down an old fellah selling socks on the quayside just before I got back on the ship, so I got one bargain at least.'

'Was he a little wizened chap – about 120 years old, bent double and with a crutch, dressed in a ragged filthy jacket and very baggy trousers which were also torn and filthy?'

'That's him. Did you get some socks too?'

'Yes, I did. After all, he stood right by the gangway – not a bad sales pitch, I'd say. You couldn't really miss him.'

'What did you give him?'

242

'What he asked for – fifty cents a pair.'

'Fool you, Harry. You're easy meat. Far too soft. You ruin it for everyone else.'

In fact, Harry had given the wretched old man a crisp ten-dollar bill for a couple of pairs only. His desperate condition and pitiful image had made Harry cringe with guilt as he had walked up the gangway behind a couple of obese passengers. They were loaded down with piles of totally unnecessary luxury items, which they'd probably discard once they got home. The total cost would most certainly have enabled the poor old man to spend his precious last days on earth in dignified comfort.

Bleep! Bleep! Bleep!

'Damn. I'm sorry, folks. Work is never done.'

Harry contrives a genuinely annoyed face, polished by years of practice.

'Excuse me a moment while I answer that...'

He gets up and walks briskly to the Maitre d's desk at the door to the restaurant.

'Good evening, *Dottore*.'

'Evening, Romero. I'll just use your phone, if I may.'

Harry dials the hospital.

'Hello, Derek. It's only me. Nothing is happening down there, is it?'

'No. We didn't call you, Doctor. All is quiet ... are you in the restaurant again?'

'You know the drill, Derek.'

Harry puts the phone down.

'Romero – do me a favour please, can you? Give the table my apologies ... you know, it's an urgent matter in the hospital.'

'Say no more, *Dottore*.'

Obscured by another pillar, they cannot see Harry as he turns and heads out of the restaurant. He will find a quiet spot in the far corner of the library where nobody is likely to disturb him, where he can aimlessly thumb through any one of a large number of giant-sized books with beautiful glossy pictures which are found in that section.

Soon he is comfortably nestled into a soft leather recliner, cradling a mammoth tome on the flora and fauna of the Antipodes. Within minutes his eyes have closed and he begins to fantasise. He sees Penny appearing like a ghostly apparition from a grey swirling mist. She is naked and floats towards him. She smiles faintly as she comes close and envelops him in an embrace. He pulls her onto him tightly and they kiss passionately. And then there is a blank. The fantasy stops suddenly. It will not move to the next frame. His eyes open involuntarily. It is as if he dare not visualise the ultimate passion and the sweet ecstasy it might yield.

He cannot understand why his mind denies him such a natural indulgence with a girl everybody agrees is ravishing beyond compare. She clearly has a marked effect on him, but his natural reactions of simple sexual desire seem to be inhibited in some mysterious way.

Fed up with the pictures of marsupials and aborigines, he picks up a large world atlas which might distract his confused thoughts. He flicks through the pages at random, stopping at countries and places he has been. Memories are invoked. Rich images of people, places and events. He relaxes again, and his eyes close and he falls asleep.

'Doctor, we're closing now. It's eleven o'clock.'

Jane Appleyard, the librarian, gently rocks his shoulder.

Harry wakes and sits bolt upright as if he is emerging from a nightmare.

'Where am I? Oh Jane, I'm sorry. I must have been dreaming.'

'Don't worry, Doctor, but we are closing now.'

'Of course, of course. I'm going. What time is it? Aah, eleven. I must be gone ... see you.'

The Lido bar is a huge area at the aft end of the ship on one deck. On the starboard side, there is a fair-sized swimming pool over which spans a special roof which can slide open in hot weather. Scattered around are deck chairs, sunbeds, tables and parasols. On the port side is a large rectangular bar which serves on four sides, and in the middle between the pool and bar is a raised wooden dance floor. The DJ is playing old Sixties rock music. It is one of the special revival nights which take place at least once a week.

Harry stands at the large glass-doored entrance and surveys the scene. It is crowded, and what few young passengers there are on board have congregated in the bar area. It is a chance to socialise with the ships' officers who are conspicuously out in force, or as Harry might prefer to say, hunting in packs. It is early yet. One or two couples gyrate in an inhibited jerky fashion in the centre of the disco floor under the rotating multi-coloured light.

Harry scans again. The overall lighting is subdued and in some corners virtually dark. He sees an arm waving on the far side. It appears to be Suzanne with Libby and Penny. Suzanne must have locked the nurses' station, which is normally open on a twenty-four-hour basis, and told the bridge duty officer where she can be contacted. Harry smiles and heads for their table.

'Good evening again, ladies – the three wise virgins – may I join you?'

Libby pulls out a chair.

'Three certainly. Wise? – I reserve judgment on that. Virgins? – no comment.'

Suzanne and Libby laugh easily. Penny forces a polite smile. She is still unused to the seemingly crude familiarity displayed by the others. She is a few years younger than Suzanne and Libby, and it is hard for her to fall in with their demeanour. Although she seems comfortable enough with these two well-travelled adventurers, Harry can sense her feeling of vulnerability, if not inadequacy, compared to them. He wishes he could reassure her that she more than compensates for her perceived failings with her freshness and natural innocent charm. She sits demurely on one side, slightly separated from the other two.

'Not getting lost so much now, I hope?' Harry says casually, trying to draw her into conversation.

'Oh, I am. Yesterday I was looking for the gym and ended up in the control room halfway down the working alley.'

245

'You found the tennis court the other day.'

'Yes! We played after lunch. It was great. Two of the engineers invited us.'

Harry senses a resurgence of the twinge of panic he'd felt when he'd watched her, unseen from the upper deck. The wolves were sniffing then, already – but then Harry knew they would be.

'Yes. I saw you.'

'Oh, did you?'

'I was up on the top sun deck – the helicopter deck to be exact, so you wouldn't have noticed me.'

Suzanne's antennae are out.

'With binoculars, I suppose, Doctor?'

'Unfortunately not,' replies Harry, parrying the thrust decisively, 'not a bad tennis player, are you?'

'I need more practice,' Penny says modestly.

Harry indulges an image of her picking up the ball at the net.

'Well, I don't think you need much practice.'

The subterranean sexual innuendo which, for once, Harry hadn't intended draws the predictable response from Suzanne.

'YOU certainly don't need any practice, do you, Doctor?'

'I'm sure I don't know what you mean – I hardly play tennis anyway. It's not my game ... you know that ... I mean ...'

Harry splutters and looks embarrassed. He is annoyed at the girls that they might paint a picture of him as an inveterate womaniser in front of Penny. Suddenly two figures in white officers' uniforms appear from the shadows as if out of thin air.

'Ladies.'

They know Suzanne and Libby well, and without even a minimum of formality, pull them up from their chairs, pre-empting any refusal.

'Go on,' says Harry, sensing an opportunity to be left alone with Penny, 'you both need the exercise.'

They join the other couples now filling the dance floor. Harry's eyes follow them. Penny sits silently.

'They'll be gone for the night, I'm afraid.'

'Really?' Penny says with a look of genuine puzzlement.

''Fraid so.'

'Do you like dancing?'

The dreadful chore is unavoidable now. In usual circumstances Harry is able to minimise or even evade the ritual of disporting himself on the disco floor. Invariably, it literally puts him under the spotlight and provides enough evidence, innocent or otherwise, to set the tongues wagging about his latest conquest – real or imagined.

'Well? What are you waiting for? Let's go.'

Harry compensates for his natural unease by acting over-enthusiastically. He simply has to accept that many eyes will be following his every movement.

He leads Penny and aims for the heaving throng on the dance floor in as casual a manner as he can. There is only space on the perimeter, so maximum exposure is unavoidable.

They both start to move, jerking about in a restrained and stiff fashion. Harry is very uncomfortable. He steals a glance at Penny, who seems to be moving in a slightly less restrained manner, but he knows that she can sense his discomfort and self-consciousness. And then suddenly, as if Harry's awkward discomforture is appreciated by the DJ, who enjoys his game of social manipulation, the loud, fast rhythm changes abruptly.

'Now ladies and gentlemen, a golden oldie...'

There is not a record that Harry can recall as ever being slower than the one that starts to play. Most of the couples leave the dance floor, and the few that remain sidle up to each other in a close embrace and smooch. But there is smooching and smooching. If it is polite non-sexual smooching, the torsos and most certainly the genital regions hardly touch. It is as if there must be an indiscernible gap which separates and eliminates the risk of a tactile response.

It is how Harry starts with Penny. But as they come necessarily closer, her smell hits his olfactory sensors, setting off a whole gamut of subcortical reflexes. Harry is in danger of being driven by his baser instincts, regardless of the prominent social exposure. Warning bells! Not here, for heaven's sake –

247

in front of so many prying eyes who will make such a meal out of it. Remember the inviolable caveat.

It is too late to impose such cold-blooded restrictions. Her aroma locks him in as firmly as if a computer sequence had been initiated by the flick of a switch. His hands move subtly and slowly, so as not to cause alarm. Stealthily, they massage her back, softly and non-threateningly, before moving imperceptibly down to her waist. That is as far as he dare go in the circumstances. The buttocks would definitely be a no-go area at this early stage and in such a highly exposed social setting. He would never hear the end of it – and besides, it would be too big a gamble to take with Penny.

Harry is content with her waist. It is narrow and firm and muscular.

Stirrings. Groin awakes. An unconscious softness rapidly escalates to a very conscious firmness. Pelvic girdle automatically grinds forward, and the firm bulge nestles snugly in her matching curve. The indiscernible gap is obliterated at a stroke, and nobody observing is any the wiser. Nothing that might be viewed as unsavoury or risqué can be interpreted from their slow and easy progress across the centre of the dance floor. Yet Harry is confident that she appreciates the surreptitious pleasure of subtle genital contact. Harry feels a gentle counter-grind. She is enjoying it!

Her dress is thin and hugs her figure, and her bra is even thinner. Such firm breasts! Such tactile pleasure! Danger! Firmness progressing to hardness. Stop pelvic grind, gentle as it is. She understands and acknowledges with the slightest of pelvic shifts.

Harry's mouth comes close to an ear. The urge to kiss her neck is irresistible. He pecks half-heartedly. She doesn't start, but Harry pulls his head up and their eyes meet for a second.

'Shall we sit down?' he says, hoping that the receding genital bulge is not too noticeable.

Their table is empty. Suzanne and Libby have definitely flown. Harry and Penny sit down and sip their drinks silently. They stare at the couples dancing. It is late, and they are both

248

tired. Minutes of extended silence pass, made easier by the loud music. When it stops, Harry turns to Penny.

'I'll walk you to your cabin?'

She nods and pushes her chair back immediately. Eyes follow their exit. Harry can think of nothing to say to her as they walk, and he feels tense and awkward. He senses she is uneasy in starting anything between them. They reach her cabin and she places the key in the door.

'Bright and early tomorrow, then,' he says as if there is no tension. She turns.

'Goodnight, Harry.'

He cannot stop his hands going to her waist. He pulls her gently towards him. She doesn't resist, and their lips naturally meet. It is a restrained and short kiss, although sensuous enough to transmit an intended message.

'Goodnight, Penny. Sleep well.'

In bed, Harry fantasises. There is an irrepressible desire to convert the forbidden fruit into carnal reality. The temptation is overwhelming. Harry compares Penny to the instant disposable sexual commodity of Thailand, where the ship will call in a few days. Luscious creatures of exquisite sexual delight they might be, but it seems that Penny's sexuality has a more indefinable quality, an enigmatic dimension which only serves to intensify the force of his attraction to her. It is far more than the carnal receptacles of Pattaya. They are merely designer fuck machines formulated for instant sexual gratification. There is a reluctance to recognise in Penny a 'lust-inducing quotient' that he might compare with the bar girls of Bangkok or Manila, but if she has such a base quality it is immeasurably enhanced by an element of innocence and purity which makes her all the more ravishing and desirable.

He cannot remember when, if ever, he has had such a feeling for a woman. But it is like a mixture of pain and pleasure – which is confusing his usual *modus operandi*. In simple crude terms he wants to fuck her desperately, just as he might fuck a whore – but he also wants to put her on a pedestal, and somehow not include her in the general category

249

of penile receptacle designed primarily to instantly satiate his lust. It is as if he wants to experience her undoubted sensuality to the full, but doesn't want to violate her in any way – and having sex would be a violation.

On the one hand she is a sex object like any other female, designed for his sexual gratification. But on the other hand, there is a conflicting discomfiture which he cannot dispel. It is as if she represents something more than just an avenue for his carnal indulgence. It is undoubtedly a novel feeling for him and is disturbing his well-established pattern of behaviour with females.

As Harry drifts into sleep his fantasy assumes control as he mentally rehearses his sexual approach, brushing aside and temporarily burying the uneasy obtrusive feelings in the deeper recesses of his subconscious.

The morning brings from the self-appointed social commentators of the ship the winks and nudges, the predictable interpretations and speculations of the previous night's events, innocent as they had appeared. Harry is used to it, and normally such prying interest flies right over his head. But today, he feels uneasy and super-sensitive that Penny might be classified as simply another quantum of carnal fodder.

He intends to maintain his silence and dignity, but is well aware that the gossip, the half-truths, not to mention the pure inventions, could provide more than enough raw material to be processed and woven into the intricate social fabric of the ship's community. Like a priceless crude oil, it would then be refined through countless recycling processes until it represented the purest high octane of truth to fuel the complex web of social behaviour on board.

In the clinic, Suzanne and Libby are diplomatic and discreet. They are sensitive to the consequences of an intra-departmental romance and can be counted upon to play down or even deny such an occurrence. Harry is pleased to see that Penny displays a similarly discreet air as if nothing had passed between them the night before. This morning she has been assigned to assist Harry in the clinic, ushering patients in and out. Occasionally she disappears into the sick bay next door to give an injection or apply a dressing. He dare not allow his eyes to fix on her for more than a fleeting fraction of a second, lest his smouldering sexual impulse is ignited.

It is routinely busy as mornings go, and by 11.30 the clinic has finished. Suzanne had gone to bed after the morning report, as she is on night duty. Libby is called to make a cabin visit on a mild case of Alzheimer's disease whose incontinence is becoming more troublesome. Harry leans back in his chair with a mug of tea and toast that has been brought by Derek.

'I missed breakfast this morning,' he says in an unaffected manner, as if the previous night had been a dream of no consequence.

'I must admit, I scoffed a full English breakfast in the Mess,' she says, looking straight at him, 'my appetite on the ship seems to be increasing out of all control – I'm sure to put on weight if I am not careful.'

'It's the sea air – happens to everyone, I'm afraid. But you needn't worry, with all that exercise you do in the gym – and face it, your genes have given you a pretty good head start.'

Harry winks and allows a gentle smile to reinforce his first prolonged eye contact of the morning.

'What are you plans this afternoon, then – tennis again?'

'Yes. We've got a foursome organised. I'm really looking forward to it.'

Damn those two randy young engineers! They're becoming a definite threat, but there seems little he can do. Before he can consciously evaluate what he is going to say, he speaks.

'Penny – would you like to come round for a drink tonight – in my cabin, that is?'

In the silence before she responds, Harry realises that he has hastily, against his better judgment, showed his hand, perhaps prematurely, even though he has not elaborated any clearly defined strategy. But he knows he needs to pre-empt the wolf pack of eager young officers snapping at her heels. It is necessary to get her onto his ground, his territory, where he can maximise his advances to her. He hopes that, despite this

251

sudden and unexpected invitation to the intimacy of his cabin, she will be interested enough to respond positively, without any feeling of alarm at the possible consequences.

She looks up in surprise. Her eyes shine brightly and her lids flutter for a moment. She falters.

'Uuuuh – well – uuuh – I, that is, we – Libby and myself have been invited to a – uuuh, cocktail party and...'

She is flustered and Harry agonises for a moment, although her eyes definitely say 'yes'.

'...all right Harry, yes, I would like that ... it would be fine. I can always go with Suzanne another night ... what time shall I come?'

'Good. That's settled then ... after dinner. Let's say around ten o'clock, if that is not too late.'

'No. That's fine.'

'There's a good in-house video showing. It will be nice to relax "at home" for a while.'

'Sure. That's fine ... do you want to play tennis with us this afternoon?'

Harry is tempted to sacrifice his siesta for once, but he knows that the young engineers will be there and he cannot afford to give them any opportunity to appear as rivals, combatants in an arena in which they would most certainly triumph. Their athletic prowess on a tennis court would most certainly eclipse anything he could offer. No. He'd play his own game at his own pace and on his own territory, in his own inimitable fashion.

'No, thanks. It's vital that I get my little siesta. I'm up at five thirty most mornings, so I really need an hour after lunch.'

At dinner in the restaurant, Harry is silent and brooding.

'You seem preoccupied,' says Desmond.

'It's been a busy day, Desmond – and a long one. In fact, I still have some important paperwork to finish off – you know, medical reports on crew members that I must have ready by the next port. So, I think I'll give coffee a miss tonight and ask you all to excuse me. I hope I'll be better company for you tomorrow.'

Harry gets up to leave. He can see that they are a little perplexed at his minimal contribution this evening.

'See you all tomorrow – have a good evening.'

Within minutes he is back in his cabin. He changes into a loose-fitting tracksuit. He looks at his watch nervously. It is 9.55. He puts on a Debussy tape and sits back to wait for Penny's arrival.

There is a knock. It is precisely ten o'clock. Harry jumps up and opens the door. She is truly stunning. Her hair, her skin, her smile, her smell – her whole being. She intoxicates him like no other woman before.

'Sit down. What can I get you?'

'A Diet Coke, please.'

'Of course, you don't drink – very wise.'

He pours himself a light beer.

'Enjoy dinner?'

'Yes. It was pretty lively in the Mess tonight.'

'Yes, I can imagine,' he says, visualising the skulking hyenas as they became bolder and bolder in their feverish desire to corner their quarry.

'When you've been at sea a while you'll appreciate a quiet evening away from the crowds.'

She sits opposite Harry in the reclining chair, her legs crossed and her knee-length dress riding up slightly to just above her smooth, rounded and well-tanned knees. Harry cannot suppress a lurid thought of what lies out of sight a little further up under her flimsy dress. Lest it show on his face, he deletes such erotic imagery from his immediate consciousness and continues the conversation.

'The day after tomorrow we arrive in Pattaya. That's an experience, I can tell you.'

'Yes, I've already heard. It sounds quite terrible – but I'm sure it is very exciting, I imagine – if you're a man, anyway!'

Harry laughs but is careful not to draw any conversation about the major activities of Pattaya, in case he reveals his own

253

intimate indulgences over the many years he has been going
there.

'I'll take you ashore if you like.'

He knows she must have been invited by half the officers in
the Mess, so he quickly elaborates on his invitation before she
can think about the answer.

'We can go for lunch – I know an excellent seafood place not
far from where the launch drops us off. It's situated on the
water – a sort of restaurant on stilts, with a beautiful view of the
bay. The cuisine is really very good – and the risk of food
poisoning pretty minimal – at least it has been the past half-
dozen times I've been there.'

'That sounds great.' Penny could hardly have refused after
that dissertation.

'Good. We should be able to get off by midday. Clinics are
normally quiet in port.'

Harry leans forward to place his glass on the coffee table.
He knows that sooner or later he is going to have to make a
move. As his head comes closer to her knees he smells her
sweet body aroma. It provides the necessary spark to ignite
his simmering arousal. He stands up unexpectedly without
speaking. Her eyes follow him with a faint alarm. Stooping
down slightly, he gently grasps one of her hands, which are
clasped and resting on her knees. He pulls her upwards, with
a carefully controlled force – strong enough to indicate the
firm intention but light enough for him to react to any
sensation of resistance. She stands easily and faces him. Any
alarm or puzzlement have evaporated by the time she has
reached full height. It is a tacit acceptance to Harry that she
will allow him to hold her.

There is total cooperation as their lips lock and their bodies
come together tightly. His genital reaction is unrestrained, as is
the pelvic grind. This time there are no prying eyes to censor.
His hands move swiftly to her buttocks. She is also cognizant of
the fact that there is no audience, and responds positively to
his pelvic pressure.

Again, Harry's thoughts swirl in confusion. He feels exquisite
pleasure, but it is tainted by a sense of guilt and concern. It is a

feeling that he doesn't want to despoil her untainted innocence, to chalk her up as simply another sexual statistic. It is a very rare – if not entirely novel – reaction. Penny senses a subtle reticence as he holds back.

'Are you all right?'

'Yes – yes, of course. I'm fine.'

They kiss again, and this time the passion rises swiftly to obliterate all negative thoughts.

'Let's sit on the couch,' Harry whispers.

They embrace again and Harry pulls her on top of him as he falls back into the niche between a cushion and the back of the sofa. His hand finds the back of her knees. The skin is soft and smooth. His hand moves upwards towards the back of her thigh. She does not resist. In a way, Harry wishes she would. He is now locked into the full sexual attack, but he is still vaguely aware that something is not quite right – and then his hands are smoothing over her firm buttocks.

Her panties are thin transparent cotton and very skimpy – barely covering the essentials of her genital anatomy. She wriggles her pelvis unconsciously. His fingers are probing her most intimate area beneath the thicker cotton gusset. Despite the extra thickness it is soaked through with her sexual secretions. A finger finds a hairy edge. It slips effortlessly under and is directed by natural contours into a hot, wet orifice. There is a groan.

'No. NO, NO. Please, Harry. No...'

She pulls away.

He realises. This is all too fast for her. She is not used to it – the shipboard dimension where time is compressed. Intimacies in a relationship which might take weeks or months ashore, can occur quite naturally in a matter of days on board a ship. But she is not yet used to sea time.

Harry sits back unperturbed. His erection is painful – and obvious to Penny.

'Harry, oh Harry – I'm so sorry. You must think I'm...'

'That's all right. I understand. I should apologise to you – really...'

'...and besides, I don't have any contraception ... and...'

255

'We might look into that,' Harry says matter-of-factly.

'I'm a bit frightened. I've never felt so ... so ... well, physically involved before. Quite honestly, I confess, I've only had sex once before, with my boyfriend at home ... it wasn't much fun, truly ... neither of us knew what we were doing...'

Penny blushes and looks down at the floor.

'What can I say? You make me feel so hot ... and...'

Harry pulls her head onto his chest and kisses the back of her neck delicately.

'Don't worry, my dear – there's plenty of time.'

There is a more than faint smell of raw sewage in the warm, humid air as the launch approaches the pontoon. Harry and Penny can already make out clearly the peddlers selling everything from stuffed cobras to T-shirts with personalised logos, waiting like a barely constrained squadron of vultures about to gorge on a vulnerable prey.

They are not on the first launch of the day. That had been hours earlier, and had been full of elderly American passengers who had boarded a couple of waiting luxury coaches which had whisked them away on a tour including a Buddhist temple, a snake farm, elephants pulling teak logs, traditional temple girls dancing and lunch in a five-star hotel. They will not see, or indeed be remotely aware of, the most important industry in Pattaya – or Thailand for that matter – sex. But then it is a principally nocturnal business. They will all be safely tucked up in their beds back on the ship when the true face of Pattaya appears at its gaudy best.

The nocturnal awakening of this sex emporium is a glittering explosion of noise and colour – when the sleeping slum emerges from its dull, grey daytime camouflage and transforms into a pulsating neon world where the delights of erotic fantasy and illusion are suitably reinforced by the reality of the sexual merchandise on offer.

They step ashore, and Harry leads Penny aggressively through the gauntlet of traders, ignoring their repeated exhortations, and heads towards the main street. Gusts of hot wind generate minor vortices of dust which swirl up from the dry, potholed road. The place is deserted. It is like a ghost town. Harry looks at his watch. One p.m. Siesta time. The bars are empty except for the few diehard dipsomaniacs who are seen slumped in various corners, committed to pouring even more poison down their inflamed gullets before the day is out.

Between the bars are innumerable tailors' shops who promise made-to-measure suits and dresses, guaranteed delivery within 24 hours at a fraction of the Western price. The proprietors are in the main Sikhs, who in their grand-looking turbans and fancy silks look strangely incongruous in such a seedy setting. The shoe shops offer hand-made snakeskin and crocodile shoes, exotic and flashy-looking, with no apologies to the conservation movement.

And then there are the lapidary shops. Emeralds. Rubies. Diamonds. Sapphires. Jade. Every species of precious stone imported from the remote mining fields of Australia to be expertly fashioned by skilled craftsmen into exquisite costume jewellery to suit every taste.

The small children are out in force, even at siesta time. Their mentors cannot risk missing the opportunity of waylaying tourists, who they know will be out in the midday sun. Dressed in rags, grinning from ear to ear, they sell chewing gum and single cigarettes to locals but beg directly from anyone who looks remotely foreign. Penny is disturbed at first, but Harry reassures her that after a while she will become immune to their constant exhortations.

There is an old coolie woman in a traditional triangular straw sunhat, who sells fruit. She is the real article, a genuine peasant from up-country and not part of any cultural ploy by the tourist board. She carries two heavy baskets which balance precariously on each end of a pole slung over her shoulders. They contain papayas, mangoes and pineapples piled so high that if it weren't for her perfect balance, would cascade into the filthy gutter.

At this time of the day it is unbearably hot, and the filth and dust on the street is made worse by the exhaust fumes of the taxis and motorcycles which scream by with irreverent contempt for the siesta. They hoot on sight at a foreigner, hoping there is a slim chance of picking up a bountiful fare.

Harry finds the restaurant. They are greeted by a tiny, frail-looking wisp of a girl, doll-like in her prettiness, who leads them through the back and outside onto a verandah. Supported on spindly stilts, it juts out into the fetid, scum-covered brown water of the bay. They sit down by the railings and can look out at the hordes of multi-coloured pleasure junks bobbing up and down at anchor.

The lobster is fresh and succulent, the salad is spotless and well-prepared. Harry leaves a generous tip. He has been quiet. Penny is too preoccupied enjoying the distractions of the exotic surroundings to feel uncomfortable with little conversation. She is unaware of the complex mixture of emotions he is experiencing as they stroll back to the launch and take the choppy ride back to the ship. It is three o'clock in the afternoon. Harry stifles a yawn and is thinking of his siesta.

They clatter up the rickety metal steps which hang precariously on the side of the ship, suspended by one-inch-thick steel hawsers that drop down from way up high on the boat deck. They hardly seem adequate to take the weight of the pontoon itself, let alone the countless overweight passengers that come off the launch. Harry is convinced that one day there will be a disaster in one of the anchor ports, where scores of vastly overweight passengers will be committed to a premature watery grave when the seemingly flimsy structure collapses.

He walks silently with Penny to her cabin. There are two hours before the clinic at five o'clock, which should give ample time for his siesta – unless Penny invites him. As she is struggling to get the key in the lock, she speaks.

'Are you coming in?'

He is not sure of the innocent nature of the invitation or whether it is subterranean language for something else. As she disappears into the closet, he perches precariously on the edge of the bed. The time doesn't seem right to make any play. He is sleepy – but perhaps she wants to play now? In his uncertainty he hears the inner voice of caution and reproof for what he might be getting into, and speaks as soon as she appears from the closet.

'Penny, I think forty winks is the order of the day. I'll get my head down back in my cabin and then see you in the clinic at five o'clock.'

'What are you doing tonight?'

'I planned to stay on board, actually – especially as I know most of the crew will be rampaging ashore. How about you?'

'Libby has promised to take me to see the lights tonight – with a crowd of other people, I think. They say I should see the special shows – and mustn't miss the kick-boxing.'

She cannot bring herself to say that she really wants to see the red light district in all its glory. Harry knows that it will be a totally new experience and a precious chance to observe at close quarters a facet of life that she may have been only vaguely aware of before.

Harry had already determined that he did not wish to be her guide around the gaudy fleshpots. There would be a conflict of emotions that would be difficult to accommodate. It would be uncomfortable, if not disturbing. The close proximity to the blatant carnal attractions, the 'receptacles' would somehow pull him away from her, and he fears he might lose the strange new emotion he had discovered in his feelings for her.

'Penny, I must go to my bed. If you're going ashore tonight you ought to take a nap as well. I promise you, it will be a long hard hectic night on the town, especially if Suzanne is the tour guide.'

'That sounds a good idea.'

As Harry begins to raise himself up from the edge of the bed, Penny spontaneously bends over before he is at full height, and looping both arms around his neck, kisses him enthusiastically. Harry is taken by surprise at her taking the lead, and his emotional confusion is reactivated and intensified. But his sense of pragmatism predominates.

After a few seconds embrace he gently pulls away.

'Must go – and you definitely need a little sleep.'

259

* * *

The next day the *Empress* ups anchor and heads for Hong Kong. Harry is waiting for the avalanche of crew attendances as the price paid for a few hours of unrestrained fun and frolics ashore in Pattaya. He will be ratty with the victims, not so much as a reproach on moral grounds, which he could hardly justify from his own safaris around the carnal watering holes of the Far East, but more from the fact that his extra workload will be trebled – and for the crew it will be entirely free!

In the morning clinic the next day he is anxious to gauge Penny's reaction to the red light district. But he is apprehensive that any such discussion might inflame the natural female antagonism towards those males of the species who plainly use bar girls as disposable objects. It would not be so much a reaction of female solidarity, but more a gesture of pity and compassion for their abject abuse by men.

'Well, ladies – did you enjoy your little excursion ashore last night?'

Libby and Suzanne had seen it all before, and their first-time shock from the sordid world of carnal pleasure had long been replaced by a detached superficial appreciation of the noise, colour, music, gaiety and sheer fantasy spectacle of the strip.

'You tell Penny, Harry – she cannot believe the Catoy show is really men . . .'

'You mean the female impersonators? 'Fraid so, Penny – everyone a full-blooded male, although they are all on female hormones and some have had breast implants, and one or two the full sex-change operation.'

'Oh – I just can't believe it. I really cannot . . . they're so beautiful and . . .'

'I know. I've made the same mistake myself . . . I mean . . . you know what I mean!'

'Yes, Harry? What exactly do you mean?' asks Libby with the carefully contrived disingenuousness of a psychoanalyst of the Freudian school.

Damn it! He doesn't want Penny to think he could possibly

approach the local fauna – female, male or otherwise. He ignores Libby's desire to be enlightened and confabulates with an explosion of filibustering words.

'Yes, absolutely unbelievable, quite remarkable, aren't they? And their miming and dancing, incredible, don't you think? So entertaining...'

'I really enjoyed it,' she says, and as Libby winks at Harry to acknowledge he is off the hook, Penny continues excitedly to relate her experience.

'The girls in the bars – there were so many – and in the street – so many – all the girls in Thailand must have been in that one street – so many – I couldn't believe it ... I mean, what do they all do?'

Harry looks at Libby and Suzanne. Surely they must have enlightened her?

'Just having fun, I suppose,' he says lamely.

'And the massage parlours – every other shop in the high street seemed to be one.'

She lowers her head slightly as if to impart a snippet of privileged information to the unenlightened.

'I've heard that they are really brothels...' She whispers earnestly, as if imparting a conspiratorial confidence that is guaranteed to shock.

'Is that so?' says Harry in an expressionless voice, trying hard not to be facetious at her expense or feed the irony that is being savoured by Libby and Suzanne. They smile a knowing smile, acknowledging his clear wish not to make a meal out of Penny's naïveté.

At the end of the clinic Harry and Penny are alone for a few moments in his office. He continues writing up patients' notes, whilst she busies herself tidying up and replenishing the stock items on his examination tray. As he writes, his mind is scheming. What should he do? Should he boldly invite her to his cabin, maintaining the momentum of his strategy? Or should he leave it a few days and allow her to settle and think on things? There is turmoil in his subconscious which is resolved by a spontaneous decision to indulge his base instincts – hang the consequences – they can take care of themselves.

'Penny, would you like to come round for a pre-dinner drink tonight?'

'Why, I'd love to. I can go to the gym tomorrow.'

'Ice and lemon?'

'Thanks.'

Penny sits on the sofa in Harry's cabin. Above her head on the wall is a reproduction oil painting of an old majestic liner being carefully manoeuvred into dock by a bevy of tugs.

'I hadn't noticed that painting before – it's beautiful.'

'Yes – it's only a reproduction, but I like it too – the old *Mauretania* coming into New York harbour. That's some years ago – well before my time, of course.'

Harry laughs. The irony doesn't escape him as he looks at the picture and then smiles at Penny. If she is the helpless, vulnerable ship, then he is the powerful tugboat which will guide her safely into his port.

'Are you going to the table tonight?'

'I can't say I feel much like it – but I suppose I'd better make the effort – I've not been for quite a few evenings, and they're all moaning a bit. Anyway, I don't need to be there until nine o'clock, so there is plenty of time to get ready.'

What he really means to say is that there is more than enough time to consolidate the physical relationship, against which he is fighting a losing battle of diminishing resistance. There is no mention of the fleeting passion a couple of nights before, when they came close to the final act. Perhaps it will be tonight. His approach would be normally cold and calculating and entail a definite strategy, but with Penny he is not able to be his usual dispassionate self. There is a strange unfamiliar feeling he has for her which seems to inhibit his regular well-worn technique. Now he is hesitant. Perhaps it is simply a question of confidence. The prize is so valuable that he dare not risk putting her off.

There is a prolonged silence. But then he does not want to talk – to woo her anymore. He feels he has performed enough of the pre-coital courtship ritual and now it is time for serious action. He wants her to yield, so that he can possess her – make her his.

She breaks the silence and says what he needs to hear to commence the coital sequence.

'Harry ... you really turned me on the other night, and...'

She falters and her cheeks flush.

It is the invitation to take up where they had left off and finish the business. Harry wastes no time.

'Next door? It's more comfortable.'

She nods without hesitation. This immediate acquiescence amplifies Harry's confidence enough to close the book on his scheming evaluation. He can depend now on the natural sequence of the biological impulse to orchestrate events without a hitch.

They stand by the bed and turn towards each other embracing and kissing passionately. Harry breaks away and starts to undress quickly down to his underpants, which barely shield his erection. Penny is quick to take the cue, and strips without fuss to her bra and panties. Harry pushes her round gently and deftly unhooks the bra. It falls to the floor and she turns back to face him. His eyes feast on her full breasts. The nipples invite his mouth, and after a few moments she groans and pulls his head up to kiss. He continues massaging the erect teats with one hand as the other slips into the top edge of her panties and soon finds the slithery midline slit. It is hot and wet and the clitoris is swollen and easily discernible. Harry senses she can hardly wait. The intensity of this passion is novel to her, and without prompting she starts to pull down her panties. They break apart momentarily and she steps out of the flimsy garment. They lock in a tight embrace again, with Harry grasping both her bare buttocks. And then she insinuates her fingers into the top of his pants and makes an attempt to pull them down. It is the signal for him to hastily remove the last vestige of covering. His swollen organ is revealed in all its glory and oscillates in Penny's direction. She draws close and it nestles comfortably in her groin.

263

Still locked in an embrace, Harry moves sideways and allows himself to fall onto the bed. Penny falls beside him with a self-conscious giggle. His hand seeks her clitoris again. Her groaning becomes loud and continuous, and her pelvic thrusts into the air are almost violent in their intensity. Harry knows that any more foreplay is superfluous. Besides, he feels so sexually aroused himself that he knows he is going to be hardly able to control his own ejaculation. But then he realises it doesn't matter because she is so close to orgasm.

She is desperate to receive him as both of her hands go to his groin and caress his pulsating organ, directing it clumsily towards her hot vaginal orifice. Harry moves from her side to lie on top of her. He adjusts his posture slightly to allow him to slip in effortlessly on a film of mucus. His pelvic thrusts are instantaneous, fast and hard. As suspected, his orgasm comes after no more than a dozen strokes. But he need not be concerned for her appreciation – she had reached her orgasmic plateau almost immediately after his full penetration, which causes her to thrash about so violently, Harry is almost thrown off the bed.

As the peak intensity of the mutual pleasure fades, Harry continues to lie on top of her, not even bothering to support his weight by his elbows. But then he becomes aware of her noisy breathing and adjusts his posture, taking most of his weight off her chest. He looks down on her. For a moment their eyes meet. He stretches down, and they exchange a soft kiss.

'Oh Harry, Harry, Harry.' No other words come.

'Penny ... Penny ... this is the most ...' He cannot finish the sentence. He rolls to one side on his back to wallow in the sheer sensual pleasure and utter satiation. Her head nestles in one shoulder.

They lie for some time not speaking or moving, in a hazy semi-somnolence, simply savouring the post-coital fulfilment. Harry, in his semi-dream state, analyses the quality of the sexual experience. For once it was not simply a convenient receptacle to receive his ejaculate. There is something more. He cannot define it, but whatever it is, it has immeasurably enhanced the overall experience of the sexual act and brought a new dimension which, pleasurable as it seems, vaguely disturbs him.

He looks at his watch.

'Christ! Eight thirty.'

He startles Penny from her drowsiness.

'What's the matter?' she says with alarm.

'The table – I said I would go tonight. Quick, a shower.' He jumps up and goes to the bathroom. When he comes out five minutes later, vigorously rubbing his head with a towel, Penny is dressed and ready to go.

'I've just time to get to the mess for dinner – I'll take a quick shower in my cabin,' she adds, not wishing Harry to suppose she is defaulting on hygiene.

'Uuuh Penny … if you want – I mean, if you would, or … you know, perhaps we could … I mean, you might want to …'

Penny looks up at the ceiling and frowns in a theatrical show of frustration, as if she is computing the logistics of what the recent events have more or less confirmed will be a foregone conclusion.

'Of course, Harry – I'll come back and see you after dinner – oh, and should I bring my toothbrush?'

Harry smiles. It is the end of the beginning.

'Evening, folks!'

'Hiya, Harry!'

Desmond speaks.

'We missed you again. What have you been up to? Did you enjoy Pattaya?'

The chuckle and twinkle in his eye asks all of the subliminal questions. Harry knows it is a circumlocutory probe into matters sexual.

'In actual fact, I didn't go ashore in the evening, so I guess I missed most of the fun.'

'You mean you missed the Thai boxing,' says Louise enthusiastically.

''Fraid so – but I have seen it before – many times.'

Desmond tries another more direct tack.

'What about the other attractions?'

Harry senses that Desmond is going to behave this evening after his embarrassing performance the other night, so he will be content to hear Harry's set-pieces on the infamous seedy Thai resort and not risk a further unpleasant scene. Harry answers by beginning a short monologue which seems appropriate. He falls back on his well-worn repertoire of expressions and descriptions and pithy anecdotes which draws the anticipated appreciative responses and invites comments on their experiences of the seedy resort. It is a lighthearted and carefully self-censored exchange, so predictable in its style and content, rich in clichés and awash with smug truisms. Such a debriefing session might be seen as almost mandatory, once the rich and respectable First World passengers are safely cocooned back in their luxurious floating palace, light years away from their brief skirmish with the sordid wretchedness of the Third World.

They prattle on, regurgitating and redigesting the fun of witnessing at first-hand the uninhibited spectacle of Third World gaiety, a grim gaiety barely hidden to anyone who might care to scratch beneath the paper thin veneer. It is the harsh reality of survival – a reality of desperation, thinly veiled by the colour, the noise and the bright lights.

'How's your new nurse?' asks Louise, 'You said you were expecting one to join in Singapore, didn't you?'

Harry cannot conceal his reaction. The subtle change in colour, more a glow than a full blush, is a sure sign which Louise is quick to register.

'Pretty, is she?'

'Uuuh – uuh, conventionally so, I suppose.'

He regains his equilibrium, but her eyes tell him that she is cognizant of his attempted camouflage. Harry senses she is going to delve deeper, and pre-empts her before she can speak.

'Well – you know – yes, I would say she is pretty attractive – yes – certainly,' he says, as dispassionately as possible.

But Desmond picks up the scent and wastes no time.

'I saw you both ashore.'

'Yes, Desmond. It was in the daytime. We went to see if we could get some material for her mother. You know. She asked me if I knew any good shops, and I thought the easiest way was to show her ... anyway, I often go ashore with the nurses.'

'As a twosome or threesome?'

'Either. Actually, she is a rather shy girl and it is all very new to her ... I mean, this travelling around the world ... so I thought she needed an escort and besides, I wanted myself to ...'

Harry is struggling vainly to throw Desmond off the scent. He could never possibly confide what he is beginning to feel for Penny or even suggest that there was any empathy between them.

'That's nice for you, Harry,' Louise says charitably. She senses his growing discomfort, and makes the necessary rescue. 'What do you recommend tonight?'

Harry is appreciative and indebted.

'Let's see – the Beef Wellington is usually pretty good, although the Fillet of Dover Sole as a main course is better for your cholesterol – and is calorie-controlled, of course. I'm going to have the Nasi Goreng. It might be a bit too spicy for some people, but I love it.'

The main course comes. Conversation dies away. Harry eats his food in silence. He cannot think of anything except Penny. He relives the events that have taken place in his cabin just an hour or so before. He knows she will come tonight and stay with him. And then there is the warning not to get involved.

The waiter takes the order for dessert, but Harry has had enough – of food and company. He prepares his departure.

'Must go, folks – no dessert or coffee for me – got a lot of paperwork I'm afraid, so I'll look forward to seeing you all tomorrow.'

He is up and gone before anyone can delay his exit with more aimless conversation. He goes straight to his cabin, where he undresses and puts on a dressing gown. He switches on the video.

Penny arrives at around 11.30. After the gentle knock, the door opens slowly and she walks in before even he can greet

267

her. She is dressed in a trainer suit and carries a small toilet bag.

'What are you watching?'

'Some old Western – you know, you've seen one, you've seen them all.'

'You look tired.'

'Getting old, my dear. It's been a long day. I think that's a suitable cue to go to bed, don't you?'

She smiles, and her face cannot hide a hint of nervous excitement.

'Yes, that sounds a good idea.'

In the bedroom they undress silently and climb into bed. They tuck themselves snugly under the sheets. The sensation he cannot explain or identify from previous experience causes him to ponder what it is about this woman that is so different from the countless other partners he has had. She does not simply represent another receptacle lying next to him. There is something else, something he cannot deny, that disturbs him in a strange way. Her sexual qualities have certainly had a profound effect on him, and the physical attraction is very strong – but it is not just that. By definition, he thinks – if it is something more than physical, then it must be 'metaphysical' – is it what people mean when they talk of a spiritual element to human existence? Something intangible or so complex and far removed from physical forces that it cannot be explained in mere physical terms? Whatever it might be, a sensitive spot in his psyche has been activated which he cannot fully understand.

'So what is your mother like – don't tell me – she's beautiful.'

'Yes, she is – very, very beautiful.'

'Is she like you?'

'Well, people say I'm her double – that we are as alike as two peas in a pod. They sometimes joke if we are twins, which of course is very flattering for her. Yes, I suppose we are very alike physically. It's funny, I don't look like my father at all – although we are more alike in other ways – you know, temperament and the like. I suppose it goes that way in families, doesn't it? I've always joked with friends that it must have been

268

the milkman – but I wouldn't say such a thing in front of mother – I did once, and she seemed to take it so badly that I made sure I never made that joke ever again!

'Although my mother and I look so much alike, in all truth, I am much closer to Daddy. My brother also looks like Mother and not much like Father, but he is much closer to her than he is to Father. I suppose I am his favourite. He spoils me quite a bit ... we really are close.'

'Genes, my dear – it's all in the genes, I guess – how people turn out, even though it's so very unpredictable.'

'How do you mean?'

'Genetic throwbacks – the random mixing of the genes at fertilisation – unleashing characteristics which are locked forever in the cells' chromosomes – the key of life, the eternal blueprint and all that. You must remember some of that from your general training?'

'Yes.'

'You see, it's the genes that are immortal, not the mere human machines that carry them from one generation to the next. They're selfish little blighters, and they merely exploit every human being until death so that they can live forever. I'm sorry – I'm getting a bit carried away. Anyway – I bet if she is only just a little bit like you, then she will be absolutely gorgeous ...'

Harry visualises an older woman, probably around his own age or maybe a little older, and speculates how attractive and well-preserved she might look.

'Let's sleep. We've a lot of sick sailors and the grim harvest of Pattaya to reap tomorrow.'

'Goodnight, Harry.'

CHAPTER 10

TRUE LOVE

No sooner met but they looked; no sooner looked but they loved; no sooner loved but they sighed; no sooner sighed but they asked one and other the reason; no sooner knew the reason but they sort the remedy.

As You Like It, William Shakespeare (1564–1616)

If I had no duties, and no reference to futurity, I would spend my life in driving briskly in a post-chaise with a pretty woman.

Samuel Johnson (1709–1784)

Three weeks after Pattaya Harry and Penny are inseparable. The ship has continued its meander around some of the major Asian ports on its leisurely world cruise. During the three days it was alongside in Hong Kong, a small army of Chinese managed to put a fresh coat of black paint on the hull before it sailed up to Shanghai in the Chinese People's Republic and then on to Pusan in Korea. The final Far Eastern ports before crossing the Pacific to Hawaii were Osaka and Yokohama.

They have been able to go ashore in every port. Harry had fixed it for Penny, despite the fact that usually the three nurses took turns and didn't always get off at every port. But Suzanne and Libby had gone out of their way to accommodate the blossoming romance. Admittedly, in the beginning they had expressed some reserve, if not a little cynicism, knowing full well the way romances could sour so quickly on board. Their concern because of the effect such a liaison, if it terminated, could have on the medical department, has gradually evaporated as they witness each day Harry and Penny becoming more and more committed. They had never seen such a thing with Harry before – or indeed, ever thought they would.

Penny has moved into his cabin. So far the arrangement has not caused any problems. Suzanne and Libby might have altered their perceptions to appreciate the seriousness of the relationship, but the staff Captain has buttonholed Harry on several occasions to remind him of the golden rule – although his warnings have become less sarcastic and sceptical as the survival time of the love affair increases. In the beginning the gossip around the ship about the doctor's new bit of fluff was a major topic of conversation, and bets were taken, but now it attracts less and less attention, and by the time the ship reaches Hawaii, interest has all but fizzled out.

Penny is very excited about going ashore in Honolulu and seeing for real, places she'd only read or been able to dream about. It is seven o'clock in the morning as the *Empress* edges slowly past the famous Aloha Tower and settles snugly into her berth. There is a swing band of sorts which plays a medley of Glenn Miller tunes – an attempt to inspire an atmosphere of the Forties and Fifties which has nostalgic appeal for the older generation of passengers.

Harry and Penny lean over the side from the bridge wing to gain a bird's-eye view of the band and the gathering crowds who are waving enthusiastically from the quayside 100 feet below. They can see a long line of coaches snaking back on itself, waiting to fill up with the hundreds of passengers who will tour the island. The veterans amongst them will most certainly be going to pay their respects to the floating museum of the sunken SS *Arizona*, the Second World War battleship which remains semi-submerged exactly where it was sunk by Japanese planes during the attack on Pearl Harbor on that fateful day in 1941.

Harry will not be taking Penny to see the famous war memorial. They plan a day at Waikiki beach. He knows it will be crowded, as it is the favorite tourist spot, but he has promised Penny he will take her there so she can take the necessary snapshots.

The last clinic patient is seen by 10.30. Penny had not been too busy and had managed to snatch a few hours sleep. Now she is free for the rest of the day.

'Suzanne, you're the boss now – it should be quiet, as most people will be off the ship.'

'Where will you two be going?'

'We can walk to Waikiki from here – it's about three miles. When we get there we should be about ready for a seafood

274

lunch – and then a paddle in the water – you know, do the tourist thing – and then we'll get a cab back in time for my little siesta ... it could be a tiring day, but we'll do our best to cope...'

'I feel so sorry for you, Doctor. Try and enjoy yourselves, won't you?'

Back in Harry's cabin they change into shorts, T-shirts and trainers. Armed with towels and sunglasses and with Harry sporting a sun visor, they look like a couple of typical cruisers about to head for a day of fun and sun in exotic Honolulu.

'We'd better go off the crew gangway on 5 deck forward – don't want passengers to recognise us or think we having a good time, do we?'

'Let's go then,' says Penny cheerfully.

They stroll along 2 deck, holding hands comfortably. In the beginning, such a blatant show of commitment would have drawn endless comment from the social commentators of the ship. In the time-warp of a shipboard romance, three weeks is half a lifetime. The fact that they are still seen happily together has earned them full recognition, albeit grudgingly from the social pack, which is always ready and eager to pass judgment on the amorous activities of others.

On the ship, everybody's business is everybody's business. It was inevitable simply from the confined nature of the environment – where everyone worked and slept and lived out their lives in such a limited space, surrounded by an inhospitable and endless expanse of ocean for months at a time. It was only when social attachments become more serious and sustained for longer periods than one-night stands, that personal sensitivities were respected and comments and criticisms from the pack were eschewed.

Penny and Harry had successfully got over the hump, so to speak, of being in the social spotlight. The stability of their relationship has become an accepted feature of the ship's social milieu. The only occasional sarcastic comment tinged with an unmistakable streak of envy, might come from a junior engineer who had thought himself a hot favourite in the initial scramble for Penny's favours. But it is water off a duck's back to Harry. He ignores such sour grapes, providing the jokes do not become too personal or offensive.

They mount the rickety gangway, which vibrates alarmingly as crew members scurry in both directions in a never-ending stream. Harry walks in front of Penny as they join the single file of crew hurrying down the gangway.

At the bottom of the flimsy structure he sees a bearded man in his early twenties, wearing a large gold earring and with his dark brown hair neatly tied back in a ponytail – not unlike the traditional sailor of old. He is waiting impatiently, with a look of barely controlled exasperation on his face, for the stream of people flowing endlessly off the gangway onto the quay. There is a large kitbag at his feet, and he is bending down fiddling with a strap, partially blocking Harry as he is about to make the last step onto terra firma. The two end steps rattle loudly, heralding Harry's intention, and just as he is about to jump the final step, the man looks up abruptly and moves aside. Penny is talking at Harry's back and is amused at some commotion going on at the taxi rank. Harry is aware of her giggle, but doesn't respond to it. His attention is momentarily distracted by the broad-shouldered young man who has stood in his way, waiting to board the ship. Harry assumes he is a new crew member about to join the ship. Their eyes meet briefly, and Harry freezes for a second.

'Get a move on, slowcoach,' urges Penny impatiently.

As they pass, Harry notices that the sailor's attention rivets on Penny as she hops down onto the quay, almost tripping over his bag.

'Sorry . . .' he says, violently pulling the bag aside. He appears embarrassed and flustered.

'That's quite all right,' says Penny cheerfully, with only a cursory glance as she and Harry walk past him.

But Harry does not miss the way the young man's eyes fix on her. He blushes, and his face comes alive in the way most men react on first sight of a strikingly good-looking female. Penny doesn't appear to notice. Her attention is still drawn to the two eccentric-looking geriatrics, gaily-clad in Hawaiian shirts, who are arguing with their taxi driver. Harry is never jealous when

276

another man admires his woman. He is flattered and never feels threatened even by a younger, and perhaps more handsome man. It appears that Penny had not even noticed him, but as they get out of earshot her casual remark reminds Harry that healthy young women are hardly ever not likely to notice a handsome potential suitor.

'Must be a new crew member joining,' she says as if she herself has been an integral part of the ship's company since the beginning of time.

'Yes, probably,' he answers automatically, as a strange sensation following the fleeting eye contact lingers and distracts his concentration for a moment. There is a feeling of déjà vu, but he cannot recall where or when. Penny senses his pre-occupation as they walk on in silence.

'Are you all right?'

'It's just that – well – that chap ... I feel I've seen him somewhere before – you know that feeling you get sometimes ... the mind playing tricks, I suppose. Anyway, it doesn't matter ... let's go and enjoy a day at Waikiki.'

The days pass quickly after the ship leaves the Hawaiian islands and heads east across the Pacific towards the West Coast of America. It remains warm and sunny, and the sea is calm every day. Clinics are not busy, and there is much free time. Harry and Penny spend even more time together, and the relationship seems to strengthen as each day passes.

Harry has begun to think about their age difference. But then he consoles himself. Penny appears naturally mature beyond her years, whilst he has refused to grow up and enter middle age gracefully. And besides, he has always kept himself in good condition.

In the brief moments when he is alone walking on the deck or working out in the gym, he thinks how lucky he is that perhaps he has found the person he has been searching for subconsciously all these years. Just being close to her makes him feel happy and contented. For once in his life, he has no yearning for any other woman, he cannot possibly be tempted.

Penny satisfies all his needs. Apart from the mutual physical attraction that has not waned and has in fact intensified, there is unquestionably the other dimension, an 'extra' dimension which he cannot recall ever experiencing before with another woman. It defies his description, except that he knows that there is a warmth, a fusion of minds, an ethereal empathy – a closeness of spirit – a term he is reluctant to use – which seems to transcend the bodily side of their relationship.

He confesses, almost grudgingly to himself, that there seems to be some sort of metaphysical, even perhaps mystical quality to the way they interact – although his natural cynicism and scepticism that such hypothetical dimensions exist make him feel uncomfortable. Thoughts that he would normally categorise as in the realms of primitive superstition engender in him a conflict of feelings, including a faint guilt, for allowing such irrational, unscientific notions to creep into his analytical thinking processes.

Harry's all-consuming feelings for Penny now direct his thoughts to the future. For the first time, he has started thinking about leaving the sea and settling into a more conventional lifestyle, landbased. He tries to imagine a life ashore with Penny – perhaps even marriage and children. Before meeting her, such a thought filled him with horror. Now, for the first time in his life, such an institution takes on a definite appeal – with Penny as the possible partner.

He has woken early this morning. He is alone in bed, as Penny is working the night duty. His waking thoughts dwell on the change that has occurred so quickly and fundamentally in his attitude to life. Maybe the whole thing is a flash in the pan, and he is suffering from the delusion of total infatuation with a beautiful girl half his age, who hangs on his every word and who satisfies his every desire.

If he is wise, he reminds himself, he should resist the urge to make any drastic changes in his lifestyle. Why not simply enjoy the ephemeral pleasures of cruising around the world snugly cocooned in a ship – a million miles away from the toil and troubles and harsh realities of life – as if time and reality are suspended forever?

He stirs from his rumination and rolls over towards the door, which has closed quietly. He opens his eyes from the half-sleep and lifts his head to see the clock.

'Is that you, my darling?' he enquires softly.

'Yes – I've brought you some freshly brewed coffee,' comes a whisper from the dayroom, 'are you awake?'

'I was just about to get up.'

Penny appears at the curtain which separates the dayroom from the bedroom. Harry pulls himself to a sitting position.

'Just what the doctor ordered...'

He takes the coffee and places it on the bedside cabinet. Penny bends over towards him, and as they kiss he pulls her down on top of him.

'A bit smelly, I'm afraid. I need a shower before I go to bed.'

Harry sniffs at her chest, twitching his nose theatrically.

'Seems all right to me.'

'Let me get changed.'

She pulls away and stands up and starts to undo the buttons on her tunic.

'Were you busy last night, then?'

'So-so – the usual dribs and drabs until about four o'clock – and then the fight...'

'Oh yes,' Harry leans forward, 'what was all that about?'

'There was a fight in the Pig. A bit of a battle, by all accounts ... you know, bottles, glasses, chairs – everything. Fortunately, nobody was seriously hurt, otherwise I'm afraid I would have had to have called you out.'

'So glad you didn't. Four a.m. is not my best time ... anyway, what was it all about?'

'It seems there was an argument between a couple of the diehard deckhands – you know – the heavy drinkers with a pretty tough reputation...'

'Degenerate rabble, you mean?'

'Well, not all of them ... anyway, it was between them and a new deckhand, the one I eventually patched up, in fact. He was very well-spoken and apart from his earring, ponytail and powerful build, most unlike any of the other seamen I've met...'

279

'So what was it about?'

'He said they had made fun of him, the way he spoke, and accused him of being too snooty ... naturally he didn't like that, and when he told them it wasn't his fault he'd had a good education, they took it as an insult, that they hadn't – and so attacked him. I talked with some other crew later, in the hospital, and by all accounts he was ferocious and was able to deal with both of his attackers until he was eventually restrained by others.'

'What condition was he in when you saw him?'

'A bit bruised and battered about the face, with some superficial cuts which I managed to suture. I think his beard protected his face, even though there was a laceration on his chin. I had to shave off quite a bit to expose ... it's funny, even though his face was swollen, after I'd shaved off a good part of his beard there was a faint resemblance to you ... as you might have looked twenty years ago.'

There is a twinkle in Penny's eye. Harry pulls her close.

'Good physique, handsome, eh?'

'Only kidding ... nowhere near as handsome as you – especially with half his beard removed. I advised him to shave the rest off, otherwise someone is likely to provoke another fight with him.'

'And you say he was well-spoken?'

'Yes. He didn't sound like your average sailor at all. It's funny, though, I must confess when we were talking I felt a strange sensation, as if we had met before somewhere – although of course we never have...'

'What do you mean?'

'I don't know – it was the way he looked at me. It's difficult to describe, but his stare seemed to reach right down deep inside – it felt a little bit spooky – I know that sounds daft...'

'C'mon, tell the truth, you fancied him and he, not surprisingly, fancied you...'

'No, honestly – I don't think it was that. It was definitely something else ... strange, really. I just can't describe the feeling ... it was a little weird, though.'

'Don't be silly. A hunky macho sailor who'd been brawling

was grateful for the undivided attention of the beautiful, compassionate nursing sister ... and his pitiful condition and undying gratitude simply brought out the mother instinct in you.'

Penny smiles serenely.

'He was too young for me, anyway – I prefer older men.'

She leans down and kisses Harry.

'Anyway, I advised him to come back and see you about the swollen eye and cheek, in case there might be a fracture. I said he must come back within a week to have his sutures out.'

'All right, that's enough about work. Look – it's seven o'clock, and I'll have to get up shortly and you'll have to go to bed. There's just time for a quick cuddle.'

She slips the shapeless nurse's tunic quickly over her head and pulls back the bed cover. Her body is perfection. Harry stares unashamedly at her contours as she bends down and climbs into bed next to him.

'Harry, you're so warm,' she purrs as she snuggles up.

For once, he ignores his erection. He is content to hold her close. As she nestles comfortably in the crook of his arm, he can see she is ready for sleep. After a few minutes he detaches himself as slowly and gently as possible, and reluctantly climbs out. There is a senior officers' meeting in the Captain's cabin before he starts the morning clinic, and he mustn't be late.

By ten o'clock he is in his consulting room in the ship's hospital to start the grind of seeing patients. Harry goes through his usual routines, and there is nothing out of the ordinary in the cases that present until Libby ushers in a tall, broad-shouldered, muscular-looking individual with an earring and a ponytail. He speaks without invitation.

'My name is Jason Brown. I'm a deckhand.'

Harry looks up from the desk, where he is completing the notes of the previous patient.

'Oh – hello ... what can I do for you? I can see you must be the one who ran into the proverbial door last night. Let me see.'

Harry invites him to sit in the chair adjacent to his desk and leans across to examine his face. The bruises are painfully evident around both eyes. There is a superficial gash on his left cheek and a deeper one on his chin, which has been sutured.

Harry leans back in his chair.

'Some door, eh!'

'There were three or four of them in the end, Doctor,' says the young man in a sombre tone.

'You're new to the ship, aren't you?'

He nods sullenly.

'I see the Sister shaved half of your beard off – I imagine you might want to shave the rest, don't you?'

'I will later,' he replies, without the merest flicker of humour.

'What was the argument over?'

'I've no idea. Perhaps it is because I have recently joined the ship – you know – some sort of ritual nonsense – I really don't know. They were all completely drunk – and wild. I admit I'd had a couple of pints, but that was all. I most certainly was not looking for trouble, believe me.'

'Ship's life,' says Harry philosophically. 'Let's have a look at that bruised cheek and eye.'

Harry stands up and goes behind to palpate gently around his left zygoma and the infra-orbital margin.

'Aarrrrgh – that was painful.'

'Sore, eh?'

'Yes.'

'Zygoma – cheek a bit tender too? No double vision? Follow my finger with your eyes – good.'

Harry points an index finger upwards in front of his face.

'Hold your head still.'

He notes that his pupils are equal and react to light normally.

'Tongue out, waggle from side to side. Screw your eyes up tight – good. Shrug your shoulders – good. That's fine.'

It is a quick assessment of his cranial nerve function and is routine for all head injuries. Harry can find no signs of significance.

'Although you're a bit tender around the eye socket margin,

282

I don't think there is any fracture,' he says authoritatively, looking into the young man's eyes again.

Those eyes. That look. The lids are swollen and blue-black and half-closed, but Harry finds he is disturbed by a message in them that he cannot understand. He realises it is the same young man standing at the end of the gangway in Honolulu who was waiting to board when Penny tripped over his bag. He is less easily recognizable with all the bruising and swelling and slightly bizarre appearance of the half-shaven beard – but nevertheless, the strange sensation that he had felt then is reactivated now as Harry completes his physical examination. His eyes appear to be asking a question. There is a searching quality in them, earnest if not intense, and Harry is made slightly uncomfortable by the effect it is having on him.

'So you've recently joined, have you?'

'Yes.'

'Have you been at sea for long?'

'About three years now.'

'With the same company?'

'No – I worked with several other shipping lines before I joined Norsk International about eighteen months ago. Since then I've been on most of the ships in the cruise fleet.'

'If you don't mind me saying, you don't sound very much like the average seaman we get on here.'

'I went to a minor public school in Worcester, not one of the well-known ones, but good enough for me to get three A levels. I had a chance of a place at Oxford or Cambridge to read law, but decided I needed to grow up a bit first, and so I came away to sea.'

'Very interesting,' Harry nods his head in measured appreciation, 'but three years? Don't you think you should be going up to university now?'

'I got bitten by the wanderlust spirit, I suppose. I keep meaning to go ashore once and for all but I cannot stop signing on again. After a month or two at home I seem to get restless. I'm not sure I could ever settle down to a normal sort of life again.'

'Nonsense. You can't waste your life, and certainly not your

283

education, playing around at sea forever. If I were you I'd start thinking seriously about completing your education – at least not wasting the opportunity of going to university. It'll broaden your horizons so much more than the many physical ones you've seen in your three years at sea.'

'I don't know, Doctor – I really don't know what to say.'

'Well you tell me, young man – what are your hopes and dreams for the future? Just what are you searching for, if anything, at sea?'

'I ... I really do not know ... I was searching for something in the beginning, but you wouldn't understand that ... I have come to realise it is an impossible search, an impossible dream. I've lost sight of what I was originally looking for – I'm sorry if that sounds a bit mystical, but I have to accept now that I cannot find what I think I was looking for – if ever I was certain it existed in the first place ... I'm sorry – that doesn't make sense, I know...'

'Not sure what you're looking for eh, young man? Well, if I were you, I'd finish this voyage and get the hell out of it. For God's sake, seize the opportunity to go to university and complete your studies...'

'Is that all?'

'Yes – for today, anyway. You must return in around five days to have your sutures removed, although you can come any time to have your dressing changed by the Nursing Sister.'

'Thank you, Doctor.'

He stands up abruptly and turns to go through the door.

'And try to steer clear of any more trouble.'

'I'll do my best...' he says making a half-turn at the door. Harry catches his half-profile for a split second before he turns away. That profile! It sparks a distant memory from his subconscious. He feels a faint alarm, and there is a strange sensation of familiarity evoked. It prompts him to speak without thinking.

'Have you ever been to the Far East?'

'Yes, of course – many times.'

'Where?'

'Most parts of Asia and South-East Asia.'

'Where exactly?'

'You know, China, Thailand, Singapore, most ports in Indonesia, the major Japanese ports, Taiwan, Hong Kong, the Philippines...'

Philippines. Philippines. Harry's mind is asking questions automatically without conscious thought. There is a vague unease, and the strange feeling intensifies with the mention of the Philippines.

'Ever been to Manila?'

'Oh yes – quite a few times – it's one of my favorite ports. I went there on my first ship, actually – had a hell of a time...'

'When was that?'

'I suppose not quite three years ago – but why do you ask?'

'Just wondered. Just wondered – that's all.'

CHAPTER 11

REVELATIONS

None of you shall approach to any that is near of kin to him, to uncover their nakedness: I am the Lord.

Leviticus 18: 6

'What does it say?'

'Hang on a minute, give me a chance to open it.'

There is a prolonged silence as her eyes scan the telegram. And then without any warning her lips start to quiver and tears well up.

'What on earth is it? Tell me – what's the matter – why are you upset?'

'Oh dear, oh dear – it's Nana – my grandmother – my father's mother ... she's gone...'

Penny sobs uncontrollably.

'I feel so silly, I'm sorry,' she says in a voice which is shaky and emotional, 'it's not a complete surprise – she's had a pretty serious heart condition for years, and her angina has been getting much worse for the last few months. She's actually had a couple of heart attacks and...'

'Here's a tissue. Now you have a good cry – come and sit down.'

It is almost 9 a.m. and the ship has docked in Los Angeles. Penny and Harry are drinking coffee in the hospital kitchen. Port docking days are usually eagerly awaited, in view of the expected mail from home. They had been especially looking forward to Los Angeles for the excursion they had planned – a special tour of Hollywood and the Universal studios. Later they might go to Malibu Beach if there was time but this news has put the damper on everything.

'Let's go next door and tell Suzanne and Libby. We'll

289

complete the handover and then we can decide what has to be done. Now – don't you worry about a thing.'

Suzanne and Libby put their arms around Penny when they see her crying as Harry tells them the bad news.

'Ladies, of course Penny will have to go home. I'm sure we can cope on the ship without her for a couple of weeks or so, don't you?'

'No problem at all,' says Libby reassuringly.

'And you can return in just under three weeks, when we're scheduled to arrive in Southampton at the end of the world cruise,' says Harry cheerfully, 'so that's settled.'

'But there'll just be Suzanne and Libby – it's not possible and ... how do I get home? Oh, I can't ... I can't ... I'm so sorry...'

'Getting home is a minor detail. I'll ring the crew purser, and he will book the flights today in no time ... and I'll speak with the staff Captain to make sure it is authorised as a compassionate case, and then the company will pay the air fare. Now, first things first. You'd better phone home and let them know that you got the telegram, and tell them you will be on your way very soon. You can ring them later when the flight details have been confirmed. You go up to the radio room now, and I'll ring the chief radio officer to make sure he records it as a compassionate call – satellite costs a small fortune ... go now. We won't be busy this morning, so we don't need you. Libby can stay up a few more hours anyway – can't you, Lib?'

'Of course. It was pretty quiet last night, anyway – I actually got a few hours sleep on the couch.'

Penny wipes her eyes and nose with a tissue and looks at Harry and then Suzanne and Libby, as if to speak. Harry doesn't give her the chance.

'Go on. Go now – the sooner the better. I'll catch up with you later. Ladies, I'll be in my cabin.'

In his cabin, Harry sinks back into the sofa and sighs deeply, alone with his thoughts. There is a feeling of uncertainty accentuated by highly charged emotion, which is making him feel especially vulnerable. He is no longer in charge of his life – his destiny – whereas, before Penny appeared on the scene, he had always been strictly in control. He takes more deep breaths, slowly and deliberately trying to induce in himself a sense of calm so that he can analyse carefully the new direction he has taken in life.

It would seem that his general outlook has been dramatically altered in the space of one month by a beautiful young woman who is half his age. She may show a maturity beyond her years, but if he was ruthlessly honest with himself, she is a world apart, with a fresh, unsophisticated innocence, an innocence that has been defiled in the pursuit of his carnal pleasure ... but is she not different? Has she not affected him in a way he could never have predicted? ...How? Why?

He had lost count of the number of beautiful young girls who'd passed through his hands over the years. Some he had felt stronger feelings for than others, but never, never had a woman been able to peel away the protective layers of his inner psyche, and expose the inner core – to upset his well-worn perception of the fairer sex – and, as a direct result, his total emotional equilibrium. In the past, she would have simply been another statistic – used for a convenient time slot until he'd become tired of her – and then disposed of, to be replaced by a fresh sample.

Perhaps he is changing as he gets older? Maybe the natural maturing process that occurs in men at a much younger age – to prepare them for nest-building, mating and child-rearing – and loyalty to one partner, has come late for him. His life had been one long retarded adolescence – but now, it seems, this young woman may have effected the final metamorphosis into a mature breeding male.

But how can one month be long enough to have orchestrated such a fundamental change – such a deep emotional commitment? Doubts creep into his mind about the nature of his feelings for Penny. Is it not simply a prolonged infatuation, fuelled and refuelled by her vibrant youthfulness and striking beauty? Or is there something more, a strange new entity which has ignited a whole cascade of emotions and generated a new awareness which he has never experienced before?

He is beginning to convince himself that it is not simply the

291

physical allure of a beautiful young female. He'd had so many, one much like the other ... his instincts of scientific rational analysis continue to delve deeper into his innermost psychic recesses. It is an attempt to articulate the mysterious and novel emotions that have sprouted undeniably – as if from heavily dormant buds buried in his previously impenetrable subconscious.

Within the limitations of conventional language and definition, his conclusions, fanciful and unprovable as they may seem, draw on the terms 'metaphysical', or indeed, 'spiritual' – whatever those terms mean in actuality. He is uneasy with this train of thought, as it doesn't fit with his ideas of logic and reality. Such words have always been synonymous with the mumbo-jumbo world of clairvoyance and mysticism – or even mainstream religion, for that matter – where the essence of the creed is represented by a ritualised submission to some mysterious abstract force which totally defies reality and can never be subjected to rigorous logical scientific argument.

Harry's eyes begin to close as his thought processes drift haphazardly. It had been a late night, and he had stayed longer than he'd intended in the Mess, gossiping with other officers. Even though it is only 10.30 in the morning, he cannot resist the desire to sleep.

Uninvited images appear. Totally unconnected with his present line of thought, he sees himself in the clinic, examining a patient. It is the young seaman who had been involved in the fight. Harry re-examines his facial injuries carefully and recounts the conversation that passed between them. Why this man? Why should he occupy any space in his subconscious? And the strange sensation he'd felt when he'd looked into his eyes – it is invoked again. And Manila – why on earth had he asked him if he'd ever been to Manila? What did he care?

But now, as Harry sinks further into a state of unconsciousness, the deeper recesses of his mind are probed and there appears a faint trace of a memory of an incident which evoked a similar sensation. He had been on one of his regular forays in the red light area and he'd seen a young man passing in the shadows of the night. It becomes clearer now, how he had

292

chased after him, despite the alarm and consternation of his two exotic companions. And then he had mistakenly confronted an American in the street, which had caused some embarrassment.

The memory had been long since buried and forgotten – but now it resurfaces and is rekindled, apparently by the young seaman in the clinic, who is not at all a typical seaman. Quite unexpectedly and inexplicably, he had asked him if he had ever been in the Far East, and he'd said he'd been in Manila many times, including on his first trip at sea. It would have coincided with that time of this strange recollection. Could it have been him that he'd passed by in that dark street in Manila, appearing for a few moments before disappearing into the shadows of the night?

Harry stirs. His mind is playing silly tricks on him. What a remote and nonsensical coincidence that would be! But he recalls the very odd sensation that he'd felt during their brief passing. It had been strange enough and disturbing enough to distract him from his two lustful companions and chase after the stranger, only to make a complete fool of himself shortly after. And now, this articulate, wild-looking young man, who claims he could study to become a lawyer if he so wishes, evokes almost identical responses.

Harry attempts to rationalise. Why shouldn't one individual exert a certain unpredictable effect on another? There were no rules to forbid it, and the common experience of so many witnesses tells of how meeting certain individuals can precipitate an uncertain and unpredictable reaction, even before they come within range of conversation. And people have hypothesised an invisible physical aura, perhaps some sort of electrical field of force surrounding individuals. As two people come close, such fields of force would impinge and interact to produce an electrical response which is ultimately manifested as neurological activity in the brain – the conscious experience?

But Harry reminds himself that this train of ideas is the province of mystics and charlatans. Most reputable scientists poured scorn on such wishy-washy notions, their only cynical concession being that so-called 'paranormal phenomena' might allude to a dimension worthy of a little lighthearted research.

But maybe there is an important, mysterious force that interacts between people, which is seemingly invisible and cannot be described in conventional physical terms. Was it some sort of aura – or perhaps a 'spiritual' calling card might be a more appropriate term? Maybe every individual has his or her own unique 'spiritual calling card' – a supersensitive receiver and emitter that can tune into the frequency of the spiritual entity of others.

Before his daydreaming can address such a concept, the shrill ring of the phone startles him from his somnolence. It is the staff Captain who, from the tone of his voice, is wearing his official hat.

'Doctor, I've decided in this case, that Miss Reeves' repatriation can be considered as of a compassionate nature – although, as you would be the first to appreciate, it is not adhering strictly to the guidelines of immediate next-of-kin ... but in the circumstances I can authorise ...'

'Thank you very much. I am very grateful to you, staff Captain.'

'I take it she will be ready to rejoin when we arrive back in Southampton?'

'Well, yes – that's the plan. The funeral is next week, and we won't be back in the UK until a week after that – so there is plenty of time – I don't know what you are worrying about.'

'Fine. Don't forget, she must see the purser for flight details, passport, tickets etc. I believe there might be a BA flight at four o'clock this afternoon.'

'That would be good. I can go to the airport with her.'

At the airport, Penny is tearful again.

'I feel so guilty, Harry. I've been having such a wonderful time. It's been like one long happy dream since I left England ... and poor Nana was so poorly, and I didn't even manage to see her before I left ... and now she has died, and I wasn't there ... and I'm leaving you ... oh, Harry, Harry.'

'There there,' he pulls her close, 'it's all part of life, I'm afraid, my darling. Goodness knows, you've seen enough of it in hospitals. I know it's different when it's your own, but you know what I mean. Don't worry, you'll be home for the funeral, and it will be exciting to see the family ... two weeks will fly by, and then we'll be together again. You'll rejoin in Southampton, and everything will be the same as before, I promise. Now, c'mon, dry your eyes before you get on the plane.'

Penny sniffs and blows her nose.

Harry looks at the TV monitor overhead.

'Your flight is boarding now. You'd better go. And don't forget – two weeks will whistle by ... have a safe journey...'

They embrace for the last time and exchange a fleeting kiss.

She walks towards the departure gate and shows her boarding card to the attendant. As she passes through quickly, she turns for a second and blows one last kiss. Harry waves and shouts.

'Safe journey ... see you soon ... all my love...'

And then she has gone, and an immediate heavy sadness descends on Harry. He stands motionless, staring at the departure gate wishing that he could simply walk through and go with her.

He takes a cab back to the *Empress* his mind swirling with a complexity of emotions as he tries to predict what it will be like without Penny for over two weeks. In the short period they had been together, they had established a strong bond, the intensity of which he had never before experienced. And he thinks now of the tearful reunion that Penny will have with her family and the sombre ritual of the funeral of her beloved grandmother.

Penny is surprised at the number of friends of her grandmother who have come to the funeral. And she does not even know half of the family members present – the aunts, uncles and distant cousins that she had not even seen before ... strange events, funerals, she thinks as she dutifully turns the pages in the musty-smelling hymn book. Most family members, even distant relatives, feel obliged to pay their last respects – and they likewise hardly know each other. There are awkward and uncomfortable moments as the mourners meet before and after the service. Names are not remembered. There are botched introductions followed by embarrassing silences. And now the chief mourners, the inner circle of family and privileged friends, are back at Penny's parents' house. Penny has taken her coat to the upstairs bedroom. As she walks in, a voice cries out.

'Penny! Darling! How lovely to see you, my girl.'

It is her other grandmother, that is, her mother's mother. She turns from the wardrobe with arms open to embrace Penny, who still has the watery-eyed look of the close family mourners.

'There there, my dear. You'll get over it,' she says matter-of-factly with little emotion. But then she is well into her seventies and has in the last few years attended many funerals. Besides, it was not a blood relative, but merely the mother of her son-in-law, whom she hardly knew. She tries to modulate her alacrity and what might be perceived as a lack of appropriate emotion, but Penny senses the truth of the situation.

'Nan, you've never really liked Dad or his family, have you?' she says with a candour that takes even her grandmother by surprise.

'You mustn't say that, my dear. Of course I love your father. He has been a good husband to your mother and a loving father to his children, so how could I not like him?'

Her face is flushed and she is hesitant. The words are empty and without feeling.

'Of course we have had our differences – your father and I, that is ... but we've always managed to overcome ... I mean to say, eventually accommodate those differences...'

'Yes, I understand, Nan – but be honest, you've never really liked Dad, have you?'

'It's difficult for me, Penny ... I cannot explain exactly.'

There is a long pause. Penny senses her grandmother wants to say something, but is holding back.

'Tell me, Nan – why?'

296

There is an even longer silence as the old woman purses her lips and heaves an exaggerated sigh. Her face shows she is making a decision whether to yield to Penny's forceful interrogation or stay firm and close the subject.

'Your father, my dear – I know you love him very much – so I do not want to say anything that will upset you – but ... well, the truth is – I could never accept that he was the right choice for my daughter – your mother, that is. I'm truly sorry if that sounds harsh and cruel ... perhaps I shouldn't say any more.'

'No – please go on, Nan, I want to hear.'

'Your mother was such a lovely sporty and adventurous young girl, full of the zest for life, and it was a surprise to your grandfather and I when she became interested in your father. He was very conventional and quiet – and dare I say – or so we thought at the time – just too boring for our daughter. I know it sounds silly, but he was almost too well-behaved and agreeable – which I know is the sort of thing a prospective mother-in-law would hardly ever say. It's just that he wasn't interested in any of the things she loved doing, and really, we thought, that in their best interests, they were totally unsuited for marriage. I must confess though, as it turned out to be, they have made a successful life together, and I am very happy for that. And of course we have you and your brother. I shouldn't say any more ... I've had too much sherry and it makes me talk too much ...'

'Is there anything else to say, Nan? Please tell me if there is something you think I should know.'

'My lovely Penny. You were so full of energy from the moment we all stared down at you in your crib. I can see you now – you were such a beautiful baby – your mother was so deleriously happy when she had you ... and naturally when you grew up you so clearly proved to have inherited your mother's sense of fun and adventurous spirit – perhaps even more so. Look at you now – sailing around the world on a luxury cruise liner, and still so young. I envy you, my dear, but I am so happy for you. All I can say is, thankfully you're not like your father, if you don't mind me saying so, Penny dear – absolutely no sense of adventure there, I'm afraid. You've

297

plainly got that in abundance, so much of it. But then you showed it as a child – that wanderlust spirit … I wonder sometimes – as well as your mother, you must have inherited it from your real f- … oh dear, now what have I said?'

'Penny looks puzzled and then turns a ghostly pale as she realises what she thinks her grandmother has just said.

'What do you mean, Nan?'

'It doesn't matter, my dear. It was nothing.'

'Please, Nan. You were about to say something about…'

'It was a slip of the tongue, my dear. It is nothing of importance.'

'NAN – please. PLEASE.'

'Don't shout, dear. You frighten me.'

'I'm sorry, Nan – but you must tell me. You were going to say "real father" weren't you? What on earth do you mean? Have I got another father?'

'Sit down, Penny. Sit down and listen.'

The little grey-haired old lady slowly lowers herself into the chair and assumes a posture that displays clearly that she is about to say something of dramatic importance.

'Penny, my dear – you are adopted. Your father, your adoptive father that is, is NOT your real father…'

'I can't believe…'

'Let me finish. Please. Just listen for a moment. Your mother longed for children, but tragically they never came. After five years of childless marriage, she was desperate. I don't think your father was quite so anxious, but anyway they adopted you and a few years later, your brother Mark … so I'm afraid you're both from different fathers, and your "father" isn't your real father, I'm sorry to say. I really didn't want to tell you, but honestly, you forced my hand, didn't you? Your mother will be furious. I must admit, I thought you and Mark knew anyway, because your mother said years ago that she intended to tell you both when you reached an age you'd be able to understand.'

'We never knew, I can tell you, Nan.'

'Oh well, it's too late now – I've told you, and it's probably a good thing too.'

298

'But Nan, I love Daddy so much. He means everything to me. Poor Daddy ... poor poor Daddy.'

'I'm sorry, – I shouldn't have said those things about your father. He is a good man and a loving father – he has given you both a good life. You must realise that fact. Nothing can change that.'

'Nan, what do you think my real father is like?'

'Oh this is getting silly now. I really don't know. I dare not speculate on such a thing. You've certainly got your looks from your mother and a part of your sense of adventure, that's for sure – but the restless spirit – that's something else. I guess it might come from him whoever he is ... your true father, that is.'

'Could I find out who he is?'

'I shouldn't even think of such a thing, my dear. Apart from anything else, it would be unbearably cruel to your mother – and of course your father – no, put it out of your mind. It would serve no useful purpose at all.'

The look of utter bewilderment on Penny's face changes to one of puzzlement as she tries to digest everything that her Nan has just confided.

'But Nan, I don't understand what you've just said.'

'What do you mean – I thought it was quite clear.'

'Well – you said I was adopted and my father is not my real father ... and yet – mother is my real mother. I mean, she was definitely pregnant for me. I've seen the pictures. And God, everyone says we look like twins so how can I be adopted? It doesn't make sense.'

'Ah well, Penny dear, it's a little more complicated. In all honesty, I couldn't begin to explain the exact details, so really, I shouldn't say any more about it. I've said far too much already. I think it's time you had a word with your mother. Oh dear, I wish I hadn't said anything now. She'll be so angry with me ... let's go downstairs – and please, Penny, don't say anything about our conversation until I've gone.'

'All right Nan, I promise.'

As they leave the bedroom her Nan's expression has become serious and Penny's face is a mixture of perplexion and hurt.

She has learned that her dear beloved father is not her real father and that she is adopted. That is disturbing enough, but doesn't explain how she is still the natural daughter of her mother.

'I'll wash up.'

Penny gathers the piles of dirty plates and cutlery from the table. There had been a veritable banquet of food, and the sombre sadness of the occasion had not dampened appetites.

'I'll wipe then, dear. I'm so glad it's all over. What a relief!'

Her mother's eyes are moist as she picks up a large plate and starts to wipe vigorously, as if she is wiping away the tension and grief of the funeral ritual.

'We've hardly had a chance to talk – you've got so much to tell me about your adventures at sea – and your new boyfriend! You haven't said how old he is or what he looks like. I mean, is he handsome? I'm sure he is. And he's the ship's doctor – well, you know what they say...'

'Please Mum, I promise I'll tell you everything, but first you must tell me something.'

Her mother appears alarmed at the seriousness in the tone of Penny's voice.

'Tell you what, Penny love?'

'What "adopted" means.'

'What on earth are you talking about?'

'I'm sure you know.'

'I'm sure I don't my dear. Please explain. You've got me worried now.'

'Nan tells me I'm adopted. How can that be? You are my real mother, and I assume Dad is my real father. It just doesn't make sense. I don't understand.'

'Let's go into the lounge, I'll need to pour myself a stiff drink. This will take some time. I guess we should have told you years ago, and your brother. We should have realised that it was bound to come out sooner or later – it's just that we – that is, your father and I, couldn't bring ourselves to tell you. We thought it could be glossed over, buried with time and become unimportant – never mentioned, forgotten. Nobody would ever possibly know the truth. But now – my mother, your Nan – has said something which has confused you...'

'Nan didn't mean to say anything. It slipped out – she'd had a few sherries – we were simply talking about character and personality...'

'Yes, I've often wondered what sort of man your true father was. Wild and adventurous, I'd imagine, judging from your character and behaviour...'

'So Nan was speaking the truth? But I don't understand. How can it be? You weren't married before Father.'

'AID. Artificial Insemination by Donor. That's the stork that brought you into the world. A private Harley Street infertility clinic. There were lots of them in the mid Sixties, and I was desperate to get pregnant. Eventually, after years of heartache, I – with your father, of course – decided to try these clinics. We were frightened at first. And when the clinic we chose dis- covered your father was infertile and I was "normal" it was a terrible blow to him. But after the initial shock he took it well, and was happy and supportive for me to go through the business of being fertilised by a semen specimen from another man – a completely anonymous stranger, that is.

'You have to realise, that for any man it is quite a blow to, to – his manhood if you like – although in my eyes, your father was no less a man than the man I'd married, and he certainly proved to be no less than the perfect father to both you and Mark...' Her voice trails and tears well up.

'He has always looked upon you and Mark as his true children. Right from the very beginning it required tremen- dous strength from him to give me all the support I needed to go through the ghastly business of AID. Trips to London every month. All the disappointments which in the beginning only added to the misery. Unimaginable heartache. But then there came the joy with pregnancy and the absolute ecstasy with your birth. But I think there was more of that feeling from me than your father – well, you understand what I'm saying. Even so, he was delighted for me, and for us both, because it was the realisation of a dream. And when your brother Mark came

301

along, the picture was complete and we were, and of course still are, very happy.

'I think your father's real joy and contentment of fatherhood came with seeing me so happy as a mother and then of being involved as the father who brought you both up right from the very beginning, as if you came from him. It didn't seem to make any difference, and after a little while the nature of your origin became forgotten and irrelevant.'

Penny sighs deeply and sits silently as the facts sink in to her consciousness.

'I cannot believe it. All these years. And father and I are so close. How can it be? How could I possibly come from some-one else?'

'It's a fact, Penny my love. We should have told you a long time ago. I'm sorry that you had to find out like this – and at such a sad time for us all. Maybe it's all for the better now. I must say, I feel relieved and...'

'Tell me, the clinic in London – the one that you went to – I mean the man, the donor, the person who...'

'Your real father? Absolutely anonymous, strictly confiden-tial. I certainly never had a clue, and the clinic could never tell us. We will never know.'

'Why?'

'I was told from the very beginning that such information was an absolute confidential secret between the clinic and the donor. It had to be that way. All we were told was that the donors were usually medical students from London Teaching Hospitals. Maybe that's how you've got your interest in nursing – who knows?'

'It's incredible, Mother. I just can't take it in. I feel so confused now – my "real" father...'

'It's not "real", in the sense of the reality of here and now, if you see what I mean. As the doctor in the clinic told me in the beginning, when I'd had second thoughts, the young men in question were simply "sperm machines" – that's what he actually called them – sperm machines supplying a vital ingredient for my anticipated conception. He said they were merely mechanical or physiological fathers. Fathers, but not fathers in the true and full sense of the word. You know – not fathers in the sense of nurturing and bringing up a child, as in real fatherhood.'

'Yes but surely the genes, the character – and the inherited features – everything, it's from him, the anonymous donor. You can't alter that can you?'

'Well, I honestly don't know. I must confess, I often wondered in the beginning what your "donor" was like. You were such a beautiful, healthy child but you bore no resemblance to your father, your "second" father, shall we say.'

'People would often remark, jokingly of course, that it must have been the milkman. I can see the funny side of it now, but at the time it never failed to touch a sensitive spot. Fortunately, your father was able to appreciate the joke that others didn't realise they were making, but I think deep down, it hurt him that he wasn't your real father. As you got older and we all grew together more like a typical family, then it was hardly ever mentioned again and was completely forgotten, as if it had never happened.

'Who knows where this anonymous benefactor might be now, or what he looks like or what he is doing? Probably he is a conventional middle-aged man, happily settled down somewhere with his own family, leading an ordinary life just like the rest of us. He will have forgotten that time in his youth when he provided such a valuable service to women desperate to become pregnant – at almost any price. And he will never know what a beautiful daughter he has helped create, a daughter who has brought so much happiness to two very lucky parents. In a funny sort of way, I feel sad for him. It's as if he has lost something priceless which he has never had – if that makes sense.'

'It is so hard to believe. It's incredible. First my Nan dies – and then this.' She cannot stem the tears any longer.

'Come here, my dear.'

Her mother hugs her.

'Here, wipe those silly tears. Forget all that nonsense, and tell me about your wonderfully exciting life on board and all the new friends – not to mention your new boyfriend.'

Penny is grateful for the distraction from the confusing thoughts implanted by the astounding truth of her origins, and she begins to chronicle in fine detail her life on board the luxury cruise liner from the moment she joined in Singapore.

'…and so you see, although Harry is quite a bit older he's very young at heart and physically could pass as thirty – easily. Honestly Mother, you wouldn't believe it if you saw him…'

'But Penny, it's only a month, and you're so young. You've lots of time, and I'm sure there are many handsome, intelligent bachelors just lining up to meet you. Treat it as a sea-going romance, and don't get too serious. I don't want you to get hurt in any way, that's all. Now tell me, what are your plans?'

'I have to rejoin the *Empress* next week in Southampton. It will be sailing to New York, and I think there is a cruise to the Caribbean before returning across the Atlantic early next month. My official leave is due in about five weeks' time, and then I'll be home again.'

'That all sounds so exciting. Your father and I are so happy for you. He talks about you to everyone – I even have to tell him to shut up sometimes. But oh, Penny, he is so proud of his daughter, you wouldn't believe it. And remember, you are HIS daughter. You must never reveal that you know this secret. It would serve no useful purpose, and I know it would break your father's heart.'

'Of course I understand. And I agree. Anyway, Dad is Dad – and he is MY Dad – that's easy. It makes me love him more than ever.'

'God bless you. Now – enough of this serious talk. You mentioned earlier that you needed to see Dr Thomas. Have you made an appointment yet?'

'Yes. At 9.15 tomorrow morning.'

'I know it's not my business – and you are a grown girl now, but I am still your mother and – everything is all right, is it, dear?'

'Oh, you are a silly old worry-pot! It's nothing, really. It's just that I've had an upset stomach for a week now and I've been feeling a bit sick and off my food. I imagine I've picked up one of those exotic bugs from all the foreign ports we've visited.

We get lots of cases on board, you know. At least I haven't got diarrhoea. I'm sure Dr Thomas will put me right.'

'Good. That's a relief. But make sure you get it sorted out before you return to the ship.'

'Come in. Lovely to see you, my girl.'

'Hello, Dr Thomas.'

'Take a seat. I'm sorry to hear about your grandmother.'

Penny nods in silent appreciation as she sits down in the patient's chair adjacent to the ancient wooden desk, behind which sits the avuncular grey-haired physician who has looked after her since she was a new-born babe.

'How's life on the ocean wave?' he says, failing to suppress a twinkle in the eye.

'I'm really enjoying it. It's fabulous.'

'Well, my dear, you look far too healthy to be visiting me. You are positively beaming. But what can I do for you?'

'It started a couple of days before I left the ship in Los Angeles...'

'It's all right for some.'

'You know, I had to fly home for Nana's funeral. Anyway, it was the nausea that upset me the most. I assumed I had a stomach upset – you know, we get lots of it on the ship. But I didn't have any diarrhoea. One or two cramps maybe, that's all. Half the ship seems to suffer from those symptoms at one time or another. We visit so many exotic places, where they say the food and water is not safe or as hygienically treated as it should be.'

'Uuum. And how do you feel now?'

'There's no bowel upset and I don't have any pains or cramps, but I do feel nauseated at times. Not all the time – just now and again. I'm not really off my food, except when I'm feeling sick.'

'You're not taking any medications, you know the Pill or anything like that are you?'

'No. Nothing.'

'I know you're not allergic to anything. Let's have a little

305

look at you anyway, young lady. Hop onto the couch. No need to get undressed. Just loosen the top of your skirt – that's fine. As perfect a healthy suntanned specimen as I've ever seen. Sorry, a bit of pressure. I'll feel gently. No more than that.'

He begins to palpate each abdominal quadrant methodically.

'No tenderness?'

'No, just a bit ticklish,' says Penny, stifling a giggle.

'Good. A bit squelchy in the ileo-caecal region, but apart from that, nothing. Periods OK?'

'Yes. I think so. Yes, in fact I'm a little late this month, but that is not unusual. It's anything from four to six weeks at the best of times, so I'm not particularly worried.'

'And of course you've changed your job – and lifestyle pretty drastically. Have you got a boyfriend on the ship?'

'Yes. In fact, he is the ship's doctor. He's lovely.' Penny diverts her eyes and blushes through her suntan.

'I'm sure he is Penny, – and I'm sure you are both very responsible, eh?'

'What do you mean?'

'Well, I've looked after you since you were a tiny tot, so I think we should know each other pretty well by now. Of course, you're a big girl now, and a fully qualified nurse, mature and responsible – look Penny, I'm talking about contraception.'

Penny lowers her head and blushes again.

'You said you are taking no pills?'

'Yes. Nothing.'

'Now – you and your boyfriend – I take it you are having sexual relations?'

Penny's blush deepens.

'Yes. We are.'

'Does he take any precautions?'

'I'm not sure, I mean I've not really thought about it – I – I don't think so, uuum...'

'You don't think so! He doesn't use a condom?'

'No.'

'And now we have to get specific, I'm afraid Penny. I know it

306

is embarrassing for you, but it is very important. Does he withdraw just prior to ejaculation?'

'N – no, I don't think so.'

'All right, I understand. Now I know we have never fitted a coil for you – and I take it you have not had one fitted elsewhere?'

'No.'

'And you have been having frequent sexual relations for how long?'

'About five weeks.'

'I see.'

Penny's blush recedes and her complexion converts to an ashen grey despite the suntan, as she realises what Dr Thomas is suggesting.

'Penny, pregnancy is always possible in a fertile, sexually active young woman, especially if there appears to be no protection – that is contraception. I must confess, I am a little surprised – what with you a nurse and your boyfriend a doctor. If you don't mind me saying, it's a little irresponsible, don't you think?'

She is silent. She looks down at the desk and tries to speak, but the words do not come.

'It can certainly explain your nausea – I'm not saying it is, but we must rule it out.'

'Dr Thomas, I – I just don't know what to say. I feel so – so ...'

'Look, don't worry. There is no need to panic. Go away today and bring me a fresh early-morning urine specimen tomorrow, and we'll take it from there, all right?'

'But, but – what if I'm pregnant?'

'Don't jump the gun. We'll meet that problem if it arises, but in the meantime, let's not presume it until we have the test result.'

'Don't bother, Penny dear, I'll answer it.'

'Hello Mrs Reeves, this is Dr Thomas's receptionist. Is Penny in?'

307

'Would you like to speak to her?'

'Yes please.'

'I'll fetch her for you – hold on. Penny, it's the surgery.'

'I'll take it up here.'

'Hello Penny, Dr Thomas would like a word.'

'Hello my dear – are you alone?'

'Yes – Mother is in the kitchen.'

'Listen carefully. You will have to come and see me as soon as possible to do some routine blood tests, because I am sure you will be anxious to rejoin the ship soon. Naturally we can discuss what you might do at the same time. There are several options which we must discuss carefully before you decide.'

'What do you mean?'

'Penny, your pregnancy test is strongly positive.'

CHAPTER 12

BLOOD TEST

And Lot went up out of Zoar, and dwelt in the mountain, and his two daughters with him; for he feared to dwell in Zoar: and he dwelt in a cave, he and his two daughters.

And the first born said unto the younger, Our father is old, and there is not a man in the earth to come into us after the manner of all the earth:

Come, let us make our father drink wine, and we shall lie with him, that we may preserve the seed of our father.

And they made their father drink wine that night: and the firstborn went in, and lay with her father; and he perceived not when she lay down and not when she arose.

And it came to pass on the morrow, that the firstborn said unto the younger, Behold, I am yesternight with my father: let us make him drink wine this night also; and go thou in and lie with him, that we may preserve the seed of our father.

And they made their father drink wine that night also; and the younger arose, and lay with him; and he perceived not when she lay down, nor when she arose.

Thus were both daughters of Lot with child by their father.

Genesis 19: 30–36

The *Empress* docks in Southampton. It is sunny, with ample patches of blue sky and enough wispy cloud moving briskly on the stiff breeze to add an extra dimension to the dull horizon of drab grey dockside sheds and the mountains of containers stretching as far as the eye can see. The crisp chill of a late spring morning is evaporating as the sun gets higher, and Harry is able to discard his jacket without feeling cold.

The expectation of seeing Penny again gives him a hollow feeling in his stomach. He leans over the rail high up on the boat deck and looks down at the scores of expectant faces on the quayside. Fork-lift trucks have already begun the job of loading and unloading. Very soon now the ship should be cleared by customs and immigration so that the crew and passengers can disembark.

He can see her! She sees him! He waves frantically. Even from that distance he can see how her soft silky hair glistens in the sunlight. She is still tanned from her weeks in the tropics and appears even more beautiful than when he last saw her. It seems an age ago.

With her crew pass she can get on board quickly. He feels nervous. It had been a short shipboard romance broken by over two weeks of seperation, and now he is fearful of whether there will still be the same mutual feeling. She is, and has been one girl amongst so many. What is so special about her, and why does he feel so committed? He is aware that it is out of character, and it engenders in him a sensation of doubt and uncertainty.

Now, he is at the top of the crew gangway and she is at the other end. Ignoring the bustling stream moving in both directions, they fight their way to the middle where they embrace tightly. It blocks the flow of human traffic in both directions, and unless they move on quickly the good humour will soon turn to irritation.

All doubts about the renewal of their commitment are evaporated in an instant. Once they have forced theirselves through the endless tide of bodies and landed safely inside the shell door, he showers her with kisses. That fragrance. Those eyes. The firm body. Such youthfulness. He didn't deserve it.

'Oh Harry, I missed you so much. Did you miss me?'

It is sweet music to his ears.

He nods, not a little self-consciously. There are too many curious onlookers witnessing their reunion.

'Let's go to my cabin. It's far too crowded here.'

The lift is unattainable, so they take the stairs up through the lower decks and along the labyrinth of alleyways, still threading their way through a surge of humanity anxious to disembark.

His cabin is a glorious haven of privacy. He closes the door and lets out a long sigh, as much in nervousness as relief.

Without thought or ceremony their lips meet passionately and set the seal on their rapidly rekindled feeling for each other. He breaks off and stands back to admire her, feast on her from head to toe.

'You – you look so well – so fit and healthy – and radiant. Yes, I think that's the word, my love – radiant.'

She looks down at the floor with a contrived look of innocent demureness.

'Oh, I'm sorry – how did the funeral go?'

'It was okay. Honestly, I met relatives I didn't know I had – and I learnt something truly amazing ... but then I'm not sure that I should tell you ...'

'Now don't tease me. What was it? Are you going to inherit a long-lost fortune or something?'

'Nothing as lucky as that. No, it's something you couldn't possibly guess. Perhaps you wouldn't even be interested – it's not really that important – certainly not as important as the other bit of news I've got to tell you…'

'Oh Christ, this sounds intriguing. C'mon, young lady, you know how impatient I am.'

'Well, it was at the funeral – or I should say back at the house where the close friends and relatives had gathered. I went upstairs to hang my coat and found my grandmother, the maternal one that is – you know, my mother's mother…'

Penny tells him the whole story of her mother's revelation, finally finishing almost breathless with excitement and an exaggerated sense of drama in her voice: 'Oh Harry, it explains so many things – you know, about different temperaments and personalities – and as Nan said, my "adventurous spirit", which dear Daddy didn't seem to have. All that mother could say was that whoever had been the donor, he most certainly would have had an adventurous spirit. Isn't that amazing?'

'Fascinating. Absolutely incredible.'

Images of his own involvement in the AID business all those years ago flash before him. Those cold winter mornings when it was necessary to produce an adequate semen sample and then carry it by hand in a warm coat pocket on the crowded underground to the clinic in Harley Street. God, that was well over 20 years ago – around the same time that Penny was talking about when the whole business of AID was beginning to boom.

He is tempted to recall his own experiences and intimate involvement as a medical student. But he holds back. He cannot reveal such a thing to her. It might upset her that he had donated to so many women and produced so many anonymous offspring.

'Absolutely fascinating,' he repeats with conviction, 'I can tell you one thing, whoever he was, he must have been intelligent, handsome, if not beautiful – and full of the zest for life. Now, is that a compliment or what?'

'Ha ha, don't be so silly. Actually, I look very much like my mother, so quite probably I have very few of his features – excepting the adventurous spirit, of course!'

313

'Anyway, it makes little difference. The donor might be your biological father, but your "real" father, the one who's provided for you and nurtured you all your life – that's the one you've got now.'

'Yes, I accept that, and love my father even more. Even so, it all came as a bit of a shock, I must confess.'

'Now, after that little tale, you deserve a drink. I could do with one myself. What'll you have?'

'Just a tonic – with ice and lemon, if you've got it.'

'Now, you said there was another piece of news you had for me?'

'I went to see my doctor...'

'But I thought I was your doctor!'

'Don't be silly, Harry. You know what I mean.'

'Well, I can't see that there's much wrong with you, young lady,' he says forcefully, feigning offence that she had to seek the attention of another practitioner.

Her face assumes a dramatic pose, and she sits bolt upright as if she is about to make an important pronouncement.

'Well – what on earth did you go and see him for?'

'Can't you guess?'

'Haven't got a clue – c'mon, stop teasing me.'

There is a faint smile appearing and her eyes are glued to his.

'I'm pregnant.'

He does not move. Even his eyelids seem paralysed and he cannot blink.

'What! Of course! All that blessed nausea on the ship before you left – it must have been morning sickness and we didn't even realise.'

'I'm pregnant. Pregnant and so happy.'

His immediate mental reaction is confused. In fact, his mind is a complete muddle. He is apprehensive. This has not happened to him before, at least not in these circumstances.

As he looks at Penny's unrestrained joy, there comes over him a creeping feeling of desire to share it with her and indulge uninhibitedly in such news. But he is bewildered. His face shows it.

314

'Harry? Harry? Are you all right? Did you hear what I said? I am pregnant – with your child.'

'Are you – are you sure?' is all he can whisper.

'Of course I'm sure. I've had all the tests. Aren't you happy?' She is perplexed by his blank stare of consternation.

It begins to sink in. But he cannot assimilate it easily. It is an entirely new experience he is unable to relate to previous experiences. Finally he allows his emotions to assume control.

'Penny. Penny darling.'

He pulls her towards him. 'Oh Penny, I just simply can't believe it, it's...'

'Does it make you happy?'

He senses concern in her voice.

'Deleriously so – of course – I mean – I really cannot – it's such a shock and, and...'

He holds her at arm's length.

'It's absolutely wonderful news. The best I've ever had in all my life – truly, truly.'

He pulls her towards him again and showers her face with kisses in a show of uninhibited affection. But then he pulls away. Practical considerations are creeping into his thoughts.

'What does your mother say?'

'I haven't told her yet. Maybe after she's met you – whenever we'll be able to arrange that. But you haven't told me yet if you still love me.'

His sensual kiss square on her lips answers her question. She breaks away.

'Guess what? My doctor, my "other" doctor that is, says that I am a rare blood group – I must say, I never knew – but anyway he said the laboratory would like a blood sample from the prospective father. I told him all about you, and he said he would like a sample from you at the earliest convenience.'

'Oh yes? What's that all about, then? They don't think I'm likely to have some rare blood group as well, do they?'

'No! Don't be silly. He just said that because my group was so rare, or at least it had some extremely rare factors in it, that it was necessary to predict the liklihood of the baby's blood group in case of future transfusions. Apart from that, he did admit that the rarity of the factor made it an important opportunity to study this particular blood group and a suitable specimen of your blood would also be necessary for that. Apparently the local hospital lab had actually phoned my doctor to make the request.'

'That's fine by me. So how soon do they want it, and where?'

'Well, they said we can leave it at the Norsk shipping office when we arrive in Southampton, who can then send it by courier to London.'

'London? I thought it was your local hospital laboratory?'

'The doctor said they were sending my blood to a haematological research institute in London which made a special study of rare blood groups in pregnancy, and they would be the ones who would want your blood also. Sounds complicated – I'm sorry, Harry! I think he said it was somewhere in Harley Street.'

'Harley Street? Then it must be a private laboratory. Perhaps if they want my blood so badly I should charge them for it!'

'No, no. It's actually a government research institute, or so he told me, and it was doing important work for the Health Service.'

'Fair enough – right, we can take it today. In fact, I need to see the boss about something, so I can easily take it over myself before we sail tonight. Now, what about your future?'

'I don't need to see the doctor again for six weeks at the earliest. I've looked at the ship's schedule, and it should fit in nicely on one of our Southampton visits – I think it'll be about the time of the Mediterranean cruise. Oh Harry – I'm so happy! Promise me – does it make you happy?'

He feels strange. It is an odd sensation. He is uncertain if it is pleasure, discomforture, fear or a combination of all those emotions. It is a new experience, the prospect of parenthood, but it has come much later in his life, and maybe it is just more difficult to accomodate at his age.

'It's just come as a bit of a shock, that's all.'

Her face shows concern.

'No, no – really Penny, I am very very happy and...'

She cranes her neck upwards and fixes on Harry's eyes. She

316

can recognise that, despite his bemused expression, he is delighted with the news. She stands back relieved, and looks him up and down as a sergeant-major might a raw recruit. She laughs.

'Look at you, Harry! You've put on weight. Your face is flabby. I can hardly recognise you. If you're not careful I might not fancy you anymore – I might even start looking for a younger man...'

'Quite right too,' he answers submissively and not a little guiltily. 'I haven't been to the gym for some time – put on over ten pounds – terrible, isn't it?'

'Uuuum. You'd better get in shape, or I could definitely go off you...'

'That's it – today, I go on a crash programme – proper diet, no alcohol, vigorous exercise, gymnasium every day and of course as much sex as I have energy enough left over for...'

'Promise?'

'You just wait and see. In two weeks time I will look at least twenty years younger.'

'I'll believe it when I see it.'

'You want a younger man – you'll get one ... just you wait and see.'

'I just cannot believe it. It's impossible. It cannot be. There must be a mistake. But I've checked it four times already. The names. The samples. The circuit. The 'scope – the whole damn apparatus. It's all perfect. How can it be? It can't be...'

'What on earth are you mumbling on about, Bill?'

'Oh, hello Doctor. It's a bit of a puzzle, quite frankly. I'm sure I've done something wrong, but I can't see it. I'm in the process of analysing and matching blood samples. After the usual tissue type protocol I've done a DNA genetic fingerprint profile on two samples, and the picture I'm getting is unbelievable. I'm sure I've made a fundemental mistake somewhere in the process, but I just cannot see it.'

'I'm sorry, you've lost me – what on earth are you talking

about? You – a mistake? Highly improbable, I'd say. You're the senior technician in this lab, and if you make mistakes then the whole bloody edifice crumbles. Tell me, what's the problem? I'm sure it's something simple.'

'Well, a couple of weeks ago I did a routine analysis on a blood sample from a pregnant woman with a rare blood group, which had been sent to us from a district clinic. It's a rhesus negative base combining the extremely rare sub-group antigen specificity factor, Gamma three recessive, which is as rare as hen's teeth.

'You know we're doing a study on the genetic prevalence of this recessive characteristic, and getting our hands on this sample was a real windfall. As per protocol I naturally requested a blood sample from the putative father for sequential corrolative analysis, DNA fingerprinting etc. etc., you know, the full work up, and his specimen arrived in the lab yesterday. Since then, I've put it through the full haemotological profile, not once but four times, cross-checking my methodology each time at every single step of the process.

'The results have been totally consistent. And in particular, the DNA match has been startlingly reproducible, right down to the sub-group minor bands . . .'

'Very good – so what's the problem?'

'I've subjected the pregnant woman's blood to the same analytical profile, including the DNA fingerprinting spectrum, and . . .'

'Yes Bill, very interesting – I know you're gathering data for the paper we're going to publish – but why the sudden interest in these particular samples?'

'Come and see for yourself.'

'I am actually very busy and I must finish the report I've got to present to the society tomorrow, and I've also got a lecture to give to the PhD students at one o'clock . . .'

'Please Doctor Coombes, I know you are very busy, but I think you, as the lab director, ought to see these two samples.'

'Goodness, you are sounding very serious and official – all right, only if you've got them all set up ready in the comparative analyser. I can spare a couple of minutes, but that's all.'

318

'The samples are ready for you. You just need to simply look down the microscope.'

'Uuum. Yes.'

'Do you see?'

'Yes, I see. Two DNA spectra. Beautifully prepared, as I would expect from you. Congratulations. I've told you a million times Bill, as if you need reminding, that you are the best technician in our lab and...'

'Yes, thank you – but what can you say about the two spectra and the DNA fingerprint?'

'Let me see again. Uuum. 'D' bands, two 'Ff' bands and an Alpha-Beta-one sub-group, a small X-Delta two band, congruent symmetry on the Gamma series – yes, very clear – nicely done. You've managed to achieve a remarkable consistency in your preparative methods. These two samples are almost identical, except that is, for the aberrent Delta band in the upper spectral frequency – and perhaps the tonal quality of the staining procedure.

'We need that sort of consistency in a lab like this – our reputation depends on it – and with your skills in the new genetic fingerprinting methods, our work is becoming more and more valued internationally. But you hardly need a reminder from me of how good you are...'

'But Doctor, with all respect, you've missed the point. I'm sorry if I haven't made myself clear. You are looking at two seperate samples, labelled clearly "one" and "two"...'

'Yes, I can see that quite clearly. You've prepared two samples from blood cells of the pregnant woman with the rare blood group that we're doing studies on, and ... really, I must go. Well done again.'

'But the sections of the DNA spectra which show a remarkably similar configuration – each is from a totally different blood sample.'

'Yes – but what are you saying exactly?'

'If these were absolutely identical in every band, that is, in over thirty separate bands, not including the sub-groups, then we could say with a billion-to-one certainty that the blood samples are from the same person, can't we?'

'Go on.'

'These two samples are almost the same, except for the slight incongruity in those minor bands I mentioned. But certainly in the major Alpha, Beta-one, Kappa, Delta and Gamma bands there is an astonishing degree of compatibility which cannot be entirely explained by the...'

'Wait a minute, Bill, not so fast. These two spectra from two blood samples you are saying are from two different people...'

'Yes! Precisely.'

'You said one was from the pregnant woman.'

'Correct.'

'That's the one on the right, yes?'

'That's it.'

'And the one on the left – that's another person?'

'Most certainly. I've checked and checked. There cannot be any error.'

'But that's an incredible match in the circumstances of such a rare group. Where did you get, or I should say, who did you get the second blood sample from?'

'That's the whole point. It's from the putative father of the pregnancy.'

'What? Let me see again. I don't believe it. But there it is ... All bands identical in the major sections, and only those three sub-bands in the Alpha and Gamma sequence differ slightly. That's incredible. It's either a billion-to-one chance congruence, or, or...'

'Yes, Doctor...?'

'...or the father of the child this pregnant woman is expecting is also the father of the pregnant woman herself.'

CHAPTER 13

HARLEY STREET REVISITED

Man with all his noble qualities, with sympathy that feels for the most debased, with the benevolence which extends not only to other men but to the humblest living creature, with his god-like intellect which has penetrated into the movements and constitution of the solar system – with all these exalted powers – still bears in his bodily frame the indelible stamp of his lowly origin.

The Descent of Man, Charles Darwin (1809–1882)

'I really fancy you now, darling.'

He stands in front of the full-length mirror wearing only boxer shorts, unashamedly preening. He has lost over ten pounds in two weeks. It has made a difference. Gone are the heavy jowls and the flab around his loins. His abdominals are firm and easily palpable. The contour of his rectus abdominus is clearly visible.

'So this younger version will be satisfactory, eh?' he says to his admirer as she slides out of bed, wrapping herself in the large bath towel he has brought for her.

He kisses the back of her neck.

'Go on – you have a shower first, I've got plenty of time. I want to finish that investment article I was reading last night. It tells you how to make a fortune out of even the most modest of savings...'

'But I haven't got any savings.'

'You will when you've been around as long as I have.'

The shower turns on and Harry reclines on the bed to study the *Investor's Chronicle*.

He decides to join her before she has finished, but is determined to resist any temptation to delay their exit. He must complete half a dozen medical assessments on crew members that morning. These mandatory health checks on all merchant seamen every five years are a bore, and he wants to complete them before the passenger clinic starts at 10 a.m. In the shower, their fondling poses a threat to his tight schedule.

Despite his rock hard erection, he musters all the resources of self-discipline to suppress his volatile animal instincts lest they assume control of the situation.

Soon they are dressed and heading for the officers' dining room. It is a distance of nearly a quarter of a mile from his cabin in the stern section. They walk along the 2 deck passenger corridor, stretching virtually the whole length of the ship, to the A stairway far forward, which leads up to the officers' mess on the quarter deck. As the luxuriously carpeted passage stretches ahead of them, it is hard to believe that they are actually on a ship ploughing through the waves at a comfortable 26 knots. It was different when there was a heavy swell. Then the ship would lurch from side to side and bow to stern in a slow-motion corkscrew fashion which, at times, could be quite alarming.

It is only 7.30. Most of the passengers are still sleeping off the effects of the night before. Stewards are flurrying about all along the corridor, in and out of the staterooms, carrying laden breakfast trays for those passengers too idle or too drunk to make it to the dining room. Others brandish dusters, push vacuum cleaners or carry piles of towels and sheets ready to respond to the calls which will begin soon enough.

They stride past the purser's office at G stairway. There is a crew entrance on the starboard side of the office which is reached through a door concealed in the wooden facia of the side panelling. It serves as a short-cut to the hospital along the working alleyway down on 6 deck, and is used as an emergency. As they pass, the door opens and a figure emerges. Harry is vaguely aware through his peripheral vision that it is a deckhand whom he recognises, although the beard has gone. The bruises have disappeared, and when he turns to face the man directly, he can see that the scar on the face has healed satisfactorily.

Penny also signals recognition, and in her eyes Harry cannot miss the undisguised admiration for the handsome figure. She smiles warmly at him, and he blushes deeply.

'Good morning. I hardly recognise you without your beard – and now that the cuts and bruises have healed. You look well.'

324

'Yes – thank you, Doctor.'

The young man glances at Penny and then quickly diverts his eyes self-consciously. It is a plain signal that he is attracted to her. That is not surprising, and although it doesn't go unnoticed by Harry, it doesn't bother him. In fact, he would be disappointed if she were not attractive to other men.

The handsome young deckhand turns sharply, and bidding a muffled self-conscious 'Good morning', continues on his way in the other direction.

Penny is aware that Harry has noticed the man's reaction to seeing her, although she is uncertain if he had been able to detect any reaction she might have shown in seeing the man. She pre-empts any doubt, as if she is able to read Harry's mind.

'He looks so different without his beard – and now the wounds have healed, I must say, he is actually quite handsome, even a slight resemblance to you, Harry – now that you've lost all that weight, my dear.'

'Thanks for the compliment.'

'Seriously, there is a faint resemblance – he's a lot younger, of course...'

'Of course...'

'No, really. He has a similar nose – and the eyes, definitely the eyes, and the cheekbones – I think there is a likeness, don't you? I could quite fancy him.'

'That's fine by me. If you feel you need a newer model, one that can outperform me – then go ahead.'

She stops and turns towards him.

'You're not jealous, are you?' she teases.

'Come off it! How could I be jealous of a young whippersnapper still wet behind the ears?'

'I do believe you are a little envious, Doctor.'

'All right. I admit it. I wish I were twenty years younger. Alas, there's nothing I can do about it, is there? Can't put the clock back. But you must admit I'm in pretty good condition for my age.'

'Not bad. Not bad.'

They walk on.

A subterranean thought is reactivated in Harry as the features of the deckhand imprint clearly on his mind. There is a strange sensation of familiarity, a definite feeling of identification with the image, but he is unable to recall an event which would explain such a déjà-vu phenomenon.

The morning clinic passes routinely. Harry sees the last patient around 11.30 and then goes to the main kitchens with the hotel manager and executive chef to make a food and hygiene inspection. Penny decides to take an early lunch and then go to the upper sundeck. The weather is fine as the *Empress of the Seas* sails down the east coast of Florida, heading south for a short island-hopping cruise in the Caribbean.

'I'll see you later this afternoon, Penny – I'll be back in the cabin by 2.30 for my nap.'

'Sign of age ... only joking. You are still my number one, despite your advanced years...'

Harry clutches her around the waist firmly and pulls her towards him.

'If you weren't in such a delicate condition, young lady, I'd put you over my knee and spank you.'

Her smile obliterates any such intention, real or imagined. He is captivated by it and does not speak. She pretends to swoon, but stays firmly in his grip.

'Oh, Doctor.'

'Go away with you – and don't forget to take a good lunch – you're eating for two now.'

'Jason – what the hell are you doing? For Christ's sake, fix that block and tackle to the crossbar or you'll skull yourself with this swell and the ship rolling as it is.'

'Sorry, Jack.'

The assistant bosun and Jason Brown, the young seaman he most prefers as a mate, are in one of the lifeboats, applying a fresh coat of bright orange paint.

It is not easy work high up on the port side, where the breeze is stiff and the movements of the ship are exaggerated. It is made more difficult because Jason is preoccupied. He cannot

326

clear the image of the doctor and the nurse from his mind. He is experiencing a jumble of muddled thoughts and emotions, burning questions and suppressed desires.

How beautiful she looked this morning! Radiant. Vibrant. Graceful. Strong. Everything a man desires. But she is unreachable. Everyone knew she was the doctor's woman.

It wasn't a fair world. She is so young and beautiful – and despite his youthful appearance, he is so much older. Old enough to be her father. How can she prefer a man twice her age compared to someone like himself, who is probably close to her own? Perhaps it's the charm and experience of older men, not to mention affluence. All the attributes that age can bring which impulsive youth lacks.

But his face? Those features. He has lost weight and looks younger. The thought is reactivated. The original purpose – the search for his true identity. Is this the man? Could it possibly be? No! No! The feverish search for his real father had all but been extinguished many ships ago. It had been a fruitless, hopeless quest, prompted by a silly pipe dream founded on no more than a gossamer-thin thread of reality, a sentimental, and in the beginning highly charged, emotional idea that had driven him feverishly twice around the world. A fruitless search for an enigmatic soul who he didn't even know still existed.

He had at long last successfully buried the anguish, and seemed now to be reasonably content with life and at peace with himself. He had even started thinking of leaving the life of ships behind and continuing his studies at Law school, as his parents had originally hoped.

He has convinced himself that the four years at sea have not been wasted. Indeed, there was no doubt that he had matured, and with that, at times, painful maturing process gained priceless values from the sheer breadth of his experiences. His travels around the globe had shown him the almost limitless diversity of human culture and behaviour, and yet, in his observations, he had been able to recognise in peoples, the common thread of humanity revealing the same hopes and desires, the same fears and disappointments, the very same

327

human spirit in all. If only, he'd idealised, the nations of peoples could appreciate their unity of character, their common purpose, then perhaps it might make them less likely to fight each other...

Imperceptibly, the preoccupations and distractions of the 'University of Life', as one old semi-literate seaman described it, had drawn him away from his original purpose – the search for his genetic origin, his biological roots, his real identity – his true being – and it hadn't mattered.

It had been a search for a mysterious, ill-defined, unnamed faceless figure in an uncharted dimension, a craving to find not so much a body but a spiritual entity that he could truly call his father. Only after all this time had he become rational enough to question the validity, if not the sense of the original quest. Why had it been so damned important to him – to the exclusion of virtually everything else in his life? Now, with the passage of time, he had conquered the compulsion, the blinkered feverish drive to find and identify such a mysterious and ephemeral spirit – if indeed it existed at all.

But, but ... this man. Could he be the one? Has this unheralded and entirely unexpected re-emergence of interest been prompted by a force that might link them?

He recalls the flimsy evidence, the only hint that such a figure existed, from the information that had been grudgingly given to him at the infertility clinic by the nurse. She had felt genuinely sorry for him on that bitter winter's day, and had tossed him no more than the scrap of information that she dared – that the man who started the seed growing in his mother, the man who yielded his soul for a paltry sum of money, was a medical student – and possibly, only possibly, a doctor who went to sea some time many years ago.

It was scant and flimsy evidence to support the fantastic notion that this could be such a man.

But, but ... when he had been in his presence, just the few times in the ship's hospital after his injuries, and now, this morning for a few seconds passing on 2 deck – he could not deny he had felt a strange sensation that he could not explain.

Sheer coincidence, that's all it was! His emotions and the

328

deeply buried, virtually extinguished yearning were still capable of resurfacing uninvitedly, as if to play some sort of capricious trick on him. Such a nonsensical thought! Whimsical indulgent fantasy!

But, but ... that feeling. It is strange – and undeniably there. Disturbing and unnerving.

'Jason – JASON! I've told you – watch what you're doing, for Christ's sake. It's dangerous up here, and you'll have both of us over the side if you don't concentrate – shit, what on earth has got into to you?'

'I – I'm sorry, Jack. I was daydreaming. Don't worry, it won't happen again. I'll concentrate, I promise.'

His mind clears, and they continue their task uneventfully until midday. Jack speaks as they are about to finish.

'Are you coming to the Pig for a drink?'

'No thanks. A little exercise in the gym and then a spot of sunning on the foc'sle.'

'Suit yourself. I'll see you this afternoon.'

Penny is daydreaming. She is alone on the top sundeck, indulging in pleasurable thoughts. Thoughts of how much she enjoys life at sea, her job, the travel, the exciting exotic places she has visited around the world – and above all, how in love she is with Harry and the fact that she is now pregnant with his child.

She has told herself that the company need not know for some months yet. Their policy is compulsory resignation in such an event. She knows she can easily avoid that judgment for at least 12 weeks – before it starts to show. By that time, Harry might have ideas about leaving the sea. He could get a job ashore. She could work in a hospital, at least after two or three years, when the baby had started pre-school. She could still continue her nursing career, that is if another baby didn't come along!

Her dreams, etched in fantasy, are even more pleasurable because they could so easily become real, she tells herself.

The breeze freshens. She sits up and looks through the glass screen which shelters the port side. She stands to get a fuller view, and walks forward to the end of the sundeck and leans over the railing. She looks down to the foc'sle 50 feet below, where the ratings are permitted to sunbathe in between the anchor chains and giant capstans on the hot metal deck.

There are a number of crew stretched out, male and female, but her eyes automatically focus on one figure. She sees him lying on a white towel stark against the green-painted deck, just to the left of the port side anchor chain, away from the others. He is lying on his back. He is tanned. His body is perfection, lean and muscular, with the proportion and symmetry of a well-tuned athlete with the best of pedigrees.

She is able to indulge unobserved and alone. Although Harry is slim and in excellent shape for his age, in fact with the physique of a much younger man, this specimen lying 50 feet below, with the broad shoulders and narrow waist, has the distinct advantages of youthfulness. She lets her imagination run uncensored with no repressive interference, and inevitably her thoughts become erotic. She can sense his raw energy, even from this distance, and fantasises on the enthusiastic force he might use in lovemaking. Of course, he would be less experienced than Harry, without the finesse acquired from years of practice, but that would not matter too much. He would undoubtedly arouse her much quicker with the intensity of youth.

His smooth-tanned skin glistens in the hot sun. He stirs. He sits up and casually looks around in all directions. Penny pulls back sharply in case he should look upward. After a moment, she peeps over the railing – he has turned over on to his front and lies splayed out, with his arms above his head and his legs wide apart. The skinny swimming costume clearly displays his small, firm buttocks. She feels a fleeting sense of arousal as he fidgets to get comfortable on the hard metal surface. And now he turns over again onto his back. His head drops to one side, and she sees clearly a three-quarter profile of his face. It is quite astonishing!

There really is a likeness – only more apparent from a certain viewpoint such as this. The sharp features – high cheek

330

bones, square jaw, Roman nose – softer and less worn than Harry's – nevertheless exude a similarity which is startling.

For a few moments negative thoughts creep into her mind. She questions her committed involvement with Harry. He is much older, old enough to be her father. She is still young and attractive. There are so many younger men closer to her own age who might be more suitable. She feels a pang of uncertainty at the emotional commitment to Harry, intensified momentarily by the visual stimulus of the well-spoken deckhand below.

It had been a surprise to her when he'd said casually that he had qualified for university entrance on leaving school, and his parents had wanted him to go to Oxford or Cambridge. He had, in fact been promised an unconditional place at Cambridge, but had turned it down.

He had divulged all these facts to her when she was gently removing the sutures from his facial wounds. As far as he was concerned, he'd considered himself far too young at the time to go up to university, and he'd felt he should see a bit of the real world first. His parents, especially his father, had been firmly against such an idea, but had reluctantly conceded when he'd promised it would only be for a maximum of one year.

It had been almost four years now since he'd come away to sea, and he admitted that his parents were bitterly disappointed, if not despairing. She'd asked him how much longer he'd intended to stay at sea, but he'd been reluctant to give an answer. He wasn't sure, but he felt he needed some sort of motivation to reactivate his drive to get him out of the rut – and away from 'the seductive nature of the sea which could mesmerise a man's soul'. When he'd said that, she'd stopped pulling momentarily on the sutures. It had been such an inappropriately sophisticated and philosophical phrase that it had confused her perception of him as a deckhand, even if his claims of a private education and promised university place were true.

'Hello, Penny.'

Her indulgent reflections are interrupted abruptly by Suzanne's cheery voice.

'Thought I'd get a bit of sun before duty. I don't sleep too well after nights. It upsets my whole rhythm. Anything interesting on the foc'sle?'

Suzanne leans over.

'Oh, I see. Got the binoculars? What a hunk of torso. Say, isn't that the clever deckhand who got injured in the fight?'

'Yes – I think it could be him. He looks different now that the bruises are gone.'

'Very nice ... you know, there is a definite likeness to Harry, don't you think?'

Penny blushes as if Suzanne has somehow managed to gain uninvited entry into her thoughts.

'Oh, I don't know. Do you really think so?'

'Sure. Especially if you look from this position at his profile. Come over here – do you see what I mean?'

'Yes. I suppose with the eye of faith ... uuum.'

'But he's so dishy, isn't he?'

'That's all you ever think about...'

'And you don't, of course!'

Penny smiles.

'I'm more than happy with my doctor, thank you.'

'Well, I'll settle for that hunk down there, even if he is only a deckhand and rather young. Mind you – I noticed the way he looked at you when you treated him – I was watching when you dressed his wound one time. I think he came back for redressings more frequently than was necessary. I imagine he must fancy you. Surely you were aware of that?'

There is a hint of envy in Suzanne's voice. Penny blushes and splutters.

'Don't be silly. I hardly took any notice of him – simply got on with the job and did what was necessary.'

'Yes – of course.'

'Look, I've checked it and rechecked it ten times. I've meticulously gone through the whole damned process step by step. I've checked the original sample, the delivery docket, the main file and the storage records – absolutely everything. Every conceivable source of error I've ruled out. There has been no mistake. I'd stake my life on it. The picture – the facts are perfectly clear.'

'I believe you, Bill.'

'Well, what do you propose we do, Doctor?'

'We have no choice – we must contact the putative father. It is going to be an unpleasant task, but we have no choice. Apart for any moral or ethical reasons, there could be legal inter-pretations – and possibly complications – which must be addressed. Who knows exactly what is entailed? This has not happened before, as far as we know – certainly not where it has been clearly demonstrated by absolutely irrefutable proof.

'On the face of it, such a pregnancy is – well ... I suppose, illegal ... look, we must contact this man and as soon as possible. I know it could be a very sensitive matter ... after all, we do not know the social arrangement, do we?'

'I don't know what to think.'

'Well, if the father is consorting with his daughter, as the tests unequivocally imply, it does raise rather serious questions – God ... this is damn difficult, Bill. What the hell do we do?'

There is a prolonged silence as the two men ponder and struggle to come to terms with the discovery. Finally, Dr Coombes speaks, knowing that he must do what is necessary.

'What did you say his name was?'

'Lester. Harry Lester. In fact, it appears to be a Doctor Harry Lester. He works for a shipping company – on a liner, the *Empress of the Seas* – he's the ship's doctor, would you believe?'

'How on earth did you get that information?'

'After I'd checked and rechecked the result all those times, I thought I'd better call the hospital that sent us the sample in the first place, to see if I could delicately glean any information that might throw light on the matter. I was lucky to speak with the Sister in charge of the ante-natal clinic, and she was able to remember the pregnant woman immediately. She said that they had had a long conversation about working on board cruise ships as a doctor or nurse – apparently the pregnant woman is a nurse!'

'Oh God, what are you going to tell me next?'

'At least it shouldn't be too difficult to make contact with them, Doctor – if I call the shipping line office and find out if they are on board at the moment. I'm sure the company can give me the necessary information so that we can send a message.'

'That sounds a good idea ... we can impress upon him that he must come and see me as soon as possible. We'll keep the problem under our hats for the time being ... no one else in the lab must know.'

'No, of course not.'

'Well, that's decided. Quite frankly, I don't think there are any other options. I'll draft a suitably worded note today.'

'...and in view of the very unusual blood picture, it is imperative that you call in to see me personally at my laboratory in Harley Street as soon as possible. Please reply in the strictest confidence to the above address. Dr Simon Coombes, Director.'

The telex is noncommittal, but Harry feels a faint alarm.

'I'll need to make a satellite call. Can you get this number for me?'

'Sure thing.'

'Let me see ... what time is it in the UK? We're five hours behind them. There should be someone in the office. I'll go to my cabin, Jim, if you can put the call through to there?'

'Right you are, Harry.'

It takes around a couple of minutes for Harry to walk from the hospital on 6 deck to his cabin at the aft end on 2 deck. The chief radio officer's timing is perfect. As Harry closes the door to his cabin, the telephone rings.

'Just putting you through...'

'Thanks. Hello?'

'Harley Street Laboratory, can I help you?'

'Yes – this is a satellite call from Doctor Lester, Harry Lester, on board the *Empress of the Seas* in the Caribbean. Could you put me through to Doctor Coombes, please?'

'Certainly, sir. Just hold on a minute, please...'

'Good morning, Coombes here.'

'It's Lester, Harry Lester speaking, I got your…'

'Aah, Doctor Lester, so glad you called … where are you now?'

'Somewhere off the north coast of Puerto Rico – on our way to San Juan…'

'Well, it seems to be a pretty good connection – I can hear you perfectly Doctor Lester…'

'Good. Good … Doctor Coombes, your telex alarmed me somewhat … and I'm a little puzzled as to what it can possibly mean…'

'Yes, I am sorry to have done that – but – well – it is rather important – and – uuuh – a rather sensitive matter which is, quite frankly, far too sensitive to discuss on the telephone. To be honest, I need to see you as soon as possible. What is the earliest that could be … with the ship's schedule?'

'We're due back in Southampton in around two weeks time, but will only be staying for one day. I suppose I could shoot up to London and meet you … but it's a bit of a rush, and … is it really that necessary? Can't we deal with it over the phone?'

'No. I'm afraid not. As I said, with all due respect, the matter really does require me to see you. The issues at stake are frankly, uuuuh, what should I say…'

'It all sounds intriguing. Can you give me a hint?'

'I'm afraid I'd rather not over the telephone. You must bear with me … I'm sure when we meet, you'll understand and appreciate my caution.'

'You're beginning to worry me now, Doctor Coombes.' Harry's initial curiosity is overshadowed by an alarm which is intensified by the tone in Doctor Coombes's voice.

'I'm truly sorry for that. All I can say is that it is a matter that I am sure we can resolve when you come to see me.'

Harry focuses on the painting of the old cruise ship opposite in perplexed silence.

'I'll check the exact itinerary of the ship and let you know the dates. I promise, as soon as we dock in Southampton I should be able to get a quick clearance off the ship and catch a fast train to London.'

'Good. That's settled, then. I'll look forward to meeting you, Doctor Lester. Goodbye.'

Harry replaces the receiver and sits back in the chair. He is mystified and feeling more alarmed than when he'd first read the telex. What on earth could it be? Blood test? It could be something to do with Penny's rare blood group – maybe some incompatible factor which might cause problems in the pregnancy. Confidential that might be, but Harry thinks the doctor could have given him just a tiny inkling without compromising himself – strange, very strange.

He looks at his watch. 10 o'clock. He'd better return to the hospital and commence the clinic.

'Four people waiting, Doctor Lester.'

'Thank you, Sister.'

Harry winks at Penny.

It is a company rule that hospital staff address each formally in front of patients in the clinic. Harry doesn't adhere to such unrealistic protocols, except when it is logical to identify the Nursing Sister as such, or there is a need for himself to be recognised as the doctor to a passenger or patient who might not know him.

By 11.30 14 patients have been seen, none of whom has a serious problem.

Penny comes in the office and slumps in the chair opposite.

'That was an interesting session,' says Harry, 'five respiratory infections, four constipations, three yeast infections, two sea-sicks and a partridge in a pear tree – who says being a doctor at sea is not fun?'

Penny laughs.

'I shouldn't complain, should I? It's money all the same – enables me to live the life to which I've become accustomed...'

'What was the telex?'

'How did you know I received a telex?'

'The radio room phoned down, remember? I answered the telephone.'

336

'Of course – my short-term memory again. Anyway, it was hardly worth mentioning.'

Harry does not wish to alarm her, especially in view of the troubling conversation he had with the doctor who sent the telex. She doesn't seem interested and doesn't press him, although he knows he will have to tell her soon enough that he must go to London when they arrive in Southampton.

'In fact it was from the lab in London. Apparently a simple technical hitch – probably a stupid mistake, more like it – but anyway, they say the specimen I took them last time was not adequate for some reason, and therefore they cannot do any of the analyses they want to do. So they would appreciate another fresh sample from me . . . I'll get the early train, so I should be back by lunchtime.'

'Couldn't you simply send it by courier, from Southampton when we arrive?'

'I suppose I could – but the technician made it clear that it must be a fresh sample this time, preferably taken by them in their lab directly from the source . . . so that there is less risk of contamination or spoilage . . . you know, all those things that can happen.'

'I wouldn't mind a day out in London. We could maybe go to . . .'

'You don't need to come really. It's hardly worth it. I can get back by midday, and we could have lunch in that new Indian restaurant at the far end of the High Street.'

'Sounds OK to me.'

Harry has not the slightest notion of what problem Dr Coombes is going to discuss with him, but he has a feeling that Penny shouldn't be involved unless it is absolutely unavoidable.

Two weeks pass uneventfully. The clinic workload continues to be light, and there is only one emergency call-out late one night, to an old man in left ventricular failure which, unlike their previous cardiac emergency, they successfully reverse.

There has been ample opportunity to top up their suntans. Penny is beginning to look even more beautiful – to Harry at least. Unquestionably, she radiates a magnetic charm which,

337

combined with her singular good looks, has a marked effect on almost everyone who comes close to her.

And now, as the *Empress* glides majestically along Southampton water, it is early morning and the late spring sun, rising slowly above a blue-grey haze in the east, yields little warmth yet. There is a faint breeze from the south-west, and the air feels sharp and crisp. The light is muted, but there is no cloud, and it promises to be a fine day. The intense greenery along the shore confirms the new growth of spring. On the port side the trees and dense foliage stop abruptly as the sprawling Fawley power station comes into view. The berth is just a little further up the channel on the starboard side. Even though it is only just after 6 a.m. scores of ardent passengers crowd the decks, with their cameras flashing at everything that moves.

The mighty vessel overshoots its berth by several ship lengths so that it can make a 180 degree turn and come along port side, in order that the departure will be easier, safer and quicker.

Harry is alone on the deck, having insisted that Penny should stay in bed for another hour. He watches the frenetic activity on the quayside – the delivery lorries by the score, in neat rows stretching the length of the quay, the cranes and hoists, poised ready to transfer cargo to and from the holds, the portable gangways positioned ready to connect to the different decks – and most of all, the people – from this distance, hordes of tiny figures scurrying in all directions as if without purpose. The massive car park is already packed full, and the special Southampton to Waterloo boat train and all its 16 coaches can be seen waiting patiently on the other side of the customs terminal.

Half an hour later, Harry has said goodbye to Penny and is waiting at the crew gangway down on 5 deck as the ship is cleared by customs and security. He has changed into a suit and with the first group of crew eager to get ashore, makes his way to the crew customs shed on the dock directly opposite the gangway.

He has no luggage and passes through customs without

being stopped. On the other side of the shed is the taxi rank. He looks anxiously at his watch. He should be able to make the 7.50 express direct to London.

He is fearful, fearful that the bubble of happiness and utter contentment in which he has been living for the last couple of months – with a woman who has affected him in a unique way he has never before experienced – is going to burst. The relationship has blossomed even more since the pregnancy, and has now settled into a state of near domestic bliss. But as yet, they have not discussed anything of a permanent nature, such as marriage. It is as if it is a foregone conclusion that they will be together forever.

The fast train to London takes just over one hour. From Waterloo Station Harry gets the underground to Oxford Circus. Coming out of the subterranean rotunda station at Oxford Circus and up the steps leading into the northern end of Regent's Street evokes long-distant memories. It is well over 20 years ago that, as a medical student, he used to make a similar journey, from St Paul's along the Central line to Oxford Circus at least three times a week.

He is able to appreciate the irony of his mission today. Although not to deliver a valuable semen sample to an infertility clinic, his journey is connected with the same business, the procreation of life, only this time, his contribution has been in the time-honoured natural fashion.

He finds himself treading the exact same path, along Upper Regent Street, left into Cavendish Place and across Cavendish Square as far as the traffic lights on the other side. And then it is a sharp turn into Harley Street – one of the most famous streets in the world, where medicine is available to everyone who can afford it. There are many good doctors in this illustrious street, but there are also many less creditable practitioners, some of whom would perfectly fit the label charlatan. They use the prestige of the famous street to extract the maximum fees for the most questionable service.

Harry recalls the growing number of fertility clinics in the late Sixties and wonders how he would now categorise those practitioners who made fortunes out of the desperate plight of

339

barren couples. Perhaps the joy they undoubtedly brought to many couples justified their handsome fees for a routine technique that had been elaborated and practised down on the farm for many years before it had been offered to the human race.

There! Number 17, just a few yards up from the traffic lights. Dr Crowther couldn't possibly be still there after all these years! He must be retired, or more probably, dead. Harry crosses the road to take a closer look down memory lane. He mounts the steps at number 17 and bends forward to read the names on the shiny brass plate. There is no Dr Crowther. He wonders if there is still the same fertility clinic on the first floor. Is it possible that Liz – he remembers her name so clearly – is still working here? Highly unlikely! She'd be married to a solicitor or accountant, or perhaps a doctor, God forbid, living a life of domestic fulfilment no doubt, in an idyllic rural retreat, a million miles from the grimy capital.

And so today, he reflects on the irony that he is returning a generation later – to visit a clinic where, it appears, his contribution to the natural process is to be of more consequence than the umpteen anonymous and totally carefree visits he'd made all those years ago. Today, he is accountable for once for an act of procreation, and his concern intensifies as he gets closer to the laboratory.

He is perplexed and nervous with the director's insistence that he see him personally. He cannot help feeling tense and vulnerable, in a way perhaps that so many women had felt all those years ago, on their desperate journeys to the infertility clinics. Now he can appreciate the anguish and apprehension they must have felt.

But then as medical students, they were so cavalier about it. The depth of thought and consideration with regards to their contribution to the 'baby-farming' business extended no further than the logistics of masturbating to order in the privy of the student halls of residence.

His indulgence in the memories of his prolific activity a generation past stops abruptly when he sees the brass plate at number 123, with the name clearly emblazoned in large bold letters: 'HARLEY STREET SPECIALIST LABORATORY'. He feels a pulse of nervousness as he swallows involuntarily and steps up to ring the bell.

The door opens after a few seconds.

'Can I help you, sir?'

'Yes – I'm Harry Lester. I have an appointment with Doctor Coombes.'

'Oh yes, Doctor Lester, we're expecting you – do come this way, please.'

The matronly middle-aged receptionist ushers Harry into a gloomy, musty-smelling entrance hall, Edwardian in character, with high ceilings and elaborately carved cornices.

'His office is at the top of the stairs, directly opposite the landing. He is free now, so you can go up straight away.'

'Thank you.'

Harry ascends the narrow staircase, balustraded and thickly carpeted, slowly and with trepidation and an increased sense of foreboding. He reaches the top and immediately sees the door opposite with the name 'Dr Simon Coombes, Director', in discreet black letters. He hesitates a moment, and then knocks softly.

'Come in.'

'Doctor Coombes?'

'Yes?'

'I'm Harry Lester.'

'Aah yes, Doctor Lester, I believe – so pleased you could make it in the circumstances. I appreciate it has been a bit of a rush for you ... please sit down.'

Dr Coombes is a small man in his late fifties, not quite bald but with remnants of grey hair on either side of his head just behind his ears. His gold-rimmed half-moon spectacles perched on the end of his nose make him look professorial, although one would imagine from his ruddy-cheeked complexion and boyish features he could be a country dweller or a fisherman exposed to the ravages of a prevailing south-westerly. He wears a tie, grimy with age, but most certainly an institutional tie – probably from his alma mater and a well-worn green-brown jacket with dark leather patches on the elbow. There is a strong odour of pipe smoke in the room, and his fleeting smile as Harry sits down reveals crooked, irregular teeth which are heavily stained with nicotine. He is patently an academic through and through.

'How long is the ship in Southampton, Doctor Lester?'

'We sail at twenty hundred hours – sorry, eight o'clock this evening, so there is plenty of time.'

'Well, I do apologise for having to drag you up to London on such a beautiful spring day. I'm sure you have plenty of other things you would prefer to be doing with your brief time in port.'

Harry nods appreciatively as Dr Coombes picks up the phone.

'Gladys – can you bring some coffee, please.'

He looks up directly at Harry, raising his eyebrows in a question.

'Coffee, Doctor?'

'Harry nods, feeling decidedly less tense. The ambiance is warm and the man's manner is genuinely friendly. But just as Harry is beginning to feel relaxed, the bright friendly face and the initial cheerfulness dissipate in the instant it takes to replace the receiver. Dr Coombes sits forward, hands clenched on the pristine white blotter.

'Doctor Lester ... this is very difficult, and I don't know how to say it...'

Harry's alarm rekindles in an instant and rises to a level worse than before.

'What do you mean?' he says, trying to stop his voice croaking.

'How much do you know about consanguinity?'

'Consanguinity?'

'Yes.'

'Uuh, well ... I'm certainly no expert, but I probably know as much as any other non-expert doctor. I mean it is well-known that the Pharaohs of ancient Egypt indulged in premeditated incest, including brother-sister marriage, in order to keep power within the family – I guess that's why they all eventually died out...'

342

'Very good...'

'...and in fact, in a similar fashion, I believe the royal families of Europe are all pretty well-related, some closer than others. It is common knowledge that Queen Victoria can be identified as the common origin of the present crop of European royals...'

'Excellent Doctor Lester. You obviously know a lot about such things. But let me ask you – and please forgive me if this sounds like a *viva voce* examination – why do you suppose that consanguinous unions have not been simply deprecated in the history of mankind, but actually made taboo in even the most primitive of societies since the dawn of civilisation? I should emphasise that I am only interested in the strict biological consequences, and not the moral or ethical issues that may be at stake.'

'Well – I suppose because of the inherent risk of defective offspring from in-breeding.'

'Correct. As you know, we all carry recessive genetic traits for harmful characteristics which can be passed on to successive generations – characteristics which can vary from mild disorders of a non-life-threatening nature to those with lethal consequences. I don't need to elaborate on specific examples, but even the average man in the street is aware that there is an increased risk of mental retardation with or without other physical manifestations from incestuous breeding. To be perfectly scientific and rational, one is bound to say that it is not an absolutely inevitable consequence, and offspring may be quite normal intellectually and physically – but the chances of abnormality are certainly enhanced, if not greatly increased, in consanguinous unions, that is, incestuous relationships.'

'Yes Doctor, I am conversant with all of that ... but why?'

'As you might well remember from your medical school lectures all those years ago, one recessive gene alone will not manifest in a harmful disorder – but two recessive genes for the same characteristic – you know, one supplied by each parent – become dominant so to speak, and this can manifest in a problem in the offspring...'

Harry nods his head in agreement, wondering just where

343

such circumlocution will lead. Before he can interrupt, Dr Coombes continues.

'...in fact, Queen Victoria herself was a carrier of the haemophilia gene, which is a recessive gene linked to one of the female sex chromosomes. As you probably remember, because it is a recessive gene, females do not manifest the character, that is, haemophilia, because they are protected by the other X chromosome. On the other hand, males, with one Y chromosome and one unopposed X chromosome, suffer from the awful bleeding disorder if they have the recessive X-linked gene. So you see, it is the female who unknowingly passes this trait on to successive generations – until it pops up in a male offspring ... and there are so many other examples of disorders – but I mustn't bore you – I'm sure you can remember from those distant biochemistry lectures the so-called inborn errors of metabolism...'

'Yes but where is all this...'

'And so, I am sure you will understand and agree that the children of consanguinous, that is, incestuous unions, if they survive, have everything stacked against them. As I said, there are always the exceptions of the perfectly healthy child, but they are the exceptions that prove the rule ... do you get my point?'

'Absolutely. Fascinating. It's always nice to get a refresher course in a long-forgotten aspect of genetics,' Harry says, not bothering to hide a hint of facetiousness, 'but you haven't brought me here today to discuss such esoterics.'

'No – of course not. I'm sorry. At least not primarily – but quite frankly, what we've just talked about, Doctor Lester, is extremely relevant to your situation.'

Harry's alarm is intensified again as he involuntarily leans forward attentively.

'I'll come straight to the point – your involvement with Miss Reeves...'

There is a sudden flushing of Harry's cheeks at the mere mention of Penny's name.

'Please forgive me from stating what may seem to be the obvious ... but you ... uuuh, yourself ... and uuh, Miss Reeves are, I take it ... shall we say romantically involved?'

344

'You needn't be so coy about such a natural thing. The way you say it, anyone would think it was against the law ... of course we live together on the ship.'

'I'm sorry, Doctor Lester, it's just that we need to clarify everything one hundred per cent ... there is absolutely no room for error or misunderstanding ... please bear with me.'

Harry's anxiety is beginning to be superseded by a feeling of growing irritation with the circumlocution of the learned doctor.

'You are undoubtedly, then, the other half of her pregnancy, so to speak?'

'Of course!'

'Are you absolutely sure...?'

'Now look here...'

'I am sorry, but as I have made it clear to you, we really do have to be absolutely certain – we are talking about a very serious matter.'

A surge of adrenaline pulls Harry further forward so that he is balanced on the edge of the chair, with his nose close enough to smell the heavy pungent odour of stale tobacco-impregnated tweed.

'What do you mean? Please tell me what this is all about.'

'Doctor Lester, we have analysed the blood sample from Miss Reeves countless times. Checked. Rechecked and re-checked...'

'Yes...?'

'We have analysed your blood sample countless times. Checked. Rechecked. We are absolutely certain that we have made no error, either in our recordings or analytical methods ... you know we are a well-respected laboratory with an enormous experience...'

'Yes, yes. I know all that,' says Harry with increased anxiety and rising impatience, 'please tell me the problem.' His face is a mixture of puzzlement and undisguised anxiety. He senses a bombshell about to drop.

'Well, the two samples, one from yourself and the other from your – your ... shall we say intended? The two samples show remarkable similarities on our DNA fingerprint.'

345

Harry's anxiety is compounded and his sense of foreboding becomes acute.

'In fact, Doctor Lester, we, that is my colleagues and myself – I have shared the findings with a couple of senior colleagues – absolutely confidential, of course...'

'The findings, Doctor Coombes.'

'The DNA profile conforms to a certain unique pattern of compatibility, which leads us to one simple and unequivocal conclusion...'

'Yes?'

'Your girlfriend, the lady who is expecting your child, is in fact ... your daughter.'

Harry cannot speak. It is as if the inside of his head has exploded and only a void is left. He stares at the bald-headed director of the laboratory, who looks down at his hands resting firmly clasped on the desk. Harry is vaguely conscious of the man's wrinkled forehead, the shiny hairless dome of his scalp and the prominent black mole on one side of his nose. The mouth is closed and expressionless. He is allowing time for the ghastly information to sink in to Harry's brain before pronouncing any judgement.

Harry is vaguely aware of a distant hum of traffic and the occasional blaring horn. He is dumbstruck. Paralysed – he cannot move. His body is motionless and fixed to the chair, as if he has been transformed by an evil genie into a block of solid granite. His conscious sense, his awareness of his surroundings, is blurred. The room in which he is sitting is surreal. He continues staring blankly at the diminutive figure with the expressionless face sitting opposite, who suddenly lifts his head and fixes his gaze directly at Harry.

'I'm sorry, Doctor Lester ... truly sorry. From your reaction, it would seem that you had absolutely no previous knowledge of the kindred nature of the relationship between you and Miss Reeves.'

Harry is aware that Dr Coombes has spoken, but the words are incomprehensible.

'Doctor Lester? Doctor Lester?'

346

Harry jerks his head back as his awareness of his surroundings returns.

'Yes?'

'I assume that you were totally unaware of the ... the – biological relationship between yourself and Miss?'

'Oh God, oh God – yes ... YES ... of course ... you couldn't possibly think that I would ... oh God, this is not real. It is incredible. I don't believe it is happening. This is a dream – a nightmare – I'm sure I'll wake up in a moment ... won't I?'

'I am truly, truly sorry. I can tell you, my colleagues and I have discussed the matter at great length – and I must confess initially, we were shocked – more so because we were unsure of whether you and your ... your – lady friend had any knowledge of your kinship ...'

'Surely you didn't think we would have done this thing in the knowledge ... ?'

'I'm sorry if that offends you, but until now, we had no real information ... but it is clear that you did not know and that there must be some other strange, highly unusual social circumstance which has allowed such a thing to happen without you or Miss Reeves knowing. Are you able to throw any light on it?'

Harry is calmer now. The pain of mental anguish is almost unbearable but his mind clears. God – just an hour ago, he had been indulging in long-distant memories, wallowing in the nostalgia of his medical school days and the intimate involvement he'd had with this illustrious street.

AID – artificial insemination by donor ... BY DONOR ... BY DONOR! Oh no. Oh God. It couldn't be ... surely not? A million-to-one shot ... it couldn't be ... oh God ... it must be. It's the only explanation. The unthinkable had happened. 'Ye shall reap as ye sow'. After all these years, his activity as a regular sperm donor had reaped its grim harvest ... but surely, the chances of such a thing happening were so infinitesimally small that it was never even contemplated, let alone ever mentioned. Numbers, statistics, probabilities were never considered. Even though the carefree band of donors plugged away merrily, providing samples week after week to scores of women, the likelihood of such an event was blissfully ignored. It had never occurred to anyone, even when the clinics had proliferated and the business of inseminating women had grown to the proportions of a factory production line, to calculate the statistical probability of a consanguinous union – be it father-daughter, or brother-sister – 20-odd years down the line. It was thought to be so improbable that it was never even considered as a possibility.

Even though in the late Sixties the number of infertility clinics had greatly increased to service an ever-increasing demand, the pool of donors remained relatively small and was drawn, in the main, from just a few London medical schools. The clinics came to rely on a rather exclusive band of reliable and trustworthy donors, who had more or less cornered the market. These veritable studs could be depended on to appear, sample in hand, at very short notice. Medical students, conveniently located in two or three hospitals not far from Harley Street, were perfectly suited to the task. They had no social, moral, scientific or in fact, any other sort of objection to AID and were only too eager to guarantee a reliable service for the regular income it gave them. In those early days, there was little review of what was going on in Harley Street – the term 'medical audit' had not yet been invented. The rising number of happy pregnant couples and the suitably enriched practitioners asked no questions except the date of the last period.

'AID Doctor Coombes ... AID.'

'AID?'

'Yes – artificial insemination by donor. Many years ago, over twenty in fact, I used to be a sperm donor to the Harley Street clinics, when I was at medical school. In fact, I recall, that at one time or another, I was on the books of at least three clinics, and on average made at least three donations per week for over a period of five years.'

Dr Coombes moves his head up and down slowly, and the expression on his face changes – allowing even a tight smile to appear as if to say, yes we have the answer.

'Of course, of course – it must be. Why didn't I think of it?

348

That's it, Doctor Lester. Good God, I don't suppose anybody ever sat down and worked out the numbers.'

'In actual fact, there have been one or two occasions over the years when I have found myself speculating on the number of children that I might have around the world. I remember asking a nurse in the infertility clinic once what sort of success rate they could expect over a period of time. She wasn't able to give me a very clear figure of the percentage of successful inseminations – she said there seemed to be several factors which influenced the rate such as the time of the year, you know, spring or winter – I think spring was a more favourable time – and racial origin. Women from some races seemed to fall pregnant by AID easier than others. Don't ask me which ones, because I cannot remember.

'Anyway, I can remember years later working out approximately how many donations I'd made over a period of five years. Even allowing for the times when I was away from London, it still worked out to around one thousand in total. I could remember what the nurse had told me – she'd said, at the best time of the year – the spring – successful fertilisations occurred in about thirty per cent of cases, and at the worst time – in the winter only about ten per cent. So I worked out a rough average over the whole year of around twenty per cent, or one in five of my donations resulted in a pregnancy. That's probably a conservative estimate, but over a five-year period would be as many as two hundred pregnancies at least.

Quite a few of these women came from abroad, so that the eventual scatter of these children would be far wider than the UK. I suppose, if it was even considered at all, the probability of any offspring from the same donor meeting each other, or indeed the donor himself, was thought of as beyond the realms of all credibility...'

'Doctor Lester, this is absolutely fascinating – if you'll forgive me ... I mean – it's quite incredible. You are so correct in what you say. I must confess, I have colleagues in the infertility business, as you might appreciate, and if I remember those times, the risk of such an event was considered so small, if indeed it was considered at all – that it was entirely ignored.

349

'Things have changed, I can tell you. These days the clinics are carefully controlled. There has been quite a bit of legislation which has brought about a rigorous evaluation and continual monitoring of the business – or perhaps I should say "treatment". For instance, the clinics are limited very strictly in the number of successful conceptions from any one donor – I suppose in recognition of this unlikely but possible scenario. In fact, I believe it is something like a maximum of five pregnancies per donor. Once that number has been reached, they are struck off the books, so to speak. And they can't simply go down the street and sign on with another, because there is a tightly controlled central computer database with details of every such birth. It is, in effect, a register which prevents an "expired" donor from trying to register with another clinic. Fortunately, most, if not all of the cowboy clinics have gone out of business.'

'I suppose then, in the Sixties when I was involved, it was a bit of a free-for-all, with anybody and everybody grabbing a slice of the action...'

'Precisely ... more coffee?'

'Thank you.'

Harry sits back in his chair as Dr Coombes pours. His head is swimming again, and there is a sensation that it is all a terrible dream. The little man in the grubby tweed jacket leans back in his executive swivel chair and emits a deep sigh.

'What are we going to do Doctor Lester? This is a horrendous dilemma we are in. God help us if the press got hold of it ... of course, nothing can possibly come out of this office ... we are watertight, as it were, I assure you, and I am pretty confident you will keep your own counsel. But how about Miss Reeves? How on earth can we tackle it?'

Harry shakes his head in despair. The problem seems insurmountable. He can find no words. His mind is blank.

'I'm afraid there appears to be only one option suitable ... uuuh, logical. I'm sorry, I cannot find the right word but the only inescapable option is – termination ... that is, abortion.'

Harry is numb. He is distraught beyond description. His

350

world has turned upside down. His emotions are so charged that they totally override any expression of rational thought.

'Abortion? ABORTION? For God's sake, how can you say that so ... so easily?'

'I'm sorry. I know it is hard for you ... in all my career, nothing has ever happened like this, believe me. I feel as bad about it as you do...'

'But abortion ... that's impossible ... no, I cannot do that. What the hell am I expected to say, for God's sake?'

'I'm sorry ... but it is, I believe, the only way out of this dreadful situation. You will just have to tell Miss Reeves in some way...'

'No. No – that's impossible. What the hell am I expected to say to her, for God's sake?'

'You don't need to tell her necessarily of your kindred relationship – of course that is your choice – I think, in fact, it would be most advisable not to. Just how you solve the problem of your present liaison is something I am afraid I could not possibly advise you on ... but I am confident you will make the right decisions once your emotions have settled.'

Harry feels for once that he is on the receiving end of a doctor's platitudinous advice and appears momentarily stunned.

'Doctor Lester, I think you ought to return to the ship, think about it for a few days and then, when your mind has cleared, make a firm decision. Whatever in your wisdom you decide, I would appreciate if you would let me know, as I feel in the circumstances we have a certain responsibility ... you understand me ... in view of the illegality of the situation...'

'Illegal! ILLEGAL! Bloody hell! You've got some nerve saying that ... who gives a damn about the illegality or legality or anything else...'

'Please, please. I know this is all very stressful for you, but we must keep our heads and sense of...'

'Keep our bloody heads? What the hell am I going to do, I'm deeply committed in a very emotional way to my girlfriend who is to be the mother of our child, and I find out that she's my bloody daughter! And you sit there and tell me to keep my bloody head!'

'I am truly sorry, Doctor Lester. This is extremely difficult. But I know it is the only sensible way out of this awful dilemma. Please take my advice and think it over for a few days. As you are well aware, she is around eight weeks pregnant, so that there is at least a little breathing space for an early termination on legal medical grounds. It will, of course, be very easy to justify. We simply advise that there is a serious genetic problem – say, for instance, that there is the presence of a lethal gene which may cause intra-uterine death or severe malformation – and therefore abortion is strongly recommended...'

Harry has had enough. He stands up. His eyes are unashamedly watery. He turns and walks towards the door, saying nothing.

'Goodbye, Doctor Lester. Please let me know...'

He runs down the stairs, brushing past the receptionist and slams the front door as he emerges, breathing hard, into the street.

It was a dream. He'll wake up any moment. He is really still on the ship – which will be docking soon. And then he can go off with Penny and spend an idyllic day in the New Forest. They can have lunch in an old traditional pub deep in the National Park, and maybe cream tea and scones later in a pretty tea garden.

Dream-like, Harry steps across the road. A blaring horn from a taxi brings him to his senses. Oh God. It is reality. He wasn't dreaming the conversation that has just taken place in the doctor's office.

What the hell is he to do? His feeling of distress and helplessness threatens to overwhelm and crush him completely. Walk. WALK, for God's sake walk. Get some oxygen to the brain – to the centres of reason and logic. PENNY. He must think of Penny. Her welfare is paramount. Her emotions. Her happiness. STRATEGY. It is imperative he develop a strategy. He must work something out. He must, he MUST – and before he sees her in Southampton.

On the train he is restless and cannot think clearly. He is confused and is not able to formulate a plan. With the continuous clickety-click and the gently rocking rhythm his aching mind is soothed, and soon he drifts into a pleasant state of somnolence. His conscious thought ceases and with it, the intense anguish and turmoil. But his subconscious is working overtime. It is formatting a realistic and an entirely pragmatic approach to overcome his agonising problem.

'Southampton. This is Southampton. All stations to...'

He awakes just in time to jump down hastily onto the platform as the train pulls away. But as he gathers himself and walks briskly through the ticket barrier, he is calm. His mind is crystal-clear. A strategy is now firmly implanted in his mind which he feels a steely resolve to carry through. His despair has gone as he climbs into the back of the taxi. It has been replaced by a feeling of empty sadness and a conviction that now, he must be the pragmatist.

Once on board, he goes immediately to his cabin. Penny is not there. He assumes she is in the hospital. He picks up the phone in a bold decisive manner, determined not to deviate from his purpose.

'Harry! You're back. Is everything all right? Did the test go satisfactorily this time?'

'Yes, yes ... listen, Penny, is it quiet down there at the moment?'

'Like a graveyard.'

'Good – lock up, put the usual sign on the door, and come up to the cabin for an early afternoon tea.'

'What a super idea, oh, Harry, I missed you...'

He replaces the receiver and clenches his teeth. He stands up and begins to pace the dayroom in his quarters, telling himself he must remain calm and composed. Whatever happens, he must stay in control of the situation and make the black task facing him as painless as possible for Penny.

The door eases open and a head slowly appears around it.

'Penny!'

'Harry!'

Her face is beaming, and her eyes sparkling like incandescent beacons.

She comes towards him, arms outstretched. He puts his

arms around her waist and pulls her on, but not with the usual force and unrestrained enthusiasm that she usually expects. She senses it.

'Are you all right?... Your voice sounded a little strange over the phone.'

'Sit down. I've got something to tell you ... it's not easy, and I'm not sure how to do it.'

She draws back and her smile fades rapidly. Her eyes flash alarm and her cheeks flush. She sits on the sofa and leans forward.

'What is it?'

He composes himself and does not answer her immediately – but she is anxious and impatient.

'Come on, tell me, for goodness' sake?'

'This is so difficult ... please give me a moment...'

'What do you mean? What are you trying to say? Please tell me ... it's not us is it, Harry? Please don't say you're fed up with me – I'll die ... why do you look so miserable?'

'The blood test ... and ... and the rare blood group ... yours and mine ... they're not compatible ... the baby is almost certain to be deformed or seriously mentally retarded ... I ...'

'Oooh, Harry, Harry ... please don't ... please...'

Penny begins to sob uncontrollably. She is kneeling on the floor now in front of Harry, and buries her head in his lap. Her heavy convulsions with each sob intensify the pain that he feels.

'Dear dear Penny ... you must believe ... this is painful for me beyond anything I have ever experienced ... of course I love you very much ... more than anything on this planet. From the very bottom of my heart, nothing has changed that ... but this ... this thing is so terrible ... I just don't know what we should do ... we were so happy and ... and...'

'Harry ... Harry – are you sure? Did the doctor really say it? I mean – how do they know? How can they be so sure?'

'The specialist said it was virtually a certainty. The rare gene combination. He said it was an unbelievably small chance that two such blood groups should come together – you know – millions to one, he said ... and it just happened to be us.'

'But does it mean we can never have normal children ... and should not...?'

'I haven't thought about anything else – honestly, I cannot say.'

Her heaving sobs are replaced by a quiet whimpering. She reaches for the box of tissues on the side table. For a moment Harry's mind clears, and the resolve he felt on the train, to be determined in his pragmatism, returns.

'You know you told me that your father is not your real father, and that in fact your mother went to a special clinic to receive artificial insemination from an anonymous donor?'

'Yes?'

'Did she ever say where it was, or maybe the name of the clinic – or maybe even the name of the doctor who...'

'She said it was in London – Harley Street, I think ... in fact, I'm pretty sure – you know, where all the private doctors work. Oh, and I do remember her definitely saying it was a woman doctor. I remember her saying that, because most of the specialists were men and the woman doctor had made a point of telling her that she was the only woman in Harley Street ... oh Harry, I cannot bear this...'

'Did she tell you the doctor's name?'

'Yes – I'm sure she did. But I cannot remember it now ... but why do you ask? Why these questions? What's it got to do with us?'

Penny is calmer now. Her eyes are still red and moist, but she has stopped crying. She stands up and returns to her chair.

'I'm just interested ... you know, the donor's blood group ... it might have been unusual too ... and uuuh, one hopes it wouldn't have effected anyone else, and, and...'

Harry is rambling now – talking fiction as best he can. But she cannot know it. She must NEVER know it.

'Mishi-, Martin, no – Mallory ... I know it begins with an M but I just cannot think of it...'

'Was it Mason, perhaps?'

'That's it! That's it! Definitely ... do you think we should contact ... can she help us?'

355

'No no no. I don't think that would be of any purpose, after all these years.'

God! Shirley Mason! Harry must have visited her clinic hundreds of times in the Sixties. So many sperm donations! So many pregnancies! And, God forbid – here in front of him, the end product of one of them ... and even more incredible, it is a young woman that he himself has now impregnated – his own daughter is expecting his grandchild!

Penny's face darkens as the realisation of the terrible news Harry has brought surges like a second tidal wave over her.

'Oh Harry, Harry – what are we to do ... this is so terrible...?'

Her voice is tremulous and desperate.

In his mind he is clear. He knows it is going to be difficult to say, but he knows he must. He must.

'There is only one thing we can do ... and I think you know what that is, don't you? It is inconceivable to continue with a pregnancy which has a high chance of abnormality...'

She begins to sob again.

'Don't worry. We can try again ... it doesn't mean the end ... next time, I am sure everything will be all right...'

The words tumble out unthinkingly as he tries to placate her. But they are empty words, and he feels guilty for lying so desperately. He knows he can never contemplate a pregnancy ever again, although he dare not tell her at this moment. And worse – he knows that as far as their relationship is concerned it is the end – at least in its present form. If after all this trauma there is still an understanding, then it will be from an entirely different perspective.

The main problem he now knows he must face, is to disengage himself without ever giving her the true reason, but at the same time trying to minimise the hurt it will cause. But first, there is the immediate task of getting her consent for the procedure that they both know she must go through. She senses what Harry is about to say.

'Harry! I can't! I can't!'

'Penny – termination is essential – unavoidable ... it is the only option, painful as it must seem. You can leave the ship today and be back in two weeks when we return to Southampton...'

She screams hysterically.

'"Termination" – "termination"? You mean abortion. ABORTION!'

CHAPTER 14

NEW LOVE

And if a man shall take his sister, his father's daughter or his mother's daughter, and see her nakedness, and she see his nakedness; it is a wicked thing; and they shall be cut off in the sight of their people.

Leviticus 20: 17

It seems an interminable two weeks before the *Empress* returns to Southampton. The ship has been to New York and then completed a five-day cruise to Bermuda before making the four-and-a-half-day return trip across the Atlantic.

Harry has fretted most of the time.

As the mighty vessel glides sedately along Southampton Water, he is almost beyond himself with anticipation to see Penny again. But his desire to see her is marred by the knowledge that she might not be the same Penny who'd left the ship so hastily two weeks before. She had run down the gangway minutes before it was pulled away. She'd had no suitcase, and was so distraught that it had been torture for him to not go after her. But in the circumstances it would have been impossible for him to follow. He could not have left the *Empress* in the lurch just as she was about to sail, without a doctor – it is forbidden by strict maritime law for such a ship to leave port without a qualified medical practitioner on board.

He'd watched helplessly from the shell door on 5 deck as she'd run off the ship, eyes red and swollen, her face a picture of total anguish. It had been almost too much for him to bear as he'd stood there, paralysed by the circumstances. What had made it worse was that she had not said, or simply could not bring herself to say, what she'd intended doing. He'd just hoped she'd get home and explain everything to her parents and then follow the only choice, agonising at it seemed – to have a termination.

361

As the mooring ropes, thick as a man's arm, are looped over the huge steel bollards on the quay and twanged tight by the winches on board, Harry feels a flutter of trepidation and doubt, that she has done the right thing – and if she has, he fears what effect it will have on her general well-being – and most importantly, her psyche and the future of their relationship.

His perception of how the relationship should be is confused. There is within him a conflict of opposing forces which he is desperate to resolve, but cannot. In the two weeks she has been away from the ship, he has thought of little else than the dilemma posed. On the one hand, he wants her desperately as a woman, a lover and even a mother of his children – all those instincts, which, until she had come into his life, he had scorned contemptuously. But, on the other hand, he has begun to realise that there is something else now: feelings and perceptions in him, that he had never encountered before. Powerful, overwhelming feelings of kinship, totally devoid of any mating element. Feelings that he must protect, nurture and love in a patriarchal way, which he cannot relate to any previous personal experience – but which he is beginning to realise are the instincts of parenthood.

Oh God, how could have this happened? How can any one person be to blame? Who would have thought there was ever the slightest possibility of such a thing coming to pass? But now, he recalls the harmless fantasy of the conversation he'd had with the passengers at the table on the world cruise, and because that particular group of passengers had been on for an exceptionally long period, he could even remember their names.

It had been the effeminate Harvard professor, Desmond – or had it been the cynical eccentric, Hal Van Dicky? – he could never forget a name like that! It had been suggested that the extreme unlikelihood of ever meeting such offspring might be greatly increased by an assumption that 'like breed like'. Certain inherited characteristics and instincts, such as an inborn desire for travel and adventure, might bring the remote orbits of two such related individuals closer together.

362

This fanciful notion might be even more credible in a modern world, where there existed a limited conventional outlet for such instincts in terms of travel to foreign places. An obvious and popular outlet for a young adventurous person might be the world of the cruise line industry. Attraction to such a world might increase the chances of coming into each other's orbit. It WAS fanciful, highly improbable – but not totally impossible – there was a ring of logic to it.

All those years ago, he had literally scattered his seeds in a carefree, thoughtless manner, oblivious of any consequences there might be. Over twenty years later, it seems he had plucked the forbidden fruit once too often – and now, his irresponsible lifestyle has returned to haunt him with a vengeance.

The choice is clear, but none the simpler for that. It is still an agonising choice, whichever way he looks at it. It can hardly be reduced to a simple question of logic versus emotion. The emotional element is inextricably bound to either choice. He cannot win either way – but he does not want to lose either way.

The all-consuming dilemma has not left his thoughts for a moment since she left. Slowly and painfully, his mind has begun to rationalise the limited options open to him and then to try and formulate the necessary strategy to follow. Once she has returned, his sole purpose must be to put into effect any plan of action, ill-defined as it may be, which will have the main purpose of making her happy again.

His thoughts have been clouded repeatedly with the abhorrence of this conjugal union with his own flesh and blood – his own daughter. Even though he is hardly to blame, he has not been able to dispel the sense of guilt and revulsion. At times his conscience has threatened to drown him in tidal waves of panic, which have distracted him from his attempts to think clearly and rationally.

He'd recalled the joke amongst the cavalier band of medical students who donated semen samples regularly, how funny it might be if they should ever meet one of their offspring, especially if it were a comely female! How perverse and rebellious they were, and utterly carefree in their actions. They knew that, statistically, the chances of such an unlikely occurrence ever happening were so infinitesimally small that they could contemptuously tempt fate without ever having to face the day of reckoning. But now, that ultimate fear, fictional as it may have seemed to them in those halcyon days, has been realised.

The ship has been tied up for what seems like ages before Harry sees her. He is in the hospital pharmacy talking aimlessly to the dispenser about restocking medical supplies when she appears. She is elegantly dressed in a light brown suit of a surprisingly conservative style for her. There is no smile. She radiates an air which is sombre and formal, which disturbs Harry. His eyes immediately search for any message or feeling. She merely offers a subdued smile, and he is painfully aware that her eyes do not show their usual sparkle. There is a pervading sense of coolness. It makes him hesitant to greet her with his usual physical enthusiasm. It is clearly not the same Penny who left the ship two weeks before.

She stands motionless, expressionless at the doorway. They both start to speak at the same time.

'How are ...'

'Has it been...'

'Sorry – you first.'

'Has it been busy?' she asks in a polite, flat tone.

'Yes,' he says cheerfully, anxious to break the ice, 'we had a pretty hectic crossing. The first two days were force ten ... you know, the endless lines of green seasick passengers, the pools of vomit...'

'Please don't...'

'You can't stand in the doorway all day – come and sit down.'

She walks hesitantly towards Harry, who half-heartedly raises his arms to embrace her. As his arms encircle her, she freezes

364

but doesn't resist or pull away. It is a passive denial of his affection.

Harry kisses her fleetingly on her cheek and stands back. The sense of conflict that has been brewing up during her absence intensifies, confusing his approach towards her. He feels deeply hurt that there appears to have developed a chasm between them – and yet he cannot deny there is a sense of relief that it might signal the reversal process in their relationship, a reversal process that he knows, no matter how painful, must occur.

She sits on a small chair. Harry reaches for a stool and pulls it up towards her. Their eyes meet and she looks away. Incredibly, he feels embarrassed. How ridiculous! How can two people who were so bound up physically and spiritually a mere couple of weeks ago behave so awkwardly and diffidently, as if they'd only just met – and the flame of deep passion had never existed?

There is an unpleasant hollow feeling in his stomach, associated with an overwhelming sense of sadness and despair. The joy and excitement of the previous weeks together, that had promised such a glorious and idyllic future, look as if they have evaporated forever.

His mind searches for something to say to fill the awkward silence.

'Did you see your parents?' he asks blandly.

'Yes. I did,' she says, matching the hollowness of the enquiry.

He wants to ask her every little detail of her torment – so that he can feel it – suffer the agony she has gone through, so that he can relieve her of the burden and ease her suffering. But he is hesitant to rekindle any possible distress so soon after.

'Did you ... I mean ... was it taken ... were you ...'

'Yes! It has all been taken care of. It is finished,' she says in such an icy, unemotional tone that it is infinitely more painful to Harry than if she had spilled out all the gory details. It is as if the vital spark in her has been snuffed out.

Oh God! If only she knew the truth! But she will never know – she must never know. It would destroy her totally in the way that it threatens to destroy Harry now.

'Penny, my darling – I know what you must have been through.'

Harry leans forward to instinctively embrace her. She freezes again. There is no response. It reinforces the sense of rejection that Harry is feeling. If only she could share the other set of feelings which are now beginning to take hold. His agony is made worse by the fact that she can never know how they might love each other in the natural roles of father and daughter.

They sit in silence. Harry's emotions are on fire, so jumbled and mixed up in ferment that he is in a state of virtual paralysis.

And then, quite suddenly and spontaneously, as he focuses on her bowed head and small delicate hands clasped firmly in her lap as if in a subconscious display of penitence, his mind clears in a veritable flash of light. The strangulating noose of confusion and despair is cut at a stroke and falls away. His intense mental suffocation is instantly relieved. In the space of a few seconds his mind is crystal clear and in control. It is as if an automatic programme has been activated in his deep subconscious. The message of instruction is loud and clear and totally compelling. It says he must help her. He must make her happy in her life. It is imperative that she has every chance. His needs are unimportant and secondary to hers. She is young and healthy and has her life in front of her. She must be encouraged and guided in the right direction. She will become his overriding priority in life.

And then quite astonishingly, for no apparent reason, Penny's face lights up as if she is to be party to his salvation. She speaks.

'Harry, you remember that seaman,' she says, 'the one who was in the fight whose face I stitched and you saw the next day – you know, the well-spoken...'

'Oh yes – of course I remember – nice young chap. Highly educated, I believe. Some story about being eligible for Oxford or Cambridge but ran away to sea to seek adventure, or something like that. Is that the one you mean?'

'He stopped me as I came up the gangway. He appears to be

pretty shy and was embarrassed, but still made a point of speaking – he's quite a nice chap. He said he was thinking of leaving the sea and going to university to study law before it is too late...'

'Good for him! I'd told him so in the clinic when I last saw him, to do just that. I'm sure that will please his parents. I think he'd fallen out with them over his extended sea career, as it were – especially his father.'

'Anyway, he said that he had exhausted his original desire of running away to sea – something strange about a quest, which he didn't elaborate on – it sounded all a bit dramatic and mysterious...'

Harry senses that he has certainly made an impression on her.

'But really, it's amazing ... I even recognised some of your mannerisms in him ... I know that sounds ridiculous.'

'Yes, it does ... mind you, I think you might be right in a way – if you stay at sea long enough you take on sea-going mannerisms that you can recognise in others around you.'

'No, they really were just like ... oh, it doesn't matter. Anyway, what I was going to say, is that he had the nerve to ask me if we could meet for a drink or something! Can you believe that?'

Harry has already determined quite clearly that the educated young sailor has had more of an effect on her than she would care to admit. It could be just the sort of fortuitous coincidence which will enable him to wean her from her present relationship with himself.

'Really? Cheeky young devil.'

'He even said he knew I was "with you" and he meant no offence and that it would only be a harmless drink. Of course I said no...'

Harry smiles. But Penny is uncertain how to take it.

'What are you smiling at?' she says defensively.

'I wouldn't have minded if you had said yes – honestly. I don't mean I'm trying to get rid of you or anything ... it's just that, well ... it would be good for you ... after all, he's much nearer your age than an old fogey like me...'

'But Harry – I've never thought about our age difference – it's unimportant, you know that.'

'I know, I know, but I think it wouldn't do you any harm to socialise with some younger people – and face it, he is a particularly good specimen, I'm sure you will agree.'

The glint in Harry's eye tells Penny that he is not oblivious to the biological reality.

Penny tries to stifle an impish grin, and her crimson blush clearly signals her own evaluation of the young deckhand. It is the first sign of emotion, and Harry is relieved and yet saddened. He is talking with her in a matter-of-fact fashion about fixing up her first date, although she would never see it that way. It is as if the seal on the close bond between them is about to be broken, albeit by sleight of hand on Harry's part. There is developing a tacit understanding that it is ending, but is too painful to define in more concrete terms. Harry's eager encouragement for her to accept the invitation from another would-be suitor, lighthearted as it may seem, says all that is necessary.

Before Penny can react to his proposition, still unsure of his serious intent, Harry bamboozles her as if it has already been decided.

'Of course, he is not an officer, so he cannot go in the public rooms – and you are most certainly not expected to go into the Pig and Whistle with the ratings. Apart from anything else, as I'm sure you'll appreciate, it is likely to cause a bit of a stir – you know, in view of the social hierarchy on the ship – nursing officer going out with a humble deckhand ... very few people are going to be aware of his education. I know that sounds a bit snobbish, but you know what I mean...'

'Yes, of course, but...'

'Not to worry. We can fix something. I'll have a word with the staff Captain. He can, and frequently does, issue special dispensation for ratings or petty officers to dress up and go to the public rooms in certain circumstances. I'm sure he'll understand, especially if the request is coming from me. He owes me a few favours.'

'Just hang on a minute, Harry. I haven't agreed to anything yet. I wasn't trying to suggest ... I mean ... really, I was only saying that he had the nerve to ask me...'

Harry cuts in again.

'Don't be silly. Of course you must. It will do you good. It will do us both good ... that's settled, then.'

A surge of relief comes over Harry as Penny's face brightens up and a hint of her old sparkle reappears. Her mood has definitely uplifted – a positive indication that the dreaded ordeal of the reunion is over.

Harry's relief is tinged with sadness that their relationship, at least in the form it had been, is over. Their careful game of psychological manoeuvring has concluded that they can remain friends, but has also tacitly acknowledged the painful reality that the intense union they had known is now irrevocably finished.

Harry is confident that she will recover fully and regain her previous self with minimal harm done. It has been her first major emotional relationship with a man, and painful as it turned out, time will heal.

But she will never know the truth – the reality behind Harry's strategy. And she will never be able to appreciate or to share with him the incredible intensification of his feelings for her – feelings rooted in universal primordial instincts which have now supplanted, at inestimable emotional cost, those previous set of feelings which were based on an entirely different set of instincts.

'Right then – that is decided.'

'Yes – but I told him I couldn't.'

'Did he look disappointed?'

'Yes – crestfallen.'

'There's no problem then, is there? When you next see him – and I am sure that needn't be too long, as you know where he will be working around the decks – then when you just "happen" to pass by, you can innocently say hello with that special smile of yours. I am sure he will take it from there. Don't worry, his antennae will pick up the signals. I suppose there is a chance that he may not have the confidence to ask

369

you again, but I'm sure you will be able to drop as many hints as you like until he gets the message loud and clear.'

Penny smiles in a show of mock admonishment for Harry's matchmaking efforts. She moves towards him silently, signalling full agreement. In a show of warmth and affection that Harry had thought they had lost forever, she hugs him tightly. But even in this uninhibited embrace he can detect a subtle difference in its message. For a moment he holds her head close to his chest. His eyes are moist and he feels a lump in his throat. He pushes her gently away to hold her at arm's length and looks into her eyes. Like the embrace, the message has changed. It is as warm and committed, if not more so than before, but it carries with it also, a message that she may not be able to consciously appreciate. She responds naturally enough and offers a cheek for him to kiss.

'There! All settled. Now, down to business – we've got a hospital to run...'

Harry sees Penny every day in the hospital. The change in their relationship is firmly consolidated and soon becomes public. Within a very short time she is being pursued by the pack, the ever-patient skulking carnivores who lurked in the shadows of the ship's watering holes, waiting for any opportunity to pounce on an unsuspecting prey.

Harry is able to stand back and observe the display. He is relatively unaffected and recognises the range of antics and ploys with a fair degree of amusement. He is happy enough because Penny herself seems to be enjoying all the attention. At the Captain's cocktail party there is a veritable flurry of activity of would-be suitors who present themselves, anxious to try their luck. At one stage, Harry sees she is completely encircled by a group of young officers, all champing at the bit in their eagerness to curry her favour.

He is amused and contented with such developments. The date with the educated deckhand now seems irrelevant. She has the pick of the ship. Although he confesses a certain liking for the bright young man, as if he possesses a certain trait in his

370

character that he naturally empathises with, it is now up to Penny herself to make her own choice from the almost unlimited field. But he had promised to speak on his behalf at the next opportunity. It comes soon enough as David Carstairs, the staff Captain, sidles up to Harry at the party.

'So, Harry, I hear it's all over – the romance of the century. It's a shame. We all thought it was for real. Your long sentence of bachelorhood finally coming to an end ... what happened, then – if you don't mind me asking?'

'No – not at all.'

Even though Harry cheerfully accedes to being debriefed by the staff Captain, he is in truth uncomfortable with the proposition. He knows he cannot possibly reveal the truth. Nobody knows that Penny had an abortion. And, even more sacrosanct, he would never be able to share the secret of their true relationship.

'Well you know what it is – I get bored. She's very young ... young enough to be my daughter, in fact. She's intelligent and mature for her age, but you know, in all honesty I think there are just too many years between us – the gap is too wide to bridge...'

It sounds simple and entirely plausible, and satisfies the inquisitive staff Captain to a point.

'David – a favour.'

'Yes?'

'It's one of your seamen. Works with Jack, the assistant bosun, most of the time...'

'I know him – the well-spoken young chap who got A levels and is far too clever to be a deckhand ... what about him?'

'Well, it's a little delicate, and you might think slightly irregular. I know he is only a rating and all that but, well, he has asked Penny out, and she has not been able to say yes for obvious reasons – you know, the usual protocol, she being an officer, he a rating, the usual traditional bunkum ... you have to concede that he is a special case. Anyway, what I am asking is that they, or at least he, can be granted a special dispensation some time, to go in the public rooms – you know – on a date, for heaven's sake.'

'Now, Doctor,' the staff Captain says in his official voice without any hint of parody, 'you know that POs and above are the only crew who can qualify for that privilege – and then only on my say-so.'

Harry bites his bottom lip and thinks how pompous David Carstairs can be at times. Certainly his power on board is considerable, and next to the Master, almost as absolute. He decides to pander to his ego.

'David – you are a wonderfully popular staff Captain. I think it is because you have the strengths of great leadership, but at the same time you are able to relate to the humble man ... in other words, your unique qualities mark you out as a true leader of men – but one who still retains the common touch...'

'Okay, okay. One night, and one night only. It could set a dangerous precedent, that's the only problem. I'll have to square it with the senior convener of the union, or there really would be a stink. In fact, I have a better idea ... a way round it. Now, I believe he's been at sea for over three years – which means, providing he is considered good enough, he can be made up to deputy assistant bosun. I know he is pretty capable from what Jack has said, so it could be justified in front of the men. The important thing, is that it will automatically give him PO status – which, of course, means I can grant permission without causing any waves. A good idea, don't you think?'

'Brilliant! An absolutely splendid idea – if ever there was one.'

David Carstairs preens, in spite of the facetious hollowness of Harry's compliment.

'Just for you, Harry – nobody else,' he says.

One week after his conversation with the staff Captain, Harry has arrived a few minutes before the regular morning meeting in the hospital. Libby and Suzanne are already present, but surprisingly, Penny, who is invariably early, has not arrived yet.

'Penny's late,' he says lamely, aware that it is unusual.

There is no immediate response, but he notices Suzanne look at Libby with a knowing smile.

'Something I should know?' he gently inquires, sensing a conspiracy.

'It's none of our business, you must understand Doctor, but we did see Miss Reeves out and about last night, having what seemed like a good time with her young seaman.'

'Oh yes?'

'Actually, he looked really dishy in a suit. And he'd had his hair cut and got rid of the silly earring. Made us feel quite envious ... although he would be far too young and wet behind the ears, you understand.'

Harry's initial pang of regret is quickly replaced by a strong sense of relief and a satisfaction of the deep desire that her happiness is all that matters.

'Where were they?'

'We first sighted them in head-to-head conversation in the Yacht Club Bar, and later dancing the night away in the Eight Bells disco as if there was no tomorrow ...'

'Seems that there isn't,' Harry retorts with perfect timing as Penny appears at the door to the office.

In spite of what one would imagine the effect of a late night would have on her appearance, Harry recognises the old sparkle and radiant energy in Penny that tells him more eloquently than any words the good time she has had with a companion who has undoubtedly created a big impression. He is pleased. But he cannot help feeling a little apprehensive that she must not be used or hurt in any way. He will be cautious in any encouragement.

Feigning a disciplinary tone in his voice, he says,

'What time do you call this, Miss Reeves – ten minutes late? Burning the candle at both ends, eh?'

She looks at the other two and blushes furiously. She knows they will have volunteered a full report of the night's events. Harry saves her.

'C'mon, Penny – sit down. I can talk to you later – in private,' he says, winking at Suzanne and Libby, 'Sister Richards, please give the report.'

Later in the clinic Harry and Penny are alone waiting in between patients, and there is an opportunity to talk.

'So what was he like?'

She pauses to compose her answer.

'Well, he's very nice, I suppose – and I must say, so intelligent – and he wants to be a lawyer – and...'

Her enthusiasm overtakes her before she can get the words out. It is impossible for her to pretend it was a run-of-the-mill date.

'... and he says he plans to stay at sea for only another three months, and then he is going to...'

She is babbling now, and Harry cannot suppress a good-natured smirk.

'You're making fun of me!'

'Of course I am not – I'm just very happy for you.'

She looks into Harry's eyes and tilts her head coquettishly and realises how she is acting. As if in consolation for his dented ego, she reminds Harry how much her date had reminded her of him not just physically, but also in mannerisms.

'Really Harry, the similarities are amazing.'

'As I said before, he's taking on the old seadog persona that gets to all of us eventually – he'd better leave before it's too late to revert.'

'No, no. Seriously, I don't think it is that. It's just a slightly eerie feeling I get.'

For a moment Harry looks at her and his eyes focus on hers. This time she doesn't divert her gaze. Harry feels an overwhelming emotional surge that he wants to protect her, be her provider, her guardian ... to guide her safely through the difficulties and misfortunes and perils he knows she will come to face in life. And the message that he reads in her eyes appears to come from her inner self. It is an entirely natural message which perfectly compliments his recently emerged innate desire – the desire to act like a father to her – rather than a mate.

She continues to tell him about their evening together and the long conversation they'd had. It is very evident that he has had a marked effect on her, and Harry is cautious, if not a little

374

alarmed. She appears to be so enthusiastic about him in such a short time that he feels he ought to warn her.

'Penny – don't rush things. You've only just met him. There's a large field to choose from, and admit it, you can have the pick of the bunch if you want.'

'Don't worry, my feet are firmly stuck to the ground.'

She continues with titbits and trivia of their conversation. Everything it seems, is recounted. Harry listens patiently, nodding occasionally. He feels like a father confessor.

'...and we can go out again. The staff Captain says he can go out on Wednesday now that he is deputy assistant bosun – wasn't that a bit of luck getting promoted to a PO! Anyway, I can always invite him to my cabin, can't I? – I know I can't really go down to the crew quarters.'

'Master's standing orders are that it is forbidden for a rating or even junior petty officer to be seen to frequent officers' cabins. What I am saying is be discreet – please ... otherwise there could be problems.'

'Anyway, I wanted to tell you that he is going on leave in three weeks – and I'm thinking of requesting a special leave so we can...'

'Slow down! You've only been out with him once, for goodness sake!'

Harry is shocked by the speed of this development. Perhaps, he thinks, it might be a rebound effect after their own affair – which makes him anxious that she doesn't make any precipitous decisions that could risk her getting hurt.

'I do agree ... but I must confess, we did talk a lot when he came for his dressings ... you know, after the fight...'

She looks at the floor as if she has just confessed to a guilty secret.

'I really like him – I know it is so soon after ... and I know he likes me – I'm pretty sure of that.'

'Well, I am happy for you both – but please do not forget, be careful, be discreet – on board at least – you know the blasted protocols. I know it sounds awfully snobbish, but remember, in this environment, you are looked upon as an officer, whilst he is still a rating.'

'Petty officer.'

'I stand corrected, "petty officer" – but you know what I mean. I know that most of that palaver is nonsense and doesn't stop the sun rising in the morning, but just use your common sense, won't you, my dear?'

'Yes – "father",' she says in soft sarcasm.

An involuntary shiver passes down Harry's spine.

Time passes in that characteristic way that seafarers grow accustomed to on a voyage – each day, each 24-hour period merging into the next imperceptibly, so that one loses track of the day of the week.

Two weeks have passed since Penny went out on the town with her new beau, and it now seems ages since she'd had the conversation with Harry, analysing the first date. Strangely, he hasn't bumped into them together around the nightspots of the ship – although in the few moments when he has been alone with Penny, she has talked about little else except her new-found love.

Although Harry is happy to see her so happy, he is still reluctant to share her blind enthusiasm. Above everything, he dreads her being hurt, now, later, or in fact any time in her life. His instincts as well as experience remind him that sooner or later life has the nasty habit of throwing up unpredictable events which can shatter all illusions or realities for that matter, in a manner that can crush the strongest of spirits.

If he had to describe his feelings about Penny and Jason, he would say he was guardedly optimistic. Jason seemed to be a very pleasant young fellow who had qualities which singled him out as a worthy suitor. From what Penny has been repeating to Harry almost verbatim on a daily basis, it seems that his ambition to go to university and read for a law degree has been rekindled – no doubt aided and abetted by her. He speculates what they might be planning, but is loath to acknowledge any obvious conclusions, other than he would be leaving the sea some time in the near future. He doesn't think he could face any more emotional traumas affecting Penny's life – certainly

376

nothing as painful as what now seems to have been well and truly forgotten and buried, as if it had never happened.

The *Empress* is in mid-Atlantic, two days out from New York, heading for Southampton. The sea is calm. It is midsummer, and the late sun is setting over a cloudless horizon, throwing up a brilliant dazzling orange reflection on the glass-like smooth water. There is only the sound of a soft breeze and the distant hum of the generators as the 68000-ton monster slices its way effortlessly through the blue grey ocean at 26 knots.

Harry has finished dinner in the officers' mess. He hasn't bothered to entertain dinner companions in the passenger dining room tonight. He couldn't face another tedious evening of banal conversation – so whilst they are tucking into their main course, he is slowly walking along the boat deck outside, alone and in a reflective mood. He shields his eyes from the shimmering path of light stretching to the horizon, and in the philosophical mood he is in, finds himself indulging in the immense grandeur of ocean and setting sun.

As he comes to the aft end and crosses from port to starboard, he passes the huge plate-glass window which looks out sternwards from the piano bar out onto the tennis court. There is a partly drawn curtain and he is able to see passengers sitting at the tables from his vantage point on the steps, but they cannot see him because of the contrast of bright light inside and fast-approaching dusk outside.

There! There they are – Penny and Jason – in animated conversation. Harry stops, and from his invisible position is able to observe the couple without himself being seen. They are truly a handsome pair, he thinks – no doubt about that. Jason's head moves up and down in enthused animation, and his gestures when he seems to be expounding on a point are exaggerated with dramatic flourish.

Harry is drawn naturally to his engaging personality and is confident of the strength and goodness in his character. Penny seems to hang on every word. Harry unashamedly watches them from his vantage point and can witness for himself how close they appear to have become in the short space of time.

Jason, still talking, turns towards Harry's direction. As he turns, Harry sees clearly his three-quarter profile. He is smiling at Penny and anyone else who might be taking notice, with the air of confidence that springs from both a recognition of his own striking features and an awareness that his companion is a stunningly beautiful female who has his undivided attention.

Harry is struck by a thunderbolt! He freezes – absolutely paralysed from what he sees before him. Oh God! It cannot be! Impossible! Absolutely impossible! He must be dreaming! It is pure fantasy! The shimmering sunset, the brilliant light must have affected his visual perception. But he cannot ignore the terrible feeling of dread that has passed through the whole of his body. His legs feel like jelly. His mind is swirling now, any rational thought drowning in a deluge of crazily mixed emotions. He is in a state of utter and total confusion. He can sense his heart pounding against his chest. He gulps for air and grasps the cold steel railing.

He stares at Jason again. It is as if he is looking at himself in a mirror 25 years ago.

CHAPTER 15

FORBIDDEN LOVE

The nakedness of thy sister, the daughter of thy father, whether she be born at home, or born abroad, even her nakedness thou shalt not uncover.

Leviticus 18: 9

That time in Manila about three years back – the stranger in the night and the weird effect he had experienced when they'd eyeballed each other – it is him. It is the same sensation, only more intense this time as the visual impression impacts more clearly.

It cannot be! How could such a remote possibility come to pass? Perhaps there is some supernatural force, a metaphysical world that is invisible and separate from the human world that has tracked him down – after all this time – to exact the price for his carefree, mindless behaviour all those years ago. It is utterly beyond belief, and Harry has no rational answer to explain such a coincidence of events – except that in the limitless universe, it is supposed anything is possible ultimately.

As he stands clinging to the rail, the feeling of overwhelming despair threatens to consume him totally. For all his past misdemeanours, has he really ever done anything of such wickedness to deserve a fate so cruel? His grip tightens on the cold steel as he battles to clear his head. Perhaps his mind is playing tricks. The chances of such a thing happening is so improbable as to be of negligible consideration ... but then coincidences, unbelievable coincidences do occur. Isn't the whole of nature, let alone the ultimate mystery of the universe, one giant enormous coincidence of such unbelievable improbability, that the human brain has needed to hypothesise supernatural dimensions – dimensions which there is no hope ever of proving – in an attempt to explain the utter mystery? And on the planet earth, do not coincidences, one in a million, one in ten million, one in a hundred million, occur every minute, every hour, every day, affecting someone somewhere in the vast mass of humanity on the planet?

But not this. It can't be. He must be deluded. Just because there is a strong resemblance in physical features and they share certain mannerisms should not lead to such a fanciful outlandish conclusion. Perhaps his rational processes are somehow biased and distorted by the relationship with Penny – but surely not twice – lightning couldn't strike twice ... or could it? Could this young man be yet another legacy of his extra-curricular activity all those years ago?

Delusion. Hysteria. Fanciful nonsense brought on by the emotional events of the last few weeks. That must be the simple explanation ... but what about the strange incident in Manila and the similar feelings when he'd met him on the ship?

Harry lets lose his grip on the rail and walks back along the deck, away from the aft end towards the midship's door. By the time he has reached his cabin, he is in a cold sweat. Even though the image of Jason is still fresh in his mind, he is tempted to go back and look through the window again ... but it is not necessary. His perception has solidified.

He slumps into the armchair, burying his head in his hands. He passes into a dreamlike state where it feels as if he has left his body. His spirit has dissociated, and he looks down on himself. It cannot be happening. He will wake up refreshed any moment and wonder why he would dream such a thing. He will curse with relief at how the subconscious mind can be so wilful in the games it plays with the emotions.

But he is awake. He pinches himself, and it hurts. It is **his** problem. It was **his** making, and **he** must face it.

His thoughts spin endlessly. There is no answer! It is an impossible situation, and yet he must know for sure. It must be confirmed beyond all doubt. He raises his head and sits up straight in the chair. He must do something. He must find out. The only way he will be able to rid himself of the horrible fear that threatens to destroy him is by searching for the truth – by proving that this Jason is not of him, that the whole thing has been a ghastly trick of the mind.

He could not possibly talk with Jason himself on such a matter. There is only one thing for it – he must retrace his steps back to the infertility clinics, to see if he can find any record which would show Jason's origin. Only then can he be sure, so that he can dispel once and for all from his mind the absurdity of the notion that has gripped him.

When the *Empress* docks in Southampton on Friday he can get the early train to London, and go to Harley Street and the clinics to rule out this insane notion.

Harry opens the top drawer of his desk and pulls out a telex pad. He pauses for a moment and then begins scribbling furiously:

'Request urgent one week's leave for unexpected specialist appointment in London clinic. Apologies for short notice. Unavoidable. Please revert with confirmation asap.'

That should do it. He knows that the personnel office can sign on a suitable doctor at two minutes notice from a large pool of retired practitioners. They are only too happy to be offered the diversion of a luxury cruise on the *Empress* and get well-paid for it. One of them should easily be able to hold the fort for a week.

It is Monday morning. The rush hour is at its peak, and Harry is threading his way through hordes of commuters at Oxford Circus underground station. He walks slowly and deliberately up the grimy concrete steps, steadfastly refusing to accelerate to keep pace with the continuous stream of bodies jostling him from both directions.

At last – daylight, blue sky. It is a bright and warm midsummer day. He should be somewhere else, he thinks. Anywhere but here, walking along Upper Regent Street against a tide of humanity hell-bent on getting to work.

He is fearful of the purpose of his visit, even though compelled to see it through to the bitter end – he must find out, it is imperative – if only to justify the agony he feels. He hardly dare think of the prospects, the possibilities, if such information reveals what he fears most. It is daunting beyond belief.

He is still able to remember the clinics he did 'business' with all those years ago. Goodness knows, he had made enough journeys in the past to find his way with eyes closed. And now, he is retracing his steps as if it were only yesterday, and he was again on an errand with a plastic pot of semen carefully sequestered in a warm pocket.

Only it is not 20 years ago. It is today, here and now – and the reality threatens to totally overwhelm his senses and plunge him further into an abyss of utter despair. More doubts and fear come upon him as he nears his destination. Will the same clinics still be operating now? And if they are, how can he expect there to be any staff still employed who might remember him or consent to help him? And if there are, will they be prepared to divulge highly confidential information – information of an extremely sensitive nature – from records, which, if still in existence, have been stashed away in some cobwebbed damp cellar for years, to gather dust and fade into oblivion?

Harry begins to feel more depressed with the futility of his compulsion and what the end might or might not bring. He turns right into Harley Street and stops to gather his thoughts. Immediate memories are awakened as he focuses on the neat blocks of Georgian terraces which stretch in a dead straight line into the distance towards the northerly junction with Marylebone Road and Regents Park.

Harry reminds himself where each clinic was in the street. Harvey Wagstaff was towards the other end on the same side – he cannot recall the exact number. Shirley Mason, if he remembers correctly, should be at 106 on the other side, and Bodkins and Crowther are towards this end. He remembers their numbers clearly. They'd had by far the most visits. Bodkins was 52, and Crowther 17.

He decides to start at the far end of the street and work his way back down. He will walk positively and briskly to try and instil a feeling of purpose and positive mood, so that at least those in the clinics might feel more disposed to helping him.

After ten minutes at a brisk pace, he is almost at the other end of the street and has begun to look at the brass plates framing every doorway. He can remember to within one or two doors and he looks closely at every brass plate, but there is no sign of Harvey Wagstaff. Perhaps he has long gone. Harry is not too concerned, because he is not highest on the list in view of the small number of visits he'd made. But there is still always an outside possibility, which he has to confirm or exclude.

He reaches the junction with Marylebone Road. Nothing. He must have gone. He will try number 103 anyway, which he thinks was the most likely number.

'Good morning – Doctor Harvey Wagstaff?'

'Who?'

'Harvey Wagstaff – an infertility expert – about ten to twenty years ago?'

'Oh yes – he was further down at 93. I'm sorry, sir, he's not been there for some years now.'

'Any idea where he might have moved to?'

'I'm sorry, sir – can't help you there.'

Harry crosses over to the even-numbered side and walks slowly down to 106, which he is certain used to be Shirley Mason's. It would be an extraordinary twist of fate if his desperate enquiry yielded the dreaded result in her office.

He arrives at number 106 and hesitates on the doorstep. He is nervous, and tries to compose himself before he strikes the large brass knocker. But the door opens as he raises his hand and a young couple emerge from the gloom into the sunlit street. They appear distraught. The woman is tearful. As they walk away, Harry catches the attention of the woman showing them out before she closes the door.

'Excuse me. I'm sorry – good morning. I wonder if you could help me?'

'Yes?'

'I'm looking for Doctor Mason, Doctor Shirley Mason. I didn't see her name on the plate.'

'She retired over five years ago.'

'And the infertility clinic?'

'There are several other doctors ... would you like an appointment, sir?'

'No – no, thank you. I don't suppose you would know if she ... oh, it doesn't matter. Thank you.'

Harry's confidence and determination are wavering. The hopelessness of such a task is becoming clearly evident. But he will complete his journey and visit the last two clinics. It is an irresistible compulsion that is driving him.

He continues walking down the street, but now the contrived bounce in his step has gone. He will not admit it, but he is simply going through the motions to satisfy the obsession that is gnawing away inside of him. He is pretty certain that old Reggie Bodkins will be long dead and buried, but it is possible that his son, who was also a specialist, in practice with his father, might still be there.

And there – at the top of a long list of names etched on a shiny brass plate – 'Doctor Alistair Bodkins FRCS FRCOG' – that's him for sure, the son of old Bodkins.

A surge of renewed confidence gives him the impetus to strike the large brass knocker firmly and decisively, as if his luck is about to change.

A matronly lady, petite if not sparrow-like in proportions, opens the heavy shiny black door and peers at Harry over her gold-rimmed spectacles, which she lifts from her nose and lets drop on the cord around her neck before speaking.

'Can I help you?'

'Doctor Bodkins ... I mean the old Doctor Bodkins...'

'You mean Mister Bodkins.'

'Yes – of course, but he is a doctor...'

'That is correct, sir – but surgeons and gynaecologists are referred to as Mister...'

'I wonder if the older Mister Bodkins is still in practice here ... I – uuuh, sent him some patients quite some time ago, and...'

'You are a doctor yourself?'

'Yes.'

'I see. Well, I'm afraid he is dead now. His son, Mister Alistair Bodkins, has taken over the practice ... if you would like to make an appointment...'

'No – no, thank you. It's just that I need some information

386

on an old patient of mine. It concerns the identity of a son they had who was possibly born through the help of this clinic when the old Mister Bodkins was in practice ... it must be something like twenty years ago now.'

'I'm afraid all our records concerning past patients are strictly confidential – and besides, I really don't think there are any records still in existence going that far back in time.'

'It's very important ... perhaps Mister Bodkins keeps records – private records somewhere else?'

'I don't know. I am sorry, but I cannot help you. Now, if you will excuse me.'

'Would it be possible to have just a quick word with...'

'He's a very busy man, and the earliest appointment, and then only if it is very urgent, is over two weeks. I can book you in, if you must – but I don't think he will be in a position to help you much with records kept twenty years ago ... besides, he cannot reveal any information regarding...'

'Thank you – I get the message.'

Before Harry can even turn round to go she has begun to shut the door. If there is a secret with the young Dr Bodkins, then it will stay with him forever.

He stands down from the step and looks up at the clear blue sky. It is mid-morning now, and he is aware for the first time of the continuous traffic noise and the smell of exhaust fumes. It is made even worse in this street, congested at the best of times, by taxis dropping off clinic clientele every few doors.

The combination of sun and noxious fumes, together with the high humidity, is making Harry's task even more onerous, and his shirt is soaked with sweat. As he looks along the last hundred yards which effectively signals the end of his search, he begins to resign himself to the absurdity and utter futility of the whole business. If he is still compelled to seek a solution, then it will have to come from a completely different source.

After waiting ages for a gap in the traffic, he scuttles across the road for the last time and heads in the direction of Oxford

Circus, going past the ever-decreasing odd numbers, knowing that number 17 will be the final call. He wonders now, if it is even worth bothering. The other clinics have yielded nothing, and there is no reason to suppose he will be luckier at number 17.

He stands opposite the large shiny green door and scans the dozen or so names on the brass plate polished to perfection. As expected, there is no 'Crowther'. He moves closer and looks at every name individually – definitely no Crowther. It signals the hopelessness of his task. He has wasted an entire day on a fruitless, ill-conceived mission, and now he must sit around for nearly a week brooding on his thwarted quest, until the *Empress* returns to Southampton.

He is of two minds whether to even bother to knock on this last door or simply quit and get out of this dirty, dusty hot city. He tosses a coin in his mind. What the hell! He steps up towards the door and halfheartedly presses the bell.

He waits. No one appears. One more ring and then he will definitely leave. The door opens as his finger is released.

'I'm sorry, sir – we were busy ... can I help you?'

The pretty young face catches Harry by surprise.

'Uuuuh – yes ... do you know if there was a Doctor Crowther who used to work here?'

'I've only been here a few months so I never knew him, although he is still talked about. The doctor here now is Doctor Templeton. Would you like to come in and make an appointment?'

'Yes, thank you.'

The door closes behind Harry, and a shiver of nostalgia reminds him of the times when he used to pass through that same door over 20 years ago. The entrance hall is much the same. Even the decor has barely altered – dark heavy red wallpaper and delicate wall lights – a thick dark-patterned brown carpet stretching down the hall to the back office – a curving staircase with an ornate gold handrail leading up to the first floor and the examination and treatment rooms.

'Would you like to come this way to the reception office?'

Harry follows meekly. He has given up any likelihood of

discovering the truth, but this is the final trip down memory lane before he accepts the unalterable reality.

'Where is Doctor Crowther these days?'

'He retired many years ago – to Eastbourne, I think – but I believe he died not long after retiring. Doctor Templeton has been here for quite some time. The offices at the top of the building belong to the British Association of Cosmetic Surgeons ... they are nothing to do with us.'

'Do you keep records going back to the time of Doctor Crowther?' Harry asks casually.

'No, I don't think so. I've only seen the records of Doctor Templeton, and they only go back about ten years,' she says in a cheerful voice, seemingly unruffled by the fact that Harry is quizzing her with questions entirely unrelated to making an appointment.

'Now sir, when is it convenient for you to see Doctor Templeton?'

'Aah yes – well, actually, in fact – I don't really want an appointment ... that is to say ... what I really need, is, well ... I really wanted to get some information.'

Harry puts his cards on the table. The pretty receptionist's ready smile disappears, and the instant change in the tone of her voice signals her antennae have been deployed.

'Information? What sort of information?'

'Oh, nothing much really...' Harry falters. He reflects for a moment, is it really worth the effort? Is there not another way to end this fantasy he seems to have created for himself – once and for all? Without any conscious thought, he changes tack.

'Liz – Liz Fielder. Have you ever heard of her?'

'No – can't say I have, sir.'

'She used to work here a long time ago ... let me see – it must be well over twenty years since I...'

'There is a Mrs Beckett, Elizabeth Beckett, who has been here for a long time, but no – there's never been a Liz Fielder as far as I know.'

'What does Mrs Beckett do?'

'She is the manager-cum-administrator of the clinic. She knows everything – I think she used to be a nurse once...'

'I see. How old would she be, then?'

'I'm sorry, sir, but why are you asking all these questions?'

Harry senses that even the tolerance of the helpful young receptionist is about to run out and he will receive a final rebuff and be asked to leave. But he will pre-empt it and leave with his dignity intact.

'It doesn't matter. You've been very kind and most helpful. I'm sorry I bothered you...'

'So you don't want an appointment?'

'No, no – thank you anyway for all your trouble...'

Harry turns and walks towards the front door. Just before he has turned completely, a door behind the reception desk opens.

'Andrea, could you please...'

Harry recognises her without hesitation.

'Liz!'

'Harry! My God!'

'Harry – what on earth have you been doing all these years – the last time I saw you was a week before you sat your finals – God, it must be at least twenty years ago ... and it must have been your last visit as a medical student ... do you remember?'

'Do I remember? Of course I remember – as if it were only yesterday.'

'What on earth have you been doing all these years ... and what on earth are you doing here today?'

'It's a long long story – can we talk?'

'Of course – come this way to my office. Luckily, it is quiet today – we've actually no new appointments, and I'm using the time to do a job I've been putting off for years – to clean out all the old files that have been gathering dust since God knows when.'

'They could be what I am here for, Liz,' he says sombrely.

'What do you mean?'

'Can we go to your office?'

'Andrea, can you put the kettle on, please? This way.'

He follows her into a room on the other side of the corridor, gently closing the door behind him. She sits down behind a

390

large executive desk, motioning Harry to sit in a soft lounge chair opposite.

'You sounded serious – what is it? Is there a problem?'

Harry sits back in the chair and clasps his hands together under his chin in a reflective pose. He is going to give Liz the full story of his life in as abbreviated a version as possible. After a few moments, he begins to talk. In the space of ten minutes he has outlined his main career moves since leaving medical school and enlightened her on his final destiny as a ship's doctor. She listens without interrupting.

'... so there you have it in a nutshell ... anyway Liz, enough of me for a moment – what about you? I am amazed that you are still here at number 17 after all these years – and especially with Doctor Crowther having gone.'

'Honestly, I never planned to be here so long. In fact it could only have been a year or two after your crowd of contemporaries qualified and left the scene that I got married to Bill and had three boys, virtually one after the other. I stayed at home for over five years until the first two were at school, and then I decided I wanted to go back to work. Bill didn't want me to go, but you know, I felt bored and unfulfilled at home ... anyway, I heard that Doctor Crowther desperately needed someone to run the office and organise the clinic. It had expanded considerably since those early days when you were around.'

'But you remember me!'

'Oooh yes, how could I ever forget Harry Lester? I can picture you now ... and I remember how the quality of your samples would vary depending on whether you were talking to your girlfriend or not! And I'll tell you another thing, I was pretty sure you were splitting samples and supplying other clinics – you never would admit it, but am I right?'

Harry looks down in feigned sheepishness.

'Yes – I'll come clean ... I hereby confess to that practice – on the odd occasion, anyway. It didn't happen too often, I promise ... and I always made sure you got the biggest portion!'

'And there was another strange thing I seem to remember,

391

as we are on the subject of sample quality. There were times when you brought a very good quality sample, which we didn't need to check under the microscope. But one day Doctor Crowther decided to make some random checks on quality control, even on the good volume specimens – and it happened to be a day that you brought in one of your very best volume samples. We couldn't believe what we saw down the microscope because we knew that you had one of the highest sperm counts in our donor pool, and high volume usually correlated with a high count. That day, we managed to identify three or four haggard-looking sperms drowning in a large volume of semen – or what at least appeared to the naked eye as semen – how on earth did you do it? Go on, you can tell me now – how did you do it?'

'Robinson's Lemon Barley, Liz.'

This time, Harry is genuinely sheepish and can feel his cheeks flush.

'Only once or twice, I promise. It was in desperation – you know, double bookings, girlfriend ... honestly, I used to feel guilty doing it...'

'So that was it – that was how you did it ... a mystery solved!' Liz smiles and shakes her head in disbelief.

'How successful was I, in fact – you can tell me now, surely?'

'I can't honestly remember. It was a lot, I know that.'

'Well, how many would you guess?'

'Let's see – you were with us over five years – is that right?'

'Correct.'

'One donation per week, occasionally two. I admit that we would use one sample, if it was good enough, for two or three separate inseminations, so that could increase the final yield. Of course, not all inseminations resulted in a pregnancy – but let's say the success rate was about twenty-five per cent ... that works out about, let's see ... say a rough figure of about twenty to twenty-five per year – conservatively, which over five years makes well over a hundred...'

'Oh my God...'

The main purpose of Harry's visit reimposes itself in the

forefront of his consciousness. The dread shows on his face as his cheeks are drained white. Liz is alarmed at the sudden and marked change in Harry's expression.

'Surely it doesn't worry you, does it? At least not this long time after – it certainly didn't seem to bother you at the time.'

Harry is mute. He fixes his gaze on the edge of her desk as if momentarily in a trance.

'Are you all right, Harry?'

'Something terrible has happened. The worse thing that you or I could ever imagine ... you simply will not believe such a thing...'

In a few painful sentences Harry recounts his involvement with Penny and the awful truth that has been revealed by the pregnancy.

Liz, whose years in the infertility business have trained her for every eventuality, where she has learnt from painful experience every possible nuance in the spectrum of human emotions, is aghast at Harry's desperate plight.

'Oh my poor Harry. That is so cruel. You are right – I can hardly believe it. It's incredible. Who would have thought that anything like this could ever have happened? I know that everyone joked about it once in a while, you know, speculated – fantasised ... but we were always smug in our certainty that such a thing happening was well-nigh impossible from a statistical point of view.'

'Liz, the impossible has happened.'

'Yes – but you see, it was in the very early days, and we only checked once on those very early figures. It wasn't appreciated at the time that your little band of donors from Barts would be bringing samples so regularly for the five years you were at medical school. In those days there were no strict quotas – that all came in when you had long gone ... very tight regulations were introduced. It was made an absolute rule that one donor could only produce five viable pregnancies before being erased from the central register.'

'Central register?'

'Oh yes – all the clinics had to be linked to a centralised computer register so that it could be recorded and verified

393

exactly, the contributions made by any one donor – anywhere. The AID business had become big business – a baby-farming boom – and infertility clinics sprang up everywhere. I suppose it was realised then that regulations had to be introduced to minimise the risks of consanguinity ... are you absolutely sure?'

'No doubt about it – no question at all. The blood tests – prenatal – were analysed at the Harley Street lab – you know – DNA fingerprinting, the lot...'

Liz drops her head and is silent. There is nothing more she wants to say as the full realisation sinks in. She looks up suddenly.

'But why are you here today? I'm sure this is not just a social visit after all this time. You say it happened at another clinic, you said ... I mean – it's lovely to see you, even in these awful circumstances ... but why have you come all this way...?'

Harry shakes his head slowly.

'What is it ... what is the problem?'

'It is worse than you could ever imagine.'

'What do you mean – tell me – what is it?'

'There is another...'

'Another what?'

'Another of my offspring...'

'You're kidding?'

'Well, I'm pretty sure there is. Maybe not one hundred per cent ... I know my mind could be playing tricks, but it's more than just a hunch ... something much deeper. That is why I am here today. If it turns out that my suspicions are correct, then it will be absolutely devastating and...'

'Why, Harry? WHY? What do you mean?'

'It's a young man ... he's working on the ship also. It's quite incredible ... I think I'm going mad at times from thinking about it. I cannot escape ... it's like a bad dream. A dream that I hope I will awake from soon...'

'But you say you are not sure – a hunch. Maybe after all this emotional turmoil with your girlfriend, your mind is playing tricks on you. Perhaps you're looking at all young people of a suitable age and speculating...'

'No I haven't gone mad. I am convinced.'

'Well, what can I do?'

'I need you to check – to verify – one way or another – if he is the one.'

'Harry, you know I would do anything for you, but that is quite a tall order. Apart from being strictly against all the rules ... the ethics, the confidentiality – you know exactly what I mean – it is so long ago that it would not be on the present computer base.'

'I understand. I appreciate all that – but this is a very very special case, believe me. Surely there must be some old records kept somewhere, of those cases in the early days?'

'It's funny – a strange coincidence, perhaps – but I am just about to clear out all the old files and records from the storage cupboard. But I'm afraid I've been given strict instructions that they must be destroyed.'

'Liz – you've got to! I can't say how important it is!'

'I fully sympathise – you know I do – but are you sure it's not a strange state of mind you've got yourself into – because of your girlfriend?'

'No. I promise. Please believe me – this is real. I know I've been worried sick, and got myself into a terrible state where I cannot think clearly or rationally – but – but – I promise, it is clear enough to realise that something terrible might happen.'

'I don't know what you mean ... but I'm sorry – I cannot do it. These files have got to be confidentially destroyed ...'

'Liz, the young man ... he is now the boyfriend of my daughter ... and it looks like it is getting serious.'

They stare at each other in complete silence. Liz is unable to speak. Her mouth opens but no words come. Her colour becomes more ashen, and the look of horror in her eyes signals clearly to Harry her appreciation of his anguish. Harry remains motionless, but there is a sudden feeling of relief and a cold comfort – relief that he has at last been able to share his terrible secret.

'You see – we must check ... we must.'

She says nothing. She gets up from behind her desk and goes to a pile of dirty cardboard boxes in one corner.

'What did you say his name was?' her voice quivers.

'I didn't, but it's Jason – Jason Brown.'

She recoils as she is about to lift up the first box.

'Oh my God! Oh my God. I cannot believe it ... I cannot believe it.'

'You know ... ?'

'This is a nightmare. I don't need to search the old files. He was here. I remember as if it were yesterday ... but it must have been three or four years ago now. He was looking for his "real" father, can you believe! I didn't tell him of course, for the same reasons I gave you ... but he was so desperately sad that I think I may have said something about the donor being a medical student who may have gone to sea as a doctor – but that was all, truly ...'

Liz cannot suppress her tears any longer.

'I'm sorry,' she sniffs, reaching for a paper handkerchief, 'this has never happened before ...'

Harry puts his arm around her and pulls her into his shoulder.

'So there you have it. The whole grisly mess,' he says calmly, looking out of the window at the hustle bustle of the street, 'I said it was unbelievable ... the sort of thing you might read about in trashy novels ... naturally, I don't have to spell out the dangers of consanguinity. God knows, just the moral and ethical considerations are bad enough without thinking of the physical dangers ... oh, it's so awful ... I don't know what I can do.'

'Listen, Harry – don't be too pessimistic. Perhaps their relationship will not last. As you've said, shipboard romances are only as long as the voyage. If Jason leaves the sea to go to university, it could naturally be the end of it.'

'I can't be so optimistic about such a thing happening. When I left the ship, they seemed to be pretty engrossed in each other. Yes – sure, I have seen countless shipboard romances which have been pretty strong on board, but which have evaporated rapidly ashore ... but these two ... oh Christ, it looks so serious – as if they mean to stay together.'

Harry's face is a picture of torment and despair. His mission

396

to London has realised his worst fears, and now he must depart.

'Liz – I must go. I'll work something out ... anything – anything ... they simply cannot stay together, we know that...'

'Harry – let me know, please ... and keep in touch.'

'I will – I promise.'

Harry extends his arms and pulls Liz tightly in a final embrace. Her tears are free-flowing, and Harry's eyes are red and moist.

'I must go.'

'Goodbye, Harry. Goodbye ... take care...'

Today Harry must rejoin the ship in Southampton. Since confirming his worst fears, he has been in danger of losing his mind. He has been hardly able to sleep, and there has been no room for any other thought night and day. As the train speeds through the Hampshire countryside he is still unable to galvanise his thoughts into any coherent or precise pattern to somehow accommodate the problem that faces him.

Why him? How could this awful chance in millions affect him? Is it some sort of divine punishment for all his years of carefree, irresponsible sex? Could there really be some sort of metaphysical power, the devil himself perhaps, exacting retribution for his contemptuous denial of the traditional family life and conventional human relationships? For so many years, he had succeeded in remaining aloof from the binding constrictions, the vice-like social constraints that the vast majority of humankind blindly submitted to.

Only other people yielded passively to such forces and acted out the stressful games imposed on them – allowing the natural forces and instincts to trap them in an emotional stranglehold from which they could never escape.

But oh! How clever he had been – spreading his seed, as programmed by nature, everywhere, indifferent – if not contemptuous – of the possible consequences. NO emotional ties.

397

NO family. NO responsibility. Life has been such a blessing and he had triumphed over nature – enjoyed the pleasures, tasted the forbidden fruit with impunity ... avoided all the stresses of life's game, but played it to the full nevertheless.

But his forbidden fruit has returned with a vengeance to haunt him ... this incredible coincidence ... this cruel, vindictive twist of fate. It is a symbolic reminder in the shape of a demonic spectre issuing its dire warning to others who might be tempted. It is the omnipotent force of nature bringing him to heel. How dare he be so arrogant and carefree! The audacity of a mere mortal! One little solitary human being. Who the hell did he think he was? Such impudence – or more like stupidity! The blind arrogant delusion that he could triumph over those forces which had painstakingly evolved through countless millenia in order to perfect the perpetuation of the species ... as if he could play but not pay!

It is as if he has offended an inviolable rule of the eternal game plan, and now the all-pervading cosmic force is exacting its ruthless revenge ... but it intends to take more than its required pound of flesh. He will pay more for being so impudent. It is a just punishment and will serve as an effective deterrent to others to make sure they put any such ideas out of their heads. Don't tamper with nature, that is the message, loud and clear ... you cannot ... YOU CANNOT ... YOU CANNOT ... YOU CANNOT ... CLICKETY CLICK ... CLICKETY CLICK ... CLICKETY CLICK...

'Southampton. Southampton. This is Southampton. All stations to...'

Harry wakes with a start, just in time to grab his bag and plunge out of the carriage door, almost falling headlong onto the platform.

Back in his cabin, he lies on his bed ruminating. He despairs. How can this problem be solved? All he can think is that he must see Penny, even though he will not know what to say to her.

He lies on his bed, staring up at the deckhead oblivious of

time until he is aware of the light fading. When he sits up he looks through the porthole. He can see the orange neon lights which have come on at dusk on the far side of Southampton Water. He looks at his watch. He has missed dinner. But he is relieved. He couldn't face conversation in the mess tonight. The ship is about to sail. He will get up. Penny will be starting her night duty shortly. The hospital. He must go to the hospital. A spasm of intense anxiety shudders through his whole body.

By the time he reaches 6 deck his mind is strangely empty and devoid of thoughts or ideas. For the first time in ages, he feels a sort of calmness, a sense of resignation overtaking him as he walks through the door into the hospital.

Penny is sitting at the desk writing. She looks so beautiful. Her crisp white tunic contrasts strikingly with her perpetual suntan. For a few seconds Harry indulges in her image unnoticed, before she suddenly looks up and sees him. Her face comes alive. Her eyes sparkle. For a moment Harry is uplifted – and then the realisation of something he should do overwhelms him again and his fleeting joy is crushed.

'Harry – you're back! Did you sort out all your business problems?'

'Uuuuuh – yes – of course. All sorted out. Everything in order.'

He desperately searches for the right thing to say. A natural introduction which can lead him into telling her everything. But it will not come.

'How's Jason?' he croaks feebly.

The mere mention of his name brings an immediate flush to her face. She acts coy.

'Very well, thank you Doctor.'

'Good.'

'You know – we seem to be so well-suited. I hope it doesn't sound too corny, but it's almost as if we were made for each other ... it really is quite incredible. We get on so well and ... you must know by now ... I do adore him – and well, I think he feels the same way about me – or at least that's what he keeps telling me.'

399

Harry's face tells her that he is disturbed. But she assumes it is because of his original desire for her and subsequent envy of her new suitor.

'Oh, I'm sorry. I shouldn't talk that way. It's thoughtless of me.'

'No, no, no – I'm very happy for you both, believe me.'

'Well, you don't look very happy – if you don't mind me saying.'

'Honestly, it's something completely unconnected with you two ... still got a few things on my mind. Believe me, I'm delighted for you both.'

'I believe you – and I'm so pleased, because I want to tell you something. You know Jason will be leaving after the next voyage?'

'I didn't, actually.'

'Well, he is ... and we want to hold a party – you know, a sort of celebration thing ...'

'What will you be celebrating?'

'His leaving the sea. And I suppose I can let you into the secret ... he's been promised a place to study law at Cambridge! Isn't that wonderful?'

'Yes, of course ... it's wonderful news. I am pleased for him. He's finally seen the light. The sooner he gets on with his real life, the better.'

'I've also made a decision.'

'Yes?'

'I want to get on with my career ashore. I can confide in you now, as I am sure you will know soon enough – I've been offered a junior sister's post at Addenbrookes and ...'

'That's Cambridge, isn't it?'

'Yes.'

He is silent. She continues, oblivious to his rising alarm.

'So the day after tomorrow – in the officers' wardroom. It's all been arranged – the catering, invites – everything. Everyone will be coming. Of course, you will be guest of honour.'

Everyone is drunk. It is a near-riot. The officer's wardroom is a

400

heaving mass of inebriated bodies, human in form but reptilian in behaviour. Harry cranes his neck to look over the sea of bobbing heads for Penny and Jason. He cannot see them. He is most certainly not in any party mood, and has drunk only one light beer. His torment and anguish do not leave him for a moment. He is vaguely aware of bodies, hot and sweaty – lurching and colliding – stumbling, falling. Loud, such loud voices, so many – and even louder, deafening disco music.

The assault on Harry's senses from such a shindig only serves to exacerbate his morbidity. He decides to pay his respects to Jason and Penny and then slip away quietly to his cabin.

He sees them. There, on the other side of the dance floor, swirling around each other like a couple of wild dervishes with not a care in the world. Penny appears to be deliriously happy. Jason is obviously drunk. Harry threads his way through the tangle of souls and sidles around to the edge of the dance floor, where he is able to attract their attention. Penny sees him first and cries out enthusiastically.

'Harry!'

Jason sees him, and his already ruddy cheeks turn an instant deeper red. She tugs at his arm towards Harry.

'What a party,' Harry says unemotionally, 'don't let me stop you two dancing. I just wanted to say hello, enjoy yourselves – and don't drink too much. I won't stay long. I really do have some important letters to write, and . . .'

'Harry! C'mon – just one dance . . .'

'No – really I must go . . . next time, I promise. Look, here's our trusty assistant purser, James – he'll take you for a spin . . . I'm sure Jason won't mind.'

'Of course not . . . go on, Penny. I need the rest,' says Jason, breathing hard.

As she flits away into the heart of the throng with her new dance partner, Jason heaves an exaggerated sigh of relief.

'Phew! She's killing me, Doc. I thought I had some energy.'

He stands directly facing Harry. Their eyes meet, and for a split second Harry feels a surge of emotion that threatens to consume his whole being. He fights hard to stifle it but senses, despite Jason's advanced state of inebriation, that he too is acutely aware of a strong mutual force pulling them together as they stand and eyeball each other.

Jason speaks, but has difficulty getting the words out.

'Doctor – can I ask you a question? I mean, I need to know something ... what I'm trying to say is that there has been something bothering me for a long, long time ... it's very difficult ... it's just that, well ... you and I ... and something that should be...'

'Jason! It's your turn. You've rested long enough!'

Penny grabs Jason's arm and pulls him violently towards the dance floor. He looks perplexed and his face continues to ask the question he hadn't been able to finish. But within seconds, the magical distraction of Penny captivates his whole attention, and he is able to match her in the frenetic thrashing they call dancing. Harry withdraws and melts into the mass of bodies out of their direct vision. In a few moments he will quietly slip out of the back door and head for his quarters.

As he turns to go, the music stops abruptly. The master-of-ceremonies is the assistant cruise director, Lance Frost. He claps his hands violently.

'Shut up, everybody. Quiet ... quiet, please ... can I have your attention for a moment...'

The loud cacophony of voices hardly changes until people realise the music has stopped and Lance Frost is shouting at the top of his voice. Harry has stopped in his tracks. He sees Penny and Jason walk towards Lance and jump up, one either side of him on the small podium. Faces turn towards them and there is a loud, spontaneous 'Hush' which results in a workable silence.

'Ladies and gentlemen, this is a great party, but particularly because it is to celebrate a very special occasion. The ship's company is very happy for the two people involved, but very sad because we're going to lose our favorite Nursing Sister...'

Harry's sense of foreboding becomes acute as Lance turns to Jason and hands him the microphone. Jason is embarrassed and self-conscious despite the alcohol, and demonstrably not practiced in public speaking. His voice cracks nervously. He looks at Penny. Her eyes seem to infuse power and confidence into him as she moves closer and grasps his hand. He is able to speak.

'Friends ... everyone here ... I can't say how – how fantastic this party is for us both,' he says, looking at Penny.

Harry's fears intensify as Penny draws close to his side.

'Although I am happy tonight, I am also sad – sad because I will be leaving the *Empress* soon ... and I'm afraid Penny will be leaving too ...'

There is a loud murmur of good-humoured disapproval, and shouts of 'Shame'.

'But I want ... well, we want ... I don't know how to say it ... it's just ... well, I would like to make an announcement, that Penny and I ... that is, as soon as we leave the *Empress* ... we are going to be married.'

Two months have passed since the fateful announcement which drove the dagger further into Harry's heart. A day, an hour, a minute has not gone by where he has not been racked by the torture of the thought of what is to happen soon.

He has taken extended leave. His lengthy and loyal service to the company would have made it difficult for them to deny his request for a sabbatical period of unspecified interval in order to 'bring himself up-to-date' with current advances in medicine. But he has not devoted one minute to study. His increasing anguish has intensified to an unbearable degree as each day passes, drawing nearer and nearer to the promised event.

Two weeks to the fateful day, and Harry can bear it no longer. He must talk to somebody. Dr Coombes, the laboratory director in Harley Street – perhaps he can help him and assuage the endless torment that is destroying him. He will go to see him as soon as it can be arranged. Perhaps he will understand. Perhaps he can enlighten Harry, reassure him that it is not his doing – such distant unforeseen events totally beyond his control. Perhaps it can lessen the pain. But he is guarded as whether to tell him the whole story. Even though Dr Coombes knows about Penny, he knows nothing of Jason and the impending marriage.

He is fortunate. A brief call to Dr Coombes had enabled a swift appointment to be made, and Harry has made the journey to London and finds himself in the doctor's office.

'How nice to see you again, Doctor Lester – I must say, it's rather fortunate that my secretary had been able to squeeze you in at such short notice...'

'I am most grateful ... thank you.'

'Please sit down.'

'Now – what can I do for you?'

'I – I'm not really sure. What I mean to say ... well, is that ... I need to ask you some technical questions. I mean, I need your expert opinion on something that is bothering me ... it's not easy...'

'Is it concerning your girlfriend?'

'Uuuuh ... yes...'

Harry is nervous and barely contains his agitation, but the learned doctor cannot possibly suspect the real reason for Harry's desperate plea for help.

'...risks of consanguinity ... I mean, in truth, are they really so great?'

'Well, it would be futile to indulge in wishful thinking and the hope that any offspring from such unions would be normal. Admittedly, the risks are smaller in the first generation – but if there is continued inbreeding, any undesirable genetic characteristics will inevitably manifest. I think you are well aware from your own medical training, leaving aside any moral or legal considerations, that the closer the genetic origins of the mating couple to a common source, as it were, then the greater the chances of there being adverse inherited traits. These can range from minor features of negligible consequence, you know, for example a deviation of the distal end of a little finger, to full-blown problems which are incompatible with survival. So, it would be fair to say, that there is a range of abnormality which is entirely unpredictable in its eventual manifestation...'

'May I say, Doctor Lester, that I am pleased, and rather relieved, that you have come to see me, because I hadn't heard from you after our first meeting. I had wanted to review the situation with you and discuss the possible strategies for the future ... but if you remember, you left in rather a hurry ...'

'Yes – I must apologise for that – it was appallingly bad manners. I'm sorry.'

'Don't worry about it. I understand how you felt then ... but tell me, did Miss Reeves ... was there a satisfactory outcome?'

'Yes. She had a termination.'

'Good. Oh, I'm sorry – I don't mean it like that – you know what I mean?'

'Yes yes, of course.'

'And how did she take it?'

'How do you think?'

The balding academic looks down at the desk and nods slowly.

'I'm sorry ... but of course it was for the best – I'm sure you agree?'

'No! NO! Of course I cannot! How the hell could I?'

'I'm sorry. How is the relationship ... I mean, how is she now?'

'It is finished. She is fine.'

They sit opposite, staring down at the pristine white blotter. Neither cares to speak. As far as the learned doctor is concerned, there is little more to discuss. But Harry, who has come for succour and to be offered even the smallest glimmer of hope and a way out of his torment, has received nothing for his pains. After a prolonged pause, Dr Coombes looks up at Harry.

'Well, it was kind and thoughtful of you to come and tell me the outcome of this unpleasant business. As I said, I'm sure it is all for the best. I do hope and pray Miss Reeves will be happy and get over it ... and of course yourself. I can appreciate, it has not been easy. You can rest assured, at least – the secret is safe with me – just you and I – and my senior technician. No one else will ever know.'

'Good,' says Harry emptily, 'thank you.'

'Well, that's it. If you have no more questions, Doctor Lester, then...'

Harry had come to London with one burning question, but had been unable to ask it.

'Yes ... thank you again.'

Harry gets up slowly to leave. Dr Coombes jumps up from his desk to escort him to the door. At the top of the stairs Harry shakes his hand and finds himself speaking involuntarily.

'Oh, by the way, what are the risks of brother-sister or even half-brother-sister consanguinity?'

'Much the same in probability terms, as father-daughter, I'd say. I suppose there would be marginally less risk with half-siblings because they share the genes of only one parent – but still, the chances of the offspring being affected in some way are pretty substantial. It's certainly something that nature seems to abhor ... that is, apart from the usual moral and cultural objections, you understand...'

CHAPTER 16

THE WEDDING

And Abraham said: And yet indeed she is my sister; she is the daughter of my father, but not the daughter of my mother; and she became my wife.

Genesis 20: 11–12

'Doc – I mean Harry – Penny and I, are so happy you agreed to be best man. It's really wonderful – and means so much to both of us.'

Harry has extended his sabbatical leave. The circumstances have been such a strain that he has not been able to face the prospects of returning to sea. At times, he feels as if his life is over. It is three months now since he left the *Empress*. It has been three months of torture.

He cannot overcome the central issue of the problem – the inescapable fact that a half-brother and sister are about to be married – his son and daughter! The biological consequences of such a union are bad enough, leaving aside the clear moral and legal dilemma.

The law is unambiguous. It is illegal. The incestuous relationship is deprecated universally, and in most societies it is enshrined in prohibitive taboos.

Since the unhelpful meeting with Dr Coombes Harry has tried desperately to discuss the problem with other experts, and has sought the advice of many specialists in genetics in different institutions. Such genetic counselling would normally be an open matter for legitimately married couples, who might have a medical problem that was known and could be passed on to potential offspring. But Harry has had to concoct a hypothetical reason for his interest when he has approached these counsellors, and so he has not been able to get the response that his battered psyche desperately needs. All had unanimously emphasised the greatly increased risks of breeding between such a closely related couple, even though they conceded there was a small chance that the children would be entirely normal and exhibit the good dominant characteristics of both parents – where all the dangerous recessive genes were effectively hidden. But in reality, the chances of such good luck were minimal, and there would be a strong likelihood that one or more recessive traits would manifest in a physical or mental abnormality.

Harry has rehearsed countless options and speculated on so many possible scenarios to evolve a satisfactory solution – but it is hopeless. He is painfully aware that his despair will consume and destroy him unless he can, by some adept feat of mental gymnastics, drastically alter his perception of what is right and wrong and somehow live a life resigned to fate and what may, or may not happen in the future.

As the dreaded day draws inexorably closer and closer, he becomes more and more morose. He is incapable of doing anything. Events have simply overtaken him. There is a gradual resignation that he cannot possibly bring to bear any influence on what is happening. He still feels painful guilt from his involvement and the crucial part he played in the tragic saga, but he tries to console himself that he is innocent of any wilful wrongdoing, and no one could ever have predicted such unlikely events.

As the fateful day approaches, he senses that he is beginning to develop a feeling of passive acceptance. In the beginning, he had fought so hard against the natural forces that told him he had transgressed against nature, defied her absolute power, infringed her inviolable sexual laws and offended her so deeply. But now he tries to block out the possible consequences of such actions and come to terms with the reality which now seems inevitable.

It is to be a grand wedding. For the reception there is to be a large white marquee erected in the garden of Penny's parents. The wedding ceremony is to take place in her local parish church.

410

Harry has kept in regular contact. Ever since Penny and Jason had phoned him and begged him to be the best man, he has barely managed to conceal his smouldering anguish. In the helpless mode into which he had drifted, he'd been powerless to refuse the request to play a vital role in their union.

Most of the arrangements have been finalised by Penny's parents. Harry had driven over to their home in Broadstairs on a warm autumnal day to meet them. They were both charming and courteous. They never realised that he had been the doctor on the *Empress* who'd had a romance with Penny before Jason. Penny had never shown them a picture, and she'd covered her tracks well after the abortion.

Her 'father' was a pleasant man, very interested to hear about Harry's long career at sea, although Harry was not in a mood to offer an autobiography of a life he now deems wasted and fruitless. Penny's mother was simply an older version of Penny herself. She was about Harry's age, maybe a shade younger, but he could not help speculating how attractive she must have been as a young woman. He had suppressed all thoughts of the fact that he would be meeting the mother of his daughter.

On the eve before the wedding, Harry drives to Jason's parents' home in Stilton Keynes to discuss last-minute details for the big day. He has deliberately avoided going to see them until the last possible minute. It had been hard enough meeting Penny's parents, but her frequent phone calls had forced him to come sooner.

And now, as he opens the large wrought-iron gate, and walks slowly along the garden path to the front door, he is barely able to control the intense anxiety that has come over him. Jason's mother answers the door. She greets him warmly.

'You must be Doctor Lester. I'm Doreen Brown. It's so nice to meet you at long last. Jason never stops talking about you ... do come in.'

Harry follows Doreen Brown meekly into the lounge. He feels uncomfortable despite the warm welcome.

411

'Do sit down, Doctor Lester...'

'Harry, please – do call me Harry.'

'Harry, can I get you a drink?'

'Thank you – a scotch and soda?'

She disappears for a moment around a partition that separates the main lounge from what is obviously an extension to the house. As Harry lets his head fall back into the soft velour of the armchair and stifles a sigh, a small, portly figure emerges from the door opposite. He looks serious and is shyly hesitant, but forces a smile.

'I'm Jason's father, Roy Brown – pleased to meet you. Jason has told us so much about you that I feel I already know you. I'd like to personally thank you for making him see sense at long last and get on with his career. My wife and I ... sorry, I believe you have just met Doreen ... we are delighted that he is going up to Cambridge to read law. I can't tell you the years of disappointment I've ... that is, we've – my wife and I – have had. Frankly, we suffered over him running away to sea and wasting his life ... oh, I'm sorry – no offence intended – I mean, it's not as if you're wasting your life at sea ... it's just that ... I – I mean...'

Harry smiles at his obvious discomforture at what he perceives is a regrettable *faux pas*.

'You are quite correct in your assumption, Mister Brown. It is a decadent and wasteful existence, and I freely admit it. You do not offend me in the least. I made the decision years ago, and I have never regretted it. Who knows, Jason may become a lawyer, a barrister, a Queen's Counsel – an eminent judge even ... but one day he might decide to give it all up and run away – back to sea. It doesn't matter in the end, does it? As long as he is fulfilled...'

'I can see your point, but well, I must be honest...'

'I am very happy for him – and you, and Mrs Brown. I am confident he will shine in whatever he chooses to do. He is an exceptionally bright young man, and you must be very proud of him. You have a good son...'

'Thank you. Of course I am very proud. And you, Doctor Lester?'

'Please call me Harry.'

'And you – Harry, you yourself are not married?'

'Correct.'

'Don't you wish sometimes that you'd married and had a family?'

'No – not at all. Sure, I can see the contentment and fulfilment it has brought you as a parent – but it's not always been easy, has it?'

'No, no – I mean yes, you are quite right – it's not always been easy. In fact, Jason and I had a disagreement for a considerable time – we fell out after he went off to sea. But I'm happy to say that that is history now – all in the past. We are the greatest of friends again, and what's more, we know Penny will make him the perfect wife. We think she is absolutely gorgeous ... we all get on so well.'

'... that's right,' says Doreen Brown, who has reappeared with Harry's scotch and soda.

A door slams.

'That must be Jason,' Doreen says excitedly. 'He'll be thrilled when he sees you.'

The door swings open.

'I'm home Mum, Dad ... Harry! It's good to see you. Thank you so much for coming all this way to see us ... and I haven't been able to thank you personally for agreeing to be my best man. You know, Penny did most of the negotiation!'

'It's good to see you, Jason. You look well.'

Harry takes a step forward tentatively, and gives him a half-hearted slap on the shoulder. Jason crosses the room to kiss his mother and place his arm on his father's shoulder. He turns to face Harry.

'So – everything is fixed for tomorrow. We've got to be at the church at the latest by two o'clock. It's not so far from here. If you come by at, say, a quarter to two it should give us plenty of time. Where will you be staying?'

'I've booked in at the Black Angus, so it won't take me more than a few minutes to get here.'

'Will you excuse me, Harry, I've a Rotarian meeting that I

413

daren't miss – I'm the chairman, unfortunately – and you know...'

'Of course not, Roy. See you tomorrow ... bye.'

'See you, Doreen – and Jason ... don't forget, son, an early night. It's a big day ahead of you tomorrow.'

'Another drink, Harry?'

'Thank you.'

'Jason?'

'Beer please, Mother.'

Harry sits silently whilst Jason shouts to her, asking about the flowers for tomorrow. This time she fetches the drinks without delay. She stands at the doorway with both hands full, and looks unashamedly with pride and satisfaction and not a little sadness at her son, whom she is about to share with another woman. She then diverts her indulgent gaze towards Harry.

'You know, there really is a resemblance between you two. At the right angle it is quite amazing. You could almost be related. It's quite astonishing.'

There is an immediate flush on Jason's face, and Harry suppresses a tremor of intense anguish with a nervous laugh.

'Yes, Doreen – they said on the ship that there is a marked likeness. It's funny how nature can do that. We must have come from the same batch number...'

Doreen laughs as she places his drink down on the coffee table. Jason fidgets and is silent.

'Here's to you, Jason – and Penny.'

He picks up the scotch and soda and downs it in one.

'I'd best be going – nice to meet you, Doreen. I'll see you tomorrow.'

Harry arrives punctually the next day to collect Jason, who is already waiting and impatient to leave. Doreen and Roy have gone to the church. The front door opens no more than a second after Harry rings the bell, as if Jason was waiting on the other side.

Jason is immaculate in his morning suit. Harry is unable to

say anything, as, for a moment, his emotions threaten to erupt in an ultimate exaltation of pride. Jason stands still, framed by the doorway and smiles self-consciously at Harry. They look deep into each other's eyes, and the most powerful subliminal message passes between them. Harry reaches out and places his arm on his shoulder. How he longs to tell him the truth.

In the car they do not speak. It takes only a few minutes to drive to the thirteenth-century parish church. The black luxury sedan that Harry has hired slows down to turn into the slip road off to the left. The tyres crunch on the gravel as he pulls the limousine up behind a long row of similar vehicles stretching up to the church.

He looks at his watch. Five minutes. He switches off the engine. They sit silently for a few moments, alone in their thoughts. And then, without warning, Jason begins to speak, in a slow deliberate voice, solemn and tremulous, which barely conceals an intense emotion.

'Harry – I want to ask you a question. It's not easy, and it may seem outrageously fantastic to you ... but ... well, it's a question I've been meaning to ask you for a long, long time. Promise you will give me a straight answer, I beg you. I must know. I promise that whichever answer you give me, it will not affect Penny or our relationship ... but it will put my mind at rest, once and for all.'

Harry looks into Jason's eyes – searching eyes that strip him of all defences and reach down into his very core, that part of his being that, if he could bring himself to admit it, he might call his soul.

'Harry ... are you ... or could you be, my real father?'

Harry turns away and stares out of the car window at the lime-encrusted gravestones and the solid grey walls of the ancient church. There is a transformation in his face. Gone is the anguish – the pain. It is replaced by a serenity, a picture of peace and contentment, as if the unbearable load which has worn him down so mercilessly is about to be lifted from him.

He turns slowly to face Jason, and the gentle affectionate smile is an affirmative answer. He purses his lips and confirms softly:

'Yes, Jason. Yes.'

And then there is a sudden metamorphosis in Jason. His whole face comes alive – it transforms, as if by the wave of a magic wand, to a perfect vision of hope and pride and spiritual oneness with the figure who sits next to him. At last! It is confirmed. He has found the missing piece to the jigsaw puzzle which explains his true origin and makes him whole. He cannot hold back the tears, but it does not matter. Harry's eyes are moist as he places a hand on Jason's shoulder.

'Penny must never know this – and your mother and father likewise. NEVER. It is between us, and us alone.'

'Harry ... father, I promise ... you have made me very happy ... you cannot believe...'

And together they walk, side by side in silence down the central aisle between the old wooden pews, smiling left and right as the heads turn to follow their progress. In the few minutes since his question was answered by Harry, Jason seems to have truly metamorphosed into another being, grander and more complete than ever before.

Harry scans the crowded pews of expectant faces. They are all strangers to him, but suddenly he sees ... there! It is Liz! He can hardly believe it, but it is her – no doubt! She sits there smiling serenely, sandwiched between three young men on one side and a middle-aged man in a sombre grey suit on the other. They must be her family. He hadn't seen or spoken to her since that fateful day when he had returned to the clinic in Harley Street. But how on earth is she here today? Of course! Doreen Brown. Jason's mother. She was bound to invite Liz. A mother so proud of such a precious son. A mother who wanted one of the key figures in the miracle of her son to witness his day of glory.

In the second that their eyes meet, Liz can see the strain in Harry's face. But her fleeting compassionate smile conveys to Harry the message that soothes his anxiety. It says, 'All will be well. Our secret is safe. Torment yourself no more.'

The poignancy, the dramatic pathos of the Puccini aria is not

416

lost on Harry, as his state of extreme emotion is gently caressed, until the tears are running down his cheeks. But nobody sees. All eyes are on Jason now as they reach the altar. The minister smiles a calming smile. And then, with timing that could not have been planned to such perfection, as the tenor strains reach their crescendo peak the main door opens to reveal Penny in her glory. All heads turn back, including Jason and Harry, who look down the aisle at the vision of beauty. She is devastating in her loveliness. Jason and Harry have witnessed her entrance and now turn back to the minister.

For Harry, it is a dream. Time stands still. He can hear everything, he can hear nothing. Mesmerised, he steps forward with the ring. He steps back.

It is over. Jason kisses the bride. The triumphant wedding march booms out as the couple turn to face the congregation. And then the procession. Harry is transfixed as they glide majestically down the aisle between the smiling faces and the popping flash bulbs. He looks at them ... they are so beautiful ... so beautiful.

And he shewed me a pure river of the water of life, clear as crystal, proceeding out of the throne of God and of the Lamb.

In the midst of the street of it, and on either side of the river, was there the tree of life, which bare twelve manner of fruits, and yielded her fruit every month: and the leaves of the trees were for the healing of the nations...

Blessed are they that do his commandments, that they may have the right to the tree of life, and may enter in through the gates into the city.

Revelation 22: 1–2, 14